ABOUT THE AUTHORS

Shirley Ballas is Queen of Latin Ballroom, an author, and head judge on BBC One's prime time show *Strictly Come Dancing*. Originally from Wallasey, Shirley has been dancing since the age of seven. She is three-time 'British Open to the World' Latin American Champion, ten-time US Latin American Champion, and multiple-times British National Champion. Shirley is one of the most renowned dancers in the world.

Sheila McClure was a news and entertainment producer/cameraman for over a decade. Now she raises cows, walks her dogs and writes romcoms and cosy crime. She has also written women's fiction as Daisy Tate (*Bicycle Built for Sue* and *Happy Glampers*) and award-winning romance as Annie O'Neil.

MURDER
on the
DANCE FLOOR

SHIRLEY
BALLAS

and
SHEILA McCLURE

ONE PLACE. MANY STORIES

HQ
An imprint of HarperCollins*Publishers* Ltd
1 London Bridge Street
London SE1 9GF

www.harpercollins.co.uk

HarperCollins*Publishers*
Macken House, 39/40 Mayor Street Upper,
Dublin 1, D01 C9W8, Ireland

This edition 2023

1
First published in Great Britain by
HQ, an imprint of HarperCollins*Publishers* Ltd 2023

ISBN HB: 9780008558000
ISBN TPB: 9780008558017
ISBN SPECIAL EDITION: 9780008643379

Dear reader,

As you can imagine, fifty-odd years in the world of ballroom and Latin dance have offered me more than my fair share of hair-raising dinner party stories, but in this case . . . we have delved entirely into the world of fiction to tell this backstabbing, spine-tingling, murderous tale.

Enjoy!
Shirley

For Audrey Rich, not only an avid, dedicated reader but also an amazing mum. Thank you for your brilliant suggestions (some of which we even agreed on!) and for letting us borrow your name. We hope we've done you justice.

CAST LIST

Lily Richmond: International ballroom and Latin dance legend, amateur detective and woman of the world.

Susie Cooper: One-time dance student of Lily's, former cop, now a private detective.

Jack Kelly: A 'Ten dancer'. World champion in Latin and ballroom, and the most sought-after partner on the professional scene.

Oxana Bondarenko: Jack Kelly's new Belarusian partner.

Johanna Gunnerson: Jack's former partner who hails from Iceland.

Lily Richmond Dance Studio

Ruby Rae Coutts: Lily's protegée and live-in student.

Vladimir Zukas: Ruby Rae's Latvian dance partner.

Maisie White & Darren Potter: Dancers at Lily's dance school.

The Global Dance Council

Marmaduke 'The Duke' Fitzpatrick: Chairman of the Global Dance Council.

Cynthia Fitzpatrick: His wife.

Veronica 'Roni' Parke-West: Member of the Global Dance Council, long-term dance partner to The Duke.

Sam Pringle aka Scouser Sam: Sponsor of the Global Dance Council, scaffolder, proud father to Topaz.

Topaz Pringle: An aspiring dancer. Grew up in Liverpool, spent her teens in middle America, has recently returned home.

Kiko Yakimori: Make-up artist on the ballroom dance scene.

Ramone West: Hair stylist and make-up artist. Often works with Kiko.

Brynn Conway: Hair stylist, does a particularly enviable ponytail.

Cyril de Boeuf: Head of the Blackpool Ballroom Bonanza.

Supporting cast

Javier Ramirez de Arellano: A very easy-on-the-eyes Argentinian Tango expert.

Cristobal & Lucia Suarez: Talented Argentine 'Ten dancers' and married couple.

Mirabel & Felipe: Members of the Argentine Tango group led by Javier.

Madhav Dotiwala: Owner of Dotiwala's Detective Agency and Susie Cooper's boss. Former prison psychiatrist.

Pippa Chambers: Very keen cub *Dance Daily* reporter.

Shaz & Baz: Owners of Shaz 'n Baz's Beauty and married couple.

PART ONE

Prologue

*The United Kingdom's Open to the World Ballroom and
Latin Championships*

Whitby Pavilion

Two tips to take into consideration when committing murder
in public are as follows:

One: It should be at least a little fun. Yes, doing it that way
is more stressful than, say, a discreet alleyway knifing, but it
is ultimately so much more rewarding. Who doesn't love an
audience? A crowd to revel in your skill.

There are your old-schoolers, of course, who insist revenge
is a dish best served cold, but, really? Isn't there something
to be said for pulling it off with a bit of flair? Some panache.
A glitter bomb filled with anthrax, for example. A perfectly
timed mirror-ball drop. Tactical use of—

Ah! Mustn't give too much away.

Second? Don't get caught.

Tonight, this will be easy. The Pavilion is saturated with
hopes, dreams, and hearts pumping with venom. Couples
determined to take home the top prize, no matter the cost. The

competition isn't due to start for another hour yet, but already tempers are flaring. Tensions every bit as taut as the dancers' sequinned bra straps.

Twenty-nine highly competitive (and combative) couples vying for a single title? Agatha Christie couldn't have laid the scene any better.

All that's left to do is to find a seat, settle in and watch the show.

Chapter One

It would've shocked absolutely no one to hear that Lily Richmond was striding through the corridors of the Whitby Pavilion. Least of all Lily herself. This was, after all, the United Kingdom's Open to the World Ballroom and Latin Dance Championship – and she, a legend.

Samba queen. International Dance Champion 1983 through to 1996, when she graciously stepped aside to give others a chance to enjoy the limelight. Owner of the Lily Richmond Dance Studio, where she mentored and taught dozens of champions, many of whom were here today. And, of course, renowned ballroom dance judge. An expert whose opinion meant the world to competitors on the scene because, after all, a top mark from Lily was all the gilding one needed.

So, no. Her presence was no great surprise.

What *was* reverberating through the myriad of dancers, make-up artists, and stylists jammed into the backstage corridors and dressing rooms of the Pavilion, was the slow dawning realization that Lily Richmond had not checked in at the Sponsors' Table at any point this evening. Nor had she been announced as one of the expert judges who would stand at one of nine tactical viewing points around the lightly sprung hardwood floor, her violet eyes glued to the dancers like a hawk, marked sheets shifting from her hands to the scrutineer's, discreetly crushing – no, *realigning* – couple after couple's dreams of following in her wake.

Not even for the United Kingdom Open to the World Amateur Rising Star Latin Competition.

And my goodness, that stung.

'It's like holding the BAFTAs,' a dancer whispered as she passed, 'and forgetting to invite Dame Judi!'

In the past, Lily would have been consumed by humiliation. Not only was striking her off the list of judges a very public blow to her expertise, the timing was vicious. Shaming her just a few short weeks before the all-hallowed Blackpool Ballroom Bonanza? How very dare they.

Her first instinct had been to launch into action.

Seek revenge.

It certainly would've taken the edge off. However, it struck her as she made her way toward the dressing rooms that there was something else that could be just that little bit better.

Winning.

If her couples swept the board in place of those who danced for the powers that be, wouldn't it be fun at photo time? As she pictured the scene, a smile teased at her lips. Yes, she decided. It would. And she had nothing but full confidence in her dancers. So she'd play the game. Laugh. Smile. Wave off her 'onlooker' status as something she'd been fully briefed on. But behind the façade, if someone was really asking, there was little but fury and pain.

When the hosts of tonight's event, the Global Dance Council (or the GDC, as everyone called it), had invited her to come along, *as a judge*, she'd been told to expect something momentous to happen. Something bigger than anyone could imagine. Something life-changing, even.

Removing her from the judging panel wasn't *quite* what she'd been expecting.

A little fact-gathering was in order. No need to point fingers until she was absolutely certain who was involved.

'Excuse me, Mrs Richmond?'

'It's Ms,' Lily gently corrected.

'Pippa Chambers.' The young woman who'd just materialized beside her thrust a phone towards Lily's mouth. 'I'm from *Dance Daily*, the online paper for all things dance-related? I was wondering if you have any comments about the changes to tonight's judging panel?'

Oh, dear heavens, no. She was *not* going to discuss her fall from grace with a journalist.

Lily held up a hand and pretended someone had just flagged her further down the corridor. 'Sorry, darling. Another time?' Before Pippa could answer, she plunged back into the melee.

With just over half an hour to go before the competition began, behind the scenes was the place to be. The corridors and rooms outside the public eye, where the dancers stretched and preened and prepared.

Everyone relevant to her mission was here. Amateurs. Pros. Teachers, judges, scrutineers. An impressive number of champions from days gone by (including herself). And, of course, the shiny new sponsors. Liverpudlian scaffolders with the catchy name 'Scouser Sam's Scaffolding and Skips' according to their large, garish banner advertising a 10 per cent discount if used with the code POLEMONKEY4U.

What happened here at Whitby was important. The final litmus test for who might stand atop the winner's podium in Blackpool. (Bearing in mind that virtually anything could happen between now and then, especially when a championship was up for grabs.)

For a truly competitive ballroom dancer, performing here at Whitby was the equivalent of taking mock exams ahead of the real thing, but worse. Worse, because you performed in front of everyone you liked, disliked, admired, detested or – like Lily – kept at a very carefully measured arm's length to ensure no knives slipped into her back. The thought gripped her with an unexpected sharp pain.

Was that what this was? An attempt to completely remove her from the world of competitive ballroom dance?

She stopped by an open door to a side alley, took a quick, fortifying sip of the salty seaside air and regrouped. As she did, a couple of dancers smelling of cigarette smoke bustled through the door followed by a tall, athletic man in his late thirties with a buzz cut. His serious expression brightened when he saw her.

'Brynn,' she said, pleased to see the friendly stylist she'd worked with over the years. 'How lovely to see you, darling.'

'And you. I'm loving the sequin jumpsuit.' He fanned himself, as if her presence alone had heated up the corridor, then leant in for the customary air-kiss greeting.

Kisses complete, Brynn tipped his head towards the main ballroom. 'I'm looking forward to seeing how you score the couples tonight. The competition is looking fierce!'

Lily didn't allow her smile to falter. 'Well, you see, darling,' she said carefully, 'I'm not judging tonight, actually. I'll be enjoying the show as a bystander.'

Brynn looked shocked, but was well-mannered enough to stop short of asking Lily why she wouldn't be on the panel. 'Well deserved. I should think it'd be nice for someone as busy as you to have a night off, for once!'

Lily laughed along, refusing to betray the pain she was feeling inside. 'Indeed. I hope to catch you later, darling.'

Only once Brynn was on his way did she allow her smile to slip. She was actually quite cross with herself for not seeing this coming. For allowing so much as a blink of surprise at being 'accidentally' left off a group email informing a 'select' number of judges that 'owing to structural changes within the Global Dance Council, her niche' – (*niche!*) – 'expertise would not be required' at this year's competition.

She'd seen through the lie as easily as a bruise bled through the finest pair of nude Stretch and Hold transition tights. (Dark suntan worked best, if you were asking.)

She also knew exactly who was behind it.

Marmaduke Fitzgerald.

Second-term chairman of the GDC Board and nine-time ballroom world champion.

The big, balding, self-important creature would, at this very moment, be giddy with anticipation that she would finally, after years of niggly, two-faced bullying, lose the plot in public, thereby cementing the notion that she wasn't fit to judge. And oh, how he'd gloat if she did.

Well, too bad for him. As if she'd ever let the likes of Marmaduke see her falter. Moral outrage rarely achieved results. Least of all if you were a woman. So she would play the same game they were: the long one.

A door burst open in front of her, temporarily blinding Lily to everything apart from the sign – Cleaning Cupboard: Staff Only.

A dancer swanned out. She wore a mane of white-blonde extensions, diamanté-covered C-cups (natural), and had a neon pink feather boa floating behind her as majestically as if she were Ginger Rogers exiting the Presidential Suite of the Ritz.

Ruby Rae Coutts.

Lily's lips thinned as she guessed what Ruby Rae must've been up to in there. Through the years, she'd seen her own share of pre-competition nookie in a cupboard, but tonight her patience for it was limited. Particularly as Ruby Rae was one of hers. With tonight's turn of events, she wasn't the only one under the magnifying glass. Everyone affiliated with her was, too.

A black latex gloved hand yanked the door shut from within as Lily passed and, for the most fleeting of moments, her twenty-something protégée looked entirely happy. It was a rare sight – this simple, honest, joy – and, despite the distance she tried to maintain, Lily was warmed by it. She'd let herself love one other student like a daughter and it had been such a disaster in the end that she'd maintained a steadfast rule ever since: tough love, not gut love. When love moved beyond your heart into your core, it was impossible not to be hurt.

Either way, Ruby Rae was still a favourite. Which was fortunate, seeing as the saucy minx lived with her.

To host a live-in student – usually a rising star from another country – was not uncommon for a British coach and mentor. Over the years, Lily had housed a steady stream of students, but the last two had been devoted to this one: Miss Ruby Rae Coutts of Baton Rouge, Louisiana.

Ruby Rae had the potential to go far. Right to the top if she wanted. Born to a couple who weren't suited to parenthood, she'd been fostered from the age of three to a Daughter of the American Revolution obsessed with beauty pageants. Thanks to this woman, Ruby Rae would need counselling for the rest of her life, but she had managed to take away a few gifts. She danced like a dream, could switch personality to suit the occasion, and owned any space she occupied. Inside or out.

They'd met at a dance championship in Atlanta, Georgia three years ago where, to Lily's practised eye, it became clear that Ruby's 'team' wasn't gifted enough to bring her all the way to Blackpool, let alone to the top of the podium at the Ballroom Bonanza. She was young (eighteen) and hungry (literally and figuratively) and very, very talented. Seeing glimpses of herself in the girl – her passion, her verve, her grit – they had struck a deal. Lily would coach her, improve her teaching skills, and in exchange Ruby Rae would become a world champion, all the while making it clear on her extensive social media platform that Lily was the wind beneath her gossamer wings. Everyone a winner.

'Naughty,' said Lily, when Ruby Rae finally noticed her.

'Just keeping myself sparkling fresh,' her student shot back.

Was this the latest euphemism for sex? 'In the cleaning cupboard?'

'What better place?' Ruby Rae kicked her leg high in the air. 'See? All stretched out and rarin' to go.'

Lily rolled her eyes and glanced back at the closed door. 'Not one of ours, I hope.'

'Nope,' Ruby Rae shot back, then, in her best Southern drawl insisted, 'Anyway, a real lady never tells.'

Lily's expression made it clear she begged to differ. Secrets were not something she and Ruby Rae kept from one another. It was part of the deal. She'd have to keep a closer eye on the girl.

Ruby Rae swept her hand over her hair, so well glazed it looked shellacked, then pouted, 'Don't worry. I wouldn't do anyone you didn't want me to. You know that, right?' She edged a hint of glittery pink gloss back onto her lips, her eyes meeting Lily's just long enough to expose an undercurrent of panic.

Lily did know. She also knew the weight of being indebted to a mentor or – worse – a friend.

'Do well today, darling' she said, reinstating herself as coach.

'I always do well.'

'Yesterday's rehearsal didn't suggest as much. Sloppy toe work, floppy elbows and no hint of a smile on that pretty face of yours.'

'Vlad doesn't exactly inspire fluttery lashes and doe eyes,' her student shot back.

Lily arced a brow. Vlad the Asexual Lithuanian, Ruby Rae's current partner, was not a successful pairing. He was an exquisite dancer, but appeared to have the emotional expanse of a draw-string doll. Nevertheless, Lily knew from experience that clay was meant to be played with. Vlad had tonight to give them all he had and, if he failed, he too would land on Ruby Rae's ever-growing reject pile.

'Right you are, darling.' She gave the girl's arm a squeeze then pointed in the direction of the main ballroom. 'Remember. Toes, toes, toes.'

'Head, shoulders, knees and pose,' Ruby Rae struck one, then turned the corner onto yet another long corridor. 'Anything else I need to know?'

Ah. It appeared her little American firecracker hadn't yet heard the news. She debated her word choice.

I'm not judging today.

There's been a mistake in the roster.

You should watch how you go today. Marmaduke Fitzgerald is on the warpath.

No matter how loyal someone appeared, experience had taught her that the GDC was omnipotent. Even a semi-adopted student like Ruby Rae could prove fallible in the end.

'Ohmigawd!' Ruby Rae stopped in her tracks and grabbed Lily's arm. 'Did you see Jack's shown up with a new partner?'

'I did not.'

Now, this was interesting. Jack Kelly was many things – a gifted dancer, a smooth talker, and, most significantly, a former student actively rivalling her dance school with his own – but he was not a man who arrived with new partners on the brink of career-defining competitions. How else would he have won the Blackpool Open to the World Ballroom Bonanza seven years running? He'd had three partners in that time and this last one – an Icelandic girl called Johanna with whom he'd danced for the previous two years – had been a sure-fire ticket to the top. Surely he wouldn't have let her go? Not with so much at stake. He was seven years deep into a quest to beat the only person in the world who'd won the competition ten years in a row.

Her.

Starting with someone new at this point was a huge risk. One she never would have believed he'd take.

Ruby Rae glowed with malevolent joy. 'Yeah. Johanna's knee gave out a few months back and, rather than wait for her, he's chosen . . .' Ruby Rae paused for dramatic effect. '. . . Oxana Bondarenko.' She waited for Lily to have a reaction.

'Sorry, darling.' Lily apologized. 'You know I'm wretched with names. Any more hints?'

'Total partner-whore. Well, according to the Belarusian Professional Ballroom Facebook site anyway. The Minx from Minsk,' she said. 'Not the kind of reputation I'd want hanging round my neck.'

Lily frowned. Social media was hardly a reliable source of defining a person's character.

'Vlad's in a rage.'

'Our Vlad?' Lily raised an eyebrow. 'Why?'

Ruby Rae was gleeful again. 'Apparently, they used to compete together when they were kids. You know, Iron Wall stuff.'

'Curtain?' Lily asked.

'Whatever . . .' Ruby Rae flicked her hand, clearly enjoying being able to give a dancer's second-best gift: gossip. 'He said she gobbled up partners like candy then spat them right back out again. Not that she eats candy.' Ruby was briefly reverent. 'Apparently she is, like, totally disciplined. *Ambitious*. But I still don't get how she landed Jack.'

Lily couldn't help but notice the twist of envy wrapped round that last little titbit. She made a mental note to make some new introductions for Ruby Rae at Blackpool, with an eye to next year's competition. No point in her changing partners now. 'Why haven't we seen Oxana before?' she asked.

Ruby Rae shrugged. 'No idea. Anyway,' she flicked her thumb in the direction of the dressing rooms at the far end of the corridor, 'Vlad's determined to beat her and Jack. And we're not the only ones planning to dig them an early grave.' She rattled off the names of a few top couples. 'But the best bit?'

Lily nodded for her to go on. She might not gossip herself, but it was always wise to keep one's ear to the ground.

'Johanna's here. To watch.' Ruby Rae clapped her hands. 'So much better than a *Love Island* cat fight.' She drawled a malevolent *meow* and finished it off with some cat claw hissing noises. 'If I were Johanna? I'd be pouring arsenic in Jack's water bottle for sure.' Ruby pulled to an abrupt halt at the next set of doors, shot Lily a wicked smile, then ramped up her Southern charm. 'Pardon me, won't you, Miss Lily? I'm afraid my extracurriculars have necessitated a trip to the powder room.'

Honestly, where had the *grace* in lovemaking gone? In her day . . .

Lily cut the thought short. In her day she would've been married to whoever she was sleeping with. That's how things were back then. She hadn't been given so much as a whisper of a say as regards her career or her body. Men did that. Her coaches. The Global Dance Council. Anyway. Water under the bridge. She was the boss of her own vagina now. Choosing when and who was allowed access to it suited her quite nicely, thank you very much.

A Tannoy announcement called participants in the opening round to come to the floor. The tension backstage doubled. Times were pre-set. If you weren't there when the first notes sounded? Too bad for you.

Lily glanced at her phone. Ten more minutes. Still plenty of time left to sleuth.

Head held high, sequinned jumpsuit undone to a point of

intrigue, and platform heels ready to grind the competition into the carpet, Lily once again rearranged her expression into that of a delighted parent and hit the final stretch of corridor to the dressing rooms at her usual, cadenced pace.

Despite the ticking clock, she didn't rush. She glided. And along the way she dispensed advice. Notes on pointed toes, heel work, chins being held high. Not too high, though. Elbows. So many sloppy elbows. Elements of detail and precision that had carried her to the top.

Lashings of gratitude, hands over hearts and air-kisses piled up behind her like glossy soap bubbles as she wended her way through the throng of performers. It was a charade and they all knew it.

The GDC's decision to remove her from the judging panel had left a mark on her reputation. A dark one. And she didn't like it. Not one bit. Her personal motto had always been to stand on her own two feet, but to be kind about it. No matter which way the willow bent.

Suffice it to say, she was actively reconsidering the last part.

Chapter Two

'Thank you for your time, Mr Fitzgerald,' the reporter gushed as she held out her phone. 'Would you mind telling our readers what's in store for the Global Dance Council now that you have new sponsors?'

Marmaduke Fitzgerald positioned himself, chin poised thoughtfully atop his arched hand, in front of a large, circular, frosted window, just outside the main ballroom. This particular pose offered the *Dance Daily* journalist a striking view of his profile, with the addition of silhouetted dancers preparing to take to the floor as a relief. Not that she'd look away. From the moment he'd granted her the interview, he could tell she'd been enthralled. Giddy to be the sole object of his attention. As chairman of the Global Dance Council for some seven years now, he'd experienced moments like this so often it was almost tedious. Almost.

To the other matter. The new sponsors were . . . interesting. People who splashed cash always liked to think they had sway and, as ever, Marmaduke had a plan. A bit of chaos that would give Scouser Sam the appearance of the upper hand. Then, once tonight's shenanigans were over, he – The Duke – would restore order in his own, special way. But those plans were private. He spread his arms wide and began. 'The thing you have to understand about the world of professional ballroom dancing is—'

'Don't you mean ballroom *and* Latin, Mr Fitzgerald?' The girl – Pippa, was it? – held her phone closer to his mouth as the red recording light flashed.

'Clearly, dear. It was implied.' He'd written the bloody rule-book, for god's sake. No need to patronize him, of all people. 'And please. None of this "Mr Fitzgerald" nonsense. Those in the know call me The Duke.'

She blushed and looked away.

As well she should.

'Let me put it this way,' he began again. 'The ten approved ballroom and Latin dances are like conjoined twins – you don't get one set of five without the other.' He accidentally-on-purpose stroked her hand, the one holding the phone, as he continued in his best 'made for late-night-radio' voice, 'But make no mistake. Specializing in ballroom, or Latin,' he conceded, 'breeds champions. Champions like myself.'

Her over-plumped lips parted. Presumably to inform him that many of the so-called 'Ten-Dancers', competitors like Jack Kelly who danced both ballroom and Latin, had been crowned champions. He knew that. He wasn't a simpleton. But he was a firm believer that spreading yourself that thin didn't make anyone a true master. How could you be? Ten sets of choreography to polish to perfection. Two exquisite costumes to commission. Twice the amount of rehearsal. In his opinion – and as president of the Global Dance Council his opinion did matter – Ten-Dancers weren't and couldn't be true champions. Apart from one solitary dancer. But he wasn't about to give Lily Richmond airtime. Least of all in an article about himself. *Christ.* Even thinking about the woman drew bile.

'My dear,' he began again, 'any dancer worth their salt will use the five core ballroom dances as their bible and, with diligence, become champions because of it.'

He allowed himself a romantic sigh, then made the lightning-fast decision to pull the girl into his arms and show her what he meant. He pressed his right hand to her middle back and cupped hers (with the phone) up high, signet ring aloft. 'It's the purest form of dance, ballroom.' He swept her round the corridor, changing the rhythm of his movements as he spoke. 'How could it not be the pinnacle when it encompasses the cloudscape that is the waltz? The gift to courtship that is the foxtrot? You think Latin has passion? Pah!' He dipped her low, his lips nearly brushing hers as he stage-whispered, 'The tango *is* passion.' He pulled her upright again. 'There's the deceptively pacy Viennese waltz, and the showstopper that is the quickstep. Pure, disciplined elegance at its finest.' He released her and once again adopted the air of an erudite gentleman at leisure. 'If flashy showmanship is more comfortable terrain, go ahead and choose Latin. Samba, rumba, cha-cha-cha.' He flicked them away with the back of his hand.

'The paso doble?' asked the girl, clearly wanting to be drawn into his arms again.

'Yes. And the jive.' He suppressed a shudder. All of that knee-knocking and hand-flapping was worse than a TikTok dad dancer comparing himself to Fred Astaire. Untenable.

'So you're saying ballroom is better than Latin?'

His stiffening cock deflated. This pretty young thing was like the rest of the reporters scuttling about the place. An idiot.

'Noooo. I'm saying a *foundation* in ballroom is essential if you want to branch out to Latin.'

'. . . and become a Ten-Dancer?'

If you wanted to dilute fine wine with lemonade, sure. But he couldn't say that. Not to her, anyway. He caught sight of his reflection in a nearby mirror and gave himself a cheeky wink. Though he'd just qualified for a bus pass, you wouldn't have known it. He was looking good, feeling good, and had the power to steer this interview in any direction he wanted.

'Professional ballroom dancing,' he moved the conversation on, 'is about obedience. Being a slave to the music.' He slapped the back of his hand against his other open palm in the three same syncopated beats he'd follow in a waltz. 'It's discipline, dexterity, devotion.' His lips twitched against a smile as he silently finished, *It's also the ability to ease people out of the game who don't embrace the same vision.*

He stroked his goatee, indicating he'd given his quote and now required a contemplative silence in which to manifest yet another deep thought.

His eyes drifted to the interior window that framed the silhouettes of the dancers as they warmed up in the final moments before the competition began. Men tugging their partners close then twirling them away just before those A-cup breasts grazed their freshly waxed chests.

Conflict. That's what dance was really about. Manipulation. Mind games. Sex and power. The essence of a man's primal needs, but with a code. A long-established set of rules that some people wanted to carve into stone. Ah, well. Too bad for them. He held the reins for this particular era of dance – and long may he continue to do so.

He turned and smiled at his reflection once again.

By God, it was a joy being him.

Perky Pippa aimed her phone at her rosebud of a mouth. 'So, you've fired some of your top judges recently. Can you tell me why?'

The Duke tipped his head to the side, hoping for a peek beneath her blouse while he thought of a politic answer. But before he could latch onto anything worthwhile, a smoky 'Darling!' soared through the air.

There was a jumble of competitors up ahead, but he knew who was in their midst. Like a moth drawn to a flame, he sought her.

Lilian Richmond, as he lived and breathed.

She was doling out air-kisses and hugs to a clutch of amateur dancers, judging by the numbers pinned to their backs. Always the mother hen. As yet another dancer caught her in an embrace, each of them sure to air-kiss so as to protect their make-up, Marmaduke's eyes caught Lilian's, holding them just long enough for him to see a flare of defiance light in hers. Then, without further ado, she swept into the dressing room a few metres beyond him to a chorus of cheers.

Well, this was annoying. He'd been hoping for a public meltdown. A humiliating sob of disbelief. Perhaps a bit of begging to reconsider. With this Pippa girl here, it would've been even better. If there was one thing The Duke truly enjoyed in this life, it was someone being indebted to him. Better yet, beholden.

It was impossible to miss the burst of energy Lily's presence had elicited amongst the dancers. Surely by now they'd figured out she wasn't judging tonight and that there was no need to fawn over her.

He'd hoped removing her from the judging panel would be the knock to her pride she couldn't recover from. Make her more amenable to changes the GDC would shortly be announcing.

But here she was, dressed to kill, and with a million-dollar smile on her face. She had brass. He'd give her that.

Right. Enough. If Lily was too thick to know she didn't belong here any more, he'd spell it out clearly for her.

Without so much as a backward glance at Pippa, The Duke strode to the dressing-room door and scanned the throng of dancers. There she was. As resplendent as ever. Sequins shimmering with her every move, her body filling out the form-fitting jumpsuit to perfection. As much as he disliked her personally, he admired her verve.

'Sorry, Mr Fitzgerald. You didn't answer—'

The Duke turned and gave his trademark wink to Pippa, who'd scuttled along after him. He pressed his finger against her lips, shushing her, gratified to see a blush instantly bloom across her décolletage. 'I'm afraid time's a-ticking. Excuse me, won't you? I promised a quick word with a new Belarusian dancer. Make sure she feels welcome.'

'Can I catch up with you later?' Pippa asked, lips moving against his finger.

'*May* you?' he corrected, buying himself just a moment's more time to decide that actually, no, he didn't want to have sex with this one. 'Apologies, luvvie.' He tapped his pocket watch. 'The show's about to begin.'

Chapter Three

'That's it . . . hold still for one . . . more . . . moment.' Ramone smiled at his handiwork then leaned back, framing Oxana's face with his hands. 'What do you know? I was right again.' He looked gleeful. 'The face crystals really do add a nice touch.'

Oxana wasn't about to disagree. Ramone West – a green-eyed, mixed-race Londoner, covered in an exquisite array of ink and jewellery, was the most sought-after hair and make-up stylist on the competitive ballroom scene. So even though she'd been unsure about the face jewellery, she stayed completely still as he delicately appliquéd a gem high on her cheekbone.

When he finished, he made a twirling gesture with his finger and she turned to the mirror.

'Kiko, come and look at this! Our best work yet, if I do say so myself.'

Kiko Yakimori, Ramone's business partner, and the woman responsible for the opulent French plait braided intricately into Oxana's hair, came over to inspect the finished article. Kiko was a petite Japanese woman with dramatically dip-dyed pigtails and a thick, blunt-cut fringe. She wore a diamanté eyepatch, and delicate skull earrings swung against the pale line of her neck. Between her fashion panache and catwalk-ready make-up, she could be an art installation at a Goth Museum. Together, she and Ramone were the crème de la crème of ballroom dance beauticians. Or so Oxana had been told. But now she had proof.

The three of them gazed at her reflection together.

'Stunning,' Kiko pronounced, a rare smile crossing her usually stern features.

'Do you see what I see?' Ramone was beaming. Yes. She did. Today, for the first time in years, Oxana Bondarenko felt beautiful. Inside and out. Every single thing she'd wished for when she'd packed her bags to come to the UK was bearing fruit. Dancers parting like the Red Sea when she'd arrived. Air-kisses from not just one, but every single member of the judging panel. The way the stylists she'd originally booked had been 'disappeared' to make way for Ramone and Kiko.

After submitting to hours of their ministrations with only three precious cigarette breaks, she looked regal. A bejewelled princess from a far-off land. Classy. Worlds away from how her previous 'benefactors' in Russia had wanted her to dress. Or the North Korean ones.

Oxana had done her best to fulfil their demands. What other option did she have, with a young child and ageing parents at home? Stepping away from the competitive dance world just as she seemed on course to rise to the top had been the cruellest form of self-sabotage. But private tuition paid better. And after multiple failed trips to Los Angeles to find a new partner, she'd been broke. How was she to know things would become so . . . complicated? She'd been thrilled to book a client for an entire year. Shocked when he'd insisted on reconstructive facial surgery. A tweakment here and there was fine. Necessary, even.

But entirely resculpting the face god had given her? No. She simply couldn't, even though it had meant forfeiting a year's income in exchange for her freedom. Her only option had been to ruthlessly re-establish herself here in the European competitive ballroom scene. Make a splash with a champion. When she'd returned to Belarus three months ago, she'd been relentless in pursuit of the perfect match. Discarding partners like cheap hair extensions. She hoped she hadn't been too cruel. Prayed that, at heart, they knew she was a simple country girl with one very specific dream.

She shook the bad memories away. She was safe now. Better, even. Thanks to Marmaduke and Jack Kelly, the only person she had to be tonight was herself. Her make-up was flawless. The apples of her cheeks glowed. Her blue eyes shone. Her lips, so flushed with happiness and anticipation, required only a solitary swipe of pure, clear gloss.

And her dress! A perfect red. The bodice clung to her as if she'd been born in it. Lace and a tantalizing suggestion of skin but, like so many things, a mirage. Deep, blood-coloured satin panels cinched at her waist, merging into soft triangles of creped georgette fabric that teased into godet pleats, allowing for maximum flare when she twirled out the full expanse of the hand-stitched crinoline hem. It was the first performance frock she'd ever had made just for her. Little Oxana Bondarenko from Minsk. All of it – the primping, the preening, the attention – was emotional helium for her battered confidence after years spent bowing to the whims of the rich and arrogant men and women she'd taught. Winning tonight would mean so much more to her than it would to any of these other girls.

After years of struggling to find her place in this brutally competitive world, it was with joy, with *pleasure*, that she could finally meet her gaze in the mirror head on and acknowledge that yes, at long last, she would be a champion tonight.

She'd been told as much. Point-blank. But it was nicer not to remember that part. Better to focus on the fact that she had earned this moment in the spotlight. The same way everyone else had. With blood, sweat, and, courtesy of a few casting couch moments, an abundance of tears.

Ramone turned her around again. 'Sorry, luvvie. Can you hold still for a moment? Yes, that's right. I just want to add another one . . . Kiko? Has anyone seen Kiko?' Ramone pressed his black gloved thumb to Oxana's forehead. 'This centre crystal doesn't want to stick, does it? Don't move. I'm putting some spirit gum . . . Ahhh! There we go, my lovely. Now just give Uncle Ramone a minute to – hey, who took my hairdryer? Excuse me! Attention please. Someone has stolen my Dyson Supersonic!'

Ramone's frenetic monologue continued as Oxana's thoughts once again drifted to how, if she worked hard enough, she might one day be on a par with the Queen of the Tens herself. Lily Richmond.

Oxana was, of course, a superfan. She'd not seen her idol yet, but when she did, she hoped it would be like Meryl Streep meeting Reese Witherspoon. Two pros acknowledging one another's rightful place in the world. Maybe, if she overlooked the whole 'dancing with Jack' thing, Lily would even invite her to switch studios!

'Darling. Keep your lips still, I'm just applying some more gloss . . .'

An endorsement from Lily would truly be the (low-fat) icing on her (keto) cake. Jack was amazing, but he wasn't established the way Lily was. Not yet a legend. But he did have some very important people pulling some rather impressive strings for him.

The Duke hadn't even asked her to audition before flying her direct from Minsk to the UK four short weeks ago. When he suddenly rang her out of the blue, he said that her recent YouTube videos were all the evidence he needed to know she'd be a champion, and that she'd be the perfect partner for Jack Kelly. It meant dumping Nikita, her unofficial partner at the time. And begging her parents for yet more childcare. Not to mention listening to her grandmother's endless cautions which all ended with: *It sounds too good to be true, child.* Then, as she left, her *coup de grâce, You're buying a cat in a sack, Oxana. No idea if this character will be a gentle tabby or an angry tom.*

'*Baba*,' she'd soothed. 'He's not a tom. He's Jack Kelly. A champion.' And that was good enough for Oxana. How else to catch the eyes of the talent scouts she knew would be in tonight's audience?

If her grandmother could see her now, she would know she'd been right to pounce. It was a golden opportunity. Completely above board. Well. Mostly above board. She'd learnt long ago not to ask too many questions. Particularly when it came with a direct deposit straight into her personal account. Nikita had been angry, of course. He'd been waiting for years for her to return to competitive dancing and was furious that some British guy from the Global Dance Council had turned Oxana's head with the promise of money and stardom. *So what if our costumes are second-hand*, he'd shouted. *At least we know we're honest, good people!*

Oxana had felt a little guilty, especially as she suspected that Nikita was in love with her, as well. But . . . he was young.

These were lessons a competitive dancer had to learn. Nothing was permanent. Partnerships rarely lasted for ever. And his heart would mend.

'There you are, my lovely.' Ramone gave a satisfied nod as he turned her round one last time before she headed to the dance floor. 'Have a look. Tell me what you think.'

She blinked back genuine tears of joy. She looked perfect. Ramone accepted her beam of thanks then trotted off to help someone else. She allowed herself a moment to enjoy her own beauty. And, behind it all, her brains. The Duke, like most men, thought she was an airhead. But Oxana knew that The Duke was cunning. Sly. And, despite his promises, she had easily deduced that she was a bit-player in a much larger scheme.

Which was why she'd made her own plans. Plans with dividends big enough to warrant leaving her little girl at home. She and Jack had only had four weeks to train for this, one of the world's toughest competitions, and then would have another four to do it all again in Blackpool. An impossible timeline for some. But for a dancer like her, a woman who regularly trained up to ten hours a day? No problem. She'd smiled and acquiesced to every single 'again again again' from Jack because she wasn't just learning his choreography, she was improving as a dancer. He was an extraordinary partner. The best she'd ever had. Instinctive. Disciplined. Demanding nothing less than he himself was willing to give. Both of them literally bleeding for their craft. But the stained satin on her rehearsal shoes didn't matter. All of it was for a higher purpose.

A new beginning.

A new title: world champion.

And then, fingers crossed, the happily ever after.

Book a long-term contract with *Strictly Come Dancing*, fall in love with a celebrity chef who ran a manor house hotel and, one day, send her daughter to Oxford or Cambridge so she could become whatever she wanted while Oxana lived out her days in cottagecore heaven.

It was a lot of weight to rest on a young woman's shoulders. The win, the contract, the language barriers, the cultural differences, the patronizing way she was spoken to because of the curve of her vowels and clip of her consonants. She was foreign, not a fool.

She caught a flurry of motion out of the corner of her eye and turned. Ah! Here was the man himself. The one who'd brought her here. With so much at stake, she had to make sure that she conducted herself perfectly in front of The Duke. Assure him that his investment had been a wise one.

'Marmaduke,' she cooed as he swept into the dressing room. 'Are you feeling good tonight?' She considered adding a finger wave, but rejected it as too much. As her *Baba* once said, women who flaunt their wares shortly find they have nothing left to sell.

The Duke stopped in his tracks and beamed. 'Oxana, just who I was looking for! All the better for seeing you.' He leant in close, his lips brushing her ear as he wetly huffed, 'Remember, not a word to Jack. The lad is clueless. As ever.'

Oxana nodded tightly. Jack had no idea that the result tonight was pre-ordained, but the man was confident enough to be sure of their win, anyway. She had promised The Duke that she would give nothing away, and Oxana kept her promises. Besides, it would be far too dangerous to cross a man like him.

The Duke rocked back on his heels, gave her a head-to-toe

appraisal, and nodded his satisfaction. 'Wonderful. Mmm. Simply wonderful. I knew you were a worthwhile investment, my darling. A dancer who knows how to keep her trap shut! Glorious. Now go out there and dance like the angel you are.'

An older woman – a Zsa Zsa Gabor-type – called his name and beckoned him over to the far side of the room. 'Sorry, love, got to go,' he winked. 'Business calls.' And then, as he passed, he swept a hand along the taut swell of her left buttock before giving it a pinch. A sharp one.

Oxana smiled sweetly even as her buttock stung, and gave him a fluttery wave goodbye. There was a Marmaduke in every country she'd been to. Generally a man who never let the fact he was repulsive to most women stand in the way of exercising his power, or his groin. Once he'd gone, she pursed her lips and turned back to the mirror to admire her dress one last time. She picked up her tote bag, a luxurious white leather number edged with gold studs along the rim, which she'd been gifted by a cash-poor client who dealt in leather goods. It contained everything that was precious to her, and, as dressing rooms were notorious for casual theft, she hitched it on to her shoulder. She preened and twirled, relishing the way the red fabric of the dress clung to her slim frame. Suddenly, her reflection shimmered a little. Feeling a little faint, she stopped twirling. How strange. She blinked hard, but the edges of her vision remained blurred. It's just the adrenaline, she told herself. Nothing more than that.

Chapter Four

'Lily!' Yet another dancer gushed on her approach to the largest of the dressing rooms. 'I'm shocked! Shocked to the core!'

'Oh, darling, save your energy. I'm sure there are far more shocking things yet to come.'

Wreaking vengeance on Marmaduke Fitzgerald for one.

In actual fact, Lily was no stranger to a surprise turn of events. When, as a newlywed, she'd discovered her first husband shagging someone who wasn't her, she'd walked straight into a studio and given a samba lesson to a group of six-year-olds without so much as the bat of an eyelid. Worse had followed. But Lily Richmond didn't throw tantrums. Lily Richmond didn't scream or shout. Lily Richmond was the calm in the eye of the storm, even if she'd been the one to unleash the typhoon. And, as if she'd summoned just such a test, Jack Kelly appeared in the doorway to the very dressing room she was about to enter.

As much as she wished to be indifferent to her former pupil, she found Jack's charm, much like a puppy's, endearing. Of course, she'd known the lad since he was a boy. Trained him. Guided him through his complicated teens as if he were her own. Unleashed him on the competition circuit as an amateur, ensuring he took things step by step, only to have him turn his back on her as if she'd never meant anything to him at all. Painful, yes. But wasn't that what 'family' did? Hurt those they loved most?

What was he now? Thirty-three? No. He was thirty-four. An interesting age in a dancer's life if he'd stayed an amateur. It would be his last as a competitor in the Under-35s. Time to wave farewell to the dying tendrils of his youth. But he was a pro now. No longer categorized by age, but by pure talent alone. Had been for the seven years since he'd snipped the tie that had bound them.

He looked a proper man, now. And nicer on the eye for it. Atop a body that was fuller, stronger, was a handsome face framed by slicked-back waves of wheatsheaf-coloured hair. His bright, sapphire-blue eyes snapped with electricity as he brandished a smile that could whip the knickers off a nun.

'Lily Richmond! My wild Liverpool rose! Why aren't you . . .' Jack Kelly's eyes flicked towards the stream of competitors heading to the ballroom, then back to her and, in a moment's understanding, finished, '. . . enjoying a martini amidst all this mayhem?'

'Figure, darling,' she fibbed, patting her stomach. She'd worn the same dress size for the past forty years, and he knew as well as she did that if she was going to indulge, it would be with champagne. And never before a competition. After. Always after. 'Best of luck with the tango, yes?'

The tango was Jack Kelly's favourite dance. It was also the fault line in their relationship. *One more year to really nail it, Jack*, she'd insisted. *Then you can go pro.*

His smile faltered for a fraction of a second. No one would've noticed apart from her. How could they when they didn't really know him, or his demons, as she did? That sort of knowledge came with time, commitment, emotional investment in a young man's future. One that hadn't paid dividends.

She sometimes wondered what would have happened if she'd supported his plea to go professional before he was ready. She'd fought it, as had his partner. She'd argued that he needed the full spread before he turned pro. If he wanted, for example, to perform on television, he'd need all of the paddles reading the same number for every single dance. Ten. Ten. Ten.

His tango wouldn't have made the grade.

But, like any young buck, he'd wanted to leap and he had done so. Kicked down a carefully crafted house of cards, only to build a new one in direct competition with hers.

Jack tapped the side of his nose and winked. 'You know me, Lily. I'm always a fan of some fancy foot-play.'

A child ran up to him, calling his name on a loop. 'Uncle Jack!'

He turned, his expression completely unguarded as he lifted the little boy up into his arms and twirled him round. They laughed as he booped the lad's nose who then, in turn, tugged Jack's ears so that he would make donkey noises. He returned the boy to his mother, a student from his studio from the sounds of things.

Lily was about to tell him how nice it was to see his softer, more playful side, when an exquisitely leggy woman with a set of distinctly haughty Eastern European cheekbones twirled into his arms, a huge, gold-studded tote bag hanging from her shoulder.

'Ah, there you are my Belarusian tulip! Lily Richmond . . .'

Jack took the dancer's bag from her and gave a demi-bow. 'Have you had the pleasure of meeting Belarus's best-kept secret?'

No. She hadn't.

Lily gave his partner a lightning-quick scan. So *this* must be the beauty Ruby Rae had told her about earlier, the one who had replaced poor Johanna. Her hair had clearly been done by the best. She would know Kiko's touch anywhere. Make-up by Ramone. Again, the best. A beautiful peacock's array of jewel tones around her eyes were echoed in a spray of appliqué gems on her forehead.

And oh, the dress. It looked expensive and had very clearly been made to order. Interesting. It wasn't like Jack to fund a partner to this level. But it *was* very much like Marmaduke. Especially if he wanted something in return.

'Allow me to introduce you to my new secret weapon: Miss Oxana Bondarenko.' Jack scanned his partner's long legs, his eyes lingering at the daring central V-cut between her breasts, then looked across at Lily. 'She's got quite the way with her *boleros*.'

Lily shot him a tight smile, then shook Oxana's hand thinking, *Oh, Jack. Must we do this? Pretend we're happy for one another?*

Had he chosen another path towards independence, she jolly well might be. But when he'd left her studio to start his own, irritatingly high-end business, he'd not only taken Marmaduke Fitzgerald's money to do it, but he'd also merrily purloined her top talent along the way.

Such was the magical world of dance. Win some. Lose some. And smile, smile, smile.

'This is such an honour.' Oxana clutched Lily's hand with

both of her own. A bit too stridently for someone hoping to make a good impression. Was she tottering on her heels? *Oh, dear.* 'You are a true champion. An inspiration to me ever since I was a little girl.'

Lily's heart softened, unexpectedly touched by the heartfelt compliment. 'Thank you, darling.'

This world of theirs, so full of lavish, false flattery, rarely contained genuine warmth. She looked at the girl. Really looked at her, and was caught off guard by the intensity of her gaze. It was only a feeling, but . . . was Oxana trying to communicate something to her?

Oxana threw a glance at Jack, who'd just been pulled aside by Ramone to get a quick powder then, in a low voice, said to Lily, 'I think the dancers coming out of your studio are amazing.'

Lily offered her a reserved smile, unsure what the girl was after. Surely she knew coaching was out of the question as long as she allied herself with Jack. 'How very kind.'

'Truly. I mean it.' Oxana's expression intensified. 'Dancers like me who—'

'Dancers like you who *what*, Oxana?' Jack slipped his arm round his partner's wisp of a waist. 'Float like a cloud? Dance like a dream? Earn a spot dancing with an unparalleled world champion?'

'Yes,' Oxana's laugh was brittle. 'Exactly.' She pointed at him but looked at Lily. 'Such a humble bragger.'

Jack gave a carefree shrug. 'If you've got it, you've got it, am I right?' He flashed Lily his showbiz smile.

Lily shot him back her own version which, she was pleased to see, dimmed his. Impulse made her reach out and grab Oxana's hand before Jack could steer her away, 'If you've got the time, darling, I'm happy to meet at my studio if you'd ever like to work on anything.'

Jack barked a laugh. 'Always playing the chancer, aren't you, Lilian?'

'You know me, Jack.'

He didn't. Not any more.

Oxana's eyes pinged between the pair of them before giving another nervous laugh, and then, rather strangely, she shivered, as if someone had just poured icy water down her back. Lily frowned. The girl didn't seem entirely in control of her body. Most unusual. Despite everything, she hoped she wasn't unwell.

Oblivious, Jack held out Oxana's large tote bag. 'What do you want to do with this, my darlin'? To keep it safe.' Without waiting for a response, Jack held out the bag to Lily, indicating she should take it. 'You don't mind, do you, Lil? It'll give you something to do.'

Oxana looked hopefully at her. 'That would be so kind.'

Lily's smile remained static. 'Surely Oxana has a friend or family member who'd be happy to look after it.'

Jack pulled a sad face. 'No, our lovely Oxana's all on her own, aren't you, pet? Family's all back in Kyiv.'

Oxana smiled. 'Yes. My parents are looking after my little one at home.' She reached out to touch Lily's arm. 'You should have seen my daughter when I told her about Marm . . . *Jack's* invitation to dance with him. The both of us jumping up and down. So happy. Mummy's chance to become a star in England. What an opportunity.'

Indeed. Especially if that little slip of the tongue meant her success (or failure) was caught up in Marmaduke Fitzgerald's grubby hands. Lily was tempted to warn the girl about The

Duke, tell her to watch her back, but as much as she dispensed her hard-earned wisdom, it never failed to surprise her how few people actually listened. No doubt this girl would be the same.

Even so, or, perhaps because of it, she took the bag, assured Oxana it would be safe in her care, then delivered a few pats to Jack's forearm. 'Best of luck to you both, darlings.'

She mostly meant Oxana. She would need it. Especially if she fell for Jack, as most of his partners had a tendency to do. Lily had scooped up the tattered remains of one too many broken hearts when Jack inevitably decided to move on. It wasn't pretty.

Oh, well. She had troubles of her own today.

Air-kisses were about to be exchanged when the familiar wails of a dancer in crisis called Lily to duty. Without further ado, she plunged into the depths of the dressing room.

Chapter Five

Lily had been endowed with many gifts in life – an ability to rehearse for hours on end, a photographic memory, and eyes the colour of Liz Taylor's – but extensive mollycoddling wasn't one of them. Particularly with a competition only moments away.

Nevertheless, problems needed to be sorted and her student Maisie was in a flap.

Lily gave her a quick once-over and instantly spotted the source of alarm. 'Oh, dear. Never mind. Give us a minute and we'll have you performance-ready in no time.'

As she set Oxana's bag on the dressing table and dug into her own for her stash of safety pins, Maisie's story came tumbling out. The poor thing had burst the seams of her satin tango dress after a post-rehearsal kebab had done its worst. Her latest partner, a feckless boy called Darren – or maybe it was Dave – was having none of it, loudly announcing that he'd told her not to eat anything, that no one who *really* wanted to win ate before a comp and if she wasn't ready in five, four, three . . .

Silly kitten.

Unlike Ruby Rae, who would've worn the open seam like it was a victory, Maisie needed her costume 'just so' in order to feel like a winner. She wasn't a champion. Nor were grace and elegance at the top of her list of merits. But she was a worker. Put in the hours and endured the pain. Something Lily had learnt long ago brought results.

Lily silenced Darren (or Dave) with a look. He feigned intense interest in a hang nail.

She gave Maisie a firm look, clamped each side of the dress seam and tugged. 'Suck in, darling.'

'I am.'

'Then exhale. There's too much . . .' Another unsuccessful tug. '. . . too much *something* in there.'

'Ooh, good luck with that,' said a passing dancer, without an ounce of compassion.

Lily's eyes shot up, clocking the number pinned to the back of the man's tail suit. Forty-six.

She'd keep a special eye on him when . . .

She caught the thought in the nick of time, reminding herself, yet again, that her role as a judge no longer existed.

A flurry of motion as several more couples left the room to head to the dance floor.

'Lily?' her student whimpered.

'We'll pin it, darling,' Lily soothed as precariously perched tears threatened to undo the girl's lavishly applied mascara.

'I'm scared.'

'Perfectly natural, darling.'

'About you not being one of the judges.'

Oh, yes. That. 'See it as a special treat, love. You know I'm harder on my students than anyone else.'

Maisie nodded. Yes. She did know that.

'Ooh, by 'eck! Would you look at what the cat's brought

in? Never thought I'd see Lily Richmond brought to her knees. Anyway, off to win another trophy!' The dancer, a defector to Jack's studio, was wise enough not to look back as he and his partner swept out the doors leading to the ballroom.

'You what?' Maisie shouted after him in the way a gang member might threaten to cut someone.

Lily felt a warm hit of gratitude at the gesture but refused to acknowledge any pain the comment might have inflicted.

Years of training, discipline, and a brutal capacity for self-control, meant one of her trademark smiles acted as reflector against such remarks.

'Well, well, well!' A distinctive, aggressively plummy voice boomed from behind her. 'What have we here?'

Lily tightened her grip on the safety pins clenched between her teeth as the sea of dancers parted to reveal none other than Marmaduke Fitzgerald.

Lily disguised a sniff of disgust as exertion as she rose, took the safety pins out of her mouth, then let them fall with a clatter onto the dressing-room table.

'What are you doing?' Maisie went wide-eyed with panic.

'Needle and thread, darling. Stat.'

Maisie dived into her tote for the supplies.

'I can't find one!' She looked wildly around the room and shrieked, 'Does anyone have a spare sewing kit?'

'Will this do?'

Lily found herself eye to eye with an array of pre-threaded needles in a myriad of colours. 'Perfect.' She looked up to see Brynn, the stylist she'd bumped into earlier. Her tension eased. 'I should have known it would be you. Always someone to count on in a crisis.'

Brynn grinned. 'Pleasure. My wife taught me years ago that a sewing kit is one of the most important tools a stylist can have to hand. I carry round all sorts these days. Scissors, glue gun, mints, ciggies. The dancers are always bumming those,' he said with a fun 'what can you do' wink.

The list went on. Lily half listened as she expertly tied off the thread and neatly broke off the tail of the knot with her teeth. 'Well, you can tell your wife that she's very wise.'

'Thank you so much, Brynn,' Maisie gushed, limp with relief.

'Always a pleasure. Anyway, I'll leave you to it.' He tapped his watch. 'You know better than most that every second is a precious one.'

'Oh, dear.' Marmaduke tsked as he filled the spot Brynn had just vacated. 'Remember, there are no late starts for tardy competitors,' he sing-songed as his eyes made a lecherous journey along Maisie's form-fitting ensemble.

She could be his granddaughter, for heaven's sake!

Lily adopted an innocent tone. 'Why, Marmaduke. I thought you'd be out on the floor by now.'

He chortled gamely. 'While they performed my trademark dance? Lily. You know me better than that.'

Alas. She did. Far be it from the self-titled Duke of Ballroom Dance to grace the hall with his presence while the Over-50s did the waltz.

My presence intimidates them, she'd once heard him tell a cooing crowd of sycophants. It'd be like trying to perform death-defying stunts in front of Tom Cruise or The Rock. Simply not possible.

Posture off-centred by an over-the-belt paunch, The Duke

leaned towards her for an air-kiss. Triumph glistening from his skin, his lips twisted in a grotesque moue as he approached.

'Five minutes.' A voice on the Tannoy broke the moment, mercifully giving Lily the space to step back and away from The Duke. 'Five minutes to places for the Professional Ballroom Dance Championships . . . Round One.'

The dancers beyond her became a blur of sequins, fake tan and hairspray.

Marmaduke's gimlet gaze grew more reptilian when he spotted the needle and thread.

'As hard as you can,' Lily commanded Maisie under her breath. 'Suck!' And without so much as a second wasted, she dropped back to her knees and began to whipstitch the split seam together with performance-quality confidence.

Self-pity was something Lily never succumbed to, and she most certainly wouldn't start now. Not in front of 'Smarmaduke', as he was known in her studio. Not in front of anyone.

'Ouch!'

'Hold still, darling,' Lily commanded, then. 'Poise!'

Maisie twitched. 'How can I be poised when you're stabbing me?'

A phone flash went off. Marmaduke.

'Lilian Richmond. How *wonderful* to capture you in my favourite position.'

The stench of overripe cologne choked her as she rose – much like the phoenix from the flame – with steel in her eye.

The Duke's eyes dropped to her student's waist.

'Hiding a morsel of forbidden fruit, are we?'

He was a truly disgusting man. How his dance partner, let alone his wife, could bear him was beyond all comprehension.

'If you'll excuse us?' She pointed at the Tannoy. 'Time is ticking.'

'So useful that your mother was a seamstress, wasn't it, Lilian?' Marmaduke settled against the dressing-room table, his right leg crossing over his left, as if he had all the time in the world. 'It seems you've inherited her flair for piecework.'

The needle slipped from her fingers and fell to the floor.

'Oh, dear,' he said with a smile. 'Perhaps not.'

She turned away, unwilling to let him see his comment had landed with the full dose of poison intended.

He'd never had to earn a penny to pay for his dance lessons. His studio hire. Costumes, shoes, stylists. Not a solitary coin. His nouveau-riche parents had given him anything and everything he'd ever wanted, including a Chigwell mansion with its very own ballroom.

Lily's mother had literally drawn blood to keep her daughter in dance shoes. Working all the hours she could to pay for lessons, not to mention burning the midnight oil over countless nights to ensure her daughter's dresses were every bit as fine as those worn by the likes of the minted pros. There would never be enough money or gratitude to repay her.

'Ah, well, darling,' she said airily. 'Some of us enjoy *earning* our place in history rather than asking someone else to buy it for us.'

As she sought purchase on the needle, she afforded herself one brief but satisfactory image of stabbing it into Marmaduke's eye. Surely even he knew the golden rule of brightly toned slanging matches: Never, *ever* mention someone else's mother.

'This is the final call for dancers participating in the United Kingdom's Open to the World Professional Ballroom Dance

43

Championships . . . Round One. All performers ready to dazzle our audience and, more importantly, the judges with their waltzes, tangos, foxtrots, quicksteps and Viennese waltzes, please come to the floor.'

'Lily?' Her student was in full panic mode.

'I swear I will get a new partner *right now*,' Darren, or Dave, threatened.

'Looks like you're in a bit of a pickle, Lilian.' The Duke cut in with a nod towards Maisie. 'Always a shame to throw in the towel this close to the finish line.' He swiped his hands together as if the matter was settled. 'I'll leave you to it. Judging duties call!'

'Lily!' her student despaired. 'What am I going to do?'

Once again, Lily swept the needle through the unforgiving satin, whisking it in and out of the fabric until it blurred, tying off the thread in an invisible knot and biting it off at the nub, just as her mother had taught her.

She rose, clasped the dear girl's shoulders with her hands and looked her square in the eye. 'You're going to dance, darling,' she said. 'You're going to go out there and dance as if your life depended upon it.'

Chapter Six

Ruby Rae scanned the dance floor as she took her opening position for the waltz.

She'd aligned herself and Vlad so that, in these opening moments, she had a sweeping view of the competition. Know thy enemy, her history teacher had once said, before failing her.

The first person her eyes lit upon was the endlessly leggy, Belarusian nymph she'd seen sneaking cigarettes behind the building earlier.

Oxana Bondarenko.

If you squinted, she looked the tiniest bit like Taylor Swift. And knowing that made Ruby Rae hate her more than she already did.

'Do you see her?' Vlad hissed. There was venom in his voice. Ruby Rae still hadn't figured out why Vlad was so enraged that Oxana was here, but was hoping his rage would give his performance some much-needed fire.

'Right behind you,' she stage-whispered back.

'Shall we block them? Trip them up?'

'No.' Ruby Rae smiled. 'Oxana will get what she deserves tonight. Don't you worry.'

Vlad pulled back to look at her. 'What did you do?'

She was all innocence. 'Nothing.'

Tee hee.

She scanned the dancers again. There were, as ever, the regulars on the British scene, and, as it was an Open to the World competition, a few unfamiliar faces.

She'd already clocked some new Argentinians on the floor tonight. A gorgeous couple with a 'take no prisoners' attitude. In the warm-up dance, Jack had cut them off not once, but three times, as they'd tried to stake a claim on his favourite starting position. Dead centre.

Sitting in the front row of the stadium-style seats, Ruby Rae could see Johanna Gunnarsson, Jack's ex-partner, wearing an eye-popping neon-pink maxi-dress. She was loudly telling the people around her she was here to show her support for Jack, even though it was crystal clear to everyone that she was raging.

Up until a month ago, Johanna had been convinced Jack would wait to compete again until her knee healed after her surgery, but no. He'd gone into the bowels of Eastern Europe and found someone, a virtual *unknown* someone, forcing her to sit out the competition on her own. 'So much for "There's no I in team!"' she said to anyone who would listen. When Jack danced past her with Oxana in his arms, Ruby Rae swore she could see daggers shooting from Johanna's eyes. Daggers that were nearly as sharp as the evils coming Oxana's way from the sponsor's table. The head of the company, 'Scouser Sam' himself, had brought his extraordinarily pale daughter along with him. She looked a bit like an albino vampire and was staring at Oxana with unbridled hatred. Interesting. The girl wasn't even being subtle about it. Sucking her teeth. Scrunching her nose like she'd just smelled a ripe one.

If looks could kill . . .

Anyway. Not her problem. Ruby Rae had a competition to win.

She scanned the rest of the female dancers, ticking off potential threats one by one.

No chance.

Not even.

Nope.

Nah.

Un-uh.

Until she'd gone full circle and once again came eye to eye with *them*. Oxana and Jack. The only couple she deemed capable of pouring the same searing levels of fire and ice into a tango that she and Vlad could.

Her toes curled in fury. Separately, they didn't seem at all like an obvious match. But here, now, out on the floor, they looked ready to tear each other's clothes off. For a *waltz*.

They must've bonked. Maybe that cigarette in the alley had been a post-shag fag. Or, perhaps like boxers, Jack and Oxana were channelling their energies for a victory ride.

Ruby Rae smirked. If that was the case, they'd have to content themselves with a second-place screw today.

The DJ and drummer played their opening beats. The thrill of competition ignited in Ruby Rae like hydrogen.

This was her year. It had to be. Winning the UK Professional Ballroom and Latin Championship here in Whitby was the final stepping-stone to Blackpool, where she would triumph again and then, at long last, claim the only prize she'd desired for years: Jack Kelly.

He'd offered her the chance to dance at his studio just a few

47

days into her indentured servitude with Lily, but she'd turned him down, certain he'd take on the challenge of wooing her.

He hadn't.

When Johanna was injured, she'd prayed for him to reach out to her again. Sure, it would've put a dampener on things between her and Lily for – like – forever. But even Lily knew that sometimes winning involved stamping on a few hearts. It wasn't like people cared about anyone Beyoncé had elbowed out of the way as she soared to the top. They were just glad Beyoncé was there.

Although she would loathe Oxana's presence in Jack's arms as long as they both lived, she had to hand it to him. The leggy cow looked the real deal. Right up until you caught her eye. There was something not quite right about her. As if something rudimentary was missing. One of Ruby Rae's superpowers was looking beyond a dancer's external bravura and finding the chink in the armour. Fear. A weak spot. The human factor. But with Oxana, she found nothing; the woman's expression was completely blank. As if she'd just recently been rebooted back to factory settings. Or maybe she was just a bitch. Some of the girls were. Mean on the inside and done up to look like god's gift on the outside. She'd tried to make friends with enough of them to know.

Good cheekbones, though. Such a shame she wouldn't be here long. Not if her plan bore fruit. She sent the woman a warning glance. A taunt. *Enjoy him while you can!* Then an incantation to herself: *Float like a butterfly, sting like a bee.*

Vlad took her hand, pulled her into position and then, without another moment to wish her fellow competitors harm, the music began.

Chapter Seven

At long last! The rehearsal dances are done and the professionals are finally taking their places.

The anticipation is giddy-making. Like Christmas Eve, New Year's and Easter all wrapped up into one big, glitter-encrusted present.

Tonight's surprise will be a lesson to every person here. A reminder about the true meaning of loyalty. Honour. Fairness. You'd think these were things everyone had learnt as children, but sometimes people aren't very quick on the uptake. They need reminders. Like those persistent ads on Facebook or Twitter. Popping up over and over again to instil a core fear that life simply isn't worth living if you don't have Victoria Beckham's latest metallic eyeliner.

Ah! There they are. The happy couple. Enjoy it while you can, my lovelies. The clock is ticking.

Chapter Eight

Jack Kelly was on a high. He and Oxana had nailed the waltz and swept the floor with their foxtrot. Their dancing had been such perfection that he'd been able to block everything out. The sight of Johanna staring mutinously at him every time they twirled past. The loud, staccato huffs of irritation from the Argentines. Even the sponsor's daughter, who kept giving him the evils every time he and Oxana swept by. Marmaduke had probably promised her 'a dance with a champion' in the warm-ups but, as usual, had forgotten to pass it on. Never mind. He had to keep his focus. But, as they stood here now, bodies so close he could feel the heat transfer from hers to his, the opening strains of the song that had been chosen for the tango cracked open a memory that, if he let it, could hobble him here and now.

It came to him in flashes. As if the entire memory at once would be too much to bear. Tiny snapshots of a time when he'd studied under another mentor, held another girl in his arms, and thought a sequinned top with cut-outs the height of sophistication. A deep-rooted memory that tightened a knot in his gut he simply couldn't unravel.

If the exacting moves of the tango had allowed it, he would've physically shaken the memory away. But dance demanded precision and, by god, Jack Kelly had it in spades.

He drowned out everything but the cadence of the music and turned up the heat on his come-to-bed-with-me gaze. The one he knew melted Oxana into the dancer he had been moulding these past few weeks. The one that would cue the judges into making him the man who hoisted that triple-cupped trophy up to the heavens in four weeks' time when the Blackpool Bonanza reached its apex.

Slow . . . slow . . . quick . . . Quick? Very slow.

Oxana's energy was off. Her pacing. Her footwork. The faults were possibly invisible to an amateur but would be glaringly obvious to the judges. Which meant not placing. And Jack Kelly always placed.

'Timing,' he gritted, smiling through the complicated shift between *paso cruzado* and the swoon-worthy *castigada*.

A tumble of consonants left Oxana's mouth. Not unusual considering her Eastern European origins, but sweet Mary, Joseph and the Lord of the Dance, he wouldn't be standing for this sort of nonsense. Have some *pride*, woman!

She sent him a look that, at this count, should be infused with adoration. Instead it looked pleading. Needy.

Had form allowed it, he would've shuddered in disgust. He didn't want apologies. He wanted results!

Oxana's right leg swept out to perform a *bolero* and nipped Ruby Rae in the ankle. The feisty Yank shot him a look laced with poison and longing.

Poor lass. If she'd accepted his invitation to join him at his studio when she'd first arrived instead of sticking with Lily, she'd be doing a *triple arrastre* in his arms right now.

His senses sharpened. Perhaps he should've been more insistent. Oxana, after all, wouldn't even sleep with him.

Was that what this was about?

There was weight in Oxana's feet. Drag as he tried to deftly sweep the pair of them across the floor, first left then right then left. Moves that should appear effortless. As if he was dancing with a butterfly in heat. Instead, they were leaden, as if someone was holding a magnet under her feet and trying to suck her through the dance floor into a sludge of quicksand below.

Triple barrida.

Sloppy.

Ocho atras y envoltura.

Clingy.

Ocho atras.

Unacceptable.

She knew better than to put her full weight onto his dodgy knee. In fact, she knew better than to put her full weight on him at all.

And still they danced.

Hip work, toes, extensions. Nothing was on point the way it had been in rehearsals.

Had she disappeared earlier to sling back some of that Belarusian firewater she kept in her tote? She'd been gone ten, maybe fifteen minutes? Long enough to throw back a few shots to fight the nerves. He smelt her breath, almost praying for an explanation.

Cigarettes, definitely.

And vodka?

Surely not.

This was her first run-up to the Blackpool Ballroom Bonanza in the arms of a world champion.

Perhaps he'd misjudged her ability not to crumple under pressure.

She stumbled.

'Feet, Oxana!'

He glanced at the nearest judge.

Her attention was on a relatively unknown Argentinian couple. Dark-haired and black-eyed, she was the daughter of a pharmaceuticals billionaire. He had a matching oil-slick of hair caught up in a man bun, eyes as dark as coal, and was rumoured to have been discovered during a tenure as a taxi dancer in Buenos Aires. Their back *sacada* was mesmerizing. Rendering his and Oxana's a bald insult to the tango itself.

At least the judge had missed their cock-up. He turned his head again. Bollocks. Lily Richmond hadn't.

He'd seen her slip into the crowd opposite the sponsor's table as they'd taken their positions. He'd also caught the lethal exchange of glances between her and The Duke. But now her eyes were glued to him and his partner.

Oxana's foot nicked his as they swept through a *colgada basica*.

'Form, footwork and *passion*!' he growled through his smile.

Oxana looked as if she was going to vomit.

Lily rose to her feet.

Jack blanked her, his feet crossing left, then right, then left again. Oxana's mirroring his. Normally this would feel and look like magic. Today it was like navigating a minefield. What the hell was wrong with her? One hundred seconds. That was all he

53

asked of her. One hundred seconds of concentrated perfection before she succumbed to this hot mess of blunders.

'Precision, Oxana.' He was regretting the economy-plus airfare he'd insisted on when they'd brought her over here. She'd be going back cattle class for sure. Perhaps it was finally time to have some long overdue words with The Duke. She was, after all, his idea.

Oxana's wide eyes bored into him. She looked as if she was going to say something, but instead a spray of damp hit him full in the face. A smear of scarlet lipstick stained her front teeth.

'English!' He commanded.

'*Dopomohty*,' she managed, her tongue slug-like as it withdrew back into her mouth.

'Dopamine?'

'*Do-po-mohty*.' The word dragged against her throat as heavily as her feet lifted from the floor.

Her body grew cement-like in his arms. He hoisted her arms with his elbows as she barely managed to move her feet in short, clumsy, jerky movements.

This wasn't dance.

It was humiliation.

Fear seized him with a fresh, painful grip.

He'd never, ever been disqualified in a first round. Not even as a seven-year-old with little beyond two front eyeteeth to his name.

'Get. It. *Together*.' When they were through, her name would never cross his lips again.

She leant into him for the *volcada basica*. The first moment in the dance in which he would properly take her weight.

Jesus wept!

She slurred a few more consonants.

Kink? Keck? Ketamine?

Blinking 'eck.

What the hell had possessed the woman to take horse tranquillizers before a competition?

'Cinderella, not Shrek!' he hissed, desperate now.

Her expression looked both surprised and slumped, if such a thing were possible. Her chest pressed against his. The strain of effort to pull in oxygen transferred through to him like a fish gasping its last few, pointless breaths

And then, instead of rising and floating through a swift set of dazzling turns designed to blind the judges to the rest of the competition, she slid down the length of his body to the floor. Which did, to be fair, catch their attention.

Jack knew his instinct should be to drop down and check on her. Ascertain whether her motionless body was an extreme form of protest or a genuine cry for help.

Instead, he felt that version of himself rise up above his body just in time to see the real version nudge her with his toe.

Dancers whirled round them as she just lay there, her body perfectly still. A deflated Cinderella sprawled in a pool of scarlet satin. Nothing to protect her from the chill rising from the polished hardwood floor as the music played on.

Eventually, one by one, the dancers came to a standstill. The music petered out. The drummer held his sticks aloft of his snares.

An ungainly pair wearing reflective clothing thudded onto the floor in heavy-soled boots. One turned Oxana over, checked her mouth for obstructions, the other asked for – then called – her name. Oxana. Oxana. Can you hear me, Oxana?

They were asking Jack questions, but he had no answers.

There were sternal rubs. Fingers wrapped together to begin compressions while someone else ran for the defibrillator.

How had this happened? *Why* had this happened?

Jack looked up and found himself staring directly into Lily Richmond's eyes.

She looked immortal. All-knowing.

An icy chill swept the length of him as her eyes bore through his ultra-soft, semi-transparent, two-way stretch crepe shirt, straight through to the shadowy flickers of guilt he'd carried in his heart for years.

Exposed at last.

Maybe he was hallucinating, superimposing meaning on Lily's intense expression, but something told him that after years of dodging the bullet, his past had finally caught up with him.

His crimes against the true structure of competitive ballroom dance couldn't go unpunished especially now that Oxana, poor soul, had paid the cruellest price.

And yet, he ran. He ran as fast as he could, the strains of that ridiculous song chasing him from the ballroom, down the corridors, past the dressing rooms, waiting rooms, cafés and bars until finally, *finally*, an exit presented itself. An alley. Air. Freedom.

He slumped to the ground, unable to process what was happening. He pressed the balls of his hands to his eyes, trying to concentrate on slow, steady breaths. He remembered his first proper partner. The one with whom he'd won the Open to the World Amateur Under-21 Ballroom and Latin Championships three years running. Their shared love of dance and their more exquisite, private love for one another. The memories surged through him as if a dam had, after years of straining, burst through. And that's when Jack finally allowed himself access to the name of the song that had not only played tonight, but had played the night he and Susie Cooper had danced as he pulled the plug on what could've been the most incredible partnership of his life: '(I Just) Died in Your Arms Tonight'.

Chapter Nine

Less than a mile away . . .

'. . . and we've got number nine, ladies and gents. All on its own, number nine. That's our final ball for this round. Now, let's take a look and see who's been lucky enough to win today's jackpot . . .'

Of the many bingo halls available to punters across the north-east of England, Susie Cooper's boss had a favourite: Beachside Bingo and Bhajis in Whitby.

Master gardener, street-food fanatic and one of the leading lights of forensic psychiatry, Dr Madhav Dotiwala was, first and foremost, a funster. He'd already clocked up multiple wins, enjoyed two free portions of samosas and had slurped down at least four refills at the bottomless fizzy drinks station.

The full immersion bingo experience wasn't pure indulgence on her employer's part. But, as was often the case when he and Susie went out on surveillance, nor was it entirely about work.

You're in charge, Susie Q. I'm just a pawn in the big chessboard of life.

She didn't feel like she was in charge. Far from it. Especially now that their work as private investigators had collided with both bingo *and* first-rate snack food.

To be fair, the real reason they'd come here had been dealt with a while back. During the fifteen-minute break between the seventy-five-ball and eighty-five-ball sessions, Madhav had easily surveilled their suspect (well, more accurately, actively engaged with) and gathered all of the necessary information for their client.

Ethel Rose was an eighty-six-year-old dear from Merseyside. Her daughter had rung them earlier in the week, suspicious about the senior group her mother had recently joined. Apart from the daily promise of a hot lunch, members could sign up to minibus trips destined for all corners of the United Kingdom in search of a good time. The daughter believed it was a front for criminals intent on fleecing the elderly out of their hard-earned savings.

This was not the case. The company was entirely above-board, and a good time was precisely what Ethel Rose was having. The time of her life, in fact. Next week it was line dancing in Scarborough. Then glass-blowing in the Midlands, after a buffet lunch at a Korean restaurant purported to have the best fried chicken outside of Seoul. Life was for living, wasn't it? And as long as Ethel had breath in her body, she was going to seek out as many earthly pleasures as she could. (So long as they didn't venture south of the M25. She had her doubts about southerners and wasn't shy about airing them.)

Now, three hours on, Susie had ants in her pants.

Hours back, she had taken up a discreet position overlooking the main hall where she could observe the bigger picture, take notes, photos, trace the minivan to make sure everything was above board, research the company accounts, confirming that they, too, were on the up and up. She'd even looked into some of the other old dears along for the flutter, all the while sending text updates to Madhav who, having laid false claim to a lucky seat, had been merrily playing elbow to elbow with Ethel. This division of labour suited Susie just fine.

She glanced at her phone. Okay. Time to pull the plug. They needed to get back home to Liverpool if Madhav was going to make it back for his favourite television show. She plunged into the throng of players, hoping to catch Madhav's attention before the next round began. Amongst the sea of coiffures, a mermaid's mix of blues, pinks and seafoam greens, his thick head of salt-and-pepper hair stood out. She managed to catch his eye and give him the telltale chin lift.

Wheel's up, it said. Time to go.

Madhav waved her over. 'Are you sure you don't want to play the next session? Here, take a booklet.'

Susie shook her head no, just as she did in all the bingo halls. She wanted to get out of here. Not that it wasn't a great place, Whitby.

She liked the road trips that often came with their jobs. The long talks they had. The inevitable side trips they'd take when Madhav noticed a food truck he hadn't tried or a quirky museum he hadn't visited. This one, however, had involved time travel. A trip as fast as lightning that brought her all but nose-to-nose with her past. And, despite her best efforts, she couldn't bring herself back to the here and now.

Ballroom dance had a way of doing that to her. Both on and off the dance floor.

Hours back, as they'd headed into town, a traffic light had held them hostage as streams of men and women – all with exquisite posture and dress bags draped over their arms, bodies spray-tanned to perfection – headed into the Pavilion for the

United Kingdom's Open to the World Ballroom and Latin Championships.

Susie had literally felt ill. With such a knee-jerk reaction at the possibility of seeing *him*, the He Who Should Not Be Named in her life, she should have made an excuse. Faked an urgent text to go home. Demanded that they turn around and drive straight back to Liverpool, ignoring Madhav's inevitable interrogation. But overtime and a boiler on the blink put paid to her usual tendency to pick and choose which jobs took her away from home on a weekend. And also, there was a part of her that hadn't missed the skip in her heartbeat. The deep set of her pulse. The flare of hope that maybe, just maybe, she *would* see him.

But now all she wanted was to drive home, climb into bed and forget about the entire evening.

'What about you, Ethel?' Madhav bumped elbows with the rosy-cheeked woman beside him. 'How'd you fare?'

Ethel beamed back at him. And why shouldn't she?

Madhav was utterly charming. One hundred per cent himself, no matter who he was with. Honest, kind, extraordinarily intelligent, funny, loved a good knock-knock joke and, most pleasingly of all, he was Susie's mentor.

When she'd left the police after nearly a decade of undercover service, there had only been one private security and investigation company she'd wanted to work for: Dotiwala's Detective Agency.

Dr Madhav Dotiwala, its founder, was an icon for those who sought to excel in the world of private investigation. Their team of twenty-odd employees was made up of highly skilled former police officers, retired military specialists, career criminals with a realigned moral compass, and psychiatrists from a multiplicity of disciplines. They did anything from serving legal papers to asset recovery to flying to Sharm El-Sheikh to take pictures of someone's lying, cheating, ratbag of a spouse on holiday with their secretary.

Susie's very first solo case had been just such a scenario. Not only had she located a 'missing' employee, off on disability, she'd found him kayaking down the Mersey. She'd also taken photos of him kissing a woman half his age before athletically diving off a bridge into the river. They'd shown the photos to his wife at the same time as they'd sent the evidence to his former employer. Two birds. One stone. It really had been a red-letter day.

She'd been with Dotiwala's Detective Agency – DDA, as it was known in the trade – for five years now. And Madhav's partner for the last nine months. In two years' time, if she accepted the baton he was holding out to her, the company would be hers. Why he'd chosen her, specifically, was still a mystery. But there was still at least one hurdle to surmount: The Case That Grabbed Headlines.

Madhav wasn't a fame junkie. But he was aware that unless people knew you existed, and that you were a cut above the rest, keeping twenty people on the payroll was an impossibility. Before Susie was a shoo-in to take over, she had to solve a case that caught the nation's eye. Or, at the very least, the Greater Liverpool area. A case that would put the agency, and more specifically her, firmly on the map.

Her office phone buzzed in her pocket. A new client request, most likely. Saturday evenings generally saw a flood of pleas from disgruntled partners. Whoever was back at the office must've ducked out for a takeaway and forwarded it to her. She'd check it out once they got to the car.

She nodded at her boss's freshly dabbed booklet. 'You ready to cash in?'

Before he could answer, the phone buzzed again. No. Other pocket. Her personal phone. She wrapped her fingers round it, willing the call to be nothing out of the ordinary. A request for a pint of milk or some extra tea bags when she got back. A reminder to keep the cat inside when she opened the back door. She let it go to voicemail.

The bingo caller's voice rang around the room, 'And we're off with a duck and dive! Twenty-five. That's tuh-wen-ty-five.'

Madhav shot a yearning look towards the crowd of bingo-players, already dabbing away at their cards, then back to her. 'Sorry, Susie. Sorry, sorry.' She waited while he gave his booklets to Ethel, then together they began walking towards the main doors that led out to the seafront.

As they hit the fresh air, her phone pinged with a text message.

'Your brother?' Madhav asked.

'Probably,' she said. Chris and Susie were close. They often spoke several times a day. 'I'll ring him when we're in the car.'

Her work phone buzzed again. God, she was in demand tonight. Whoever it was clearly wasn't going to leave it alone. Sighing, she pulled the phone out of her pocket, tapped in her code, then instantly felt her blood run cold as she read.

'What is it?' Madhav pulled her to the side, his tone concerned.

'It's from the office.' She tried to keep her voice neutral, but already her heart was hammering. 'Apparently there's been a death at the Whitby Pavilion. At the dance competition.' For a moment, her heart stopped. Surely it couldn't be . . .

Another message came in and she breathed a guilty sigh of relief. The casualty was female.

'Do you want to go down there?' Madhav asked.

She shook her head. 'They're just letting us know as an FYI. The police have sent someone over to the Pavilion from the coroner's office. The North Yorkshire lot.' A third message arrived. 'It's not seen as suspicious.' It had most likely been someone's nan, or one of the Over-50s after a too-rigorous quickstep.

'Not curious?'

Oh, she was more than curious. Her entire nervous system was on fire, but driving past the Pavilion earlier today had already tugged at the seams of scars she couldn't bear to reopen.

'Nothing to do with us,' she said firmly. 'Besides, we'd better get back.'

'Well, then . . .' Madhav offered her a half-bow. 'You're the boss, Susie Q.'

She shook her finger at him. 'Not yet, I'm not.'

He barked a laugh, rubbed his hands together, then air-slicked his hair back. His way of shifting gears. 'Righty-o. We'd best get a move on. Wouldn't want to miss *Dirty Rotten Scammers* if we don't have to.'

Susie pocketed her work phone again, then remembered to check the notification on her personal phone. The message wasn't from Chris, after all. When she looked at the screen, her spine straightened and her feet shifted into first position. A Pavlovian response if ever there was one.

'Darling. Please,' read Lily Richmond's text. 'You must come. I know it's been a painful few years, but we need you. No one will believe me but you. There's been a murder on the dance floor.'

Chapter Ten

The Whitby Pavilion was awash with gossip. After the paramedics had wheeled Oxana's lifeless body out of the ballroom on a stretcher and loaded it into an ambulance, the onlookers had stood still in shocked silence. But once the ambulance had driven off and the police had taken some statements, the rumour began to spread that she'd died of a heart attack. After that, it didn't take long for the bitchy comments to begin.

Heart pounding in her throat, Lily Richmond positioned herself just so, in order to absorb it all.

'I heard she had anorexia. It's no wonder her heart was weak.'

'I'd never heard of her.'

'Russian?'

'No, from somewhere else.'

'She were a right looker, that lass. Legs for days. Prudish, though.'

'Total backstabber.'

'Seriously? I thought she was sweet. Wouldn't hurt a fly.'

'Bullshit. I heard she was the skank who did the thing with the blow-up dolls on *Belgium's Got Talent*.'

'Does this mean Jack's out of the competition? I mean . . . it's bad luck, but . . .'

'Maybe he needs a new partner . . .'

'Is that allowed?'

'Who even knows what's allowed any more?'

'Jack deserves someone who's, like, genuine. Hey, do you think if I stood here I could get one of the policemen to do a selfie with me? The blond one's hot.'

As the gossip swirled around her, Lily glanced down at the small business card she held in her shaking hands. She'd found it in Oxana's bag. When the poor girl had collapsed, she'd upended the studded tote, hoping to find something – medicine, a doctor's note, a suspicious-smelling flask, *anything* – to help explain what had just happened. Amongst the hairbrushes, moisturizers, baby wipes, spare tights, rehearsal shoes (blood-ied), banana-flavoured vape pens and make-up, she'd found a plain white card with a hand-printed message:

A CLEVER BUNNY KEEPS THEIR APPOINTMENTS

When she'd seen it, she'd felt as if her entire body had been plunged into dried ice.

Lily was convinced that Oxana had been acting strangely before she'd even taken to the dance floor. Would swear to it in a court of law. And, bearing in mind the terrified expression the girl had shot her right before she collapsed, the card's ominous message could only mean one thing: Oxana Bondarenko had not died of a heart attack. She had been murdered.

As tempting as it was to alert one of the police officers who'd taken statements, too many years in the dance world during which she'd been dismissed as hysterical, imagining things, or delusional compelled her to keep the discovery to herself until the one person she trusted to take her seriously arrived. It was clear that everyone thought Oxana's death was down to natural causes and, at the moment, all Lily had to go on was this note and a gut feeling. Susie Cooper would give the note its due weight. But would she interpret it the way Lily had? As a warning. A threat. At the very least she could dust it for fingerprints. Detectives could do that nowadays, couldn't they?

The moment she'd realized that Oxana's death was suspicious, there had been no doubt in Lily's mind who to turn to for help. With her private detective skills and the fact she'd once been a dancer herself, Susie was uniquely placed to understand the complex dynamics of the dance world, and to know that things weren't always as they seemed on the surface. She was also one of the most honourable people Lily had ever known, operating from a strong, ethical core. A rarity in their industry.

The only hitch? Lily wasn't at all sure that Susie would be willing to help – not with the way they'd left things all those years ago. She could only hope that the seriousness of the situation would outweigh their shared history, and that Susie would answer her message.

'Interesting turn of events, isn't it, Lily darling?'

The familiar voice broke through her thoughts and made her start. Lily pressed her hand to her chest to still her breath, carefully tucked the card back into the tote, then fixed a smile on her face before turning to greet her long-time rival on the dance floor: Veronica Parke-West. She was the dance world's most enthusiastic devotee to offshore plastic surgery and, of course, Marmaduke Fitzgerald's ballroom partner these past twenty-odd years. What a viperous pairing they made. 'Everything all right, Roni?' she asked sweetly. Veronica hated being called Roni.

Veronica bristled. 'Fine. Wonderful. Well, *obviously* apart from . . .' She tipped her Dolly Parton-esque coiffure towards the double doors through which Oxana's body had disappeared on the stretcher. Then she gave Lily a knowing look. 'I'm sure Marmaduke's got it all in hand.'

Lily glanced up on the stage where her nemesis stood with the evening's compere, as well as Scouser Sam the sponsor, and Scouser Sam's extraordinarily pale daughter.

Rather than appearing horrified by the evening's turn of events, for some reason the daughter was smirking, looking like the cat who had just got the cream. Marmaduke caught Lily's eye and winked. Lily shivered.

'I'm surprised Marmaduke's not with Jack,' Lily said pointedly. 'Consoling the poor lad, considering the . . . support . . . he's been shown over the years.'

Which did raise the question. Where *was* Jack? Surely he should be with the police demanding answers, or with the paramedics accompanying the poor girl to wherever they brought people after these sorts of things happened. The hospital? The police morgue? She should have found out herself. Another question to add to the growing list she had for Susie when she – hopefully – arrived.

'Yes, well . . .' Again, Veronica's eyes shot to The Duke and the sponsor's daughter. Lily followed her gaze, unsure of what Veronica was implying, but certain that The Duke was up to something. 'As I said. I'm sure he's on top of everything.'

'And by everything, you mean schmoozing the sponsor instead of looking out for the welfare of the dancers—'

'Good evening, ladies and gentlemen.' The compere's silky-smooth voice poured through the sound system. 'We hope everyone has had a chance to regroup after the evening's upsetting turn of events. I'm sure you'll all agree, the very best thing we can do to honour the memory of our dearly departed colleague, whose passion and commitment to ballroom dance was evident on the floor tonight, is to continue the competition. Before we do, let us observe a moment's silence for Oxana Bondarenko.'

Everyone in the room bowed their heads reverently. From beneath her eyelashes, Lily's gaze swept the ballroom, looking for anything out of place. A malicious expression, a gleam of triumph on someone's face, perhaps . . .

'Thank you,' whispered the compere, then, much more brightly, 'Now! Would all performers participating in the UK Open to the World Professional Ballroom Dance opening round please resume their places, beginning with the tango. Two minutes. Two minutes, please. Dancers in the United Kingdom Open to the World . . .'

Veronica's talons pressed into Lily's forearm. 'Must dash, dear. Judging duties call.' She smirked at her rival. 'What a shame I won't see you up there.'

The insult barely registered. Lily had bigger things to think about than her sacking from the panel. For the first time in her very long and incredibly focused career, she fully appreciated just how savage this world could be. Her world. She felt ashamed that an entire life could be erased with only a moment's silence to show for it. Clutching the wretched tote bag to her, she made a silent vow to Oxana's daughter to uncover the truth behind her mother's death.

She scanned the room.

Now, where the hell was Jack?

After a quick check-in with her own dancers and assuring herself that they were all right, Lily finally found Jack out in the alley. His hands were pressed against an industrial-sized bin as he retched spittle and bile into a corner. Lily watched him for a moment, assessing his reaction. Was this the behaviour of a guilty man? Or an innocent? They'd shared an odd look right after Oxana had died and she hadn't yet decided how to interpret it.

She dug into the shoulder tote and found what she was looking for. Keeping her voice neutral she handed him two extra-large wipes and said, 'A couple of these will do the job.'

He looked across at her, dazed, then took the wipes.

'Just on your cheek there. That's right.'

When he'd finished cleaning up, Lily threw the wipes in the bin and gently touched his arm. 'They've called everyone back onto the floor, Jack. To carry on with the competition,' she clarified.

His eyes widened, the bright blue of them blurred with something that looked like fear. Or perhaps it was heartbreak?

She had to ask. 'Did you love her?'

'No, but I . . . God. I didn't want her dead,' he faltered, then twisted away to dry-heave into the corner again.

She rubbed circles along his back as question after question presented itself. Had he wanted Oxana out of the competition? Dosed her with something to render her incapable of competing tonight? If that were the case, what would he gain from doing so, especially when it would involve sabotaging his own performance?

Unless – the chilling thought came to her – someone had paid him, or worse, blackmailed him, into throwing the competition. Stranger things had been known to happen, after all.

The Jack she knew – the one whose cowlick she'd smoothed into submission time and time again as a boy – he broke hearts, sure. But was he capable of murder?

When Jack had finished retching, Lily handed him a bottle of water, told him to rinse and spit then began again. 'Now, listen to me, Jack. If you don't go back in there, people could start to think there's something fishy about you disappearing.'

He backed away from her. 'I didn't do anything, Lily. Honest. Oxana just got all floppy and then . . . died.'

'It must have been awful.' Lily put her hand on his arm, steadying him. 'You know they're saying she might have had a heart attack?'

'A heart attack?' He looked at her, puzzled. 'That doesn't sound right to me.'

Lily's pulse quickened, but she was careful not to show Jack her reaction. 'Why not?'

'I think maybe she took something.' He grimaced as the memory returned. 'She was trying to say something to me before she died. I couldn't understand her. It sounded foreign. She was all slurry, but I think she was trying to say something about ketamine?'

The horse tranquilliser? 'Why on earth would she have taken ketamine right before a dance competition?'

'How would I know? All I was trying to do out there was win!'

This was by far the most honest thing she'd heard from him all night. It was all Jack Kelly had ever wanted. To win. To be crowned the very best of something. No matter the cost.

This new information confirmed her suspicions that a heart attack was unlikely, and would be useful to pass on to Susie – if she ever showed up. But there was something else she needed to know.

'Jack, if you don't mind my saying, I was a little surprised to see you out on the floor with her tonight. A relative unknown with a champion. How did you end up partnering with Oxana?'

Jack shrugged. 'She wasn't my choice. I was going to wait for Johanna to finish getting physio on her knee, but Marmaduke convinced me. Said sometimes knees took years to heal. He'd seen Oxana online and thought we'd be magic together.' He paused as another wave of emotion hit. 'He was right.'

Another suspicion clicked into place: The Duke had been the person to bring Oxana over to the competition. But did that mean he was implicated in her death? Lily's head was starting to pound.

From deep within the Pavilion, the strains of music sounded.

'C'mon.' Lily gestured towards the door. 'They've got through the tango now. Let's get back in there.'

He nodded, silently accepting that she was right.

'That's right. I've got you. This way, Jack.' She steered him out of the alley and back into the Pavilion.

Clusters of dancers fell silent as she and Jack passed with an occasional, 'Sorry, Jack', or 'You all right, mate?' floating in their wake.

Despite the outward compassion, Lily was certain they were all gleefully thinking the same thing: 'Jack Kelly, dethroned at last.'

When they entered the main ballroom, Lily was struck by the heightened atmosphere of competition. As if the evening's turn of events had concentrated everyone's desire to triumph. The winner no longer a foregone conclusion.

Briefly, she caught Ruby Rae's eye from across the floor.

She hadn't been able to find her protégée earlier when she'd been checking on her dancers.

'Are you okay?' she mouthed.

Ruby Rae gave her a quick thumbs-up and a gleeful smile. 'Never better,' she mouthed back.

Now that her biggest competitors had been removed, Lily had no doubt that the fiery Southern belle would sweep the floor with the rest of the dancers. She tried not to linger on the uncomfortable thought that Ruby Rae was looking genuinely pleased that Oxana had died.

'Lily . . .?' Jack touched her arm and gestured to a table where a few of the support staff had positioned themselves to watch the competition and, of course, be on hand for any emergency primping or costume failures.

Ramone was there with his trusty wheelie make-up case at his side. And Kiko, with a can of hairspray to the ready.

Lily turned back to discreetly return Ruby Rae's thumbs-up then gave her full attention to Jack. It would be interesting to see how he interacted with his peers. 'Let's join them, shall we? Look. You know Kiko and Ramone, of course.'

Jack nodded as they headed towards the sought-after stylists. Brynn, the man of a thousand pre-threaded needles, was also at the table. Kiko and Ramone gave little half-waves, their attention on the dancers, but Brynn gave them both a warm smile as they sat down. Jack held out a chair for Lily, then tucked himself in another one just behind hers.

'You all right there?' she asked in a low voice. 'I'm not in your way?'

'No. Perfect. All good.'

His pale complexion made it clear he wasn't, but . . . perhaps

73

a seat out of the spotlight would help. Together, they silently watched as the dancers slow-quick-quicked, chasséd and feather-finished their way through the foxtrot.

'What do you think?' she asked Jack as the dancers seamlessly transitioned into the Viennese waltz.

Jack leant forward, 'I think you're in for quite the trophy haul tonight.'

She had to agree. Ruby Rae and Vlad were on top form. No surprise there. Maisie and Darren had risen to the occasion as well. 'Do you know who these two are? Couple eighty-seven?' She pointed to a Latina woman and her partner. The pair of them held an impressive command of the floor.

Jack shifted his chair a bit to get a better view, only to receive a face-full of Ruby Rae's boa as she and Vlad effortlessly swept through a series of reverse turns in double-time. When they'd passed, he sat back in his chair. 'Argentinians,' he said. 'Cristobal and Lucia Suarez.'

Interesting. 'How do you know them?'

'They've been making some noise on social media about coming over to show us how it's really done.'

'"It"?' Lily asked, a little annoyed that Ruby Rae hadn't said anything. Social media was her department.

'Dancing.' Jack huffed out a mirthless laugh. 'Apparently, we Europeans have no clue and these two know everything.'

Lily had to admit, they were very good. Graceful, exacting, poised. Excellent footwork and arm styling. None of the silly facial expressions she didn't seem to be able to wean out of some of her own pool of talent (Darren's tongue making an appearance every time he guided Maisie into an underarm twirl, for example). They were, quite simply, a joy to watch. If there wasn't the rather pressing issue of a murder to address, she might've even let herself slip back down memory lane to a few golden days when she too had danced with a partner from Argentina.

'I'm off to the loo,' Jack whispered, rising to leave.

She put a hand on his arm. 'You all right?'

'Fine. Dandy. Just . . . you know . . .' He pointed two fingers at his eyes then aimed them out at the crowd. 'Feels like they're all staring at me. Just give us a minute, yeah?'

'I'll be right here.'

By the time he'd managed to weave through the incoming flood of amateurs to the nearest exit, the Viennese waltz had finished. The dancers made their final bows and curtseys, bright, happy smiles glowing on their faces, as if not a single one of them had seen one of their own die tonight.

As they left the floor to a roar of cheers and applause, Lily experienced the oddest moment of relief that she wasn't on the judging panel tonight. Here she was, free to watch while they had to focus on their notes, hand in their sheets and prepare new ones as the warm-up music began for the next scheduled round with the amateurs.

She was in the middle of tracking Marmaduke as he made his way from the sponsor's table to the backstage exit, when a sudden lull in the music coincided with the main door to the ballroom closing with an echoey bang. Along with everyone else, Lily's head snapped towards the noise – and then her heart skipped a beat. For who should stand framed by the doorway but her former student, now turned private investigator, Susie Cooper. She'd come, after all.

Susie was simply dressed. A wrap-around dress, low-heeled

ankle boots and her mahogany hair pulled back into her trademark low ponytail, sitting in tidy obedience at the base of her neck.

Lily felt something physically shift in her as she took in her former student, a rush of protectiveness and gratitude swell and push against the confines of her heart.

It had been years since they'd seen one another and having this moment – just a few, unchecked seconds when Susie, blinking against the ballroom's lights, had no idea she was being observed – felt strangely precious. Look at her now. Her sweet little Susie Cooper all grown up.

An unfamiliar surge of nostalgia washed through her. Transporting her back in time to her studio – still ripe with the chemical tang of fresh paint – when a father led in a shy little brown-eyed girl, who'd wanted to learn how to dance.

Lily had recently divorced her second husband. One in a shortish line of self-serving narcissists she'd been foolish enough to wed. Susie's arrival in her brand-new studio had been the salve to wounds she hadn't known needed healing.

It had been the little girl's seventh birthday. Hair in bunches and a plaster on each knee, she'd tucked herself behind her father's left thigh during the entire registration. She'd arrived in the correct shoes but had been wearing a denim mini-skirt with a sunflower appliqué on it and a checked shirt that had most likely never seen an iron. Not much changed on that front through the years they'd worked together. Bless her. The poor girl had never had the money for all of the 'essential' fripperies. The spray-tans, the false eyelashes, the glitter. Her father had done the best he could with her wild curls but, with hands like his, the man should have been a butcher, not a policeman.

Susie was wearing her hair long these days, if the swing of

her low ponytail was anything to go by. And she was curvier now, to good effect. She'd been no more than a switch of a thing when she'd first appeared in Lily's dance studio some twenty-plus years ago.

What was she now? Thirty? Thirty-one? Not a solitary wrinkle on that sweet, heart-shaped face of hers.

It was strange, seeing Susie like this. Not even close to blending in with the rest of the women. Professional dancers were striking, often breathtaking examples of femininity. From a distance, anyway. But Susie Cooper was and always had been an entirely natural beauty. Not showy. Not self-aware. But, oh! The way she'd danced. For someone who didn't believe in God-given talent, Lily would be the first to admit this girl had it in spades. She'd been born to be swept around a ballroom sheathed in gossamer and tulle. A true Cinderella, if ever there was one.

Susie, peering through the crowd, eventually spotted her and gave a cautious wave. As she picked her way through the tables towards them, Lily's heart began to pound. Had she done the right thing, calling Susie here? Stirring up all that pain from the past?

Jack returned from the Gents through a nearby door, his eyes trained on their table as he weaved through the audience, completely oblivious to the newcomer making her way towards them. Lily swallowed as, just a few feet away, Susie's eyes landed on her former dance partner.

Chapter Eleven

Susie Cooper's strongest instinct was to run for the hills.

But instead, she stood, frozen in place.

Apparently that's what happened when the man you'd tried your best to forget still had a vice grip on your heart.

So much for that pep talk she'd given herself after she'd made the decision to answer Lily's summons and send Madhav back to Liverpool with a casual, 'I'll find my own way back, ta.'

Talk about pushing herself into a corner.

Well, it was too late to change her mind now. She gave herself a sharp, brisk shake. She could do this. Confront her past and investigate an alleged crime, all in the space of an evening.

But everything she'd planned for – a confident glow, a hair flick, a few witty asides making it clear she'd moved on and was as happy as a lark without him – completely evaporated the moment her eyes met his.

The connection with those jewel-bright eyes was visceral – even if he was staring at her with undisguised shock. Lily hadn't told him she'd be coming, then.

The moment came for both of them to look away, but still, their gaze held. Her heart rate quickened. As if, at this very moment, his hands were brushing against her bare skin. His fingertips tracing along the edges of her jawline, his thumb skidding the length of her lower lip as he used to do back when . . .

She forced the memories away.

Jack Kelly had made his thoughts on their future crystal clear seven very painful years ago. The only thing she should be feeling right now was relief. Appreciation that her life no longer had him in it. He was complicated and demanding and so unbelievably focused on being a world champion that she found it impossible to believe she could have ever loved someone like that so wholeheartedly. Someone who didn't know that living an everyday life was every bit as important as competing.

Says the girl out on a Saturday night . . . at work.

She'd forgotten how blue his eyes were. The inky femininity of his lashes. How annoyingly beautiful he was. Especially when, like now, he ran his fingers through his soft, gold hair and it feathered back into place. If only his face didn't tell an entirely different story. Jack wasn't best pleased to see her.

'Susie Cooper, my darling girl!'

Susie tore her eyes from Jack's and whirled around to find Lily standing in front of her, arms wide open for a hug. 'Just look at you. You haven't aged a day since I saw you last.'

'Lily. It's good to see you.' Susie winced at the crack in her voice. As predicted, seeing Jack and then her former mentor was threatening to release a chaotic storm of emotion in her. She *had* to shove it to the side and remain professional.

'It's been far too long, my darling.' As Lily pulled her into a tight embrace, another flood of memories surged forward.

Susie's father had first brought her to Lily's studio after her mother had died. He'd stumbled through an explanation of

79

their situation, single parenting, an older boy who needed to be kept on the straight and narrow, the demands of his schedule as a beat cop and, without so much of a blink of an eye, Lily had placed a hand on her shoulder and said, *Not to worry. She'll be one of my girls now.* And from that moment on she'd been true to her word. Looked after Susie as if she'd been her own. No one could have been championed more than Lily Richmond had championed her. Right up until the day Susie had pushed her away.

As Lily pulled back from the hug, Susie could see tears in her eyes. 'I knew you'd come. I need your help, darling. There's something going on, I'm sure of it.'

Before Lily could say any more, Jack pulled up beside her to greet Susie properly. His eyes still held their haunted expression, but he'd fixed a smile on his face.

'Susie Cooper, my God. It's been years.'

'Jack. How've you been?' She was pleased with how casual she sounded. As if they were no more than old colleagues greeting each other. As Jack leaned in to greet her with the customary air-kiss, she tried not to betray the effect that being so close to him was having on her. He still wore the same aftershave.

She deserved a medal for not leaning in and taking a sniff.

Sauvage, if she remembered correctly.

Savage.

Just like him. A predatory alpha male who used a veneer of charm and 'dedication to his craft' to discard whatever or whoever stood in his way. Which reminded her . . .

She pulled back and made a jokey show of looking around him for his partner. 'Dancing solo, these days, Jack?'

He turned ashen. 'Actually . . .'

Oh, sugar.

It was Jack's partner who had died.

She swore softly under her breath. Trust her to stick her foot in it within seconds of seeing Jack bloody Kelly again after seven largely stress-free years.

'Sorry. I didn't know,' she said to Jack, eyes already shifting to Lily with a silent, *Why didn't you say?* radiating from her. She widened her stance. 'I'm guessing that's why I'm here, then?' She chanced another glance between the pair of them, thoroughly baffled. 'You said there was a murder on the dance floor?'

Chapter Twelve

Before Lily could answer Susie's question, they were surrounded by the bustle of amateur Latin dancers leaving the floor as the professionals headed back on to it in a flurry of feather arm boas, chiffon wings, and the distinctive chemical tang of hairspray.

Once the pros had taken their positions on the floor, Lily began. 'Look, darling. It's all very complicated—'

Jack interrupted in a tone utterly bereft of his usual Irish charm, 'What does Susie mean, Lily? *Murder?*' He turned to Susie, defensive. 'The police have already been.'

'I'm not with the police any more.'

'Oh?' Nerves clearly had the best of him, because he took the information and ran too far with it. 'Seven-year itch strikes again, eh?'

Susie gave him a cool look, her eyes snagging with his for a beat too long.

Lily leapt in. Best to keep things on track. 'Apologies, Jack. I should have said. Susie did so well with Merseyside she was poached for a private detective agency.'

She let the new information settle with Jack before continuing.

As Susie had let the cat out of the bag about her suspicions that Oxana's death had not been a natural one, she made a split-second decision to include Jack in the conversation. If he had been up to no good, perhaps making him feel like she trusted him would make him more likely to slip up, confess.

'The truth is, yes. I believe that Oxana Bondarenko was murdered.' Then, looking at Susie, 'To be clear, the paramedics seemed satisfied that it was a natural death. A heart attack, perhaps? But based on something Oxana tried to tell Jack here, before she collapsed, I think there was something more nefarious at play.' Not to mention the note Lily had found in Oxana's tote. She would tell Susie about that in private.

Jack looked horrified.

'It's mostly instinct at this point,' Lily added, knowing Susie would wonder why she hadn't called the police if she truly did believe it was murder. 'I thought you might help me put together a clearer picture before we began to point fingers. I will pay for your services, Susie, of course.'

Susie waved aside the suggestion of payment. She scrunched her nose then tipped her head to one side, as if physically shifting the facts into place. 'Is there anyone in particular you have in mind?' she asked. 'Someone you think might have had a motive to kill Oxana?'

Before Lily could say yes, she had several people in mind, a cloud of neon feathers flew into Susie's face.

Ruby Rae and Vlad swirled into place in front of them.

Normally Lily would've assumed this type of display was for her benefit. But after Ruby Rae's spot *volta* and underarm turn morphed into a surprisingly aggressive promenade samba walk, Lily realized that the moves were being executed with menacing precision directly in front of Susie. Instead of a bright smile, she was glaring possessive daggers at the newcomer, clearly wondering what this stranger was doing speaking to Lily and Jack. Susie gave Ruby Rae a puzzled smile. She'd been the recipient of this type of venomous posturing back when she'd been dancing with Jack, but had never taken the moments to heart. This time, however, Lily could see the look registering with Susie on a different level. One that might bode poorly for Ruby Rae.

Before she could send her student a warning glance, they were off with a side samba walk and a high kick. Vlad led them into a crisscross *botafogo* and, with Ruby Rae's eyes still on Susie, the pair nearly collided with the leggy Argentinian couple who, Lily had to admit, handled the incident with grace. The judges, astonishingly, were looking elsewhere, and missed Ruby Rae's tiny hiccup – her only one of the night. They were watching Maisie and Darren, in fact, who were performing surprisingly well. Maisie was glowing with unharnessed joy. Each of the three steps required within the lightning-fast 2/4 samba rhythm saw the pair hitting their marks with true flair. They'd make the quarter-finals round, no question. *Good girl*, Lily thought.

When she turned back to Susie and Jack, Susie was picking a brightly coloured feather out of her hair, still looking bemused. She pocketed it then, switching back into detective mode, asked Jack, 'What was it Oxana said before she collapsed that made you suspicious?'

Jack threw a panicked look at Lily.

'It's not a trick question, Jack,' Susie said, her tone patient. 'We're just talking facts here.'

Jack shook his head, as if trying to figure out which reality he was living in. The one where he was the reigning British

84

ballroom and Latin champion. The one where his partner had unexpectedly died in his arms. Or the one whose former lover and partner stood before him asking him about Oxana's murder.

'Go on, Jack.' Lily gave his arm a gentle squeeze. 'Tell Susie what you told me.'

'I wasn't sure at first,' he admitted. He stumbled through an explanation of Oxana's last moments before she collapsed: the cluster of sounds he thought were Russian or Ukrainian, maybe, and then later suspected were actually an attempt to tell him she'd been drugged.

'She wouldn't have taken it herself? The ketamine?' Susie asked.

'No.' Jack shook his head. 'At least, I don't think so. She wanted to win. She has a little girl back home who she lived for ... She ...' His face creased in anguish as the words caught up to him. 'Who's going to tell that poor wee girl? Or her parents?'

Susie reached out, as if to put a hand on Jack's arm to comfort him, but then clearly thought better of it and withdrew.

Lily tried to remind Jack that the police would handle that part, but her words were drowned out by a round of applause as the samba came to an end and the dancers repositioned themselves for the beginning of the cha-cha-cha.

Susie used the distraction to give Jack a few moments to compose himself. Once it was properly under way, she asked him, 'What time did you and Oxana arrive at the Pavilion? Would anyone have had the chance to drug her before the competition started?'

Jack ran through the day's events, all of which he and Oxana had done together. Met at his studio first thing for rehearsal, loaded up their performance gear – dressing gowns, slippers,

85

costumes, make-up cases, shoes; then the drive to Whitby. They'd arrived at the ballroom and after that had come the usual whirlwind. Wardrobe. Make-up. Hair. They'd seen and spoken to scores of people.

'And she wasn't on her own at any time?' Susie pressed.

Jack shrugged. 'She did disappear for ten or fifteen minutes after she'd had her make-up done, when she was letting the face crystals set. And a bit earlier in the day. Every now and again she'd sneak off for a vape.' He threw his hands up as if he'd suddenly had enough. 'I don't know. Honestly. She could've gone to the loo. Had a nap. Made a phone call to her little one. It wasn't like we were close. We just danced together, is all. If she really *was* murdered, then maybe it was someone from her past. Someone who wanted to win tonight. You know this world, Suze. There are a thousand backstabbers out there willing to do whatever it takes.' He pointed towards the ballroom, then froze.

Lily turned to see who had captured his attention.

Johanna Gunnarsson. Amidst the noise and whirling activity of the dancers performing the cha-cha-cha, she was still sitting in the audience on the other side of the dance floor. Her eyes were fixed on Jack, her expression as cold as ice.

Susie followed Jack and Lily's gazes. 'Who's that?' she asked, her interest piqued. 'If looks could kill, Jack . . .'

'That's my last partner, from before Oxana.' He told Susie about Johanna's knee injury and how The Duke had suggested he try out Oxana as a replacement.

'Marmaduke said the council would look kindly on me for doing the girl a favour until Johanna got better.'

'So, the competition was fixed?' Susie asked bluntly.

Jack's temper flared. 'No! It was a general comment. I've

been working my whole life for this. You of all people should know . . .'

Susie's eyes narrowed, and Jack cut short whatever he was going to say. A taut energy hummed between them, both clearly remembering those combative last few weeks between them as dance partners, their arguments over whether or not to turn pro.

Lily put a hand on his arm. The last thing they needed was for tensions to escalate. 'No one's accusing you of anything, Jack. This is about Oxana, remember? We're just telling Susie about how Marmaduke—'

'About how Marmaduke *what*?' asked the man himself.

Before Lily could figure out just how much The Duke had heard, the big lecherous lump had clamped one of his meaty paws on Jack's shoulder. 'Jack, my boy! Glad to see you're keeping your spirits up after this evening's events. The show must go on, eh? I've come to lure you away from your . . .' he shot a brief, scornful glance at their small group, '*fans* . . . and introduce you to a dancer who's been *dying* to take a spin with you during the general dance before the semis.'

Jack, to his credit, looked horrified.

'An unfortunate turn of phrase, all things considered,' Lily muttered.

Marmaduke tutted. 'Oh dear, Lilian. I hardly think our new sponsor would like to hear you referring to his beloved daughter as unfortunate. Darling Topaz is a professional dancer herself, you see. She's made quite the impression in Middle America, and she'll be opening her own studio in Liverpool soon, all being well. We were chatting earlier and thought, what better way to make her return to the British dance scene than in the arms of Jack Kelly, eh lad?'

Lily only just managed to keep her surprise in check. Wasn't this a turn-up for the books? How very interesting that Scouser Sam's daughter was a dancer, too. Was the scaffolding and skips baron sponsoring the competition in order to get her an 'in'? Lily could see Susie processing this information too, clearly making a mental note of everything her nemesis said.

Marmaduke turned his attention back to Jack, pressing his hand to his heart with a sorrowful sigh. 'Of course, we're all as desperately upset as Jack here must be about poor Oxana.'

Lily doubted that. If a heart did beat in that chest of his, she was certain it was reptilian.

Smarmaduke continued, his hand absently hammering down with greater and greater force on Jack's shoulder as he spoke. 'The poor girl must've had a heart condition. How were we to know? The fact our generous sponsors have offered to pay for her return to Belarus only speaks to the family's kindness.' He blinked away some crocodile tears. 'Not only that, but they've agreed to rescue you, Jack, in your time of need. I bring some very welcome news for you, my boy!' The Duke glanced up at the stage where Scouser Sam and Topaz were watching the group like hawks. He dropped them both a wink. Jack looked like he was about to throw up.

'We're all ears,' Lily said dryly.

'Sam has generously – *very* generously – suggested a stellar new partner for Jack here to bring to Blackpool, so that he'll be able to continue in the competition.'

Susie hiked an eyebrow, her gaze moving between Lily and The Duke.

'Let me guess,' Lily said. 'None other than Topaz herself?' In as mild a tone as she could manage, she continued, 'Surely, there'd be someone with more international experience who would be better suited to a champion such as our Jack?'

The Duke pinned his piggy little eyes on Lily. 'Topaz is the *perfect* new partner for Jack.' A sudden gleam of triumph lit in him as his gaze shot to Susie then back to Lily. He remembered her now. Lily could see it. Remembered exactly who Susie had been to Jack. Through a laugh, he wagged a *naughty-naughty* finger at her. 'I know what you're up to, Lilian. Taking advantage during a tragedy. Trying to lure Jack to your own studio during these dark, dark times. And with a rusty amateur? I won't have it, and neither should Jack. He's a man with his own free will. Aren't you, my boy?' He pulled Jack to his side in a vice-like one-armed hug. Jack, still looking shell-shocked, opened his mouth as if to speak, but nothing came out.

'Right then. Let's introduce you to Topaz, shall we?' the Duke boomed, making it clear that Jack had no choice.

Jack caught Susie's eye, a hint of desperation in his gaze. 'Susie, perhaps we can catch up later? Lily, I'll . . .'

Before he could finish the sentence, The Duke had yanked him towards the stage.

Lily closed her eyes to give herself just a moment to picture Marmaduke losing his footing and falling into the empty orchestra pit as he strode along the lip of the stage towards Scouser Sam and his darling Topaz. Perhaps they could fall in, too.

Simple pleasures.

When she opened them again, she started. Susie's cheeks were blotched with emotion as she said, 'I think we need to establish why I'm really here.'

Chapter Thirteen

'Mr Fitzgerald?' Pippa Chambers thrust the blinking red light on her phone towards The Duke as he ascended the steps to the stage for the umpteenth time. 'I was wondering if I could have a word about tonight's . . . event?'

Of all the nights to have a cub reporter on the scene. The Duke summoned a kindly smile. 'We'll be issuing a statement in due course. Keep your eye on the website, love, all right?'

He continued his ascent, pulse pounding in his throat. He needed to keep his blood pressure down, and having Jack Kelly playing the grief-stricken dancer wasn't helping things. Marmaduke's grand scheme had accelerated at a speed he hadn't been braced for, but he wasn't known as the Master of the Quick Recovery for nothing. A partner losing a shoe? Another couple elbow-bashing them in the face? Peanuts compared to the complicated choreography he was managing tonight.

The threat of Sam's earlier rage came back to him. 'You'll have my girl in the arms of that lad before the night is through, or you'll be answering to a higher power, Duke.'

He knew. He got it. The weeks of increasingly irate phone calls had been hint enough. The overnight appearance of scaffolding around his house before an important dinner party had pushed the message home. Scouser Sam was finally getting his little girl back, now that the court-imposed restraining order had been lifted. He had this one chance to win his darling princess over, or risk losing her forever to bloody America and his bitch of an ex-wife. Vindictive, money-grubbing whore, whose sole mission had been to brainwash his only child against him. Sure she was twenty-five, but the girl was vulnerable. Suffering from Stockholm syndrome, most likely. His blood ran through Topaz's veins and he planned to pulverize anyone who tried to keep her from him or, more to the point, give her cause to leave.

So now here they were, with things not playing out in quite the way Marmaduke had foreseen. One of the perils of spinning too many plates at once, he supposed. It was the cross he bore for dedicating his life to dance and all her many side plots. But! Crockery was easily replaced. There was a new lay of the land now. Topaz was here earlier than anticipated and Oxana was dead. Them's the breaks.

He'd stupidly presumed Sam had clocked how much the finality of Oxana's departure had rattled everyone, and how, with a bit of nuance, they could make the necessary coupling in a few days' time, once the furore had died down.

But no. The Liverpudlian had gone all Tony Soprano on him, reminding him, yet again, that what his little girl wanted more than anything was to dance with the world's foremost and most attractive ballroom champion: Jack Kelly.

Honestly. Why the man had felt it necessary to crack his knuckles after this pronouncement was beyond him. Sam was a tradesman. He needed his hands. Didn't he know that sort of thing brought on arthritis?

The Duke poured a glass of fizz, dug into his pocket for his trusty bottle of blood-pressure pills and tipped some into his hand, pausing only to listen to the numbers being called out for the quarter-finals. Lily's students were making quite the show tonight.

He threw his head back, popped in the pills and drained the second glass.

This entire evening was a disaster.

He'd been working on putting this particular puzzle together for months now and, of course, the one person pulling it all to pieces was Lilian Richmond. Talking to Jack. Putting him in front of his ex-partner. How bloody dare she think she could get one over on him? This time, Lilian had gone too far.

Before the night was through, he would find a way to put an end to her for good.

Chapter Fourteen

The competition continued. As the diminishing pool of amateurs made their way through the semi-final rounds, Lily sought a spot up on the risers where she could observe the dancers from above. After Jack went off with The Duke, Susie had suggested she take a look around the ballroom, and backstage, to see if she could find any other clues, making it clear she could be more subtle if she was alone. Lily was happy to leave her to it. Despite the earlier friction with Jack, and the fact that she and Susie hadn't yet had a chance to discuss their past, she was hopeful that Susie would take the job on. She certainly seemed to believe Lily that there was a possibility Oxana's death involved foul play. The Duke's strange behaviour, and insistence that Jack partner with Scouser Sam's daughter, had only fuelled their suspicions, and Lily could see that Susie was starting to feel invested in the case.

Up on the risers, she found a position where she could still see the lay of the land and have another sneaky peak in Oxana's studded tote to see if there was anything she'd missed earlier.

A whiff of the girl's perfume came to her as she settled the bag on her lap.

Oxana. She obviously hadn't known her, but it was awful to think of her all zipped up in that horrid bag and heading off to some chilly basement where she'd be left, alone, before Scouser Sam had her shipped back to Belarus.

A wash of gratitude that Lily's mother, Audrey, had finally agreed to move in with her put a pin on any more dark thoughts of that nature. Lily's father had left before she'd worn her first pair of dance slippers, and though she'd not felt his absence in terms of having a fierce champion, she knew life as a single mother had taken its toll. Audrey had always 'waved the flag' for her, and now she was looking forward to doing the same in return. This was the longest spell in her life – some ten years now – when she'd been unmarried and, though she didn't miss being under yet another insecure man's thumb, she did miss the company.

Ruby Rae, for her many merits, was not a 'cup of tea and a natter' kind of girl. Not that Lily was, but still. It would've been nice to talk properly to the girl every now and again. If she wasn't in the studio training or teaching, she was out or locked in her room. A private soul who flicked the charm off and on like a light switch. But, by god, she could dance. A reminder that you didn't have to be BFFs to admire someone.

Lily's eyes moved from one couple to the next as the professionals reclaimed the floor for the next stage of the competition. Another ballroom round with the percussionist already easing into a waltz. She propped her chin on the back of her hand (she didn't have a double chin, but nor was she willing to risk the moment one might decide to spontaneously appear) and let herself be drawn into the spectacle as, once again, the music began to play.

This was rare for her. A private moment to simply watch. From the very first day she'd discovered the world of ballroom dancing, she had been in its thrall. The sensuality. The precision. The costumes, the make-up, the freedom to explore.

Her career had led her down a yellow brick road to Italy, Spain, Argentina, Scandinavia, Japan and beyond. And what a journey it had been. She'd seen countless things she never would have believed to be true, but tonight, she had to admit, had been the most frightening.

She sought Jack and spotted him back up on the stage, speaking to the sponsor's daughter. Topaz was laughing and touching his arm in the way a woman did when she found a man attractive. He was leaning in, whispering something in her ear. More laughter. And yet . . . even from here, she could see his heart wasn't in it.

'Lilian?'

Every hair on Lily's body stood to attention.

Javier Ramirez de Arellano had that effect on her.

'Javier!' She turned to see the man himself standing behind her. 'Whatever brings you here to Whitby?' Her voice was breathy. Too breathy.

Javier was the world's leading expert on the tango. A poster boy for the type of alpha male a woman would desire. Dashing, erudite, generous and, to top it all, an unbelievably gifted ballroom dancer. He was as handsome as a film star, every bit as wealthy, and, if the rumour mill was anything to go by, newly divorced. Again. What number bride would that have been? Four? Or was it five? Not that she was judging. If she were to marry again, it would be her fourth trip down the aisle, but she wasn't and wouldn't, so it was a moot point.

Javier pointed to the dance floor. 'See those two? The man in braces and the woman wearing emerald-green?'

Yes. It was the Argentine couple she'd seen earlier. 'Exquisite dancers. I should have known you had something to do with them.'

'And those two there.' Javier pointed out another pair. Less gifted, but still, possessing a poise and acumen for the quickstep that spoke well of them, and their coach.

Her eyes remained on the younger of the two pairs as they finished the dance and leant into one another for a feather-light kiss before moving into position for the next. It was such a simple moment. Entirely organic. And it took her breath away. She pressed her hand to her chest, trying to suppress an unwelcome surge of emotion.

'Lilian?' Javier's soft voice caressed her name and, this time, was accompanied by the sensation of his touch on her shoulder.

She flinched.

'Lily?' He dropped to one knee so that he was at eye level with her. 'Are you all right?' His lightly accented voice poured through her body like molten caramel. The bastard.

She turned to him, and the instant her eyes caught the glow of his amber irises she saw that, annoyingly, he was genuinely concerned.

If she were to answer honestly, explain that no, she wasn't all right, he would care. Express worry. Pull her into his arms and comfort her if necessary. Stay with her as long as she wanted, right up until the moment he held her beating heart in his palm and then . . . No!

He'd pulled her into his arms before and her body had never forgotten it.

She'd avoided going there for over thirty years and wasn't about to crack now.

'May I?' he asked, gesturing to the empty space beside her.

'Of course. Please. Where are my manners?' She gave a stupid laugh then moved over, lodging Oxana's bag between them as she did.

As Javier sat, a gentle waft of scent swept through her nervous system. The trigger sent her mind's eye on an exceptionally evocative slideshow: sunlight-saturated, sumptuous flickers of her young body and his, the pair of them entangled in a week-long orgy for two. It was Buenos Aires in the late-1980s. After meeting at a tango intensive, during which his erection had become . . . a distraction, Javier had wordlessly led her to his nearby rooftop flat, complete with a waterbed and a well-stocked larder. Days later, the waterbed ruined and their limbs a slick of massage oil and desire, Lily had whispered to his sleeping figure that she loved him. Told him that he made her feel both feral and controlled. Wicked and divine. She'd never believed it was possible to feel so beautiful. So alive. She poured the entire contents of her fragile, naive heart out to him, right up until she saw his long, dark lashes flicker. The moment he opened those feline eyes of his, she realized what a fool she'd been.

Over the last seven days they might have shared incredible sex . . . but she'd also learnt how impossible it would be for their two worlds to become one.

He was from a wealthy family.

She was poor.

He ran in elite circles.

She knew when she was being tolerated rather than truly welcomed.

His family was staunchly aristocratic in a way that seemed very, very British. Gradually, from little clues dropped here and there, she came to realize they would never accept her. Never

97

believe she was anything but a climber. And if her teenaged marriage and divorce had taught her anything, it was that she wanted her next lover to see her as an equal.

Quite simply, loving Javier Ramirez de Arellano was a vulnerability Lily Richmond couldn't afford. And so, before he could respond to her spontaneous outpouring of love, she told him she had to go.

A few weeks later, long after she'd packed her bags and flown away, she heard he'd left Buenos Aires for his parents' sprawling cattle ranch, where he'd married a woman his parents had chosen. An 'acceptable' bride, 'well-suited' to his place in the higher echelons of Argentinian society.

The news had crushed her tender heart into a sludge of anguish and pain.

He'd divorced the girl within a year. Flown to England. Begged Lily to run away with him. They could start a dance studio. Forsake dance altogether. Whatever she wanted. He'd filled a ballroom with rose petals, sat her down and, like a reverse Prince Charming, taken off her high heels, then danced her through the petals barefoot whispering *Te adoro. Te adoro. Liliana, mi amor.*

She had married by then, so had been forced to refuse him.

He remarried.

She divorced.

He divorced . . .

. . . just in time to congratulate her on her latest round of nuptials, which had lasted for some fifteen years. The scars she carried from that one were painful enough to propel her away from the world of romance. Mostly. Sex, after all, wasn't always about love.

They'd faded out of one another's lives these past few years.

She, devoting herself to her studio and judging events like this one.

He, lost in a world of Argentinian tango and its devotees. Dancers bowing at the altar of nostalgia, sadness and romantic laments.

Waste of time, frankly. Love was pain and that was that.

'Lilian, please,' Javier persisted. 'You're worrying me. I care about you. You know that.'

Of course she did. But she also knew from the ring on his finger that rumours of his divorce were false.

She straightened. 'Have you only just arrived? Here at the ballroom, I mean.'

'Yes. Well.' He waved his hands. 'You know me. Latin timekeeping.'

Yes. She did. Always an 'I do' too late.

He explained how he was in the UK for daily training sessions with his students. Speaking of the more accomplished Argentinian couple, he said, 'I've trained Lucia from a young age.'

'And the boy?' Lily asked.

'Cristobal?' Javier smiled, cupping his knee between his hands and dropping Lily one of his slow, sexy winks. 'You'll like this. Their story.'

'Oh?'

'Mmm.' He proceeded to tell Lily how Lucia and Cristobal had met at a tango class and fallen in love. He knew that Lily would see the parallels with their own story, and that it would take her mind back once again to the seven steamy days they'd spent in bed. As he did, he let his eyes drop, following the line of her jumpsuit's central seam. As his gaze hit the zipper's apex, nestled in the centre of her décolletage, he licked his lower lip, as if remembering the taste of her skin.

Lily flushed. To compose herself, she glanced out at the floor then back to his ring finger. 'A very romantic story. And did you bring your wife with you to the UK?'

'There is no wife, Liliana.' He gave a sad laugh and held up his hand. 'This is my father's. He passed earlier this year.'

She cupped her hand round his. 'I'm so sorry.' Their eyes met and a current of electricity swept between them.

The crowd burst into applause as the dance came to an end. The first notes of the tango sounded. She dropped his hand. Flustered, she scrabbled for a different topic. 'Whilst you're here, will you only be doing private coaching?'

'Mostly. We're off to Blackpool, of course, in a few weeks' time, but I am doing some workshops.' He brightened then made a deferential mini-bow. 'The Argentine Embassy is actually hosting an event in Liverpool next week. I would love for you to be my guest. Or,' he added, knowing if he gave her the chance she'd refuse him, 'if you would allow me, I'd be honoured to offer a tango workshop at your studio.'

'Well, I don't know, Javier,' she said before she could stop herself. 'We're awfully busy these days.'

Stupid, stupid woman. Why was she always denying their connection? Surely she was at a point in her life when she could allow herself the pleasure of a man like him . . .

But it was too late to take the rejection back.

Disappointment flickered through his eyes. 'Of course you are.' He took her hand in his before raising it to his lips for the softest of kisses. 'Perhaps next time.'

For a moment the two of them watched the dancers on the floor, thinking of what might have been between them.

Then Javier changed the subject. 'I was here earlier, actually. When they were loading that poor girl into the ambulance.'

'Yes. Awful.' Lily lowered her voice, knowing she could confide in him. 'I'm not convinced it was a natural death.'

'No?' Javier's interest was piqued. 'Funny you should say that.'

Lily looked over her shoulder to see if anyone was nearby. But the risers were empty apart from the two of them. 'Why?'

'I saw, well, rather I heard something earlier that would support your theory.'

He had her full attention now.

'The Duke was chatting with a couple of people up on stage. I was with Lucia and Cristobal at the time, so was very nearby. He was speaking with a short, stocky man—'

'The new sponsor, yes.'

'Him, Veronica Parke-West, and a couple other members of the GDC.'

This must have been when she was out looking for Jack. Her heart lodged in her throat as he continued.

'The sponsor was asking whether or not it had worked. The "scare tactic". I thought it seemed odd after what had just happened.'

Lily had never heard of murder referred to as a scare tactic, but . . . she supposed it depended on the circles you ran in. 'Did they say anything else?'

At that moment, the tango came to an end. Lily glanced out at the dance floor and saw Ruby Rae and Vlad in the grip of a fiercely passionate embrace. The two Argentinian couples looked to have made a suitably dramatic finish, too. Amidst the whoops and hollers, she and Javier politely applauded the dancers. Once they'd struck new poses for the opening of the Viennese waltz, the pair resumed their conversation.

'Veronica said something, too,' Javier told her. 'Something along the lines of "She's never been able to take a hint." The Duke said he thought they were going to have to double down on the mission.'

The mission?

'Make sure things were twice as clear at the Blackpool Ballroom Bonanza. You're judging there, yes?'

'So far as I know. The GDC isn't in charge of the judges for that competition.'

'What were they talking about, Lilian?' Javier asked. 'Is this to do with you or that poor girl?'

'Both,' she whispered. It had to be.

'It seems too calculating.' Javier's eyes were on the stage. 'Even for The Duke.'

After a moment's thought she said, 'You're probably right.' He had the scruples of a python, but killing a girl to make a point? 'He'd rather have me hung from a mirror ball for all to see.'

Javier's entire body bucked against the thought. 'I would hang him before such a thing would happen.'

For just a fraction of a second, Lily allowed herself to feel protected by his declaration. Then, too frightened to give herself access to something she knew in her heart she couldn't have, she gave his knee a little pat. 'Sorry, darling. I've got to go.'

Chapter Fifteen

After sending a quick text home about her altered ETA, Susie climbed into the driver's seat of the Lily Richmond Dance School van.

She glanced across to the passenger seat. 'All right there?'

Lily clicked her buckle into place. 'Perfect, darling. Thanks for driving.'

Susie grimaced a 'you're welcome' smile. It was that or wait until morning. The last train to Liverpool had long since left the station.

As she acquainted herself with the van's controls, she thought about the evening's events, trying to decide if this was a path worth pursuing.

A possible murder case that could catapult her to the helm of Dotiwala's Detective Agency.

Or a too-complicated trip down memory lane, awash with old grievances and new rivalries.

Susie wasn't sure. She did think that Lily was on to something, though, especially once her former mentor had told her about the conversation Javier had overheard on the stage between The Duke, Scouser Sam and Veronica Parke-West.

There was undoubtedly more to this dance competition than met the eye, and Susie was inclined to believe that Oxana's death wasn't simply down to natural causes. The case had definitely roused her interest. Enough to work on it with Lily? Or was it tidier to leave the skeletons from her past hanging in her closet and keep moving on with her new life? And it wasn't just Lily. It was Jack. Seeing her former partner had shaken her. Could she really work on a case that he was so involved in? One where he was a potential suspect, even?

Whilst Susie drove, excitable post-competition chitter-chatter dominated the first hour of the journey. It eventually died away as most of the dancers either fell asleep or plugged into their earbuds, in a world of their own. Lily gazed out of the window, clearly deep in thought.

Susie glanced into the rear-view mirror at Ruby Rae who, despite her suggestion it might not be the best Health and Safety decision, was cuddling her enormous first-place trophy as if it were an Eiffel Tower-shaped pillow. She was also, at long last, asleep.

Lily looked back at her dancers, and in a soft voice said, 'They did well today, my darlings. Didn't they?'

Despite her internal battle of *should she, shouldn't she*, Susie smiled at the memory of the beaming faces up on the podium, reminding her of the days when she and Jack had been the ones up there, holding a glittering trophy aloft for all to see.

'You should be proud,' she said. 'You can see the Lily Richmond touch in all of them.'

Lily waved her remark off, but couldn't hide her smile.

Ruby Rae and Vlad's win hadn't been much of a surprise. From the little Susie had seen, they'd been on fire tonight.

'Who took second?'

'Lucia and Cristobal,' Lily said, and then, in a slightly different tone, 'they study under Javier Ramirez de Arellano.'

The name kind of rang a bell. 'Oh?'

Lily failed to take her cue to elaborate, moving on to the third-place winners instead. 'I thought Maisie was going to faint when she and Darren were called.' She gave a naughty little laugh. 'I'm surprised Marmaduke wasn't incandescent at the prize-giving.'

Susie agreed. He'd clearly been furious that Lily's dancers had done so well, but hadn't bawled out any of his dancers or the judges. In fact, he'd been incredibly distracted as he'd handed out the statues. Almost . . . spaced out. 'Did any of his dancers place?' she asked.

Lily shook her head. 'The couple who took fifth had done some training with him, but they were from Jack's school, really. There were a couple of Marmaduke's amateurs who placed, but . . .'

A *fait accompli*. Lily had won this round. On the dance front, anyway.

Susie remembered Marmaduke well from her own tenure as a dancer, and just the thought of him made her shudder. The man might be older, chubbier and balder now, but he looked meaner for it. And if he and Scouser Sam were in cahoots, well. She'd dealt with many a character like Sam, back when she'd been in the police, and it never ended well. For the police.

'You're sure you want to pursue this, Lily?' she asked.

Lily twisted in her seat to face Susie. 'Yes. Very much so. The truth is, there were any number of people who had a vested interest in seeing Oxana out of the picture.'

'To dance with Jack?'

Lily inhaled sharply. 'Yes. There's that and . . . well. This is a vicious world, darling. Even more so than when you left it. People pay to stand on top of that podium and will do terrible things to make it happen.' She lowered her voice another notch, 'And there are judges willing to accept money to make their dreams come true.'

'Really?' Susie had heard whispers before but had dismissed them.

'I'm afraid so, love. Just give me one glance at a judge's handbag or shoes and I can tell you whether or not their scoring came with a cash incentive.'

'So, do you think one of the judges might have done this? Killed Oxana? Or had her killed?'

Lily leant back in her seat, considering the question.

'It's certainly worth thinking about. Or, perhaps more to the point, we should look at the amateurs who study under them.'

'Why?'

'They're often the ones with money, darling. The ones who have the means to get the endgame they desire. It's an expensive hobby, dance. Endless lessons from the very best pros. Travelling round the world, sometimes for months at a time, to train and compete. Accommodation, food, nutritionists. The dresses, the make-up, the stylists, the shoes. Oh, god, the shoes! Professionals earn their living by teaching those who have, because they, too, must pay their bills.'

'*You* didn't.' Susie threw her a look. From memory, Susie's own father hadn't paid very much for her classes, and she didn't recall any of the other children being particularly wealthy. But Susie had also been busy with school and then, later, the police academy. Her life back then had been a constant juggling act between the 'real world' and that of the competitive dancer. But, despite the intensity of it all, Lily's studio had always been her sanctuary. A place where the rest of the world melted away the moment Jack held out his hand to her. In truth, dancing had never been about the competition element for her. It had been about the sheer elation she'd felt when Jack took her in his arms and swept her round the floor as if she were the most precious thing in the world.

Now that she thought about it, she wondered if she'd been the unwitting recipient of countless generosities throughout her years under Lily's wing. A 'job' sweeping up the studio when her father was feeling the pinch. Lily's mum Audrey's ability to 'magic up' Susie's costumes. Lily's surprise when a sponsor 'just happened' to have given her a pair of shoes in Susie's size. For someone whose profession it was to notice the details other people didn't, she saw now how blind she'd been to her own situation.

A rush of emotion lodged in her chest as it struck her just how much Lily had looked after her in those strange, rudderless years after her mum had died. And when push had come to shove, Susie had turned her back on her. In what she realized now was a show of true loyalty, Lily had respected Susie's decision to walk away.

She tuned back in to Lily's conversation. 'Before I opened the studio and met you, I taught my fair share of wealthy students. Socialites and the like.'

'In Liverpool?'

'No, darling.' Lily's voice sounded faraway now, as if she had travelled back in time. 'America. Denmark. Japan mostly.'

For over a decade, and mostly without the company of her then husband. 'But anyway, that was all years ago now.' She gave Susie's knee a brisk pat and, as she had so often in the past, guided the conversation back in the direction she wanted it to take. 'So. Yes. The amateurs are worth taking a look at. And the judges.'

'And Jack?' Susie tentatively added.

Lily winced and considered her answer before saying, 'I did wonder about him earlier tonight. He's the obvious suspect, being so close to Oxana. But I've come to think that no one can fake how shocked and upset he was. You know, no matter his involvement with the likes of Marmaduke Fitzgerald, I think Jack Kelly's worst behaviour over the past few years only goes so far as stealing my star pupils.' She lowered her voice to a whisper. 'Honestly. I have to admit, it's a wonder he hasn't got his mitts into Ruby Rae yet.'

'Would she go?'

Lily gave a near imperceptible shake of her head. 'If it meant going all the way to the top? Maybe. I like to think she's loyal, but is anyone really these days, darling?'

Susie thought again about Jack, and the way he'd gone off to speak to Topaz and never come back, despite the final urgent look he'd given her, communicating that they had unfinished business. If she needed a reminder that being number one over-rode matters of the heart like love and loyalty, she'd had one tonight when she'd clapped eyes on Jack Kelly. She slid her gaze back to Ruby Rae, her cheek pressed against the large glittery orb atop the metre-high trophy.

'I guess we'll find out.'

Chapter Sixteen

DANCE DAILY
BREAKING NEWS

As reported by Pippa Chambers

The United Kingdom Open to the World Ballroom and Latin Dance Championships in Whitby screeched to a halt early in the competition this Saturday, when famed Ten-Dancer Oxana Bondarenko tragically died mid-tango in the arms of seven-times world champion Ten-Dancer, Jack Kelly. Police, who arrived on the scene at the request of the paramedics, pronounced it a 'sudden death'. They do not believe there are suspicious circumstances.

Oxana, also the winner of the famed Miss Cha-Cha-Cha of Minsk competition (2010–12), is remembered fondly by her fellow competitors.

Johanna Gunnarsson of Iceland cried tears of sorrow as she remembered her peer. 'Because of my devastating injury, Jack was forced to dance with someone else. I could not have been more grateful to Oxana for temporarily stepping into the breach. We were the closest of friends. She had legs to die for.'

Vladimir Zukas, partner to American champion Ruby Ray Coutts, remembers taking dance lessons with Oxana as a child in her native Belarus. 'She was always going to get to the top and she did it. In Latvia we have a saying: the young ones dance as the old ones whistle. I guess she will be forever young.'

Global Dance Council Chairman Marmaduke Fitzgerald had this to say about the dancer's contribution to the world of competitive ballroom dance: 'I knew from the moment I saw her YouTube channel that she was meant to be a partner to our "prodigal son", Jack Kelly. Belarus and the dance community have lost one of its purest souls today. The only silver lining to this devastating loss is knowing she was doing what she loved most in the end. As I hope, will all of us. I know you will join me and our sponsors, Scouser Sam's Scaffolding and Skips, in a prayer that she may forever rest in peace.'

Jack Kelly was unavailable for comment.

A 'sudden death' – often attributed to a heart attack or stroke – is not a standalone incident in the dance world, but it is an infrequent occurrence. Last year, seven similar incidents were reported across the globe. Most of the deceased were competing in the Over-55s.

Bondarenko's family, who could not be reached for comment, are believed to be in Belarus.

Watch out for the full results of the competition which (spoiler alert!) will see some familiar and talented faces at the top of the podium, as well as a few new ones!

Chapter Seventeen

Ruby Rae dropped down to her knees alongside her exactingly made single bed and, after a moment's reflective silence, began to pull out her shoe boxes.

It hadn't initially been her plan to make voodoo dolls when she'd first started competing, but whoopsie-daisy. Here she was with a rather delightful array of them. And after tonight's events, topped off with her very deserved win, it felt like the perfect time to get her babies out.

They weren't *actual* voodoo dolls. She didn't stick them with pins. Okay, maybe a little, but she hadn't read any dark web guides or satanic bibles so that she could get things exactly right. She'd just been born and raised in Louisiana, where that kind of thing came with the territory.

She opened the first shoe box and smiled down at the little plastic bodies.

'Hello, my pretties.'

She beamed at them for a moment, her fingers hovering over their little satin dresses, not yet allowing herself to touch her beautiful, beautiful dolls.

When she was ready, she took out several of the figures and

arranged them on a little stage made from a long boot box and a rather beautiful Hermès silk scarf she'd stolen from one of the amateur dancers when she'd been out competing. One of many little keepsakes she'd collected through the years.

She froze when she heard the sound of footsteps in Lily's room above her. She waited for the click of the bedroom door and the five, six, seven, eight soft creaks of the floor as her mentor padded to her ginormous bed.

It was always a risk, running the downstairs shower as she did while she was in here playing. Lily could easily mistake it for the perfect time to come in and poke around her room. If she came in now, she'd discover everything, decide Ruby Rae was mental, kick her out and then she'd be homeless.

When she heard Lily turn on her television, she took out her most cherished doll: Ken. She gave his plastic helmet of blonde wavy hair a stroke. She'd tried to glue on some curls at the nape of his neck (accidentally on purpose purloined at their last competition when she'd been casually leaning in for some air-kisses and then . . . snip!), but they hadn't stuck. A glittery blue Sharpie had given him nearly the right eye colour.

She propped him up against a box of rose-gold rehearsal shoes. Time to find him a partner.

Hmmm . . . Who would Jack like to dance with tonight?

She plucked Japanese Princess Barbie out of the line-up. The doll should have more accurately been called High-Heeled Geisha Barbie, because that's what she looked like. Presumably the people who designed her thought throwing the inky-haired minx into a pair of platform shoes with a slash of eyeliner made her modern. Idiots.

Never mind. Today she would be called Princess Kiko.

She pulled out another box and lifted off the lid. A shiver of delight trilled through her. An entire box of Goth Sindy dolls. Wasn't eBay just the best place in the world?

Once she'd connected the itsy-bitsy chain links on Princess Kiko's slashed leather top and put her on the stage, she opened the last box and picked up a blonde Barbie. The one wearing a fire-engine-red bikini top and matching tulle skirt that billowed out from her teensy-tiny waist. It was amazing how very much like Oxana the doll looked.

Soooo pretty.

And then she ripped off her head.

Chapter Eighteen

Marmaduke Fitzgerald was having trouble getting to sleep. Probably shouldn't have popped the little blue pills.

He picked up his phone, started writing a text, then gave up halfway through. He didn't yet have enough pawns in place to send it.

He considered waking up his wife to see if she was up for a bit of late-night fellatio, then thought better of it. They were having friends over for a late Sunday lunch tomorrow and she'd be up early, fretting about ironing serviettes and whether to fold them into swans or whatever the hell it was she did to keep up with the goddam Joneses.

Tonight had been a disaster. Not so much the Oxana part. That had been a bit of a coup, all things considered. But the rest of it? A fiasco. Now that he thought about it, the fact Lilian had unearthed Jack's ex-partner so quickly was awfully suspect. Genius. Because it made her look so concerned. So *caring*. Not wanting poor Jack Kelly to endure one moment's worry about his next partner. Bloody bitch. Jack was his puppet to pull the strings on, not hers. This memory lane business threw a massive spanner into his plans to insert Topaz into Jack's life. It was almost as if she knew how the evening was going to play out. Classic Lilian Richmond. Feign innocence while dipping her pen in poison all along.

He imagined submerging one of those needles she'd been holding into poison then bending that sweet little derriere of hers over and . . . prick!

He instantly went hard.

What the hell. He'd give himself a hand job for a change. The half-written text to Jack instantly forgotten.

Chapter Nineteen

Despite the late hour and the inevitable early start, Susie's mind stayed active after she'd finished dropping off Lily and her dance students and finally made her way back home. How could her brain keep quiet when her old world was careering towards her new one, with a murder to solve at the heart of it?

She curled up on the sofa, fired up her laptop and began to write an email to Madhav, detailing the night's events, including a list bullet-pointing areas she wanted to look into before she met with Lily again. A pathologist's report, if there was one. Toxicology. Ditto. Background on Oxana. A call log if they could hack into her phone. She thunked her forehead. Idiot! Lily had taken the studded tote home. She made a handwritten note, reminding herself to retrieve the phone from Lily, along with the rest of Oxana's things asap. She should've got hold of that bag tonight. It had already seen a loose chain of custody. Rookie error. It wouldn't happen again.

She went back to her list.

Background and business checks on Scouser Sam, Marmaduke, the British Dance Council and, after a few moment's consideration, she added Ruby Rae to her own, handwritten list of people of interest. She was one to keep an eye on. She sent the email, put her notebook on the keypad and closed the laptop on top of it. That was all she could do tonight.

Still too restless to go straight to bed, she went upstairs, into her room, and tiptoed to her closet, where, stuffed far in the back in a dress bag, she found what she was looking for.

She slipped into the bathroom, flicked on the light and, after hanging the slightly dusty bag on the back of the door, unzipped it.

A sigh flew out of her. One weighted with memories and, yes, she'd admit it, love.

She slid the midnight-blue ballroom gown out of the protective cover and, before she could talk herself out of it, pulled off her cotton wrap-around dress and slipped it on.

It wasn't a perfect fit. Not any more. But, despite the snug sensation, she felt those faraway tingles return. The ones that whispered through her body like fairy dust, shifting the way she moved her limbs from steady and reliable to . . . effortless grace. She closed her eyes, imaging, just for a moment, how she might feel if she were to find herself in the right place at the right time in the arms of the right partner . . .

She'd had such a love affair with this feeling, all those years ago. And with Jack. She'd been dancing and living the dream. Right until it all blew up in her face.

Susie opened her eyes and stared at her reflection. She had to face facts. She was terrified of feeling as defenceless and broken as she had the day Jack Kelly had snapped her heart in two. She couldn't let it happen again. Wouldn't.

She looked at her bare toes. Pointed them. Flexed.

She nudged her big toe against the edge of the bathroom

door, pushing it open just a bit so she could see into the dark of her bedroom, to the figure lying, peacefully asleep, in the bed. She owed it to him to be 100 per cent focused on the future. Their future.

Her reflection beckoned to her again.

According to Madhav, finding closure meant facing your past head-on. Perhaps life was dropping her past in front of her so she could do just that. The hand-embroidered crystal bodice of the dress caught the shabby mirror light and sent a spray of glittering reflections around the room. Despite herself, she smiled. Maybe it was time. Especially if closure came with an added bit of sparkle. She might mention it when they caught up in the morning. Maybe.

Susie took off the dress and slid it back into the bag, then pulled on her pyjamas – an oversized, AC-12 T-shirt her dad had got her a few Christmases back, and a pair of polka-dotted bottoms by George. Back in her room, she blinked against the threat of tears as she looked upon the figure sleeping in her bed. She'd once thought herself incapable of this type of love again. The kind that felt as essential as oxygen or a heartbeat. It was the type of love that could make her heart burst with joy or, without a moment's thought, see her throwing herself in front of a speeding car if it meant saving his life rather than hers.

She reached out to touch his red-gold hair, then pulled her hand away. She wasn't entirely sure what her heart was doing right now – tearing apart or holding fast. It was exactly how she'd felt earlier tonight when Jack Kelly had leant towards her, his lips almost brushing her cheek. As if her world was finally, at long last, going to become whole again. Or, more likely, completely blow apart.

The promise of his touch had detonated something in her. Destroyed her common sense and dislodged a fragment of emotional shrapnel that, like a soldier once wounded in battle, she'd thought had long since been sealed in tough, resilient scar tissue. But no. Here it was again.

Living proof that people didn't learn from their mistakes.

She climbed into bed and clicked out the bedside lamp, careful not to disturb the covers too much as she did so, or the sleeping figure beside her – that of her beloved little boy. The son Jack Kelly must never know was his.

Chapter Twenty

Jack lay in bed staring at the three dots endlessly blooping below his last message to Marmaduke. He'd thought he'd known how bad the strain of extreme stress was before, but flipping heck, he'd not had a clue.

One dead partner. The reappearance of another one he'd never believed he'd see again. And the presentation of a brand-new one, not so much dangled in front of him as shoved at him with a list of conditions that gave him no wiggle-room whatsoever.

And still, he'd managed to say no to The Duke.

He'd never really done that before. For the last seven years, they'd co-existed in a loosely defined partnership, the two of them. The Duke handled spreadsheets and property taxes and all the other bits and bobs he'd taken off Jack's hands owing to his 'difficulty with numbers', while Jack's solitary job had been to dance. Well, win, really. Which he had done. Right up until a few hours ago when Oxana had dropped dead in his arms.

And who should appear during the midst of the most epically banjaxed moment of his life but the only woman in the world he'd ever hoped to impress. Like, *really* impress. On a cellular level.

Susan Grace Cooper.

She still took his breath away. Maybe more so now that she had taken those steps away from competitive dance and proved there was life beyond it. *Jaysus.* Just lying here thinking about her pressed the air out of his lungs. She was the one living person whose approval meant the world to him. She was also the one person who was more painful to see than anyone else he'd ever disappointed. And it was a long list.

Saying that, seeing her had freed something in him. Cracked open the part of him that had to admit that, maybe, at long last, things had gone too far. Which was why, when he'd got back to Liverpool a few hours ago, he'd texted Marmaduke to say that, with regret, he'd declined Scouser Sam and Topaz's 'generous' offer.

And now these three little message bubbles were taunting him. Teasing at the frayed edges of his nerves. Hadn't he fulfilled his brief? Visited the darker edges of competitive performance enough times to last a lifetime?

Maybe this was the moment his mother had warned him of. The one when he would need to take stock of the decisions he'd made in life and, quite possibly, look to a higher power?

He threw back his duvet and went to the window, squinting through the murky darkness.

The fog shifted and there it was. The Metropolitan Cathedral of Christ the King or, as it was known locally, 'Paddy's Wigwam'. He'd actually been recently. For a beer fest down in the crypt. Brilliant craic it'd been, too. Singing, dancing, the lot. He'd had to double his run for a week to get the carbs he'd drunk off the scales, but it had been worth it.

A run. That's what he needed. A run would clear his mind.

He tugged on some joggers, pulled on a hoody, and grabbed a baseball cap that Swarovski had sent him after he wore one of their bespoke shirts a couple of years back when he'd appeared on *Strictly*.

By the time he hit the promenade, the cooler than normal April air iced away all the thoughts that had kept him awake.

That's it, Jack, he told himself. Keep on running and they won't catch up with you. Never have. Never will.

As the dots bounced away on his phone he ran two miles, three, four until, on a road not too far from the Merseyside Police Sports and Social Association, he turned off onto a small industrial estate where the Jack Kelly Ballroom Dance Studio lay. If he couldn't work it out, he'd dance it out. Only . . .

Only he couldn't.

Jutting out of the smashed remains of the floor-to-ceiling window showcasing his main rehearsal studio was a very large, quite immovable, industrial-sized skip.

Chapter Twenty-One

And as dawn breaks on yet another day in the magical world of professional ballroom dance, it is impossible to feel anything less than giddy with delight.

What chaos! What mayhem! And ever so much fun it doesn't seem right to stop at just one.

So many dancers. So little loyalty.

The only question now is . . . who's next?

PART TWO

Chapter Twenty-Two

'Daddyyyyyy,' mewed Topaz Pringle, as she swanned straight through the door that divided each of their enormous presidential suites without so much as a knock of warning. She barely glanced at Veronica Parke-West, who was desperately clutching the high-thread-count sheets to her wrinkly, cadaverous body. Time really hadn't served the former world champion well. Whoever had 'done' her back in the day should be doing time for crimes against facial reconstruction.

Never mind. Not her problem. She clattered her diamanté-embellished nails along the coffee pod selection and stopped on Irish cream. Mmm. Yes. That would do nicely.

'How's my little-bittle princess this fine morning?'

Topaz scowled. Clearly her father didn't understand what an *epic failure* yesterday had been. Jack wasn't meant to tell her he'd 'think about' things. He was meant to fall over himself with gratitude that she wanted him for a partner.

'Not happy,' she whined, throwing him a sorrowful, doe-eyed look. Her new semi-permanent lashes really helped with the effect.

'Oh, now, buttercup, that won't do.' Sam batted about for his boxers. They'd been flung on a chair in the bay window.

Rather than ask Topaz to hand him said boxers (he knew her well enough now to know which father–daughter lines were sacred), he instructed her to look away while he 'got his bits in order' which, ewww, gross! Her father's wrinkly danglies were definitely not on her 'to-see' list.

She stuffed the pod into the coffee maker. Over the loud exertion of the Nespresso machine, which always made her think of George Clooney, she bellowed, 'What are you going to do now?'

'Not to worry, poppet,' her father soothed. 'Veronica and I put some wheels in motion yesterday that should have Jack Kelly begging to hold you in his arms at Blackpool. It might take a few days, but I think you'll find it pays dividends.'

She was about to harrumph, but then remembered she had an appointment to get hyaluronic acid injections and a laser lip lift tomorrow, so having a couple of days for the puffiness to die down might be a good thing. Not that she was going to admit as much in front of the bony-looking crow in her father's bed. What even was she? A thousand?

The machine spluttered out the final drips of inky caffeine into the hand-crafted artisan mug. Topaz took a sip of the boozy, scented coffee. As the warm liquid swirled around her empty tummy and she felt the first hits of the sugar buzz, she smiled. Mmm. Hot and bothered. Just the way she felt when she was near Jack Kelly. God, he was fit. Better than on his Insta site, and she should know because she was his Number One Fan. And on YouTube. And Twitter.

She couldn't wait until he fell in love with her IRL. She had a huge tube of strawberry daiquiri-flavoured oil ready and waiting to slather all over that perfectly waxed chest of his, before slithering up and down his taut body like a sexy boa constrictor.

He'd been properly out of it after his partner had clocked it. Annoying, since she'd been all but guaranteed that one dance in the general round would see him begging to be her partner. After that, the rest of the plan was meant to be easy-peasy. They'd train for the Blackpool Ballroom Bonanza, have loads of hot sex, rehearse in a lake like Patrick Swayze and Jennifer Grey. She'd lose, like, maybe a stone, and then they'd win Blackpool followed by *Britain's Got Talent*. They'd be rich and famous and have a million followers on Insta, then move to Marbella where they would live happily ever after.

She flicked her index finger towards Veronica without looking at her. 'What's she going to do to sort it?'

'That's just it, Princess.' Sam went to brush his daughter's ash-blonde extensions back over her shoulders. She pushed his hand away. His fat worker-man's fingers always got caught in them. 'Roni here has organized for one of Javier Ramirez's star pupils to come to your studio.'

'Ramirez de *Arellano*,' corrected Veronica. 'The brightest light in the world of tango. You're lucky to—'

Sam waved a *shut it* hand at her, eyes still on his daughter. 'He's also going to invite us to that big Argentinian event.'

'What Argentinian event?'

Veronica flourished her ropey old lady arms into an arc and gave a double finger snap '¡*Oye! Argentina!*'

Gross. And also, WTF? 'Could you speak English, please?'

'That's the name of it. ¡*Oye! Argentina!*' She snapped her fingers again. 'It's an exclusive black-tie evening put on by the Argentine government to showcase the products they import,' Veronica explained.

It sounded completely boring. 'What do they import?' Topaz

asked, seized by a need to prove to Veronica she wasn't just a pretty face. But mostly to find out what importing meant.

Veronica shrugged. 'Tango.'

'What? The drink?'

'The dance, darling. One which you will be doing with one of their experts.'

Topaz brightened. 'Jack?'

'No. Jack will be there – anyone who's anyone will be there. You'll be doing a demonstration dance with Felipe. The star pupil I was just mentioning.'

'He's not the one that placed,' she whined.

'No,' Veronica said in one of those drawn-out, patient voices that meant she actually thought Topaz was stupid. 'That was Cristobal Suarez.'

Topaz gave a petulant little foot stomp. Why didn't anyone understand she would only win Jack Kelly's heart if she danced with the best?

She took another sip of her coffee, decided it was disgusting and deposited the mug with a slosh on the marble countertop. 'What's the point of going, anyway?'

Her father put on his concerned daddy face, trying to soothe her. 'Jack Kelly will see you dance and—'

This wasn't the time to be playing the long game. 'It's four freaking weeks to Blackpool, Father!'

Scouser Sam flicked a glance at Veronica. 'He'll be there, Princess. And you and Felipe will do your dance in front of everyone, which is when Jack will realize he's made a very bad mistake and be begging you to be his partner.'

Topaz's hackles flew up. 'I'm not going on a stage being

anything less than perfect!' She was shit at the tango. This was a horrible idea.

'You will, Princess. You are,' her father wheedled. 'Felipe's going to meet you at your studio for training from Monday morning, and every morning thereafter, so the two of you can get yourselves sorted.'

Her trout pout ballooned. 'What about hair? Make-up? I'll need a new dress.'

'All in hand, buttercup. All in hand. Roni here's using the most exclusive numbers in her little black book.'

They both looked to Veronica who was wincing.

'Aren't you, sweetheart?' Scouser Sam demanded.

Veronica rallied. 'The very best.'

'See, my little butternut squash? Daddy's doing everything he can so that his little girl's dreams all come true.'

Topaz looked between the pair. While she resented being likened to a butternut squash (totally a pear shape and that was repulsive), there was a note of urgency behind her father's assurances. She considered him for a moment. Having spent the bulk of her life being droned at about all his faults by her mother – now safely ensconced in a McMansion in Wisconsin with her disgusting excuse of a third husband . . . total perv – she took everything her biological father said with a grain of salt. Which, considering how much salt could bloat, meant a lot. But, unlike her letch of a stepfather, who had pretty much kicked her out so she would 'properly understand the value of a dollar', Sam was very free with his cash, no matter what she wanted. Which was why she gave his cheek a pat and said, 'Daddy. You're so clever.'

Chapter Twenty-Three

The only thing Lily Richmond was accustomed to finding at her front door on a Sunday morning was a stack of papers.

Today, however, she found Jack Kelly practising his samba bounce on the curved path leading up to her covered porch. He was entirely engrossed in the move, one of the more complicated elements in a samba that separated the wheat from the chaff at competitions.

His was good. It should be. She'd taught him the step. High heels. Ball of the foot light but grounded. A quick but distinct pelvis roll on the 'and' part of the one-two count. Solid recovery. Complete control of the torso on the ball change.

Despite the dancing, he wore a haunted expression. She herself had tossed and turned well into the early hours, but Jack didn't appear to have slept at all. 'I hope the neighbours don't think you're one of mine, darling,' she said to him. 'That arm styling is a bit wild.'

He looked bewildered at first that he should find her here, at her own front door. And then, in a quick moment of recovery, crossed to her in three long-legged steps, 'Lily. Thank God you're up.' He pressed his hand to his chest. 'I know your time is precious and that this'll sound utterly mad coming from me, but . . . I've seen the light.'

Once Lily had unlocked the studio, switched on all the lights, boiled the kettle and given Jack a strong mug of sweet builder's tea, made the way her mum had taught her (*leave that teabag in until the spoon stands up in it, love*), she finally sat down at the kitchen island opposite Jack with a steaming mug of Horlicks.

If he was here to confess to murder, she would need a cup of comfort in her hands.

But something about his demeanour told her that wasn't why he was here at all.

He was agitated. His demeanour more like an action hero freshly emerged from a disaster scene rather than what he really was: a sleep-deprived thirty-something who'd just finished what looked like a rather gruelling Sunday morning run from his place to hers. His musculature was taut, entirely at attention. Irises focused, alert to everything around him. A smear of blood swept across his cheek, presumably from the grazes on his hands she was just now noticing. He looked ready to take on an army if it would have him. What on earth had happened?

'The world of ballroom dance is under threat,' he declared.

Now. Lily loved a dramatic pronouncement as much as the next person, but surely Jack saw this was a time to focus one's attention, not broaden it.

'Are you talking about Oxana? I know it was a big shock, darling, but—'

He shook off the question. 'My studio's been destroyed and I'm through with Marmaduke.'

The first blast of news curtailed her elation at the second. 'What happened?'

'Scouser Sam and his lot have trashed it.' Jack told her about the state of carnage his studio was in. The skip through the front window. Sledgehammers to the smaller studios' beautifully sprung wood floors. Broken mirrors everywhere. 'They took my computer as well. All of my students' information. Booking system. The lot.'

A chill swept through her. She could see Scouser Sam being behind something like vandalism. But taking the computer? That seemed to speak to something else, something more sinister. 'Why do you think Sam is responsible?' she asked.

Jack looked at her as if she had missed the most vital of clues. 'Apart from the fact it was one of his skips through the front window?'

'Yes,' Lily said. 'There are thousands of the things scattered round the city. It seems a mad thing for him to do if you had already agreed to—'

'—dance with Topaz at Blackpool?' He looked her straight in the eye, glimmers of the Jack she used to teach right here in this studio coming to the fore. 'That's just it, Lil. I said I wouldn't do it. I texted Marmaduke last night when I got home.'

Lily forced herself not to blink in surprise. How extraordinary. Jack was finally standing up to the competitive dance world's biggest bully.

Instead, she mustered a neutral, 'Oh?'

Jack ran his hand through his red-gold hair and explained, 'I know it's what Marmaduke wanted. What they all wanted,

134

but . . . in good conscience, I couldn't agree to it. Topaz . . . she's not up to that level of competition, Lil.'

Lily had seen the general dance last night and, indeed, the only place Topaz would be winning a professional competition was in a category of one. She asked, 'You weren't tempted to placate the sponsor? Play the politics?'

Jack bridled at the suggestion he'd choose politicking over craft. 'Putting Topaz through a public humiliation wouldn't speak well of me, my studio, or the Global Dance Council.' He jabbed his index finger against the countertop. 'The Duke shouldn't have made promises to someone who he hadn't seen dance. Besides, Oxana had only died a few hours earlier. I know I'm not god's gift to decorum, but it just wasn't appropriate.' He fixed his gaze to Lily's. 'I'm beginning to get the feeling Marmaduke doesn't care about us dancers. That we're pawns in a bigger scheme with him pulling the puppet strings.' He paused for effect. 'And someone like that shouldn't be leading the GDC.'

'Oh. Well, now.' Lily straightened, biting back a commentary on the role she thought Marmaduke was playing in this ever-increasing disaster, not to mention the dark intentions of the GDC. She thought for a moment and then asked, 'Do you think the attack on your studio might be related to Oxana's death? Both events some sort of warning to you?' She was thinking, of course, of the note.

A Clever Bunny Keeps Their Appointments.

What could it mean, and was it in any way related to this latest turn of events? The theft of Jack's laptop?

Jack gave an agitated shrug. 'No idea.'

Both of them were silent for a moment. Lily took a sip of

her drink and, carefully, asked, 'What did you and Topaz talk about, apart from dance, when Marmaduke whisked you away? Did she say anything about Oxana's death?'

'No.' Jack shook his head. 'All she talked about was Blackpool. On and on about how she'd no interest in the amateur scene and that she knew she'd shine as an international pro.' He stopped for a moment, remembering. 'She also talked about how she was famous on Instagram. She's got thousands of followers, apparently.' His expression suggested the followers might not be there because they were in awe of Topaz's talent.

Lily took the lid off a tin of chia seed and agave syrup flap-jacks that a student's mum had brought in, and put it in front of him. 'Did she mention any haters?' There were personality clashes online all the time. And not just on the ballroom-dancing sites. She herself had been victim of some rather vitriolic cyber-bullying, and knew just how brutal a toll it could take.

'She didn't,' Jack said, and then, more darkly, 'you think that one of her followers could have targeted my studio? Instead of Scouser Sam getting his revenge?'

Lily shrugged. 'It's possible, darling. There are some very strange people on the internet.'

They both straightened as the front door clanged shut. Lily stood, adopting a business-like air. 'I'm afraid we're a bit pressed for time. Have you called the bizzies? About your studio?'

'No. No police.' Jack's jaw set in a way that dared her to suggest it again.

'Susie?' she chanced.

'God no.' He scrubbed his hand over his face, as if to wipe away the complicated emotions her name elicited. 'You could've warned me, you know. That she was coming.'

'Would you have stayed?'

His change of expression suggested that she had made the right call. And then, as it softened, she saw something else. Regret.

She felt for him, Jack. He and Susie had been a proper team. One of those couples who had genuinely been the halves to a whole. She realized now that Jack was the one who had come off worse for the separation.

Ruby Rae and Maisie burst into the kitchen, eyes widening as they registered the fact that Jack Kelly was there.

To explain his presence, Lily resorted to a bit of improv. 'Hello, darlings! We've scored a bit of a coup today. Jack here is going to be giving some of his classes out of the studio for the next few weeks.'

Jack looked at her in surprise, and then nodded. They both knew it was generous of her to offer up her studio, considering they'd been competitors for years, not to mention the fact that he had poached some of her top talent in the past. But, right now, it felt as if the two of them were on the same team – something that hadn't happened for a very long time – and she could tell that he was grateful.

'Result!' crowed Ruby Rae with a triumphant hip swivel. 'I bagsy the first couples demonstration.' She smirked at Maisie. 'You snooze you lose, twinkle-toes.'

Chapter Twenty-Four

'Who's the hungriest bear in the house?'

Susie's little boy squealed with laughter as he squirmed beneath another raft of tickles. He leapt out of bed growling, 'I'm the hungriest bear in the house!'

'No, *I* am!' Susie chased him down the stairs then, catching him up into a cuddle, pretended to eat his arm to an ever-increasing set of giggles.

'More, Mummy!' Kian begged.

'Mummy bear needs a cup of tea to wash down the rest of her little boy!' She put him down, indulging him with one more roar as he ran across the open-plan kitchen to the lounge area, where he took sanctuary behind one of the curtains.

'Mummmmmyyyyyy,' her son pleaded from behind the curtain. 'Scare me!'

'I'm supposed to protect you, not scare you, silly-billy.'

'You're the silly-billy.'

She made hand-claws and emitted an embarrassingly lack-lustre, 'Rowr.'

Kian left his curtain cave with a sorrowful shake of his head, patted her arm with a tender, 'It's okay, Mummy. We can try something else.'

She scooped him up into her arms and whirled him round and round until – just like that – she was reminded of Jack Kelly using remarkably similar techniques to put a smile on her face. He'd always been spectacular at easing her from a *bad day at work* mood into rehearsal mood. Cajoling. Teasing. Twirling her round and round the studio until, eventually, the combination of the music, his grace, his smile, his heartbeat and hers all joined as one until the only thing in the world she wanted was to be in his arms. How extraordinary that she'd convinced herself she'd wiped those years clean. She laughed to herself. As her son – their son – would say, 'You're a silly, silly, billy, Mummy.' And he'd be right. After yesterday, the memories were coming thick and fast. But Kian didn't need to know that.

'Little bears belong in little bear dens!' she cried, tumbling the pair of them onto the sofa where, after covering him in throw cushions, the only thing sticking out was a red-gold tangle of bedhead hair. She used her fingers to tease it into something slightly less wild.

Then she mussed it up again. This was Sunday morning at home! Pyjama-time. Precious mother–son moments that pumped through her blood like oxygen.

Anyway, screw Jack Kelly for invading her Sunday morning. Ever since Kian had been toddling about, pudgy fingers clinging to hers, Sunday mornings had been sacred in this house. Anyone involved in her life knew this. Even her father and brother, whose own terraced house backed on to hers, knew better than to come over on a Sunday morning.

The routine never varied. Pancakes. Bacon. (Both with

syrup.) All-day pyjamas and Disney Plus (the one household luxury, beyond the nub of Charlotte Tilbury eyeliner in her bathroom). She left Kian to play with his action figures and looked at her phone as she headed to the kitchen to make the pancake batter.

Quick meet later tonight, darling? I have more clues that I need help putting into order.

She didn't answer the message.

As she whisked a pair of eggs into the flour and milk, she glanced at her son who was kneeling in front of the coffee table, having brought more action figures into the battle. 'Die, little green man, or . . .' he glanced up at her and grinned, '. . . or my mummy will put you in prison like she does all baddies!'

Susie grinned back. Even at his young age, Kian understood that policing was in her blood. Her dad was an ex-copper. Her brother was still serving. She'd done a few years before becoming a detective, believing it would give her a bit more flexibility as regards the time she had with her son. That hadn't worked out so well, but . . . best-laid plans and all that.

Would knowing Jack have changed anything for Kian? Perhaps the action figures would be having a dance-off right now. Or maybe, instead of *Big Hero 6*, *Beauty and the Beast* would be playing on the telly.

A routine she and Jack had done using music from the latter sprung to mind. Her playing Beauty and Jack, her gorgeous, diamond-in-the-rough Beast. Had she really made the right decision? Walking away?

Another memory surfaced. The café where they'd drunk countless cups of tea behind the large, steamed-up windows. 'I don't want any of it, Suze. No waiting. No mortgages. No jobs outside the industry. Nothing that will tie us down until we're world champions!'

She hadn't been raised to think like that. Quite the opposite, in fact. Losing her mum so early had given her entire family an innate need for safety nets. Security. But if being a detective had taught her anything, it was that looking at just the one side of the coin only gave you half the story. Perhaps she shouldn't have made the decision for both of them. Telling Jack he was right. That he should go pro. Be the world champion. But that he wouldn't be doing either of those things with her. And then walking out of the café without so much as a backwards glance.

She watched her son wiggle one of his front teeth.

'Be careful, or it might fall out before breakfast!'

Kian looked equal parts horrified and excited. 'I'd still be able to eat pancakes, right?'

'Better not take the risk,' she teased. It had been loose for a few days now. The first of many, she thought, in yet another phase in his rapidly changing life.

Her stomach churned. Whatever she felt about Jack, she had to allow the dangerous thought that perhaps keeping his son from him hadn't been her best course of action. At the time, she'd thought of it as a preventative measure, stopping both of them from getting hurt in the future. But now she wondered what Kian might have missed out on.

Her heart strained with love for him. Her one hundred and seven centimetres of pure joy. He had Jack's eyes. His hair. His natural poise. But he was also a sensitive little thing. Noticed things about people other boys didn't. He was a carer, and the last thing she wanted was to see him hurt. Which could happen if she got further entangled in this case, and spending time with the father he'd never known.

She watched as tiny bubbles appeared then burst around the edges of the pancakes. Would taking on Lily's case be her best course of action? Or her craziest? This had all come about so fast. Maybe she needed more time. Or maybe, she thought as she flipped the first pancake and saw that, for the first time ever it was perfect, it was time to take a risk.

Chapter Twenty-Five

Lily pressed the bell at Number 23 Brookend Lane and popped on a bright, happy smile. It was critical that this meeting with Susie went well. She'd taken hours to respond to Lily's text. To the point that Lily had begun to wonder if she was going to back out of their agreement to pursue Oxana's killer. Now that she had finally responded, Lily was desperate to tell her everything Jack had relayed earlier and to discuss the new developments. She needed Susie's view on it all.

Susie pulled the door open and put her index finger to her lips, ushering Lily in. 'I've just put Kian down,' she whispered, pointing upstairs.

Ah. She was in protective mode.

Lily followed her in, readjusting her emotions as she did. Sometimes the fact other people had children didn't get to her. Right now, infuriatingly, it stung.

She did a double take at a photo hanging on the wall featuring a little boy blowing a kiss at whoever was taking the photo. Kian. It had to be. He was a gorgeous little thing and a dead ringer for Jack.

She thought of the tiny, newborn version of this little boy.

The one she'd held in her arms right up until she'd insisted to Susie that she owed it to her son to give him a father – and then the two of them had fallen out. Lily could see now that she'd brought too much of her own unresolved feelings and history into it. Just because she hadn't grown up with her father, didn't mean Susie and her family couldn't give the little boy a perfectly happy childhood. Maybe then they'd still have been in one another's lives.

Or, perhaps what she was feeling was simpler than that. Heartache that Susie had something she never would.

She supposed she deserved it after falling for over a decade's worth of lies from her last husband, but sometimes shouldering the blame didn't seem all that fair. Particularly as it turned out he had a family of four back home in Australia. Ah, well. That was then, and right now she had a murder investigation to concentrate on.

'I won't be long, I promise,' she whispered to Susie. 'And you know me . . . always light, light, light on my feet.'

She was surprised to see Susie smile at the memory. One ingrained in all of Lily's former students, no doubt. 'Light, light, light on those feet! No one wants to listen to a herd of elephants waltz!'

She glanced around the welcoming, open-plan living area as Susie led her past a coat rack covered with little boy jackets and, below it, a row of children's and women's shoes all in an orderly row tucked beneath the radiator. No others that she could see. It looked like Susie and Kian lived alone, no partner on the scene.

'There have been some . . . developments,' Lily began. 'With our case.'

Susie frowned. 'Tea?'

'No, thank you, darling, I'm more of a Horlicks girl.'

Susie checked inside her cupboards then, with an apologetic wince, offered, 'Water?'

'Perfect.' Lily settled herself on one of the kitchen island chairs and took a sip of the water. 'Jack came by my house this morning and I'm afraid things have become a little . . . complicated for him.'

Susie's eyes shot to Lily's, but she said nothing, so Lily explained about Jack refusing to partner Topaz, the skip and destruction and theft, and how the skip bore Scouser Sam's stencil. And how, very interestingly, Jack seemed to be turning away from Marmaduke.

Susie wrapped her hands around her mug of tea and joined Lily at the kitchen island. 'Do we think that this is linked to Oxana's death? It sounds to me like the sponsor is trying to scare Jack into partnering his daughter.'

'Possibly,' Lily said. 'You may be right. But the two things happening in one night, Jack's partner dying and then his studio being destroyed – is it coincidence, or intentional?'

Susie contemplated this. 'Perhaps hurting Jack is the real motive here. We can't rule anything out. Is Jack . . . is he okay? He hasn't gone back to his flat alone, has he?' She didn't look at Lily as she said this, clearly trying to appear casual.

'He's fine, darling. I left him at mine, where he'll be safe.'

'Good.' Susie sat back, thinking. 'We'd best look at the big picture here. Not rule anything out.'

'Or anyone,' added Lily.

Susie tapped the side of her nose. 'Exactly. So . . .' She grabbed a notebook and a pen. 'Scouser Sam is definitely a suspect. He has a clear motive: remove Oxana so that Jack can dance with his daughter.'

'Should we add Topaz?'

'Yes,' Susie nodded, writing. 'Absolutely. We need to consider anyone who might have had a reason to kill Oxana.'

'Exactly what I was thinking earlier.' Lily felt pleased that all those true-crime shows she watched were paying dividends; she was starting to think like a detective.

Susie continued to make notes. 'There are a few things to check out on my end. We're still waiting to hear if the Yorkshire Constabulary are doing a pathology report. There are the digital forensics to dig into.'

'Phone logs?' Lily asked.

'Absolutely. Finances. Living arrangements. We need to speak with her family. The other competitors.' She tapped her pen against her lip as she thought of more options.

'Maybe she said something to Kiko and Ramone,' Lily suggested. 'You know how stylists can draw blood from a stone.'

'Yes. Definitely. We'll interview them.' Susie wrote down their names then gave Lily a pointed look. 'I'd like to go through her tote, which I believe is still in your custody?'

Lily airily ignored the vaguely accusatory tone. They were on the same side here. 'Sorry, darling. It's been a busy day. Back-to-back lessons as well as all the hoo-hah with Jack.' That. And she hadn't yet had a chance to go through it a second time. Tonight, she promised herself. And then she'd hand it over to Susie.

After a moment's silence Susie said, 'Madhav is going to draw up a proper psychological profile of the killer for us. It's interesting that Oxana's death was public – very public – and it seems likely that the killer orchestrated it that way. If we also factor in that note you told me about, the one about a "clever bunny", it's reasonable to think that revenge is a possible motive.' She looked up from her notes. 'What about Johanna Gunnarsson? She has a clear motive: revenge for being dropped by Jack.'

'Ah. Yes.' Lily sat back in her chair. 'Jack and I had wondered the same thing, given how upset she was with him for competing without her.'

'Enough to kill?'

Lily held out her hands. 'People have murdered for less, darling. They'd been partners for the last couple of years and did look set to win Blackpool again this year. If Jack hadn't actually told her he'd be competing, I can see why she'd be fuming.'

'Again,' Susie pressed, 'enough to kill? Or to put a skip through his studio windows?'

Lily tapped the list. 'Icelanders aren't known for their Nordic Noir for nothing.'

Susie wrote down Johanna's name then, pen poised to write another, said, 'And, of course, there's the head of the GDC himself to consider. Marmaduke.'

'Well, we know my thoughts on him, darling, don't we? Although . . .' Lily did hate offering anything that spoke to his defence, but . . . 'Why would he pay for Oxana to come over from Belarus only to kill her?'

Susie shrugged. 'Some people look on others as expendable.'

Lily made a noise, indicating it was possible, but even so, it didn't quite fit with Marmaduke's normal modus operandi. He enjoyed digging the knife in. Prolonging the pain. Perhaps he'd had one plan and Scouser Sam another and the two had collided. After all, she didn't know when the scaffolder had come on the scene. She jotted down a note to herself on her phone. Susie didn't have to do all the work on this.

'What about the Argentinians – the dancers who placed second? Didn't you say they were wealthy? Had something to prove?'

'Yes, but . . .' Lily cut off her defence of Javier and his students, opting for a more neutral, 'Yes, but they proved it really, didn't they? Cristobal and Lucia anyway. Very talented, the pair of them.'

Susie gave her a look, like, *C'mon. Who likes second?* She wrote down their names then asked, 'What about Vlad? Didn't you say he danced with Oxana back when they were young?'

'Yes. Perhaps not as a couple, but certainly they were aware of one another.' In just the same way Marmaduke Fitzgerald had been aware of her. 'According to Ruby Rae, he wasn't Oxana's biggest fan. We can certainly ask.'

'And Ruby Rae?' Susie asked in a slightly more cautious tone. 'You think she's on the up and up?'

Lily gave a short sharp bark of laughter. 'She's ambitious, darling. Likes a trophy. Possibly a touch more amoral than I'd care to admit, but I don't think she'd resort to murder to get what she wanted.'

Susie held her gaze for a moment and then wrote down Vlad and Ruby Rae's names.

Lily bit back a protest. Putting down her own dancers' names made the surreal nature of the past couple of days startlingly more real. 'Only, Ruby Rae and Vlad were dancing. Surely, they couldn't have been responsible.'

Susie shot her a look that suggested Lilian was being naive.

'Jack mentioned he thought she might be drugged. Have you heard of needle spiking?'

'No, but it sounds awful.'

'It is,' Susie confirmed. 'A plague on the nightclub scene. The goal is to inject people – usually women – as you pass them to watch them pass out later. Just a small prick. They feel a pinch, nothing more. Usually it's a date-rape drug. Rohypnol and the like. Then the next thing the victim knows, if they're lucky, they're waking up in the back of an ambulance.'

Lily shuddered. She knew the world could be a cruel place, but pricking women with needles? She hated to think anyone involved in the world of ballroom dance could be so vicious.

Shelving the grim thought, Lily picked up her phone and, on a hunch, opened Instagram, while Susie continued to systematically craft their 'to-do' list.

'We'll have to wait for a toxicology report, of course. Realistically?' Susie tapped the list with her pen. 'I think the main thing we have to run on right now is motive and, given Jack's refusal to dance with Topaz . . .'

Lily held up her phone, 'Look. These were posted today.'

They both stared at the screen as Lily thumbed through the photos. They were of Topaz and Felipe – one of Javier's dancers – rehearsing at a studio she didn't recognize. Possibly the new one Marmaduke had mentioned?

'It looks like Topaz has found herself a new dance partner.'

'She did that rather sharpish,' Susie said. 'Who is he?'

'Felipe, if I remember correctly. One of the Argentine dancers from last night,' Lily said, shifting the image up so she could read the comments below. 'The one who took fourth. Ah! It looks like they're going to the black-tie event together.'

'What event?'

Lily explained about the glitzy evening that would showcase Argentina's exports including, but not limited to, the tango.

'Not exactly the biggest money-spinner, the tango,' Susie said.

'No, but it is the most interesting,' Lily countered, a little testily. 'Anyway, it looks like they'll have Topaz performing with Felipe as part of a display of "successful international relations", demonstrating Argentina's successful partnership with Britain.'

'Hmm.' Susie tapped her pen on her chin. 'Are we thinking Scouser Sam might have engineered this partnership, too?' Furrows appeared between Susie's eyebrows as she thought about it.

'Darling, don't frown,' Lily instructed automatically.

'What? Why?'

Lily pointed at her own, smooth forehead. 'Keeps the lines at bay. It's something to bear in mind for the future.'

Susie shot her a confused look and then another one, understanding. She started laughing. 'Lily! I'm not getting Botox.'

'I never said anything about Botox.'

'You didn't have to.' Susie was properly giggling now, teasing, 'I could see it in your eyes.'

Lily raised her hands up in protest. 'Honestly.' She spoke from the heart. 'You're a beautiful woman, Susie Cooper. I wouldn't change a thing about you.'

A deeper understanding passed between them then. One that teased at the surface of what Lily had always hoped was an unbreakable bond. But, as neither of them were prone to bursting into tears or falling into one another's arms to sob and admit just how very much they'd missed each other, Lily simply said, 'Anyway, there are a variety of techniques to keep a face young that don't involve injections.'

Susie gave her a *yeah, right* roll of the eyes, then, back to business, pointed at Lily's phone. 'Do you know who else is going to this tango thing?'

'Yes. It's quite a to-do apparently. Some prominent local business owners and politicians are expected to attend. To our end, Marmaduke will be there. And Javier Ramirez de Arellano, of course.'

Susie quirked an eyebrow. She knew that there was history between Lily and Javier, but little beyond the crib notes.

Rather than go into anything personal, Lily explained, 'He's in charge of the dancers who will be performing. In fact, quite a few of the dancers from last night will be there, as well as some of the support teams. Hair and make-up and the like.'

'For a trade show?'

'A black-tie gala. Let's face it. No one's going to go all ga-ga over soybeans, so there's going to be a huge tango display and then they'll invite the punters to have a go after. You know, let them all have a spin with a professional dancer.'

'Is Jack going?'

'Yes. He won't be performing, but he is on the roster of dancers who'll guide the punters through a tango or two.' When Susie frowned at this, Lily added, 'He thought hiding away would make him look guilty, so he wants to attend.'

Susie asked, 'Are *you* going?'

Lily turned cagey. 'I hadn't planned on it.'

Susie threw up her hands. 'Why not? Everyone you think might be involved in this is going to be there.'

Lily sniffed. She was hardly going to admit that she was

trying to get out of seeing Javier again. Her long-ago lover was still one of life's finer temptations and best entirely avoided. Like croissants, or very fine wine. A moment on the lips, and all that.

'Lily Richmond,' Susie adopted the demeanour of a stern schoolmarm, 'I've never known you to pass up an opportunity to dance, let alone teach it. What is the real reason you aren't going to the Argentine gala?'

Lily pursed her lips, then – knowing Susie needed honesty – admitted, 'Well, I could go, darling, but it's invitation only, and that would mean asking Javier to make me his plus-one.'

They shared a look.

Susie got it. She always had. Understood in a trice when something or, in this case, *someone* came with too many complications.

Susie chewed on her lip for a moment then said, 'Look. I understand that it might be difficult . . . but it sounds like the perfect evening to get some more information from people of interest in the case.' She hit the table decisively. 'I think we should both try and get an invitation. I'll be undercover; it's the perfect opportunity to ask some questions and see if anyone's looking guilty.'

'What do you need me for, darling?' Lily knew she was pushing it but continued anyway. 'I don't have your expertise.'

Susie shook her head, a smile on her lips. 'Lily, if you want to pursue this, we have to work as a team. I don't know who half the people are on the dance circuit. I'm going to need you there to help me. So, I'm afraid if you want to get to the bottom of this, you'll have to put on your big-girl pants, ring Javier, and get your name attached to that plus one.'

Lily felt a wash of sunshine fill her chest. Her little strop about Javier had inadvertently brought about the one moment she'd been hoping for when she'd decided to message Susie. The moment when they became a proper team again.

She fought the urge to beam. 'Very well. You win.' She was all business now. 'I'll text Javier.'

'Now we just have to figure out how to get me in,' Susie mused.

'Oh, well, that's easy,' Lily said. 'Jack has a plus-one. You can be his.' Susie's face immediately dropped, and Lily could see the conflicted emotions in her eyes. 'What were we just saying about big-girl pants?'

Susie good-naturedly rolled her eyes. 'Fair enough. Sometimes we have to do things that we don't like, don't we? In order to get the baddie.'

'Exactly. I'll let Jack know that you'll be taking his ticket.' Lily immediately fell back into her role of dance coach as she tapped at her phone. 'You'll have to wear something a bit sparkly . . . easy to move in. If you don't have anything that suits, I've got plenty down at the studio.' She got up from the stool, pressed send and then, not wanting to push her luck said, 'I'll leave you to it, darling. We can meet up on the morning of the event.'

'Or tomorrow when you'll be bringing Oxana's tote over?' Susie reminded her.

'Precisely.' Once she'd had a proper nosey. 'And we'll stay in touch with any developments in the case?' It was a rhetorical question. She put her hand on the door handle and, after a quick glance up the stairwell towards that little boy she ached to meet one day, whispered, 'Oh, and darling? Wear heels. There just might be a bit of dancing.'

Chapter Twenty-Six

Jack had been standing at the top of the grand stairwell of Liverpool's Town Hall for about twenty minutes. Everyone he knew was here and had clocked the fact that he was on his own. All of which was making him feel like a proper eejit. If this was Susie's way of showing him who was in charge, this whole 'let's find the murderer' masterplan wasn't going to work. His annoyance shape-shifted into something else. An acknowledgement that Susie *was* the authority in this case. Late or not, the truth was, he needed her.

He struck what he hoped looked like a casual pose, leaning against the banister, as a seemingly endless stream of well-heeled guests entered the grand hall, all dressed to the nines for ¡*Oye! Argentina!*

Exclamation points weren't the only thing the country did to excess. The generally austere marble interior was vibrant with colour, made up to look like a bustling, night-time Argentine market square, complete with swags of brightly coloured bunting and whorls of fairy lights strung along a series of mini-market stalls showcasing the country's wares. Weaving amongst the guests were servers dressed in traditional costumes, carrying trays heaving with savoury delicacies. It was, to be fair, incredibly inviting.

Not that Jack was enjoying any of the opulent decor or the fanfare each of the beautifully turned-out guests was lapping up, like the free-flowing fizz and wine. Proof, if he needed any, that he wasn't in true Jack Kelly mode. Normally, he would've been down there charming and chatting and pre-booking dances for the tutorials.

His nerves really were getting the better of him. From the moment Lily had sprung the news that Susie would be coming as his plus-one, he'd been on edge. Dread mingled with curiosity at the thought of spending the evening with his former lover.

Tonight could finally be his opportunity to get some answers.

After seven years of shutting down the painful memories, he thought he'd managed to get over it. But his reaction to seeing her on the night of the competition was proof positive that all he'd done was bury his emotions.

So, yes. He had questions. He wanted to know how Susie had been able to turn her back on him. Just up and walk away. Sure, he'd made ultimatums. Insisted that they go pro. But he'd also been in love with her. She should have known he was only pushing them hard because he believed in them and their future.

Even so, he'd lain awake these past few nights wondering if maybe he should've come up with some sort of grand gesture to show Susie that when she'd stood up and walked away that night, she'd torn his heart in two.

Jack scanned the lobby below him once again, his heart rate accelerating at each false sighting. There were plenty of brunettes in evening wear pouring in. But still no sign of her, or of Lily.

Though he didn't feel it, he knew he looked the business tonight. Brynn had done his hair with his usual light touch. Ramone had groomed his eyebrows to cover-model levels. His outfit was perfect. Such was the promise of his custom-tailored Untangomas tango trousers and his black, long-sleeved, V-necked, semi-transparent, torso-hugging shirt. Polyester, but still. The only fires he'd be close to tonight, he'd be starting. That was the idea, anyway. Lily had told him the plan, and he was primed to help her and Susie with the case by observing his fellow dancers without them noticing, looking out for clues or anything untoward. Dancing with a couple of suspects and, as casually as he could, gathering more information.

From his vantage point up here, he'd already seen a few interesting interactions. Johanna had passed by him, leaning heavily on a new sparkly cane as if she was not one, but three glasses of fizz down the hatch. She'd given him what he'd now come to think of as her customary death-stare. Hatred mixed with longing. Ruby Rae and Vlad had swanned in, but, at a signal from the stylist Ramone, had swept past the swarm of servers and into the small ballroom that had been set aside as a dressing room for the dancers. Scouser Sam had arrived in a snug-fitting camel-velvet tuxedo, awkwardly escorting none other than Veronica Parke-West. Their entrance had certainly raised a few eyebrows, including his own. Even Marmaduke had choked on his empanada when he'd seen the pair of them together.

There was just one person he hadn't seen yet – someone he was definitely hoping to avoid.

'Jack! Hiiii!'

Oh, God. Too late. He pasted on a smile as Topaz and her

extensions made an excruciatingly long, stiletto-heeled ascent up the stairs. With each step, she had to yank down the back of the . . . was it even a skirt? More like a feathery fanny pelmet. Two little strips of satin barely covered her enhanced breasts. He hoped like hell she wasn't planning on dancing in that. The three opening back steps and a side drag might be all it needed to fall off.

'Jack, *hi*. How are you?' Topaz planted a rubbery kiss on his cheek before coquettishly asking, 'I hope you're planning on getting a front-row seat for the tango display?'

'Wouldn't miss it,' he said, desperately scanning the lobby downstairs for Susie.

'It's such a shame you're only doing the common people dance.' She flicked her diamanté nails at the guests – some of the most monied, and titled, people in the north of England.

'Ah, well. You know how it goes. Win some, lose some.'

She pouted. 'We both know that's not true. Anyway, what do you think of my outfit?' She struck a pose that very nearly resulted in a costume failure, then looked him dead in the eye. 'I chose it just for you.'

'How . . . lovely.' Dear God, kill him now.

'I should probably go get my hair finished off.' She raked a hand through her voluminous extensions, fluffing them seductively. 'You'll save a dance for me, won't you? After you've done your bit with the punters? I'm *so* looking forward to us getting up close and personal again.' She ran her hand down his arm and squeezed suggestively.

Resisting the urge to pull away, Jack reminded himself that he did very much want to find out who killed Oxana. So, through as much of a smile as he could muster, he patted her hand and said, 'Sure. Absolutely.'

157

At that moment, a familiar voice boomed out in greeting, 'Jack, my boy!' Marmaduke appeared from behind him, thumping him on the back. From his jolly tone, most people around them would never know that he was absolutely furious with his protégé. But Jack knew the tone well. The artificially bright voice meant that The Duke was truly livid about Jack's refusal to do his bidding.

As Marmaduke curled his arm around Jack's neck in what was more of a wrestling clinch than a hug, he noticed who was standing beside him. 'Topaz.' He lavished her with an admiring gaze. 'You're looking exquisite tonight. Ready for the big demonstration?'

'*So* ready,' Topaz preened, swatting at Marmaduke as if he was a naughty rascal for even suggesting otherwise.

'I saw your father arriving with Veronica earlier.'

His tone caught Jack's attention. So he had been right in noticing that The Duke had been surprised at the pair's arrival.

'Yeah.' Topaz faked a yawn. 'Veronica and Daddy are, like, joined at the hip these days. Or, you know.' She pointed at her crotch. 'Joined at the something else.'

Jack and The Duke shared a look. It was clear neither man had wanted that particular picture planted in their mind's eye.

Just then, Jack spied Felipe scanning the crowd from the dressing-room door, clearly looking for Topaz. He frowned when he saw her with the two men, and dramatically tapped his wrist as if to say, *Time's a ticking, Chiquitita!*

'Oh my *gawd*!' Topaz huffed. 'Better go. I thought the Latins were meant to be more chill, am I right?'

After they exchanged air-kisses, made doubly awkward because Jack's neck was still in the crook of Marmaduke's arm, Topaz ran her nails along the expanse of her generous bosom, gestured down at her teensy-tiny dress and gave Jack a saucy wink before mouthing, 'This could all be yours.' Then she swept away with an exaggerated wiggle to her walk.

After she'd gone, Jack managed to duck out of Marmaduke's wrestling hold.

With Topaz out of earshot, Marmaduke dropped his friendly demeanour and brought his face very close to Jack's. 'I don't know what you're playing at, lad, but I suggest you rethink the idea of dancing with Topaz in Blackpool. She's raring to go and, more to the point, it keeps our sponsor happy. I haven't been spinning plates on your behalf all these years only for you to bugger it all up for me now.'

'Oh?' Jack stood his ground, pretending he wasn't at all freaked out by Marmaduke's spittle-heavy threat. The simmering anger coming from the man was a far cry from the generosity that Marmaduke had shown him over the last seven years. It gave the very distinct impression that the only reason The Duke had been so kind to him was because Jack had always done his bidding. Lily was right. The Duke was not to be trusted. 'Do you mean bugger it up for you? Or the Global Dance Council?'

'Of course I mean the bloody GDC,' Marmaduke hissed into his face. 'What else would I mean?'

Jack thought of the brand-new Bentley that The Duke drove. The hand-tailored clothes he always wore. The private residences he had scattered about the country, including one here in Liverpool for 'occasional' use. Was it really all inherited wealth? Or had Marmaduke, as Lily had insinuated, been lining his pockets with money intended for the greater good of the GDC? In other words, was Scouser Sam sponsoring the dancers, or Marmaduke himself?

Marmaduke clearly intended the question to be rhetorical, because he continued in the same slithery voice, 'Later tonight, once you've done your tutorials, you'd better make sure Topaz is in your arms and not with one of these greasy *gauchos*, you hear? Otherwise that studio of yours might soon be decorated with a "For Sale" sign.'

The pronouncements should have brought him up short. But at that moment, something, or rather, some*one,* pulled his full attention elsewhere. He turned away from Marmaduke, leaving the man diving into his pocket for his blood-pressure pills.

Below them, Susie Cooper had just walked in.

Amidst Liverpool's glitterati, all decked out in their sparkliest evening gowns and tuxes, and the scores of dancers all dressed to dazzle, Susie was the brightest of them all. As he took her in – her mahogany hair in an up-do, her subtle make-up, the way her front tooth still snagged on her lower lip when she was nervous – her dark eyes met his and, in that moment, he knew what the difference was between Susie Cooper and everyone else. Not one of them had made his heart skip a beat.

Chapter Twenty-Seven

From the moment Susie entered the Town Hall, her pulse began pounding in her throat.

It wasn't just the unfamiliarity of the glitzy surroundings that was throwing her off kilter. The very obvious wealth of the other guests. Or even the luxurious feel of her form-fitting dress that sang to an all but forgotten part of her, the part that felt feminine. Empowered by her own beauty.

It was Jack Kelly who had her standing frozen in place.

How could she not be? He was buffed and polished and looking like a film star atop the grand stairwell. And he was looking directly at her.

It had been years since a man had looked at her the way he was looking at her now. If ever. It was . . . charged. As if he was wondering how he had ever let her go. But this was stupid wishful thinking on her part, of course. Jack Kelly didn't love her and probably never had. He loved ballroom dance, and that was it. He had made that point particularly clear when he'd put an ultimatum to her all those years ago: go pro, or go solo.

Keeping that thought at the forefront of all others was

critical if she was to get out of this case emotionally intact. If she couldn't do it for herself, she had to do it for Kian.

The way Jack was looking at her, though . . .

'Come on, darling.' Lily, who was beside her, had clearly noticed the way she'd stilled when she and Jack had locked eyes. 'Let's not stumble at the first hurdle. Perhaps our Jack has already gleaned something interesting from Marmaduke.'

Possibly. Marmaduke, who was next to Jack, definitely seemed out of sorts. And, after a brief exchange, so did Jack. Throughout it all, Jack's eyes never left Susie's. The Duke looked visibly annoyed as Jack disappeared into the crowd to make his way over to them.

He arrived in a cloud of Sauvage and charm. For Lily, anyway. The pair exchanged air-kisses and *how are you, darlings*.

'Lily Richmond,' Jack snapped into the opening pose of a tango. 'I don't think you could have conjured up an event more suited to your prowess on the dance floor. And look at you!' He clutched his hands to his heart. 'Dressed to kill.'

Susie winced but Lily took the comment as it was intended and laughed. She looked down at her one-of-a-kind frock as if seeing it for the first time. 'This old thing?'

They all knew it was anything but. Flame-red and a perfect complement to her colouring, it was the kind of gown that drew sighs from women, who imagined what they might feel like wearing it, and a tactical shift of trousers for the men, who wondered what it might be like to take her out of it.

Lily complimented Jack on his outfit, at which point he turned to Susie and, instead of leaning in and kissing her cheek, tapped his watch with a pointed, 'You're late.'

So much for thinking that he'd been looking at her longingly.

Susie gave him a tight smile. 'Just been doing some fact-gathering to find out who killed your partner. Sorry to inconvenience you.'

'You could've called.'

'*You* could've said, "Hello, Susie, so nice to see you."'

'Now, darlings,' soothed a distracted Lily. She was scanning the room, presumably for Javier.

There was a brief, awkward silence. Then: 'You look nice as well,' Jack said grudgingly as if he felt obliged by the rules of common courtesy to compliment her too. But his gaze told a different story as it swept across her outfit.

Susie had borrowed it from Lily's arsenal at the studio in the end, her own small retinue of performance dresses just that tiny bit too snug to be comfortable in, let alone to dance in. This particular dress was a knee-length, ebony body-con number that hugged her curves. It was fringed with Swarovski crystals and shot through with gold accents. With her hair styled and make-up done for the first time in she didn't know how long, she had felt beautiful. Less so, now that she was front line, receiving Jack Kelly's seriously mixed messages.

She nodded to his outfit. 'You too,' she said, mimicking the exact insincere tone he'd used. Their eyes met and connected, tension simmering between them.

He was still the most attractive man she'd ever known. This close, he made her skin tingle in all the right ways. And she hated him for it.

Susie forced herself to return Jack's intense gaze with her own, steady one. Maybe he was doing the same thing she was – searching her face for answers.

His expression softened slightly. 'Suze, I . . .'

She looked away. *This is work*, she reminded herself tersely. *Just another job.* Ignoring anything personal between them was the only way she'd shift her professional mojo back into place. *Of all the things you know how to do, it's this.*

She should've told Lily she'd come as one of the waiting staff. The shoes would've been more comfortable, and she wouldn't have to remain emotionally neutral as her old life crashed into her new one.

'Suze—'

She needed to head off whatever Jack was about to say. 'You've got lipstick . . .' Susie touched her own cheek to indicate where he had a mark on his.

He looked at her, not quite comprehending.

She tapped her cheek again. 'One of your girlfriends has left a little marker.' She cringed inside as she watched her snippy tone register. She wasn't meant to care about Jack. And, more importantly, he wasn't supposed to know she did.

'Not a girlfriend. Topaz.' He went to swipe at it with his sleeve but Lily stopped him. 'I've got a wipe here in my bag somewhere.'

Despite the tension, Susie and Jack smiled at each other. Lily and her wipes.

Jack gestured at the small, crystal-encrusted clutch Lily was digging through. 'What else have you got in there, Lil?'

'Oh, you know, darling,' she said breezily. 'Lippie, phone, chainsaw.'

Jack laughed. Susie smiled. Their eyes caught again, and Susie was mortified to realize she was blushing under his gaze.

She took the fresh wipe from Lily and busied herself teasing away the smear of lipstick high on Jack's cheek. 'There you are.' A spritz of heat spread through her when, as she handed him the wipe, their fingers brushed. Heaven help her when it was time to dance together later. She gave him a perfunctory nod. 'Good as new.'

'Thanks, Mum,' Jack deadpanned.

Susie's eyes shot to his. Did he know—? No. Of course he didn't. He couldn't.

The moment was interrupted by a waiter sidling up beside them. 'Barbacoa?' he offered. They all refused. No dancer ate beef before hitting the floor. Not even at a gala of this calibre. Susie used the interruption to reassemble herself in her professional capacity. 'We've got some bad news,' she said to Jack. She and Lily had spoken to Madhav just before arriving at the hall.

Jack frowned and nodded for her to go ahead.

'As Oxana's death was deemed natural, the North Yorkshire constabulary released her body. She's been sent back to her family in Belarus. Without an autopsy.'

'Scouser Sam?' Jack's eyes darted between Susie and Lily.

Lily nodded. 'Yes. He was true to his word.'

'To cover up the murder, do you think?' Jack persisted.

Susie gestured for him to keep his voice down. They were supposed to be undercover here. 'Maybe. Although, he did say in the *Dance Daily* that he would make arrangements for her body, so . . .' She aimed a pointed look at Jack. 'One of us should have a conversation with him tonight. See if we can get anything out of him.'

Jack put up his hands. 'I'm not your man on that one. Skip or not, Sam has it in for me at the moment.'

Susie glanced at Lily.

'What?' Jack clearly knew complicity when he saw it.

'Well, the thing is, darling,' Lily gave his arm a soothing squeeze, 'we think you're exactly the right person to speak to him. You're the one he's most invested in.'

'But he might . . .' The light dawned. 'He might lose his cool and say more than he means to with me because of promises he's made to Topaz.' He huffed out a sigh. 'I still think it's mad that all these other people think they can pick partners for me. It's not like they own me.'

Susie tried to keep her expression neutral. In a way, Marmaduke – and by proxy, Scouser Sam – *did* own Jack. From what she'd seen, little had changed for Jack since the two of them had danced together back in amateurs. All he'd ever wanted was to rehearse and compete. The other stuff – the boring stuff like finding the money to pay for things – he'd happily left to others. Despite their own fractious past, she felt for him. If he'd known a dead partner and a destroyed studio was the price he would pay, he might have listened when she'd gone on at him about the importance of being able to stand on your own two feet.

As if he'd read her thoughts, Jack ran his hand through his hair and, with a reluctant grimace said, 'Right. Fine. I don't know where he is now. He and Veronica Parke-West swanned in earlier. I haven't seen them since.'

'Oh?' Lily clearly found the coupling interesting.

Susie nodded for Jack to continue.

'I thought with Felipe on the scene I'd be off the hook, but when I saw Topaz earlier, she made it very clear she still wants me as a dance partner. And The Duke still wants me to do it, too.' He pulled a face. 'Says it's for the greater good of the GDC, but I'm not so sure about that.'

'Interesting that they're still pushing for it,' Susie mused. 'Have you seen anyone else?'

'Most of the dancers from the other night are here. Oh, and Johanna. Let's just say it's a good thing looks can't kill.'

Susie went into detective mode. 'If you concentrate on Sam and Topaz, Lily and I can see what we can dig up with the others. Agreed?'

'Liliana! *Bien*. You made it.' Javier emerged from the crowd looking like catnip for middle-aged women. His performance-ready tuxedo was immaculate. His presence commanding and yet, warm, welcoming. His ink-black hair was slicked back, highlighting his high cheekbones, the alpha-male cut of his jaw and, pleasingly, a dimple of delight at seeing Lily. 'Look at you.' He took her hand and kissed it, then stepped back so that he could admire her. '*Estás muy bella*. As if you've arrived direct from heaven.'

Susie waited for Lily to lacerate him with a witty comeback. Of the many gifts Lily possessed, taking compliments wasn't one of them. But none was forthcoming. Was . . . was Lily Richmond *tongue-tied*?

'Javier,' Lily finally managed with a coquettish shake of her hair. 'Do you remember Jack Kelly and Susie Cooper?'

'Of course!' Javier said after a moment of silently adding seven years to each of them. 'You two were atop a podium last time I saw you both. What a partnership you made!'

There was an awkward silence, during which Susie and Jack didn't dare look at each other.

Javier turned to Lily. 'Seeing these two dominate the amateurs at Blackpool isn't the only thing I remember about that trip, Liliana.'

Lily blushed and looked down as the two of them shared some private memory.

Well, well, well, thought Susie. It looked like she wasn't the only one getting butterflies courtesy of her plus one.

After conversation moved on to some of the masterclasses Javier and his team were giving in the area, Susie stepped away from the group to take a moment to look round the hall. She wanted to ascertain the whereabouts of the rest of the people on her suspects list.

Jack had already clocked Marmaduke, Scouser Sam, Topaz, Felipe, Johanna Gunnarsson and Veronica Parke-West. He'd also seen Vlad and Ruby Rae going off to get hair and make-up done earlier. But what about the other dancers? Judging by the outfits, some of them were clearly working the room, but Susie hadn't yet seen Cristobal and Lucia Suarez. Perhaps it was worth sliding off and speaking to the stylists. They'd only just come on the ballroom scene when she had left it, so perhaps she could introduce herself as a potential new client?

'Lily, would you mind if I—' Susie began, just as Lily turned to her to make her own excuses.

'Javier and I were thinking we might . . .' Lily was saying, her cheeks nearly as crimson as Susie's had been a few moments earlier. She'd slipped her hand into the crook of Javier's arm and, to someone who didn't know them, they looked very much an established couple. One in the flush of first love? It was hard to tell. There was clearly a mutual attraction. This was a side of her former teacher she'd never seen before. A tiny glimpse behind Lily's disciplined façade. She liked it.

'Sorry,' Susie said. 'You were saying?'

Lily swept an invisible speck off her dress. 'Yes. Javier and

I were just going to the ballroom where the tango demonstration will be taking place. To check on the dancers,' Lily added in a way that intimated she knew she was behaving a bit like a giddy teen, but that she hadn't forgotten the main reason they were here.

Jack proffered his elbow to Susie. 'I think that's the perfect cue for me and my date here to take a turn round the hall.'

'I thought we might pay the stylists a visit, actually,' she said.

'Our Suze never did go bold enough with the eyeshadow.' Jack dropped a wink in Lily and Javier's direction.

'There's two hours of my life I'm never getting back again,' Susie grumbled, referring to her earlier make-up session.

'Hey,' Jack whispered, 'this is for show. Your eyeshadow's fine.'

'Well, your spray-tan's blotchy,' she shot back, still stinging.

'And *you* look like you've been holidaying in the Arctic,' he retorted, withdrawing his arm from her touch.

They glared at each other.

And just like that, Susie found it much, much easier not to feel any tingles at all.

Chapter Twenty-Eight

What became very clear as Javier and Lily worked their way around the massive ballroom and towards the hall, was that Javier knew absolutely *everyone*.

Right off the bat, he introduced her to the Argentine ambassador, to an opulently dressed couple who owned a swathe of gold mines, and to an old school friend, a billionaire who had made her fortune in the pharmaceuticals industry. Reminders, as if Lily needed them, that the social circles Javier had grown up in were far different to her own. *Never mind*, she told herself as they wove through the stalls celebrating Argentina's expansive array of exports. *You're adults now. There's no longer any need to worry about Mummy and Daddy's approval if he proposes.*

'Lily?' Javier had clearly sensed the flash of tension that had just shot down her spine.

Why did the man have to be so perfect? So attentive? She was here to find a murderer, not to rekindle long-dead dreams.

She feigned a sudden and intense interest in a woman cutting a pineapple with a machete. Of all the things that would happen between herself and Javier tonight, or any day hereafter, a proposal would not be one of them.

She shook off the thought, and they walked on. 'Well, this is all very nice,' Lily said. It wasn't all sheepskins and barbecues, as she'd assumed. 'Such a bounty.'

Corn, soybeans, wheat, wine, precious minerals – and then some.

'Argentina is a very beautiful place to live,' Javier said in that low, gravelly voice of his. 'Everything a person could want for a happy life.'

'Yes.' Lily refused to meet his eye. 'If only it wasn't so very far away from England.' As painful as it was, she couldn't fall back under Javier's spell. If Oxana hadn't been killed, she wouldn't have accepted his invitation. Plain as. She removed her hand from his arm.

Unfazed, Javier put his hand on the small of her back. 'Perhaps we can find you something here that will remind you of everything Argentina promises.' As if he'd already planned this moment, he led her to a jewellery stall. Sapphires and diamonds twinkled up at her, nestled amongst a dazzling display of agates, crystals and amethysts. Lily had never been wealthy enough to buy a vast array of jewellery, but she had to admit she had a weakness for a bit of sparkle. After a quick nod of assent from the vendor, Javier held up a necklace for Lily to inspect.

'Oh!' Lily inhaled.

'Exquisite, isn't it?' He wasn't looking at the necklace.

Feeling that annoying blush of hers deepen, she reached out to touch the thick hoops of Argentine-mined gold which, link after link, led to the most beautiful violet-coloured stone she had ever seen. Below the stone hung several delicate strands, dangling in a loose, rose-gold tassel.

'Lily, please. You must try it on.' Without giving her a chance to answer, Javier moved behind her so that he could put the necklace around her neck, both of them now facing the jeweller's mirror. 'This stone is a perfect match for those eyes of yours.'

Before she could protest, she felt the gemstone slide into place in the dip between her collarbones. In the mirror, she saw his amber eyes glow with approval. The gold tassels teased at the sensitive skin at the edge of her breasts. She drew in a breath as his fingertips grazed the nape of her neck, then, once the clasp had been fastened, traced the length of the chain where it rested against her spine. She allowed herself to wonder what it might feel like if he did the same with his lips.

A tiny moan of pleasure escaped her lips.

A staccato burst of Spanish broke the moment. Lily turned and saw Lucia and Cristobal Suarez. Though she'd seen them once before, she was startled afresh by what an attractive couple they made. Cristobal could easily make the cover of a romance novel. Dark, inky hair. Impenetrably dark eyes. Full lips quirked into a devil-may-care smile. He was tall and lean. Just the right amount of muscular. He was visual ambrosia. Dancing with him would turn any woman into a puddle of desire and longing.

Lucia was the type of woman who knew how to make an entrance. She was dressed to the nines in a diamanté-embellished, barely there dress in midnight blue. Her golden-hued, enviable body was all legs and limbs, brought together by beautifully honed curves. Her eyes, unlike her partner's, were wary. She shifted her thick, jet-black plait over her shoulder as she gave Lily a dismissive up-and-down inspection. 'Javier, you didn't tell us you had an old lover hidden away here in the depths of England.'

Lily stiffened, but before she could reply with a choice retort Javier, ever the diplomat, stepped in to soothe the frothed waters. 'An esteemed peer,' he corrected Lucia. 'I'm surprised you don't know Lily Richmond by sight.'

He took a step back, allowing them all the space to admire Lily, who was grateful that she'd made the decision to wear this, one of her very best frocks. It glittered and clung in all the right places as those little gold tassels shifted naughtily between her breasts.

Lucia pulled a mock-thinking face, as if she had no idea who Lily was.

Some women, Lily thought, really didn't like other women. Whether or not they were competition.

Cristobal suddenly lit up. 'Lily Richmond!' He struck a pose. '*La Reina de la rumba!*'

All the Latin ballroom dances, actually, but she wasn't one to brag.

He took her hand and kissed it as if he were a Regency suitor, his gallantry making up for his partner's frostiness.

'The queen of the rumba, yes,' Javier echoed. He unfastened the necklace from Lily's throat, his breath whispering along her neck as he quietly promised, 'One day I will buy you such a necklace.'

Lily ignored the promise. She'd been through enough 'one days' with Javier to know follow-through wasn't his strong suit. She focused her attention on the young tango stars. This was her chance to try to get some information out of them, to feed back to Susie later. See if they knew anything.

'Congratulations on your placing at Whitby,' she said. 'You made quite a show against some tough competition.'

Lucia scrunched her nose, shooting a few indiscreet daggers at Javier. 'It wasn't what we'd been led to expect.'

Cristobal disagreed, 'Second place was fine. The perfect ruse to keep our competition in the dark about the thrills we have yet to release in Blackpool, eh *bonita*? Señora Richmond, *per favor*. Let me give you a flavour.'

He took Lily into his arms and, with a quick sidestep, recentred his body weight before leading her in a swift double *planeo*. A move that was both simple and smooth but, above all, sensual. A reminder, as if she needed it, that the tango wasn't all about rigid lines and brusque, borderline brutal passion. It was about softness and sensuality. Stirrings in the most intimate of places. Going beyond the rhythm to the very essence of its origins: love and desire. Lily had to admit she was impressed.

The young buck returned her to Javier's side, stepped back and, with a simple bow said, 'A little taste of what's yet to come.'

'If that's the kind of teaser you're offering,' Lily countered, 'I'll be waiting for Blackpool with bated breath. Any more hints?'

Lucia made an impatient, unhappy sound.

Cristobal dropped Lily a sexy wink as he slid his arm around Lucia's waist. 'That's for us to know and the judging panel to find out.'

Javier stepped in then, and, if she wasn't mistaken, almost possessively tucked Lily's hand back into the crook of his arm. 'Lily will be one of the judges,' he warned. 'She's well known for being very, very unswayable.'

Was Javier jealous?

If so, she liked it.

'Well, I shall look forward to seeing you both perform.

Now,' Lily adopted a concerned expression and circled back to her main task: fact-gathering. 'Whitby . . . You weren't put off by . . . events?'

Lucia made a *pah*! noise, as if dancers were always dropping dead when she competed.

Cristobal dipped his head in a show of sombre reflection. 'Heartbreaking,' he said, his free hand thumping against his chest. 'Such a talented dancer.'

'Oh, Cristobal.' Lily reached out and touched his arm, knowing it would irritate Lucia. 'My condolences. I didn't realize you had known Oxana well.'

From the corner of her eye she could see Lucia curling her upper lip.

Lily's heart rate accelerated. Was she close to getting a clue? Cristobal lifted his gaze to meet hers and then smiled brightly. 'Never met her.'

Okay. That still didn't mean he didn't know anything. She tried to probe a little further. 'Shame. She was such a kind girl. We had a lovely chat in the dressing rooms.'

Lucia held up a hand, as if she was already bored to tears by the line of enquiry. 'All that clack-clack-clack disturbs me before a performance.' Looking down her nose at Lily she said, 'We found another room where we Argentinians were able to change in peace.'

'Oh?' One where, perhaps, it was easier to hide a syringe filled with poison? 'I always liked being part of the pre-competition buzz. Everyone else's nervous energy helped focus me.'

Lucia shot Lily a fierce, back-off look. 'We are artists, not performing monkeys. We bring quality to our performance. Not chaos.'

Before Lily could ask what she meant by that, a maître d' called out from the ballroom doorway that the dancing would begin in a few minutes.

'*Vamanos!*' Javier clapped his hands, bringing the session to a close. 'You'd best get to the anteroom. Nearly showtime.'

'See you in there, Javier,' said Cristobal, giving both of them a gallant mini-bow. 'Señora Richmond, a pleasure to make your acquaintance.'

'Likewise,' called Lily as he swept Lucia away, his partner merely inclining her head in Lily and Javier's direction.

Javier had a slightly strange expression on his face as he looked after them.

'Everything all right, darling?' Lily asked.

'*Sí.*' Javier turned to her, his features serious. 'Although, I think I've just learnt that I like having you all to myself.'

She tried to pretend his words had no effect on her. 'Well, now, that's a lovely sentiment, but if the dancing's about to begin, we really should go into the ballroom.'

'Not before we clarify one thing.'

'Oh?' Lily arced an imperious eyebrow at him. She sensed a declaration was about to be made. Was this what she wanted from him? To be claimed as his own? 'And what would that be?'

'You're my guest tonight and, as such, you're here to dance with me.'

A hot flare of desire lit inside her. Yes. *This* was what the tango was about. Possession. Desperation. Pain. 'I can dance with whoever I like, darling. It's a free world.'

'You can,' he conceded, then drew her into his arms and swiftly led her through a far more erotic rendition of the double *planeo* than Cristobal had. The steps were the same but it

176

was the fact that Javier was holding her in his arms that was different. She felt her resolve liquefy as his leg lifted and, with a tuck and shift, swept the length of hers. His solid torso arched towards her until even her areolas stood at attention. His eyes never left hers, as if his main goal was to sear his open desire directly into her optic nerves. *There will never be a day in my life when I don't want you*, they said. At which point, he released her and took a pointed step back. 'You can dance with whoever you desire, Liliana. But will you?' And then, with a possessive hand on her back, he led her deeper into the crowd.

Chapter Twenty-Nine

What a shithole.

Topaz heaved out an aggrieved sigh. So much for an elite night out.

The dance demonstration was due to start in ten minutes and, instead of being primped and pampered by someone who had their own make-up line or a super-expensive shampoo as she had been led to believe by dried-up apple-face Roni, she was in a makeshift dressing room, with *other* people (smelly) and, after false starts with not one, but three other stylists, was currently being assaulted with a *used* brush by this Kiko chick. Allegedly she was the best on the scene, but honestly? Topaz wasn't buying it. Kiko had one eye. Not a look that worked for everyone.

A flurry of motion at the entrance to the dressing room snagged her attention.

'Move,' she instructed Kiko. 'No, not there. Over here, so I can see.'

Ooh! Now things were getting interesting.

Jack Kelly had just walked in with his date, the chubster from the other night in Whitby. The one who'd kept trying to talk to Jack, when he should have been talking to her, Topaz. Were they *together* together? God, she hoped not. If claws needed to come out tonight, the only person getting them into Jack Kelly was her.

Topaz repositioned herself so that when Jack looked over, he might notice, if he hadn't earlier, that her dress was practically transparent. She wiggled her fingers at him in greeting.

Nope. No response.

Never mind. She'd been practising this routine with Felipe like an actual slave, and, to her surprise, was feeling pretty good about it. Once Jack saw her out there on the dance floor, everything would start falling into place. She was going to knock his socks off.

She reached for the clay beaker full of weird Argentine tea sitting beside her. The Latins mainlined the stuff and, as a key player in the showcase team, she'd been kept topped up with it all night, too. It was a national drink called maté, apparently. Even though it smelled rank, she actually really wanted some. She was feeling super-dehydrated all of a sudden. And a bit dizzy. Maybe she shouldn't have had the beef earlier.

It was funny though, she was trying to grab the beaker but she couldn't . . . quite . . . reach it. Not with Kiko hovering around her like an angry mosquito.

The make-up artist smelled funny. Like bitterness and rage.

A bit like the maté, actually. But, unlike Kiko who was a total downer, maté gave you a buzz and helped burn 25 per cent more fat when you danced. Felipe drank gallons of the stuff and had, like, zero body fat. All of them did. The Argentines. All week long she'd watched them wandering round with their skinny little bodies, carrying their special little cups and sucking on their fancy silver straws, like they were all part of some massive beauty cult. So far, all it made her do was wee.

'Quit moving,' Kiko instructed, blocking her view of Jack.

'Quit taking so long,' Topaz sniped.

'I'm doing you a favour.' Kiko pincered a hair bead with a pair of tweezers, then held it in a way that made Topaz wonder if Kiko was going to stab her in the eye. Then she'd only have one eye, like Kiko herself. Freak.

'What's the story with your eye patch, anyway?' Topaz demanded.

'Dancer elbowed me in the face.' Kiko sounded like she was still extra pissed about it.

'Who?' Topaz asked, hungry for gossip. 'Anyone here?'

'No one you know.'

Topaz's eyes shifted across the room to . . . ohhhh . . . The Skank. The blonde who'd won the Whitby competition, and who'd glared daggers at Topaz whenever she was talking to Jack.

Ruby Rae Coutts.

That girl gave her the creeps. No wonder, considering her background. Veronica had told Topaz all about her. Some sort of foundling child who Lily Richmond had adopted from god-knows-where, apparently. Nice hair extensions, though.

Just then Ruby Rae caught her staring. *Crap in a bucket.* Even though Ramone was painting her sparkle lip gloss on, Ruby Rae managed to mouth, 'Beee-yatch.'

Topaz flipped her the bird then huffed, 'Kiko. My dad's paying you a lot for the pleasure of doing this, so . . . chop, chop.' She readjusted herself to better see Jack and instantly felt sick. He was looking at The Skank! But . . . ohhh. Was that a little ripple of tension spread across his shoulders?

Hmmm.

Jack got tense around Ruby Rae. Interesting.

Maybe she'd got it wrong. Maybe Jack had come back here to protect her from Ruby Rae, who was clearly *raging* that Topaz was going to be in the demo dance and not her. Well, it wasn't Topaz's fault that her dad was rich and Ruby Rae was an orphan.

'Stop slumping!' Kiko flicked Topaz between the shoulder blades to get her to straighten.

'Ow! I'm not!'

'Are too,' Kiko snapped back. 'Drink some more of that.' She tipped her head towards the maté. 'You need more energy.'

'*You* need some manners!'

Fuming, Topaz lurched forward, grabbed the beaker, and took a sip of the tea. God, she felt like shit. Like her lungs had decided to shrink.

She tried to place the cup back down on the counter, but instead spilt it with a spluttered, 'Gah!'

What the actual . . .?

She tried to ask for a towel but couldn't get the words out. It just came out as a grunt as she lurched up from the chair, batting Kiko aside.

Everyone was close. Too close.

Why the hell was it so hot in here?

'Stand back. Someone's having a tanty,' she heard Kiko say.

Of course she was! She couldn't breathe! It was boiling in here.

Jack finally turned in her direction. *Awww.* He looked concerned. About fucking time. *Oh, crumbs.* Topaz lurched forward and grabbed hold of his shirt, trying to clutch handfuls of fabric in order to stay upright, but his top really was quite form-fitting. She couldn't get purchase.

She became aware of Jack's date, the chubby girl, moving in.

Fuck off! she thought. *He's mine!* But for some reason the words didn't come out of her mouth.

Topaz thumped her chest and began emitting a strange, high-pitched wheeze each time her fist connected with her sternum.

'She looks like she's choking,' Jack said.

He actually seemed really worried, now. She *knew* it! He'd totally been playing the 'treat 'em mean, keep 'em keen game. Naughty, naughty.

'Her face is turning red.'

'Do you think she needs the Heimlich?'

Jack's date stood right in front of her. 'Topaz? Are you choking?' When Topaz tried and failed to tell them that no, of course she wasn't choking; except for that beef, she was on the eleventh hour of a liquid fast. The chubster moved behind her, put her arms around her and heaved.

'I don't think she's choking.' The chubster released her. 'Something else is wrong.'

Wrong?

No. Jack was here. He was finally . . . god. She really couldn't get a breath in. And things were getting a bit bleary.

She swooned, and the next thing she knew, she was in Jack's arms.

Mmm . . . nice.

Then she was on a sofa and Jack had moved away. Less nice. Why did it feel like someone was sitting on her? And what was that noise? A strange bellowing. Like a moose. Or a hippo.

Jack's date was kneeling beside her, pressing her fingers to her throat and asking really obvious questions like, 'Topaz, can you hear me?' Of course she could. She wasn't deaf.

She could hear other voices, too.

'Someone phone an ambulance!'

'Stylists get taught first aid, right?'

'Ramone, c'mere. Kiko! Brynn! Can someone help?'

'Jack,' Topaz said dreamily. She felt a bit high. She probably shouldn't have popped those pills Felipe had given her earlier. Oh, well. Just a tiny little nap before the show and everything would be fine.

She looked up and saw other faces leaning in, examining her. Kiko. Ramone. The Duke. Veronica. Lily Richmond. And oooh. There he was. Jack Kelly. *Such* a pretty man.

This was more like it. Being the centre of attention. She'd have to remember this when she woke up. Post to everyone on Insta that, at long last, Topaz Pringle had arrived.

Chapter Thirty

By the time the ambulance had come, the official time of death had been recorded, and Topaz had been zipped into a body bag and taken away on a gurney, the bulk of the guests at the Town Hall had left.

Even so, an air of chaos remained, and Lily Richmond was feeling distinctly unsettled. Witnessing two deaths less than a week apart would do that to you.

Amidst the police tape and interviews and fingerprint-dusting and the cacophony of tearful dancers, stylists, PR girls and punters swirling around the crime scene, Lily found Susie.

Her one-time protégée was, as ever, the calm in the midst of a storm. She stood in a discreet nook of the dressing area, quietly observing the events unfolding.

It had been this aura of composure that had drawn Lily to her from the off, even as a little girl. A poised presence that, at first, went unnoticed, and then, as one became aware of her, drew you in.

Lily joined her, and together the two women watched the crime-scene investigators set out number tags, and take photos of, amongst other things, Topaz's tote bag, the maté cup she'd been using and even Kiko's make-up and hair-styling kit.

Ramone, Kiko and Brynn were currently in a huddle with a uniformed policewoman who, notebook in hand, was asking them questions, while Jack was handing over his shirt, the one that Topaz had grabbed, to a man in a white coverall in the corner in exchange for a Merseyside Police shirt. Another uniformed policeman introduced himself and, taking out his own notebook, began to interview him. Ruby Rae and Vlad were pointing out to the police everything they thought had belonged to Topaz. Lily and Susie had already been interviewed, truthfully recounting all the information they could. One moment Topaz had seemed fine, the next she seemed to be having some sort of fit and then, simply . . . died.

'I don't suppose you ever get used to this, do you, darling?' she said to Susie. 'Body bags and all that.'

Susie crinkled her nose. 'I think I'd be in the wrong job if it didn't bother me. Seeing someone die like that.' She turned to Lily, and with a sweet, almost protective air asked, 'Are you all right? Two deaths so close together could rattle even the strongest of folk.'

Despite the nod to her personal strength, Lily shivered. 'Do you think the same person is behind them?' she asked Susie. 'There's no way that Topaz's death was a natural one, right?'

Susie's eyes remained glued to a visibly distressed Jack as he answered question after question. 'I can't be sure of anything at this point,' she said. 'But two young, female dancers in their prime, collapsing one after the other? It seems extremely likely that there's a link.'

There was a moment's silence as they both considered what that could mean.

'I won't pretend I took to Topaz,' Lily said, 'but I certainly didn't predict this, let alone wish it on her. And her poor father. I've never heard a man howl in pain like that before. It definitely puts events in a different light.' By which she meant, Scouser Sam just might have to be struck off the suspects list.

Susie agreed. 'I've seen my share of crocodile tears in this job, but hand on heart? I don't believe Scouser Sam had anything to do with his daughter's death.'

'No. I agree.' Lily was no fan of Scouser Sam, but his grief had been palpable. Painful to watch, really. 'If the two deaths are linked, then perhaps Sam had nothing to do with Oxana's, either,' she mused. 'There are clearly more balls in the air than I'd originally thought.'

Susie gave a grim nod. 'Agreed.' And then, after a quick look round asked, 'Where's Javier?'

'He's taking some of the Argentine dancers back to their accommodation. There was a kerfuffle over the maté, apparently.'

'People thought it was poisoned?' Susie guessed.

'Exactly. Which led to a rush on the loos to . . . you know . . .' Lily mimicked making herself throw up. 'Everyone's fine,' she added. 'They've ruled out the possibility that there was anything wrong with the maté. Kiko told me earlier that she'd been drinking it from the same jug Topaz had been served with.'

'Interesting. Well, it's useful that we can rule out the maté,' Susie replied. She fell silent for a moment, watching Jack speak to the police officer whilst running his hand agitatedly through his hair.

'He looks upset,' Lily observed.

'Of course he does!' Susie said defensively. 'He's had two partners – well, designated partners – die on him. And when you take into account the fact that his studio was trashed . . .' She stopped herself.

'It's all right to be worried about him you know, darling?'

'I'm not, it's just . . .' Susie's cheeks pinked, and she fell silent.

Trying to get Susie to admit she still had feelings for Jack would only send her running for the hills, so Lily returned to discussing logistics. Facts.

'If the maté wasn't poisoned, then we should be looking for what else might have killed Topaz.'

'Exactly.' Susie nodded to the taped-off area where Topaz had died and the forensics team were hard at work. 'It'll be interesting to see what the police come up with.'

Lily pointed at a young investigator methodically going through each drawer of Kiko's beauty case. 'Is that protocol?' Lily asked. 'Going through everything right here?'

'It is when they think the death is suspicious.'

Lily's thoughts returned to the horrible moments before Topaz had died. 'And you're completely sure she didn't choke on something?' she asked.

'Absolutely,' Susie answered solidly. 'It looked like she was choking, but she definitely wasn't. I checked for an obstruction. Did the Heimlich. And when Brynn came up to help, he did, too. No. It was something else. Something . . .' She screwed up her face as if debating whether or not to admit to her true thoughts.

'Go on.'

Susie explained, 'Well, when Brynn and I were doing CPR, some of Topaz's lipstick came off. Her lips were blue. Which means something was stopping her from breathing.'

How odd. Particularly if it wasn't as a result of an obstructed airway. Lily thought for a moment then said, 'Could drugs have caused that? Bearing in mind that Oxana might've been slipped something, too.'

Susie frowned. 'It's so frustrating that we couldn't get a toxicology report done.' Regrouping, she answered Lily's question. 'Drugs will send you to sleep before they kill you. The ones that I know about, anyway. It's definitely something to look into. I'll see if I can call in some favours to get a copy of Topaz's toxicology report, when it happens.'

'I wish we could have a look through her belongings,' Lily said. 'See if there's anything untoward.' Like a note, for example.

As if she knew exactly what Lily was thinking, Susie said, 'We should be getting Oxana's phone records and email and diary access tomorrow from Madhav. It'll be interesting to see if anything there links to the note you found in her tote bag.'

'A clever bunny keeps their appointments,' recited Lily from memory. 'It does make me think, if we find that Oxana had any appointments in her diary from the last couple of weeks, we should pay whoever she'd arranged to see a visit.'

'Good thinking,' Susie said approvingly. Her expression changed, as if she'd just thought of something. 'Hang on. I've got an idea. There *is* something of Topaz's that we might be able to look at before the police get to it . . .'

She turned on her heel and walked out of the anteroom with a purposeful stride. Intrigued, Lily followed her. Susie made her way through the main hall, the beautiful stalls looking a little sad now that everyone had left, and to the coat-check area that was near the front of the building.

Behind the girl manning the coat-check, there was only a small selection of coats and bags left hanging on a railing. Amongst them was a leopard-print coat with hot-pink lapels that looked like it could only have belonged to one person they knew.

Ah. Lily could see what Susie was planning.

Susie suddenly began to put on a huge display of digging through her small clutch.

'Oh no!' she cried in a proper Scouser girl-on-the-razzle voice. 'I must've lost my ticket in the loo when I was putting on my lippie.' She pointed to the leopard-print coat and made a 'pretty please' face at the coat-check girl. 'Do you think that I could just grab my coat? It's right there.'

When the girl looked a bit unsure, Susie smiled sweetly and, as she pulled a fiver out of her purse said, 'I still have tip money.'

'Here you go.' The coat-check girl took the money and unceremoniously handed Susie the coat. 'The sooner these are gone, the sooner I can go home.'

'Mwah,' Susie blew her a kiss in thanks. 'Thanks, babes.'

Lily hid a grin. This little display went a long way to explaining Susie's rapid ascent through the undercover department.

Just then, Jack joined them. He looked relieved to see them and, Lily noted, much more tired than he had an hour earlier. His hair was more tousled than it had been and, as if to show them how it got that way, he scrubbed both of his hands against his head, as if trying to keep himself in the here and now.

'What was that about?' Jack asked, pointing to the coat. He

followed Susie and Lily as they headed outside before anyone realized they'd effectively stolen it.

'Just looking for evidence before the police get their hands on it. Don't worry, I'll return it once we've had a look.' Susie pulled a couple of protective gloves out of her clutch and, after slipping them on, felt inside the pockets of Topaz's coat. She pulled out a bright pink lipstick, a pack of chewing gum, what seemed like an endless supply of tissues . . .

'Aha!' she said with a note of triumph. 'There's something else here.' With care, she pulled out a stiff white business card.

Lily's breath caught in her throat as she held it out for them all to read.

A CLEVER JACK KNOWS HOW TO MANAGE THEIR TIME

'Well.' Susie's face was pale. 'This puts a new slant on things.'

Jack looked from one to the other, confused. Lily hadn't told him about the card she'd found in Oxana's bag. 'What do you think it means?'

Lily and Jack both looked to Susie. She was, after all, the expert. 'I think it means that our suspicions are correct . . . It's very likely that these deaths are connected. Oxana received one of these note cards, too. And I'm guessing the murderer sent them.'

Chapter Thirty-One

Later, having slipped Topaz's coat back on the rack while the coat-check girl was having a moan with a colleague on the doors, Lily, Susie and Jack shared a silent cab ride back to Lily's house. Jack was staying there temporarily, and for Susie it would only be a short ride to her house afterwards, once they'd discussed the latest turn of events. She felt terrible leaving Kian for so long, but knew that her dad, a night owl, was happy to babysit for as long as she needed him to, and that her little boy would have been fast asleep for hours by now and wouldn't know the difference.

She threw a guilty look in Jack's direction as she accepted a warm mug of hot chocolate from him. Kian wasn't just her little boy. He was theirs.

She slammed that emotional door shut as fast as she'd opened it. Hashing out the past wasn't why they were here. Solving not one, but two possible murders was.

So here they were, each perched on a stool at Lily's kitchen island, hands wrapped around mugs of dark hot chocolate, trying to process the latest events.

Lily's phone buzzed on the counter, breaking the silence. She read the message to herself, but Susie noticed enough of a shift in her posture to presume who had sent it.

'Javier?' she guessed.

'Mmm,' Lily said, scanning the note once again.

'Anything interesting?'

'Not really,' Lily said cagily, before turning the phone face down on the counter. 'He's sorry things ended so horribly for Topaz and that we didn't get a chance to dance.'

To Susie's surprise, Jack nodded his head in agreement. 'I was looking forward to that,' he said, his eyes meeting Susie's across the island.

'Dancing with Topaz?' she asked, even though she knew that wasn't what he'd meant.

'No,' Jack protested, and then, as if clarifying the point was suddenly too much, he dropped his head into his hands with a heartfelt, 'I just can't believe it. Poor Topaz. Poor Oxana. Who would want to hurt dancers like this?'

Susie had no idea, but tonight, with Topaz's death . . . the murder spree of two suddenly felt much more like an open-ended mission.

'I hate to say this, Jack,' Susie began carefully. 'But I think you need to watch your back.'

He sat up straight. She had his full attention.

As delicately as she could, she continued, 'Especially if you mean to keep on competing. It might be coincidence, but right now, from where I'm standing, you're the most obvious link between the two women.'

Lily pressed her hand to her chest. 'Are you saying that Jack should stop competing for the time being?'

'But I . . .' Jack threw a desperate look at Lily. 'I'm so close to matching your record. If I don't go, I have to start again. At the bottom. I *have* to dance this year.'

'Even if it means putting yourself in danger?' Susie asked.

'Well, no, but I . . . Suze. C'mon. You of all people know the answer to that.'

'And you of all people know what I think about it!' she shot back.

Jack shook his head despairingly. Again, he appealed to Lily. 'What would you do?'

From the way her expression shifted from empathetic to torn, it was easy to see Lily understood Jack's dilemma. And, to be fair, Susie got it, too. As mad as it might seem to someone on the 'outside', there wasn't anything that could keep a true professional ballroom dancer away from the world's largest competition. Particularly when they had this once-in-a-lifetime chance to reign as the world's foremost champion.

'Anyway.' Jack's face suddenly lit up with a thought. 'If we're going to find the killer, I *should* be competing, right? It would be the best way to get on the inside of what's going on. To trip them up.'

Susie considered the point before reluctantly conceding, 'It's risky . . . but you're right.'

She sucked in a breath, silently cursing herself for agreeing with Jack.

Before she could take it back and offer another solution, Lily said, 'Look, both of you. I have an idea.' She turned to Susie. 'What Jack says is true. We *do* need him.' She held up a finger when Susie tried to interrupt. 'As one of the competitive dancers, he'll be far better placed to pick up clues than I will as a teacher and a judge.'

'But—' Susie tried.

'Lil, can I just—' Jack began.

'You'll need a partner,' Lily said to him, continuing as if neither of them had spoken. 'One Marmaduke has nothing to do with. Or Scouser Sam. Or Johanna, for that matter.' Her voice grew stronger as the idea gained traction. 'You need someone entirely unconnected to the GDC who can train with you and hit champion standards in less than four weeks.'

'Absolutely impossible,' Jack said miserably.

'And *you*,' Lily said, looking at Susie again, 'need to infiltrate the competition. It's the only way to get close enough to all the suspects.' She took one of each of Susie's and Jack's hands in hers. 'Darlings. Listen. Given everything that's happened . . . I think there's only one way to catch this murderer.'

'How?' Jack asked.

Susie's stomach churned. She was fairly certain she knew what was coming because, against her will, she was thinking it, too.

Lily looked between the pair of them. 'I know it will take some work, some setting aside of differences, but I truly think the only way we're going to find this killer is if the two of you dance together in Blackpool.'

Chapter Thirty-Two

*Another dancer disposed of. Another slate wiped nice and
clean. Nothing to see here, PC Plod!*
And that, as they say, is that.

Chapter Thirty-Three

On second thought . . . no.
Honestly, these past few days have been the best fun, and so
cathartic! Clutter-clearing at its most primitive level.
No. This isn't over.
Not. Just. Yet.
Perhaps a little trip to the seaside is in order.
I do like to be beside the sea!

Chapter Thirty-Four

DANCE DAILY

BREAKING NEWS

As reported by Pippa Chambers

A second death has rocked the world of ballroom dance mere days after Oxana Bondarenko lost her life at the Whitby Pavilion United Kingdom Open to the World Dance Championships.

Topaz Pringle, Insta-influencer and Midwestern ballroom dancer, tragically passed away just moments before she was due to perform at ¡*Oye! Argentina!*, an event celebrating trade between the UK and the land of tango, which was held at Liverpool's Town Hall. Her death was called by officials just past nine o'clock, despite valiant efforts to save her life by seven-times world champion Ten-Dancer, Jack Kelly, and friend.

Topaz enjoyed a golden childhood in her native Liverpool with her father, Samuel Leslie Pringle of Scouser Sam's

Scaffolding and Skips. After his daughter spent her formative years in America, Sam tearfully told a crowd of onlookers that, when she returned, he'd been given a new lease of life. Global Dance Council stalwart Veronica Parke-West was there to console him.

Many of Topaz's fellow dancers said she was over the moon to be returning home to the United Kingdom, particularly as she had been planning on dancing at this year's Blackpool Ballroom Bonanza with long-time champion Jack Kelly.

Reports on the cause of death are conflicting. Stylist Kiko Yakimori, who was with Topaz when she fell ill, believed she was choking on a piece of *barbacoa* (beef). Argentine natives, Lucia and Cristobal Suarez, contested the assertion, claiming they'd heard Topaz was a vegan and, on the advice of her partner Felipe Blanco, had been on a maté fasting diet.

Ruby Rae Coutts, a former beauty pageant star from Louisiana, speculated that perhaps Topaz's past as a cheerleader had followed her across the Atlantic. 'Some people just can't let go,' she said. Through a deep well of emotion, she added, 'It was so tragic she didn't perform. We were all really looking forward to seeing her represent the UK tonight. No one danced the way Topaz could.'

She wasn't the only one struggling to contain their emotions. Johanna Gunnarsson of Iceland wept tears of sorrow as she remembered her peer. 'Because of my devastating injury, Jack was forced to dance with someone else. I could not have been more grateful to Topaz for temporarily stepping into the breach. We were the closest of friends and shared a mutual passion for the beauty industry.'

Jack Kelly was being interviewed by police when this article was due to go to press so was unavailable for comment.

In a statement released by the Global Dance Council, GDC Chairman Marmaduke Fitzgerald had this to say about the dancer's contribution to the world of competitive ballroom dance: 'I knew from the moment I saw Topaz on Instagram that she was meant to be a partner to our "prodigal son" Jack Kelly. Middle America and the dance community have lost one of its purest souls. The only silver lining to this devastating loss is knowing she was preparing to do what she loved most in the end. As I hope, will all of us. I know you will join me and our sponsors, Scouser Sam's Scaffolding and Skips, in a prayer that she may forever rest in peace.'

Watch out for updates on couples heading to the Blackpool Ballroom Bonanza as the 'and a five, six, seven, eight' countdown begins!

PART THREE

Chapter Thirty-Five

'All right, Suzie Q,' Madhav rubbed his hands together then gave them a solid clap, 'excellent handover. I think we can safely say we're fully briefed on everything now.'

'I'm happy to answer any questions,' Susie said. 'Any questions at all.'

The team's surreptitious looks suggested Susie had very possibly over-micromanaged the handover. But, honestly, the devil really was in the detail in this line of work.

She glanced at the clock. Ten a.m. She had used up the two days' 'allowance' Lily had given her to sort out her particulars and was already late getting to the studio. Madhav was right. She could not have been more thorough. And yet . . .

She tapped one of the files. 'Remember, this guy here usually sees his mistress between two and four when his wife is on the school run. She's a vegan so sometimes—'

'All right,' Madhav cut in, giving her a *we're finished now* pat on the back. 'Time to let everyone get back to work and, Susie Q, that includes you.'

Susie's palms began to sweat. She'd spent the last forty-eight hours desperately trying to conjure up some other way of going undercover – anything to avoid getting back on the dance floor. But, try as she might, she could see no other way. She had to be in the game to catch the killer.

She stretched her leg away from her and gave it an awkward jiggle. *Why* had she put her leotard on underneath her work dress? Rookie mistake. Even though she'd ordered a new one, to allow for her curvier body shape, she'd forgotten how the little beasts had a tendency to . . . erm . . . travel. How was she going to pick it out of her bum in front of Jack without dying of mortification?

And just like that, the nerves that had kept her up half the night were back.

Was she going to be able to take down the murderer? Or would being with Jack destroy her first?

She pushed the thought away, tapping on the paperwork for an embezzlement case she'd been working on at a local fried-chicken chain. 'This guy is fairly clued up, so you want to make sure—'

'We're all rooting for you. On stage and off.' Madhav scooped together her case files and handed them to a detective heading out of the room. He shooed the rest of his team back to their desks and, in a quieter tone said, 'If there's anything you'd like to talk about at any stage of this, I'm always at the end of the phone.'

'I think I'm a bit nervous,' she admitted.

'Course you are. How many detectives do you know who've gone undercover in an elite dance competition for the express purpose of finding a serial killer?'

It wasn't just that. Winning at Blackpool meant everything to Jack and she couldn't bear the thought of letting him down – no matter how odd things were between them. There was no way she could half-arse her way through the competition. She was going to have to dance – *really dance* – like the champion she'd once been. But it had been seven years . . . what if she couldn't do it any more?

'I just hope I can fit in some actual detective work amongst the insane rehearsal schedule Jack and Lily have devised.'

Madhav leant back against the desk and crossed one foot over the other. 'I don't know if I ever told you this, Susie, but one of the things that impressed me most about your CV was the fact that you managed to juggle school, cadets, and then the police academy, all the while maintaining a rigorous rehearsal and performance schedule. That's a lot of multi-tasking. Three entirely separate worlds, maintained to perfection.'

Not so perfect in the end.

When she realized Madhav was hoping for a response, she said, 'I almost didn't put any of the dancing stuff on there because it seemed . . .' Too full of glitter and sequins? 'It wasn't exactly hard core.'

'Nonsense. You trained every bit as hard as an Olympic hopeful. You made sacrifices, pushed yourself hard to achieve your goals, and didn't let adversity stop you from trying again.'

Madhav was wrong. She *had* let adversity stop her.

The thought pierced her heart. Getting pregnant hadn't been 'adversity'. It had shone a light on the things that were important to her and the things that were important to Jack. Just because the two hadn't matched up in the end didn't mean she'd come out worse off.

'This'll be fine, right?' she asked as Madhav gently began to steer her towards the door.

'Absolutely,' her boss assured her. 'And in moments where you think it won't be? Just remember—'

'"The greatest mistake you can make in life is to continually fear you will make one."' She quoted Madhav's favourite philosopher.

'Good girl.' He gave her a hug and then held her at arm's length so he could look her in the eye. 'I would tell you this isn't about life or death, but . . . well, we both know that's not true. I *will* tell you I believe in you.'

She bit down on her lip to keep a surge of emotion at bay. She remembered the day her grief-stricken father had brought her to Lily's studio for the first time. There, amidst the bewildering anguish of losing her mother, she had unexpectedly found the one magical place in the world where, from the moment she put on her rehearsal shoes, she felt entirely whole. A place where people believed in her.

Dance had always been more to her than twirling round in a beautiful dress. It had been about learning from Lily, a woman who selflessly gave her time and energies to a grieving young girl with no money. It had been about falling in love for the first and only time with a boy who thought she could do no wrong. And it had been about those sweet, wonderful moments when she, Jack and Lily had held up yet another trophy for the photographers, and Susie took a private moment to whisper: *This is for you, Mum.*

'Right you are, guv,' Susie eventually managed. She pointed two fingers at her eyes then at him. 'I'll keep my eyes on the prize.'

'That's right, Susie Q. But also, if you can, try and have a little fun.'

She barked out a laugh. Three and a half weeks to become a genuine contender for the Open to the World Professional Ballroom and Latin Dance Championships at the Blackpool Bonanza and also catch a murderer? Easy-peasy.

Maybe, she thought, as Madhav made a big show of opening the door and ushering her through it, maybe by confronting her past, she'd come out stronger.

And then, before she had a chance to find any more excuses to stay, the door clicked shut behind her, leaving Susie Cooper to face her biggest fears head on.

Chapter Thirty-Six

'C'mon, Suze. Let's have another go.'

Jack was desperately trying to convince himself that his entire life's work was not spiralling down the drain. But, one week into their rigorous rehearsal schedule, the mirrors lining the studio that he and Susie occupied were making it an increasingly difficult delusion to maintain.

'I don't think that's how we did it.' Susie pulled away from him, again, arms defensively crossing her chest.

'It is, Suze,' he insisted. 'We literally just watched the video.' Then, more gently, 'Look. Cut yourself some slack. It's been seven years since we've done this routine. It makes sense that you're rusty.'

She flared. 'I'm not rusty. You're not remembering it properly.'

'*Me?*' He was pure disbelief. '*I* don't remember how to do it?' His feet flashed through the basic footwork by rote. Rock-replace-side-close-side. He added the personalized flourishes that he knew caught the eyes of judges, finishing with the Turkish towel. 'You know this, Suze. Stop thinking so much.'

He held out his hand to her.

She flinched.

'I don't have the plague, Suze. C'mon. Let's try it again.'

'I don't think the peek-a-boo works as is,' Susie countered with a surprisingly good hair flick.

'A peek-a-boo should be followed by a sweetheart.' *Obviously.*

'Not everything *has* to be the way you dictate it.'

'It does when I'm the one choreographing it.'

She harrumphed and stomped off to get her water bottle.

Normally, if he reached this kind of impasse with a student, Jack would suggest doing something fun. Have a little boogie to an Abba song, do a few cartwheels. Maybe have a stab at the karaoke machine. But Susie didn't seem remotely interested in finding a better headspace, and without Lily here to back him up, the simple truth was they didn't have time to 'find the joy'. They only had time to dance.

'Right.' He stepped into position for the basic once she'd had her drink. 'Four, one start, two, three, four—'

Susie shrugged out of his arms again. 'Stop that.'

'Stop what?'

'You keep digging your fingers into my shoulder blade.'

He hadn't been. Had he? Maybe he'd been guiding her, but . . . Lily's voice came to him: *Dance is resistance* and *surrender.*

Susie was all resistance, so Jack would have to be the one to surrender. He held up his hands. 'Tell me, Suze. I'm begging you. Tell me what to do so we can make some progress and I'll do it.'

A flash of something almost like hurt cut through her eyes and, just like that, Jack wished he could erase the previous few hours and ask if they could please, *please*, start again.

'Knock knock,' Lily rapped on the door to their studio. 'Madhav's here with some news. You two up for a break?'

'Yes.' Susie was already halfway to the door.

'No,' Jack called after her retreating back, shooting Lily a look.

Lily walked into the studio, giving Susie a quick, maternal back-rub as they passed one another. After a glance at Jack, and cocking an ear at the speaker, she held her arms in position. Then, as she had a thousand times before, she counted them in. Together, effortlessly, they executed a flawless cha-cha-cha. 'Give her a bit of time,' she said as they swept their arms out into a New York, then, after a swift underarm turn, took a step to the side for a bright, smiling hand-to-hand.

He'd forgotten how phenomenal it was to dance with Lily. How a lesson with her was like rising to a higher plane, where even the most difficult of steps felt entirely natural. She was the best ballroom and Latin dancer in the world and this, here and now, was a masterclass in perfection. A reminder that, with enough diligence, and the right partner, he had it in him to excel.

But Lily wasn't going to be his partner at Blackpool.

'We don't have time for faffing about, Lil,' Jack said, leading the pair of them into an in-place basic before a few blink-and-you-missed-them spot turns. 'Susie's great. You know I think the world of her dancing. But she's got a lot of catching up to do.'

'And she'll get there.' Lily swivelled her hips for a shoulder-to-shoulder before stopping short and giving him a reassuring pat on the chest. 'You need to help her find a way to tap into that chemistry you two share. That's what truly separates one couple from another at any level.'

He snorted. 'I'd have better luck drilling for oil in the centre of Liverpool, Lil. She can't stand me.' Making eye contact with her in the mirror as he led her into a Cuban break, he said,

'Having someone openly loathe you isn't exactly the type of chemistry the judges are after.'

As they reversed the move, Lily parried, 'That's *precisely* the chemistry you need to bring on the dance floor.'

'You're joking. Side side, ronde, hip twist.'

'I'm completely serious.' She whipped through a spiral turn and, as they closed the dance with a fan ending, Lily nodded towards the door, indicating they should go. 'Dance is about having complicated feelings for one another. Love. Hate. Passion. Fear. And with Susie, it's more difficult.'

'Why?'

'Because neither of you are pretending.'

Two bottles of water, seventy 'counter push-ups' and ten squats later, Jack was growing antsy. The gist of the meeting could be summed up like this: Susie's boss hadn't uncovered any significant evidence. So if Oxana's 'digital forensics' – whatever the hell they were – were a dead zone, why weren't they back in the studio dancing?

'And there was nothing in her diary?' Susie asked, reaching for one of the almond flour keto muffins Jack had brought from a local bakery. Lily deftly shifted a snack pack of carrot sticks and hummus in front of her.

Brave.

And a little mean. Susie's curves suited her. She looked good. Even if she was shooting daggers at him half the time.

'You've got to look after your knees, darling,' Lily quipped when Susie arched an eyebrow.

'These are keto,' Jack said, grabbing a muffin and taking a bite.

Susie shot him a *thanks for trying* look. It wasn't a full smile, but it was something.

'The phone was a burner, so nothing beyond a few phone numbers,' Madhav confirmed.

After taking a melodramatic crunch of one of the carrot batons, Susie turned her attention back to her boss. 'Oxana probably had the burner because it was cheaper. Maybe she integrated it with a digital calendar she might've been using back home? Something that could be held in a cloud?'

Madhav shook his head. 'We thought that as well, but couldn't find anything.'

He began to detail how they'd triangulated something and beamed something else up to a satellite so his tech team could try to find out what murdered ballroom dancers from Belarus got up to when they weren't rehearsing.

Jack could've told them if they'd bothered asking.

When they started going through her Facebook history for the third time, he finally lost it.

'Don't you get it? *All she did was dance!*' Jack shot a pointed look at Susie. 'She didn't go out, she didn't have a secret life as a pole dancer. She didn't hang out with the girls at bottomless brunch. We had four weeks to get ready for Whitby, so we did what people who want to be champions do. We danced.'

Susie registered the comment with another pronounced chomp on her carrot. 'What about her bank account?' she asked Madhav, her eyes still on Jack.

'Ah, well, now we did find something interesting there, beyond the monthly stipend from Marmaduke.'

Lily examined the sheet Madhav had just produced then shared a look with Susie. 'A cash withdrawal for five hundred pounds two days before the competition.' It was a lot of money for someone on a tight budget.

'What would she have spent five hundred pounds on?' Susie asked.

'She didn't,' Lily said, pointing at Oxana's purse which was lined up on the counter amongst some other items from her tote bag. 'Not all of it, anyway. There's two hundred pounds in there. And some change.'

'Well.' Madhav pulled out a flyer and tapped it. 'We think she might have been planning on spending it here.'

They all leant in to look: Shaz 'n Baz's Beauty.

There was a long list of treatments – facials, manis, pedis, fillers, threading, and on it went. At the top of the sheet was a handwritten time and date.

'The same day Oxana made the withdrawal. Is that definitely her writing?'

Jack confirmed it was. 'But we wouldn't have had time for her to get five hundred quid's worth of spa treatments then.'

Madhav looked at his phone. 'Apologies, everyone. I have another appointment to get to. Susie Q, shall I leave these things here for you to have a longer look?' He gestured to the evidence. 'We can meet at the office, have a confab later?'

She'll be rehearsing later, Jack said under his breath.

Susie glanced at him and then cheerily agreed to an early evening meet with her boss. After he left, the group fell into a studied silence, eyes scanning the row of evidence spread out like a snail trail leading them absolutely nowhere closer to finding who killed Oxana.

'You said you were rehearsing all the time,' Susie eventually said to Jack. She spoke carefully, as if she were trying to put pieces of a puzzle together. 'But was there anything in your schedule that day that might have made her think she had time to get a treatment?'

'If she did, it would've been a short one,' Jack grumbled, but he pulled his phone off the counter and thumbed through the dates anyhow.

Bingo.

'I had a meeting with Marmaduke.' The one where he'd first mentioned Topaz. He turned his phone round so they could see. 'It was fifteen minutes, followed by rehearsal with Oxana. With that short a break, she wouldn't have left the studio.'

Lily peered at the phone then asked, 'Do you remember any other time she could've gone out?'

Jack ran back through the day as best he could but, despite his detailed list of students, meetings and rehearsals, his memory had blurred the day into one endless stream of competition prep. A surge of frustration swept through him. Whether or not Oxana had kept an appointment at a beautician's was irrelevant at this point. The only thing this endless speculating was reminding him of was the fact that they weren't doing the one thing they should be right now. Rehearsing.

He grabbed Oxana's empty tote, the closest thing to him amongst the collection of 'evidence'. 'All I can remember is that she came into the studio at dawn with this – ' he shook the bag, hard – 'on her shoulder, and . . .'

He stopped. There was a *plip, plip*, as first one, then another, small blue and white capsules fell from the bag onto the counter.

'What are those?'

'Hang on!' Lily stopped him from reaching out to grab one and, after rifling through a couple of drawers, triumphantly flourished an item. 'Tweezers,' she said. 'Most useful item in a woman's armoury.'

Susie smiled and snapped open a spare evidence bag from the things Madhav had left, then held it out so that Lily could place the capsules inside. She sealed it, then held them up to the light.

'They look like the diet pills I . . .' Lily cut herself short.

'What, Lil?' Jack asked.

She sighed and shook her head, apparently reluctant to continue.

Susie glanced at Jack, puzzled. 'Lily, if you know something that could help . . .'

'All right!' she said sharply, then raised her chin and pulled her shoulders back as if daring them to challenge her. 'They look very similar to some diet pills that I took, a long time ago, in . . .' she took a deep breath, 'Argentina.'

'You mean . . .?'

She nodded at Susie. 'Yes, I think they must've belonged to your Argentinian rivals.' Lily gestured to the pills. 'I remember the two halves in blue and white – just like the flag. And the writing on the side is Spanish, see?'

As if anticipating the obvious next question, Lily went on, 'And before you ask, Javier was furious when he found out I'd been taking pills. His sister died because of them.'

They all took a moment to digest this.

'Why *did* you take them?' Jack eventually asked. 'You've always been tiny.'

'Oh, darling.' Lily gave his hand a pat. 'You know this world.' She didn't elaborate.

'So . . .' Susie said, 'just to be clear: you don't think Javier would've given these to Oxana?'

'Absolutely not,' Lily replied, firmly. 'If you'd have seen his face that day . . . No.' She gave them both one of her *this subject is closed* looks. 'And Javier has always been very strict with his students. If they're using pills, they'll be doing it behind his back.'

Susie gave her a nod, indicating they'd tread carefully. 'Jack, do you remember Oxana speaking to any of the Argentinians when you were at Whitby?'

Before he could answer, Lily's phone rang. She squinted at the screen then frowned. 'It's unlisted.' She pressed the answer button and put the call on speaker. 'Hello, yes. This is Lily Richmond.'

They all froze as a staticky, mechanized voice began to speak. The kind usually heard making ransom demands in television thrillers. 'I know what you're planning for Blackpool,' it began. Lily grabbed each of their hands as the voice continued. 'Jack better be nimble. Susie better be quick. Or else Lily will be jumping over the candlestick!'

Lily's nails dug into Jack's hand. A ripple of goosebumps shot down his spine as, to his surprise, Susie reached out and took his other hand and gave it a squeeze. She was scared. They all were.

'Topaz's murder definitely wasn't the last,' Susie finally said. 'And it sounds like whoever's next . . . is going to be one of us.'

Chapter Thirty-Seven

Lily watched Jack and Susie rehearsing through the glass window into the studio. It was three days since they'd received the terrifying phone call, and they'd been dancing non-stop. Today was the foxtrot. They'd chosen a slow, languorous song with lyrics speaking to new beginnings and fresh starts. She hoped that for both of them the song rang true. They'd been such a lovely couple back in the day. Despite Lily's best attempts to understand Susie's long-ago decision, her heart ached for Jack. He deserved the chance to prove himself as a father.

But! Not her business.

She knocked on the door and entered without waiting for permission. Owning the studio came with certain privileges.

They acknowledged her arrival with a nod but carried on dancing, even though they'd been at it for hours.

Where it had been squalls and stand-offs prior to the frightening call, the energy in the studio had shifted to a more studied diligence. They weren't gazing adoringly into one another's eyes. Nor were they tapping into the passion she knew simmered, well masked, beneath the surface. But at least Susie had stopped pushing Jack away. Physically, anyway.

Death threats, she was learning, had a way of clarifying one's priorities.

She glanced at the wall clock. Eight p.m. With any luck, they'd put an end to this mystery tonight.

After a slightly clumsy spiral spin, Jack's right arm swept around Susie's waist, holding her hips to his as she allowed her torso to shift up and into a backbend spin for the dance's final flourish. When Susie rose, her fingertips airbrushing the contours of Jack's stubbled jawline, Lily thought she just might be bearing witness to a thawing.

'Lovely princess spin, darlings,' she said.

They parted and offered her the traditional bow and curtsey for her insight.

'It's not there yet,' said Susie, pulling on a shapeless jumper over her leotard.

'No,' Lily agreed. 'But nor was Rome built in a day.' She tipped her head towards the main studio. 'Javier and his students have arrived. Are you two ready?'

Jack's body language shifted from paramour to protector. 'And they think they're here for a masterclass?'

Susie shot him a look. They'd been through the plan earlier. They would, as and when the evening allowed, individually quiz Javier's dancers about the diet pills they'd found in Oxana's bag. Lily, of course, would be the one to talk to Javier. A task she was dreading.

'Something like that,' Lily said, leading them out of the studio. 'It's more . . . well . . .' Despite the gravity of the situation, the part of her that had fallen under the spell of Latin dance was already alight with anticipation. 'Let's see how we go, shall we?'

'Liliana!' Javier cut through the crowd of twenty or so dancers and, after a low, courtly bow, kissed her hand. They'd not seen one another since Topaz's death, but the texts they'd shared had been tinged with that touch of longing that so often permeated their real-life meetings. He was all suave sophistication and coiled energy tonight. Almost, but not quite, on edge.

'Shall you and I do our demonstration first, or shall we see how our students fare under their mentors' exacting gazes during this gathering of friends?'

She barked with laughter and gave Javier a *good one* smile. 'Darling, I don't know about your eyesight, but from the looks on these dancers' faces, I'm not entirely persuaded that they're looking at this as a friendly session.'

'Tango is hardly a dance of peace,' he countered.

'Nor is it one of domination,' she shot back.

'True,' he said, looking out to the dancers as they warmed up in front of the mirrors – Argentines on one side of the room, Lily's dancers on the other. 'That's very true.' He propped his elbow on his arm and tucked his thumb under his chin, as if he was about to say something very wise and insightful. She waited for him to continue, but, after spending far too many seconds staring at the pads of his fingertips lazily skidding along the fullness of his lower lip, she realized he had already begun to tango with her.

Game on, *mi amor.*

Lily looked out into the main studio, a cavernous, high-ceilinged, thick-planked affair that had once borne the weight of a hundred pews and all the sinners who sat on them.

The atmosphere already felt alive. Electric.

Casually asking people if they carried around a stash of lethal diet pills would be tricky.

'I think we should unleash our students first. Let them show us what they're about,' Lily said. She shot Javier a cheeky smile. 'After all, they might teach us a thing or two.'

'Doubtful,' Javier said, his eyes taking a lazy, sultry journey from the neckline of her simple black dress, all the way down to the knee-length hem. It wasn't a revealing frock, but what it did show – a hint of cleavage, a slash of thigh, a glimpse of possibility at the small of her back – was enough to make a point. There was nothing simple about Lily Richmond.

At Javier's signal, a guitarist climbed up onto a small stage that had once been the pulpit and plucked out a few opening chords. He was followed by a woman with a violin and a weather-worn silver fox carrying a *bandoneon*, the Argentine version of an accordion.

Everyone stood to attention.

'Right, everyone!' Lily called out after accepting Javier's hand as she climbed up onto one of the few remaining pews. 'Welcome to our informal *práctica*. We thought, Javier and I, that as many of you are thousands of miles from home, it might be nice to have a night dancing amongst your peers without the edge of competition.'

There was a murmuring that, although indistinct, made it clear this was no 'casual' gathering. This was a chance for people dancing in Blackpool to really eye up the competition. And, to be fair, Lily knew she would be doing the same.

The music began.

She instantly sought out Susie and Jack. They were holding

their own, she was pleased to see. Perhaps not with the high levels of emotional phosphorescence lighting up some of the other couples, but she could tell that the charged environment had ignited Susie's competitive side. A relief. Jack, after all, was a long-time champion, and he wouldn't be happy with anything less than a complete run of firsts on the judge's scorecards.

Ruby Rae, as usual, was gunning for a fight. With Jack back in the competition, coming second was a possibility. She might even be eyeing third if the talented Argentine couple danced as beautifully as they were tonight.

Cristobal and Lucia were on fire. He, an exotic creature, born to enthral crowds of tango fans on the cobbled streets of Buenos Aires. She, a sinewy snake charmer who'd never known failure. They were mesmerizing to watch.

Javier pointed at a late arrival using a leopard-print cane. 'Who's this?'

'Johanna Gunnarsson,' Lily explained. 'You might've seen her at Whitby. She used to dance with Jack Kelly before hurting her knee.'

The Icelandic girl struck a pitiable pose on the only comfortable chair in the studio – an old leather wingback that one of Lily's amateurs had left to her in his will. She had waltzed with the old gent every Tuesday afternoon for precisely fifteen minutes, because it reminded him of the tea dances he'd gone to at the Adelphi Hotel with his late wife.

Unreasonably, Lily willed Johanna out of her chair. Something told her Jack's former partner was playing a part rather than truly trying to stay abreast of the competitive circuit. Perhaps she was even here spying for someone else. Marmaduke? The murderer?

'Jack is the lad who lost his—'

'Partners,' Lily finished for him. 'Oxana first and then, though they never had the chance to dance together, Topaz.' She watched him carefully to see if the names or pairings elicited anything.

Apart from a sorrowful shaking of the head, nothing.

Lily screwed up the courage to ask Javier about the pills. She hadn't been lying to Susie and Jack when she told them that he had abhorred her taking them, but could it really be true that his dancers used them without his knowledge?

'I hope we haven't frightened any of your dancers off with these mysterious deaths.'

Javier pressed his hand to his chest and bowed his head. 'Two tragic losses, to be sure. But they are unconnected, no?'

Well, that depended on whether or not the toxicology report on Topaz came up with amphetamines. They'd never really know with Oxana, but the fact she had the pills in her bag was a strong indicator she may have taken some. Strong enough to accuse Javier or his students of murder?

Lily closed her eyes and recalled Javier's anguished expression when he'd realized she had been taking the pills that had killed his sister. Was she brave enough to open that weighted chest of grief again?

She opened her eyes and looked at him. His expression brightened as each pair of dancers swept past. He was a true slave to the tango and she adored him for it.

No. She couldn't do it. He'd loved his sister and she, Lily, had loved him. He was her weakness. She was going to have to leave today's sleuthing to Susie and Jack. Anyway, she reasoned, Susie's brother, Chris, was going to be getting them a copy of

Topaz's report soon. If necessary, she'd ask him at that point, once she had more facts.

Silently, they watched the couples dance. There was something unsettled about the performances. Sharp, distinct moves came with a discordant edge to them. Fluid, graceful steps were, even for the tango, too deep. Too powerful. The energy on the floor felt . . . primitive. Raw and sexual. As if death had unleashed something in the dancers that they needed to expel from their bodies before returning to the precision and clarity that made them champions. Or almost-champions.

Lily's attention was caught once more by Javier's mesmerizing star couple, who were dancing near Jack and Susie. She watched with admiration as Lucia streaked her leg out in a lightning-fast *latigazo*, a whipping of the leg, followed by a strong *media luna*. While the other dancers seemed skittish, Lucia remained controlled, precise. But then, as her foot swept the floor in a circular motion, she caught Susie's ankle. A rare mistake? Susie cried out as she flew, unchecked, to the floor. The music, and the dancing, abruptly stopped.

Lily gasped as Susie pressed herself up and gingerly put her hand to her nose – it came away covered in blood.

She knew exactly what would happen next.

'You did that on purpose!' Jack jabbed an accusatory finger at Lucia.

Ah, there it was. And as if on cue . . .

Cristobal came forward to defend his partner. Jack, not to be out-macho'd, squared up to meet him. Vlad and Darren came forward to flank him. Felipe moved to Cristobal's side. Where just moments before the air had been alive with passion and longing, now it vibrated with the threat of violence. Lily glanced at Javier, wondering if they should intervene. He was halfway to his feet when—

'Stop it.'

Susie stood and calmly inserted herself between the two opposing groups, each hand raised as if to push back the competing waves of testosterone. After a moment, she turned to Jack and held his gaze: 'I'm fine,' she said, so softly Lily could barely hear her. 'I just need some ice. Let's go.' She reached out a hand to him.

Jack frowned. Then he nodded, took her hand and allowed her to lead him to the kitchen.

Lily couldn't remember the last time she'd been so proud. Susie had never been one for drawing the spotlight onto herself, apart from during a competition. Clearly, dancing wasn't the only thing that could build confidence and poise. Police work could too.

It took a water break and a change in the lighting (from atmospherically dusky, to 100-watt bulbs) to calm everyone down.

Javier clapped his hands, pulling the attention of the dancers to him. First in Spanish and then in English, he explained that he and Lily would show them the true essence of the tango. He invited everyone to sit around the edges of the dance floor, changed the lighting yet again so that there was a solitary pool of light in the centre of the room and then, shifting himself into position, held out his hand for Lily to join him. She hesitated at first, and then, seeing Susie and

Jack enter from a far door, stepped towards Javier as the first notes were plucked on the guitar.

She stepped into the circle of light. Javier pulled her in close to him. Close enough to feel the cadenced beat of his heart, the warmth of his breath on her bare neck. Lily willed the rest of the world away. The tango, if done correctly, should be pure sensation. It demanded a different sort of focus. A heightened awareness of your partner and where they might lead you, rather than relying on a foundation of traditional steps. It required instinct and trust.

Yes, in a competition there were prescribed steps, phrasing and form to follow. But right here, right now, knowing there was a murderer running loose amongst their ranks, Lily wondered if this dance could be the perfect means of revealing whether or not Javier had had a hand in it.

She looked into his eyes.

They were aglow with desire.

As her erogenous zones hummed with longing, a lightning crack of pain flashed through her.

He was the one man she'd always longed for, but could she trust him?

Before the music had time to consume him, Lily plucked the scarlet kerchief from Javier's breast pocket and handed it to him.

'Blindfold me.'

There was a ripple of interest from the students.

Javier arched an eyebrow, but, after she'd turned her back to him, did as she said.

His fingertips grazed the base of her neck after he'd secured the silk band over her eyes. Traced the same delicate line as the gold necklace he'd promised to buy her one day.

She sensed, rather than saw or heard him move in front of her. A smile teased at her lips as she held out her hand and found his exactly where she thought it would be. The guitarist began to pluck the strings of his instrument once again, seamlessly joined by first the violin and then, at last, as if their souls were finally being given a voice, the *bandoneon*.

They began to dance.

They stuck to basic moves in the beginning, Lily naming them aloud as Javier led her into them. Walks and chassés, promenade links that forced their energies to gather in their cores. Even though the tango was a dance conducted torso to torso, in this case, Lily felt as if she and Javier were magnets pointing in opposite directions, each of them charged with an energy so powerful they knew that if they actually, finally, joined as one, it might be the ending of them. Such was the lure of the tango.

Natural twist turns, brush taps, overstays, pivots and whisk endings all melted into one another, as if they'd been formed from a pool of essential elements. His scent became her scent. Her breath became his. Two halves finally becoming whole.

At a certain point she must've stopped talking, because she felt rather than heard Javier take over. The names of the steps ribboning through her in their Spanish form. *Espejo* – to mirror. *Llevada* – to carry. *Mordida* – the little bite.

When Javier trapped her foot between both of his, she suddenly ached to be alone with him. To have this – whatever it was they shared – progress into something much more intimate.

When they finished dancing and she had pulled the blindfold from her eyes, there was silence and then, as if at last the group of warring dancers had found the one thing they shared, they roared with pleasure.

In the foyer, as everyone bundled into their coats and headed out to the small but luxurious coach that Javier and his students had been using to tour round the United Kingdom, Lily tamped down her frustration. She was annoyed that the evening's turn of events and her cold feet had meant she was no further forward in finding out if Javier and his dancers were doling out amphetamines.

'Join me tonight.' Javier had both of her hands cupped in his, his lips brushing against the tips of her templed fingers as he spoke.

It would be the easiest thing in the world to say yes. 'Sorry, darling. I've . . .' Something caught her attention through the large plates of glass that stood between them and the main studio.

'Got plans?' Javier sighed out the rest of her excuse for her.

'No, I . . .' She answered honestly because . . . what on earth?

Lily's student Maisie came running through the studio, out into the foyer and then straight past them through to the dressing room.

Lucia followed her, the same haughty, supercilious expression on her face that she'd worn after Susie had risen from the floor, her face streaked with blood.

She was an excellent example of why Lily sometimes found it difficult to trust women. In this world anyway. She wanted to. With all her heart. If anything, the women involved in the world of ballroom dance should unite, not only for their safety, but for the strength it would give them – many voices rising up against the power-base of men who'd laid down the rules for so long.

But this was a vicious world when it came down to it. Exclusive. And at the end of the day, there was only room for one couple at the top of that podium in Blackpool. It was easy enough to see Lucia was already picturing herself and Cristobal kissing that golden cup.

Well, screw you sister, thought Lily. To Javier she said, 'Rain check?' Then kissed his cheek and went to find Maisie.

She was alone in the dressing room and it was easy enough to divine what had passed between her and Lucia from the way she was standing in front of the mirror. Sucking in her cheeks, her stomach, balling her hands into fists so she could pummel her athletic thighs.

When she caught Lily's reflection in the mirror she wheeled round. 'Look!' She held out her hand, where Lily saw two very familiar-looking capsules roll to a stop between her heart- and life-lines.

Chapter Thirty-Eight

'Water?'

Susie nodded and held out her hands for the bottle Jack was throwing her.

'Good session,' he said after they'd both drunk deeply.

It had been, and, despite her strongest intentions not to blush with pleasure, her cheeks pinked at the compliment.

'How's the . . .?' He pointed at his nose then hers.

'Not too bad. I hope the bruises will be gone by the time we get to Blackpool.'

He examined her more closely. 'I'm sure one of the stylists will have something to cover them up if not. Crystals or make-up or something.' He dropped her a wink. 'You could always wear a superhero mask.'

Susie grinned at the idea and was just about to tell him the story she'd told Kian to explain her fading black eyes before remembering she didn't share stories about her – their – son.

For the nine millionth time she wondered, *Am I doing the right thing*?

'I wanted to talk to you about something, Suze.'

He looked nervous. He wasn't alone. Since the mysterious

call, the only time any of them weren't feeling on edge was when they were dancing. It struck her that what had started off as the worst part of her day – rehearsal – had somehow become the balm. The only time she felt truly safe.

While the tango night hadn't worked out exactly as Susie had planned (there had been no way she could question Lucia and Cristobal after her 'trip', and Lily had mumbled something about the timing not being right to quiz Javier), thanks to poor Maisie, they now had a solid link between the pills and the Argentine dancers. Madhav had taken the sample Lily had bagged up and was having them analysed but, just like the police, his team was busy and she was in a queue along with the rest of his detectives. If they were what she thought they were, the breakdown would reveal the water-soluble capsule contained little but pure amphetamine. Speed to give the dancers that extra boost they needed because of the calories they weren't ingesting. Or, very possibly, a drug to accelerate a painfully thin dancer's heart beyond its capabilities.

Jack grabbed a prop chair – something that would've been used in a cabaret-style number – then twirled it round and sat on it backwards, the curved wooden boughs serving as a divider between them. She sat on the floor and began to do some cool-down stretches. Ten days in to their rehearsals, her limbs already felt more athletic, and, despite herself, she liked it. Who knew what her body would be like in just over two weeks' time when Jack led her onto the beautifully sprung floors at Blackpool Tower? Even thinking about all that lay ahead felt empowering. And then she looked up. Right there, directly in her line of vision, all she could see was the spread of Jack's thighs.

Her thoughts crashed from their lofty heights to a more

primitive destination. A place between her own thighs that she really hadn't hoped to awaken during their rehearsals. She pressed her legs together and developed an intense interest in her toes.

Jack cleared his throat, another indicator of his nerves. 'I wanted to tell you why doing this – going to Blackpool – is so important for me.'

She looked up. 'It's to match Lily's record, right? Ten times a Ten champion?'

'I . . . Yes and no. Yes I want to win – it'd be an amazing record to equal – but now it's more . . .' He scrubbed his hand along the back of his neck. 'I let myself be dazzled by The Duke.'

'Marmaduke?' Susie said, though she knew that was who he meant.

Jack nodded. 'He was the one pushing the pro-line back then when we were . . . you know.'

'Together?' she suggested.

He winced his affirmation and continued, 'He kept telling me I could have my own studio. My own line of dance wear. He dangled all sorts of things he knew I wanted in front of me.'

Susie felt her muscles clench.

'No.' Jack read her mind. 'Not women.' Almost in passing he added, 'It was always you, Suze. But no, it was the fame I wanted. The recognition. I wanted . . .' The words caught in his throat.

'You wanted to be a champion,' she finished for him. At the highest level. And he'd been willing to put on the blinkers and pursue it the way Dorothy and her ragtag bunch of friends had sought Oz. 'And you are, Jack. You're the champion you always wanted to be.'

'No, that's just it, Suze. I'm not.'

She pulled her elbow up and over her head and pressed on it, willing her shoulder blades to travel back down her spine. 'You are, Jack,' she protested. 'You've won at Blackpool countless times.'

'Not with you,' he said, quietly. He drew a deep breath, then repeated with more heat, 'Not with you.'

Suddenly, Susie could feel Jack's eyes on her bare skin, where her top had hitched up as she stretched. A trickle of sweat wove its way along the sensitive skin between her breasts as she straightened. He tracked her movement, looking at her the way no man had in years, let alone since she'd had a child. Something about motherhood and work and just trying to get on with things had made her lose touch with her body. They were well aware of one another now.

She switched elbows, hoping Jack couldn't see her erratic pulse pounding through the stupidly thin top she was wearing.

'You won, Jack,' she said, trying to regain control of the conversation. 'You won those competitions fair and square.'

He scrunched up his face as if the victories were a bad taste in his mouth.

'I wanted them for *us*. Two scrappy kids who had no business being at the top of the podium. Owning it, you know? Having all those people say, do you see that boy there from Ireland? God knows where he would've ended up if his grandfather hadn't taken him to a ballroom dance class.'

She smiled as she remembered his grandfather. He was handsome, like Jack. In a Harrison Ford kind of way. One of those men you instantly knew would be there for you. Digging plasters out of his pockets for blistered heels. Ice creams waiting for them in the back of the car when rehearsal had been a disaster. Wise words when a competition hadn't delivered a first.

He had an ability to be present. There. He was, quite simply, one of the kindest men in the world.

Kian Kelly.

When she'd first held their son in her arms, it was the first and only name that had come to her.

Desperate not to let Jack see her eyes well up at the many lovely memories she had of him and their time together, she pulled her feet in, pressed the soles together and tipped her head down for a spinal stretch.

'That's where I got it all wrong, Suze,' Jack was saying.

'What do you mean?'

'I was only thinking of myself. Of the endgame. All this business with Oxana and Topaz and Scouser Sam, it's made me untangle some knots in my head.'

'Like?' she asked, eyes fastidiously trained on her feet.

'I guess I don't feel I've won all those competitions honestly, you know? I mean, part of me knows. After all,' he shot his palms into an ironic jazz-hands waggle. 'I'm Jack Kelly.'

She looked at him and laughed. 'So modest.'

The smile faded as quickly as it had appeared. 'Only, being with you again has made me see that my motivation for winning all those trophies was off.' He pressed his fist to his chest. 'I was dancing for stuff. For glory.'

Susie frowned. 'You worked for those trophies,' she reminded him. 'And you know you're a better dancer than most of those folk.'

'Sure, but . . . I hadn't realized just how much I wanted to win them with you by my side.'

Susie looked away. What was she meant to say? That the day she'd left him, her heart had cracked in two and never fully mended? That dancing with him again was equal parts pleasure and pain? That the part of her that wanted to open herself up to him again was being put to the test every single day, literally straining at the seams?

'God, I miss him,' Jack said. 'I know it's corny, but he was the world's best granddad. Always knew what to say when I got myself in a muddle.'

Susie looked up. 'He hasn't . . . Oh, no. *Jack*. He's gone?'

His face told her everything she needed to know.

'Aye, so . . .' Jack said. He rubbed his fingers along his chin a few times then got up from the chair. 'Here. I'll help you with your stretches. Cross your legs.'

After swiping at her cheeks with the backs of her hands, Susie did as he said.

'Give me your hands.' She did and, before he eased her forward into a full, deep stretch, their eyes caught. For the first time since they'd come back into one another's lives, she felt them exchange a shared understanding. They'd missed one another. Missed this. Sharing hopes, fears, loss. They'd been one another's cornerstones back in the day. Now she had to admit it, from the day she'd turned her back on Jack Kelly, nothing had been quite the same.

'Knock knock!' Lily came in, holding Susie's phone. Her eyes pinged between the two of them, the clasped hands, the intense expressions. 'Sorry, darling. You left this in my office and it's been buzzing at me.'

Susie clambered up and took it, not sure if she was relieved at the reprieve or annoyed. 'It's my brother.' She looked at Lily and Jack. 'Maybe it's about the toxicology report.'

She walked to the far end of the studio as she listened to the message, aware Chris could easily be calling about Kian.

He and her dad had been taking the lion's share of babysitting duties while she pursued this case, and neither of them were particularly happy that Jack Kelly was back on the scene. But it wasn't a personal message.

She listened to it a second time then strode back to Jack and Lily and pressed play. After the message finished, they all stared at one another.

Topaz and Oxana's deaths were connected.

'So . . . I'm not very up on technical names,' Lily said, 'but I take it that they found amphetamines in Topaz's system.'

'Yes,' Susie confirmed. 'Fenproporex. It's an anorectic – an appetite suppressant. A dangerous one.'

'Is it something that could have killed Oxana, too?'

Susie shrugged. 'I'm still waiting on Madhav's guys to let me know if the ones Oxana had matched Maisie's. Then we can compare them to Topaz's. The pills Topaz took are scary, though. They can cause hallucinations, convulsions, comas and, in some cases, death.'

Jack rubbed his hands over his head, as if trying to crush the facts into a space that didn't want to allow room for them. 'So they both died because they wanted to be skinnier than they already were?'

'I can't speak for them, but honestly? The diet pills are probably what kept Topaz alive for an extra twenty minutes or so.'

'What?'

Susie held out her phone again and pressed play. After they'd listened to the message one more time, Jack and Lily looked none the wiser.

'Topaz had BoNT-A injected into her bloodstream,' Susie explained. 'Botulism toxin type A.'

Jack frowned. 'Isn't botulism the thing in . . .' He pulled his face back, as if he was in a wind tunnel.

'Stop that, darling, the wind might change,' Lily murmured under her breath.

'Botox, yes,' Susie said, glaring at them both. 'Although, it's just a brand name that's become widely used. Like Hoover. The actual toxin is used in a few similar brands. It's something that the government's been trying to regulate because too many back-alley operators are putting people at risk.'

Lily winced. 'It doesn't sound a nice way to go.'

'It isn't,' Susie confirmed. 'It's respiratory paralysis. In other words, your lungs stop working.'

Jack took in a deep breath, as if needing to remind himself that his own lungs still worked. He closed his eyes and said, 'I think that must've been what happened to Oxana.'

'What makes you say that?' Susie asked.

'The way she was before she died. She was full of nervous energy for the first few dances and then . . .' He mimicked a goldfish out of water then, suddenly overcome, pressed his fingers against his eyes and groaned. 'God, how awful.'

After a moment's silent reflection, Lily cleared her throat and met Susie's gaze with a look weighted with meaning. 'You don't have to do this, you know. Go forward with the investigation.'

Susie knew what she was saying. She had a son to look after.

Despite the risk, Susie knew it was one she wanted to take. She'd been in the police when her son was born and confronted dangerous situations every shift. That hadn't been why she'd stepped away. It had been the scheduling. Pragmatics. The desire to clean the streets of folk who made lives a misery for innocent people still lived strong in her. 'I'm still game,' she said. 'Jack? I'd understand if you didn't want to. After all, we were all named in that last phone call.'

'I'm not letting you do this on your own,' he bridled. 'Not a chance.'

Susie was about to say that of the two of them, she was definitely the one more likely to be able to fend for herself should something dangerous cross their path, but something told her to back down. Not take away from his instinct to want to look after her. After all, if she died, Jack would be Kian's next of kin.

Before the mental image of Jack and Kian together had a chance to sear itself on her consciousness, Lily had taken hold of her elbow and was guiding them through to the kitchen, where a ream of papers was spread out on the island.

'Now. I've pulled some strings and got you a date to take your professional exam,' Lily was saying, pure business. 'It'll be the real deal. Not a casting couch. Not a "cup of tea exam".'

Susie shuddered, thinking of the lengths some dancers were willing to go to achieve their dreams. Back in the day, she'd heard rumours about people buying their way into the pros, or even sleeping with the powers that be. She'd been naive back then, but now knew enough about how the world worked to understand that the dancers who took that route were most likely coerced; manipulated into thinking they had no other choice. It made her blood boil.

'We can go pro-am if you want, Suze,' Jack said, interrupting her dark thoughts. 'I'll stay professional, you stay in the amateurs. That's an option at Blackpool.'

'Not the option you need to match the record,' Susie replied. 'I'll take the exam. And I wouldn't be happy if I thought I was being given "special favours".'

Jack wasn't relenting. 'Suze, listen. I don't want you thinking I've bullied you into this.'

'No way.' She wouldn't let him play the sacrificial lamb at this juncture. 'You've got a record to match. I don't think Lily will begrudge you the win, seeing as we're doing all this under extraordinary circumstances.'

'That's one way to put it,' said Jack. He looked nervous. And he should be. Someone out there was giving lethal botulism injections to a specific set of ballroom dancers. The notes and messages made it clear it wasn't just some charlatan. It was someone intent on causing chaos and fear. Someone intent on killing again.

Susie scanned the paperwork and let out a low whistle. 'Three days before we go to Blackpool? That's a bit tight.' Two short weeks away.

'You've come along at a rate of knots, darling, but there are still some elements of proficiency that need bucking up and some teaching hours to log. I've set up a couple of classes you could lead,' Lily explained.

Susie fought the urge to ask what needed improving. She knew what Lily would say, *The passion, darling. Where's the heart of the dance? People need to feel what you feel. Eyes are the windows to the soul.*

'Who am I going to teach?'

Lily shifted another sheet of paper in front of her.

'Juniors and juveniles?'

'They need training every bit as much as the next person, darling. And besides, the Under-Twelves are only allowed to do the basic steps from the technique book, so it'll be good for you.'

True. And the students would likely be less intimidating

than some of the adult amateurs Jack taught. She'd watched a few of his lessons and his students were good. Really good. And very demanding.

'Right.' Susie began to make notes of her own. 'So, a truck-load of rehearsal before the pro exams . . .'

'And the written exams,' Lily said.

'Fine.' She was good at that sort of thing.

'And the only other thing I'd like you both to bear in mind is that it won't just be me judging at Blackpool.'

Jack rolled his eyes. 'That's pretty standard form, Lil.'

'I know, I'm just saying; it will mean I'll be out on the floor for the entire competition. And a reminder to Susie that you'll both be working hard, too. This isn't telly, darling. You haven't done this type of competition in a long time. Your stamina will be put to the test. It's seven rounds, and twice the work for you and Jack as you're doing ballroom and Latin. Five dances. A fifteen-minute break. Five more dances. A fifteen-minute break. Over and over until the final.'

Jack cut in, 'There are the amateur and pro-am rounds as well. We'll get a bit of breathing room then.'

Lily gave an acquiescent nod. 'True. But I'm going to have to judge some of them and stay on the floor for the rounds I don't. More to the point, I'm not allowed to speak to anyone. You two are going to have to hunt for this murderer by yourselves, unless they swan out into the middle of the dance floor and announce themselves.'

'If it's Marmaduke, it just might happen,' Jack quipped, and then, as he took on the gravity of his statement – that his mentor of these past few years just might have been killing his partners, too – he gave the counter a thump with his fist.

'Veronica is judging as well,' Lily said, to move the conversation along. She listed a few other stalwarts. 'This is a big competition, so there will be eleven of us in total. I'm sure there will be some people, loyalists to Marmaduke, who will be actively looking for the two of you to slip up. Judges who will want any excuse to mark you down.'

Susie swallowed. She closed her eyes and pictured the scene, so different from the dance competitions on television. Dancers were after firsts instead of tens. And not only that, you needed a majority of judges to give the top marks. At this level, there were more judges to please.

The eleven judges, seasoned professionals all, would be stationed at tactical viewing points around the floor, eyes peeled to catch each and every mistake. Missteps. Poor arm styling. Clumsy footwork. Each round, they ranked dancers from first to sixth. They needed as many firsts as they could get. Whoever consistently ranked highest, won.

Susie was going to be dancing against pros after a seven-year hiatus. Was this insanity?

No. It was work. And she had to remind herself of that.

Lily continued with a knowing tap of her finger against the side of her nose. 'It's not all doom and gloom, darlings. Remember, this competition is different from most of the other UK events.'

'In what way?' Susie asked.

'In Blackpool, Marmaduke isn't holding the reins.'

Chapter Thirty-Nine

'Is she here yet?'

'I can't see. I've got an eye mask on.'

The Duke made a noisy show of looking himself, even though, from under her mask, Veronica knew he was mid-cycle on the massage chair. Such were the perils of having a facial, a mani and a pedi all at the same time.

His timing, however, was fortuitous. 'Thanks, love.' He winked at the spa girl approaching him. 'Just the champagne, not the crisps this time. Waistline.' As if she cared. Everyone loved a man in power, even if he was the size of a house. He threw back half the glass before shooting another impatient glance at the front door of Shaz 'n Baz's Beauty.

'If you could just keep still . . .' the facialist said, through increasingly gritted teeth.

'You do your bit and I'll do mine,' he snapped. He hated it when the 'girls' were over thirty. With the amount of money he'd poured into this place over the years, you'd think Shaz and Baz would've figured out his preferences by now.

'She'll be here,' Veronica soothed as she removed her mask to accept a vodka tonic slushy in a hot-pink sippy cup. 'Thank you, darling. Shaz!' she called out. 'Do you have any of those pop chips thingamies?'

'Anything for our regulars,' Shaz swooped in with her baby-voiced coo. 'Can I get you anything, Duke? A cashmere blanket? We could order in some sushi if you like? Oh, my! Your hands are looking good.'

This was more like it. Service from the boss.

'Could you tell the girl French ombré, please, sweetie?' Veronica asked her.

Marmaduke closed his eyes and tried to let Veronica's endless chatter fade into the background, relishing the assault on his spine from the massage rollers . . .

'With the glitter *and* the gem accents,' Veronica added. 'I'm never sure my accent translates to . . .' her voice dropped to a whisper, '*the Vietnamese*. Oh!' Full volume again. 'How're the new lips working out?'

'Baz says it's like kissing the insides of a lava lamp!' Shaz beamed.

'Fab-u-lous!'

Veronica's phone pinged and The Duke abandoned his half-hearted attempt at relaxation.

'It's not *him* again, is it?' he asked, sitting upright.

Veronica attempted to arch an eyebrow. 'Since when do you refer to our good friend Sam Pringle as "him"?'

'Since he became your bloody North Star, that's when. Or should I say . . .' he lowered his voice, 'your North Pole.' He jerked his pelvis to illustrate what he meant and felt a twinge in his back. God*damn* middle age.

Veronica swatted at his arm. 'Someone has to make sure that sponsorship money he promised keeps on coming.'

Marmaduke scowled and drained his glass, tapping the edge of it to summon one of the girls.

'Sorry, sorry, sorry,' Johanna called from the door. At last.

Her diamanté cane made her look more like a three-legged footballer's wife than a former world champion ballroom dancer. In fact, she was looking a bit feral today. As if she'd been dragged through a hedge backwards, then run through town in nothing but a trench coat.

'Here.' He flapped the list of treatments at her. 'We're having facials. Choose your poison.'

Johanna flicked half a metre's worth of golden hair, which might or might not have been her own, over her shoulder. She looked him in the eye and fashioned her perfect bee-stung mouth into a shape that was pure invitation. 'Are you saying I look old, Duke?'

He'd show her just how young *he* was later when he pronged her in one of the massage rooms. For now, though, they had business to attend to. 'Never.' He patted the faux-leather arm-chair between his and Veronica's. 'Put that baby on vibrate, stick your tootsies in the water and let's get to work.'

Once they were all settled, a fleet of beauticians silently buffing and polishing, Marmaduke began to explain why he'd called them all here. 'I have a plan to get rid of Lily at Blackpool.'

It was still in amoeba form, but they didn't need to know that.

Veronica giggled and clapped while Johanna looked between them as if she was watching a tennis match being played with grenades. 'Why?' she asked.

The Duke drained another glass. 'Progress,' he lied. By progress he meant *power* – and with someone like Lily Richmond on the scene, he'd always be a hair's breadth from true overlord status. 'The woman's so bloody self-righteous. Too dedicated to "tradition".' She was, in short, the only woman in the industry who didn't do what he told her to. Lily and that old fart Cyril de Boeuf were all that stood between him and dance domination. Cyril had run the Ballroom Bonanza since its inception. The man was incorruptible. There wasn't a bribe in the world that would interest him. Extraordinary. 'Tradition isn't what our world needs,' Marmaduke continued as if orating to a crowd of thousands. 'It needs forward-thinking progressives who know how to lure in the fat cats. Ballroom dance can't stay stuck back in the 1950s. Ow! Jesus Christ woman! What is that? A cactus?'

He repositioned himself in the chair, striking what he hoped was a reflective pose, although with this geriatric crone hovering over him with medieval instruments of torture, it took some effort.

The truth was, he was broke. And he wasn't about to sacrifice the lifestyle he'd become accustomed to by sticking to the rulebook, thank you very much. The plans he'd put in place with Jack Kelly had blown up in his face, so he'd had to come up with a new one. It was devious and self-serving, but who cared?

He closed his eyes and pictured the future. The GDC would be defunct. He would run the only competition that mattered: Dancing with The Duke. Each and every dance, trademarked with specialized moves he himself had crafted. Money would pour in from royalties as dancers across the globe participated in branded competitions. He'd be bigger than Starbucks. KFC. Subway, even.

He could see it perfectly: his name in lights, ticker-taping round the Tower at Blackpool. *The Duke of Dance's World*

Championships: the premier international ballroom dance extravaganza.

They'd kick things off with the Royal Waltz, then swiftly move on to the Fitzgerald Foxtrot, The Dirty Duke's Cha-Cha-Cha, finishing with the Tipsy Tango and the Essex Smooth. Jack was meant to have been his poster boy. His chief salesman. But he'd use Johanna instead. Wring her dry until he found someone new. By this time next year, he'd have achieved it all without so much as a sniff of Lily Richmond to ruin his plans.

Johanna circled her choice of treatment in lip liner and waved the menu at Shaz. 'I don't think Lily was alive in the 1950s,' she said to The Duke. 'She's younger than you, right?'

'Not the takeaway I was aiming for,' he snapped. 'It's *your* future I'm interested in, Johanna. As a dancer and, one of these days, as a judge. I've had my eye on you and I foresee a long, esteemed career beneath that magic mirror ball we all love so much.'

He had her attention now. And, hopefully, her blind loyalty. With that gammy knee of hers, the simple truth was that she'd have to suck up to someone.

'Now,' he continued, 'Veronica and I were wondering what you know about this Susie character. The one dancing with Jack.'

Johanna slumped back in her chair. 'Nothing really. She came out of nowhere.' She traced one of her fingertips along her glossy lower lip.

'Not true,' said The Duke, holding out his glass again and, this time, popping a couple of blue pills into his mouth along with the first swig. 'She used to dance amateurs with Jack, back when he was training with Lily.'

'Did she?' Johanna yelped. 'Oh, god. That's a lot of needles.'

They all looked at the tray of pre-charged syringes being held aloft by a man who looked so much like Magic Mike that Marmaduke did a double take.

'What are you having, darling?' Veronica asked. 'I'm certified to do them if you don't trust this gorgeous specimen.' She licked her lips and gave a little tiger growl.

'Dermas,' Johanna said. 'I've had them before on my labial folds and they were ace.' She grinned up at the Adonis. 'I think I'm good with this one. You just relax, Roni.'

Marmaduke pushed up his chair to watch proceedings. His facialist took the control and lowered it again. 'It's time for your lymphatic drainage massage, Mr Duke.'

'What were you saying about that cow dancing with Jack?' Johanna asked as Magic Mike approached her with a loaded syringe.

The Duke explained, 'She used to dance on the amateur scene but then disappeared.'

It wasn't uncommon. Sometimes people got a job. Moved. Got married. Did both, as Lily had. Swept off to Japan with her plonker of an Aussie for one very blissful decade – until he dumped her and she came back to the UK on a mission to ruin everyone's lives. And by *everyone*, he meant him.

But that hadn't been the case with Susie. She and Jack had regularly won their competitions. And even before he'd lured Jack away from Lily's studio all those years ago, she'd gone. Marmaduke had not thought much about it, to be honest. One of the many marvellous things about being a male in this world was that women were at your mercy. You could do what you wanted – seduce them, bin them – and they had to take it.

A male partner, especially an attractive, kind-hearted one like Jack, was like gold dust. There would've been a catfight over him when he'd begun his own studio, whether or not he'd had a partner. The fact that this Susie character had disappeared from the scene had simply made things cleaner.

'I've not heard anything,' Veronica said. 'But I wonder if perhaps she wasn't holed up with one of those oligarch types Oxana used to teach.'

Johanna's ear pricked up at this little nugget. 'I always wanted one of those gigs because the pay sounds lush, but then I heard that you have to put out. Do you think Oxana . . .?'

'Now, now.' Veronica pretended to grow a conscience. 'Let's let sleeping dogs lie.'

The Duke brightened. 'No! Let's wake them up a bit.'

'What do you mean?' Johanna asked through clenched teeth as she received another syringe's worth of filler.

'Well . . .' he spoke as he thought. 'What if some of the other judges were to hear some . . . less than flattering things about Susie? You know the GDC has a reputation to maintain. A moral integrity to uphold.'

'Yeah, but Blackpool isn't a GDC event, is it?'

'No, but . . .' It would be, once his plan bore fruit. And then, of course, it would become a Dancing with The Duke event. 'Perhaps it might be useful to spread a few little white lies. In aid of your journey to, one day, re-partner with Jack, obviously,' he added.

Johanna lurched forward. 'Can you use *both* pinks on my toes? I'm going for a Barbiecore look.'

'Has Jack said anything to you about possibly partnering again?' The Duke pressed.

'No,' Johanna harrumphed. 'I tried really hard to find out where he stood on things, but getting information from him is impossible.'

Blast. 'You didn't discuss anything at all?' He was furious at Jack for shutting him out. Enraged that Jack hadn't come to him when his studio was destroyed and then, later, when Topaz died.

'What about his plans for Blackpool?' Veronica prompted. 'Did Jack say if he was dancing in the pros?'

'He is,' The Duke confirmed through the steaming hot towel that had just been placed over his face. 'Hoping to, anyway. Lily has signed up this Susie girl to take the pro-exam.'

'I didn't get a notice,' Veronica griped through her own towel.

'The devious wench has pulled some strings, hasn't she?' Marmaduke would've done the same thing in her shoes, but that was beside the point.

'If the two of them drop dead in the middle of the first round, I'd be the first to do a victory dance.'

Marmaduke and Veronica pushed themselves up to exchange a look.

'Kidding,' sulked Johanna. 'Obviously.' She shrugged and sighed. 'I've sent Jack a bunch of texts since Whitby, but he doesn't really say anything.'

'What *does* he say?' Veronica pressed.

Johanna gave a despairing wail, 'He said he'd help me find a new partner when I was back up on my feet again.' The wail became a whimper. 'Can I get some of those ice things for my eyes?'

'Cryotherapy wands?' Shaz asked.

'Yeah, those,' Johanna said resentfully as if it was Shaz's fault she'd burst into tears. 'I don't want to look puffy when I leave.'

If there was one thing that rendered Marmaduke flaccid, it was a woman in tears. He dug into his pocket, found the rattling little bottle and, without looking, popped another pill. He'd set his sights on Veronica today instead. It'd been a while. Perhaps it was time to remind her just how fun a post-mani-pedi romp in the sack could be.

They sat through the rest of their treatments in relative silence. Once they'd gathered in the foyer, The Duke sent Johanna on her way with a swot to the derriere and a reminder: 'I'm relying on you, sweetheart. Keep your ear to the ground, those succulent lips of yours to the grapevine and, I promise you, you'll be back up on that podium again in no time.'

He waited for her to hobble out of the shop before turning to Roni. 'You know, the wife and I have a suite down at The Adelphi. She's just sent a text saying she's warming up the bed.'

Veronica frowned as if she didn't understand.

The Duke was suddenly short on patience. 'C'mon, Roni. It's been ages since we've had a throuple. Liven up a man's afternoon, won't you?'

'Oh, well, I . . . the thing is, I was going to go shopping for a dress this afternoon.'

He saw an opportunity and launched himself at it. 'I'd be more than happy to zip you into your gowns in the dressing room.' As soon as the Viagra kicked in, he would screw her senseless on a carpet of satin Valentinos.

'Duke?' Veronica leant in. 'Are you all right?'

He had been a moment ago. But now? Not so much. His pulse was thudding against his throat as a strange roiling sensation began in his stomach. His breath came in short, sharp gasps.

'Darling, you're not looking very well. Here.' Veronica

249

pressed a glass bottle of something repulsive-looking into his hand. 'It's kombucha. Have a drink while I find your blood-pressure pills.'

He lurched towards the wall, knocking over a potted palm and a trio of succulents. He clapped one hand on his chest and reached for the pills Roni was holding, swallowing them in a oner.

'There you are, Duke. That's right.'

He was vaguely aware of some of the salon staff gathering and calls for someone to ring for an ambulance, but his attention was on Roni, his lifelong cohort, who, instead of looking stricken, was holding one of his pills up to the light.

And then, as each breath became more difficult to take than the last . . . darkness.

Chapter Forty

'Tea, darling?' Lily popped the kettle on.

'No, ta.' Susie wanted to say yes; she'd struggled to get Kian out of bed for his early drop-off at school this morning and was desperate for the hit of caffeine. Not so desperate that she was willing to have it sloshing around her stomach during rehearsal, though. She glanced up at the screens to see who else was in the studio. She'd hated that other people could see her and Jack rehearsing when she'd first seen Lily's security system, but now that they'd had that terrifying call, she was grateful for it.

The studio she and Jack were meant to rehearse in was empty. The large studio had been taken over by the Under-12s and their parents. Brynn and Kiko had come along to lead a workshop on the latest hairstyles.

The smallest studio was, as ever, occupied by Ruby Rae and Vlad, who were in the throes of a fairly torrid paso doble.

'So we think the Argentines are to blame?' Lily said after she'd made herself a cup of black instant and began doing heel lifts at one end of the kitchen island. It was more of a statement than a question, really.

Susie grimaced. 'It's an easy leap to make. According to the report, the amphetamines in Topaz's system were the same as the ones in Oxana's bag and the capsules Lucia gave Maisie.'

'That poor girl.' Lily performed an uncharacteristic sign of the cross. 'She could have died.'

'She probably would've only suffered a few hours of nervous energy. Remember,' Susie pulled Topaz's pathology report out of her shoulder bag, 'Topaz's actual cause of death was the botulism.'

'Yes, but whoever gave her the Botox also gave her the pills. And Oxana, I'm guessing. To make sure they lived long enough to die in public.'

'Well . . .' Susie chewed on her lip as she considered the hypothesis. 'It does make the most sense that that is what their intention was. Particularly when you factor in the notes. The murderer is seeking some sort of revenge. Demanding some form of acknowledgement. From us, too. But what?'

'Well, if it is one of the Argentines, I'm guessing it's winning first place.' Lily grimaced. 'Why they'd need their victims to die in public is a mystery, though.'

Susie shrugged. 'Dancers are performers. They like an audience.' Susie thought for a moment, then carefully said, 'If it isn't the Argentine dancers, maybe it's one of their team?'

Lily shot her a look then massaged her temples. 'I have to admit, darling, I'm still struggling to believe Javier is mixed up in something like this.'

Susie read between the lines to the heart of her concern: Lily was desperate for Javier to be innocent.

'I can't imagine that he is,' Susie said, truthfully. 'Who knows? Maybe it's one of the musicians doing it as an act of unrequited love for one of the dancers? Although, I don't think they were at Whitby . . . so that still leaves us with Lucia and Cristobal, and possibly Felipe and his partner from Whitby.'

Lily took a sip of her coffee then changed the subject. 'How much botulism was Topaz given?'

Susie thumbed through her phone. 'It says here a lethal dose is seventy thousand millionths of a gram.' She pinched her fingers together. 'That would be invisible to the human eye in powder form.'

'But it was injected into Topaz?'

'Yes, that's right. The units were made soluble with saline or water.' Susie put the papers away when she heard some students outside the kitchen. She waited to continue until they'd gone into the changing rooms. 'Each of those tiny vials has something like fifty to a hundred units in it. I would imagine they used about fifteen or twenty vials' worth to kill her.'

Lily cut in, 'It takes up to fifty vials to sort out a forehead, darling.'

Susie didn't ask her how she knew. 'Remember, they're tiny, the vials. And cosmetic injections are done safely and subcutaneously. Under the skin. This was a back-alley job. Death was their endgame, not to make their target more youthful. The murderer injected it directly into Topaz's bloodstream. Completely different. Whoever it was knew how much they needed to use in order to kill someone. They probably charged up a single syringe and went straight for a vein . . .' She mimicked injecting the lethal dose in one swift movement.

Lily wrapped her arms around herself and shuddered. 'Those poor, poor girls. I know it's not the point, but I'm going the non-injectable route from here-on-in.'

253

Susie gave her a sad smile. 'You're so beautiful, Lily. You shouldn't worry about things like that.'

Lily softened and, in a moment she rarely allowed herself, took Susie's hand in hers and said, 'I've missed you, darling. Our chats.'

A wash of shame crashed through her. Lily had championed her from that very first day Susie had arrived here in this studio. It had been more bare bones then. Less glitzy. No marble-topped kitchen islands or saunas in the changing rooms. But, despite all the water that had passed beneath the bridge, Lily was no less generous with her heart and her time.

'I . . .' Susie began. How to apologize for cutting the woman out of her life who had all but raised her?

Lily took the decision out of her hands by pointing at the clock. 'You'd best be getting on. Jack'll be waiting.'

'I mean it,' Susie said. 'About you being beautiful.'

Lily gave her hand a pat then busied herself washing her mug. 'Sadly, darling, it doesn't matter what you think. This world is all about the optics. People don't take to wrinkly women unless they're a character actress portraying someone very rich or someone very poor.' She struck a pose. 'My job as a professional dancer is not only to be perfect out there on the dance floor, but to *look* the best as well. I'm in my early sixties. I have to conjure an illusion for women dreaming that they, too, would look like this if only they knew the finer points of the American smooth.' She danced a few steps with an invisible partner.

Susie applauded.

Jack appeared at the window of the kitchen door, knocked on it, then pointed towards the studio. She gave him a double thumbs-up. He smiled then headed off.

It took a second for Susie to realize that their tiny exchange had given her butterflies. She'd have to quell those before she reached the studio.

Two hours later Susie was still fighting those fluttering butterfly wings dancing about her insides.

Something had softened in Jack these past few days and, unlike when they'd first begun rehearsing, his instructions and insistence that they revisit intimate moves felt less of a challenge and more of an invitation.

But as much as instinct was urging her to accept each and every one of them, there was something far more important at stake. Kian's safety.

Jack had a target on his back. Just like she did. But she'd been trained to keep herself and her loved ones safe. As had her father and brother. And also? Her father and brother were the only family Kian knew. He felt safe with them. Loved. Whole.

Adding Jack to the mix would shake up his world and, more pressingly, increase the risk that the murderer might include Kian in his sight lines.

Jack looked up from his rehearsal playlist. 'Let's try the samba, shall we?'

Susie took another drink of water and nodded. 'Sounds good.'

He put on 'Magalenha' by Sergio Mendes. The music instantly poured into her. The drums and his voice gave the song a primitive element that instantly transported her somewhere dark and sexy and warm. The opposite of the rainy spring day outside the studio.

The choreography was some of her favourite. Sensual and athletic. It demanded that you either gave into it or walked away. It also didn't involve too much physical contact. As such, she felt free for the very first time to give herself wholly to it. And, when the choreography demanded it, happy to press her back to Jack's chest as he swept her torso and arms round in a move that reminded her of how feminine she'd once felt in his arms. Beautiful even.

The door banged against the wall and Ruby Rae stood framed in the doorway.

'Oh. My. Gawd.' She pulled an I'm-so-shocked-I-can't-even-speak face. And then continued, 'Marmaduke's died.'

Susie's mouth went dry. She looked at Jack. The blood had drained from his face. 'When?' The man was vile, and a suspect, but . . . she had never once imagined he'd fall foul of the murderer. 'Is he . . . how did it . . .?'

Ruby Rae cackled. 'Look at you two. You look like I just told you your mama had died.'

Jack took a step towards Susie. She held out her hand to stop him, finding just enough comfort in his protective move to keep the sting of tears at bay. Ruby Rae wasn't to know her mum had died.

Ruby Rae sniffed. 'Oh, don't take things so seriously. The Duke ain't dead. He's in the hospital.'

'Why?'

'He . . .' Ruby Rae started to giggle. 'He . . .' Again giggles overtook her.

'He *what*?' Jack and Susie asked as one.

'He was getting a facial and took too much Viagra with his blood-pressure pills and . . . and . . .' Tears were running down her face now. 'He almost beta-blocked himself to death!' She allowed her hysteria to consume her, spitting out the occasional phrase like, 'Veronica was there,' and, 'Won't be using Shaz 'n Baz's any more' and, 'Viagra! The dirty old coot!'

As she cackled and babbled, Jack and Susie shared a look of disbelief and then, as it registered that it hadn't been the murderer striking again, relief. But also . . . it did mean Marmaduke could still be a suspect. Their list was every bit as long as it had been from the off.

'Don't let me interrupt,' Ruby Rae said, stepping to the mirror to fix her make-up. 'You two carry on.'

'I thought you and Vlad were rehearsing,' Jack said.

'Done now. Hard to polish perfection.' She did a leg lift that, even Susie had to admit, proved her point. Ruby Rae whirled round and, leaning her back against the mirror, flickered her fingers at the two of them. 'What were you two working on?'

'Samba,' Jack said.

'Show me.'

'Oh, I . . .' Susie began as Jack pressed play. Despite her reluctance to dance in front of both a rival and a suspect, Susie knew she'd be doing this exact dance in front of a crowd and all the suspects in just over a week's time. Might as well start getting used to it.

As they danced, Ruby Rae took it upon herself to offer a commentary. 'Interesting leg work, Suze,' she'd say. Or, 'Wow, Jack. You must be really strong to pull off that lift.' It was when she said, 'It's so brave to wear your hair like that,' that Susie really felt the tension seeping back in. When they finished the dance – it hadn't been their best version by a long shot – Ruby Rae fake cheered and did the kind of clapping you do when you've actually been bored to death. But another round of applause caught her attention. Brynn the stylist was in the doorway, shoulder propped against the frame.

'That was lovely, you two. You'll kill it in Blackpool.'

Ruby Rae glared at him and swanned out with a sing-songed, 'Not if Vlad and I have anything to say about it!'

Jack glanced at his watch. 'Sorry, Suze. I've got a class downstairs to take.' To Brynn he said, 'I take it the hair session's over?'

'Yes, indeedy,' Brynn confirmed, pointing at his wheelie case of supplies. 'Another set of empowered mums are heading home, armed and prepared to spray their children's hair into submission.'

Though she'd been resisting the urge to examine her own untameable ponytail, Susie did it anyway. Rat's nest would've been a kind way to describe it.

'Want me to have a look?' Brynn asked, pointing at his case again. 'I've got a few free minutes before I'm due elsewhere.'

Susie shot him a grateful look. 'Would you mind?'

'Not in the slightest.'

He grabbed the prop chair Jack often used and set it in front of the mirror. 'Have a seat, my lovely.'

She turned to face her own reflection. Brown hair. Brown eyes. Chubby cheeks. She sighed. She didn't look a thing like the rest of the competitors. Sleek, beautifully done up, athletically toned women who would probably have to stop themselves from sneering when she stepped out onto the dance floor with Jack Kelly.

'Here,' Brynn said, slipping the elastic band from her hair. 'Put that on your wrist. I've lost thousands over the years. Now, what's all of that sighing about? Look at all this hair!' He fluffed it out, sprayed something on it and started brushing it in long, luxurious, practised strokes. 'Honestly.' He glanced at her reflection. 'The only other person I know who has this much of their own, luscious, thick hair is my wife.'

'Oh?'

'Mmm.' He shifted a thick chunk of it over her shoulder. 'See? Beautiful.'

Despite herself, she stroked it. It did look shinier. And felt silkier. 'What did you spray on it?'

He held up a bottle. 'Detangling and toning mist. Learn to love it.' He handed her the bottle. 'This is your friend.'

Susie tried to hand it back. 'No, no.' He held up his hands. 'Take it. Honestly. It's just so lovely to have someone who isn't so . . .' he glanced at the door where Ruby Rae could be heard shouting at Vlad to hurry the fuck up, they didn't have all day. 'It's lovely to have one of the good ones back in the game.'

She smiled at him. 'You remember me from back then?'

'Course I do!' He patted her shoulder, then slipped his brush back into his case. 'Sorry, love. I've got to pop off, but honestly? If you need any help or want to run through some styles, just give me a shout and I'd be happy to meet up and turn all this gorgeousness into something that'll work in a competition. Lily has my number if you need it.'

She thanked him and followed him out as far as the kitchen. For once it was empty and, after popping on the kettle for that long-awaited cup of tea, she sat herself down at the island and looked up at the monitors again.

Lily was in a studio with Ruby Rae and Vlad. Apparently there *were* a few improvements to be made on perfection.

Maisie and Darren were now in the smallest studio, working out the finer points of a complicated-looking lift. Maisie would have some crackerjack bruises by the end of the session.

And Jack was teaching a class of six-year-olds the quickstep. She knew she shouldn't stay and watch it. She had reams of paperwork back at the office to deal with. Her house was a mess. Her son deserved a proper, well-cooked meal when he got back tonight, instead of one of the pizzas her father and brother regularly made him. But Jack was so sweet with them. So gentle and kind. Patient. He made it fun for them. Exactly the same way Lily had always made it pure joy for her back in the day.

She held her breath when, as they all took partners to try out the new steps, one little red-haired girl was left standing on her own. She was looking this way and that, pretending to be brave, but, despite her best intention, ended up succumbing to a lip wobble.

Jack stepped into the breach. The smile on her face when he took her into his arms! Even the hardest of hearts would've sighed.

All of which she took as her cue to leave. She dumped the remains of her tea down the sink, scrubbed her mug clean, popped it on the draining board and left without a backward glance.

Chapter Forty-One

'Can't . . . breathe!'

Ruby Rae fought the instinct to panic.

It wouldn't help.

If anything, it ruined things.

She knew this from experience.

Kiko shot her a severe look and then, as she so often did when she was tying her up, blew her a kiss.

'Can't . . . breathe . . .' She tried again.

Kiko stood back and examined her, her eye shifting along the ropes restraining Ruby Rae's body the way a painter might, or a sculptor, because Kiko was an artist in everything she did. Today she was wearing a simple black eye patch, no make-up, and her favourite dress. A simple A-line shift that grazed the tops of her bare thighs. It was imprinted with a velvety lop-eared rabbit bound in silk rope.

Kiko's gaze settled on Ruby Rae's chest. There was a double skein of rope both above and below her breasts. Her nipples were caught tight in this year's stocking stuffer: handmade, flower-shaped screw clamps. Her chest rose and fell with each short, sharp inhalation.

A slight shift in Kiko's posture indicated she'd made a decision. 'Can you try for one more knot? You know how to breathe through it. You're my clever little bunny.'

Ruby Rae nodded. She'd do anything Kiko asked of her.

Kiko was pushing herself today. Trying out new knots she'd learned in Kinbaku-bi class, or, as it was known in the west, Shibari: the beautiful art of tight binding.

It was how they spoke to one another, she and Kiko. Through the binding, the knots, the pain, and the subsequent connectivity they felt when Kiko – a tiny little slip of thing –suspended her lover in the air, rendering her entirely powerless. Ruby Rae was at her mercy. And she trusted her with every cell in her body.

Kiko tugged the final knot into place at the top of the four coils of rope binding her ankles together. Ruby Rae struggled. Shibari might not be the art of binding a prisoner of war, but it had sprung from the practice. And struggling against the restraints was half the fun.

'Breathe the pain into me,' Kiko soothed. 'We'll share it.' This was probably the last time Kiko could tie her before Blackpool – the rope burns needed time to fade.

'Make it last,' she begged Kiko. 'Make it last all night.'

Kiko smiled, then teased Ruby Rae's lips apart with her tongue. 'Okay, bunny, I'm going to lift you now.'

As Ruby Rae's arms were pulled up into the air and her derriere lifted ever so slightly away from the floor, the pain was instant and exquisite. All-consuming. She keened into Kiko's mouth.

Kiko grabbed her red leather flogger and gave it a light snap against Ruby Rae's bare bottom. 'I told you: *quiet*. The neighbours are having a dinner party.'

Ruby Rae bit the inside of her cheek and drew blood as, yet again, the ropes swept her body further away from the ground.

Ruby Rae had been in this position a dozen times before. More, even. But today, for some reason, the look in Kiko's eye when she'd cinched the first knot into place had made her heart race, rather than flutter.

Or perhaps the look had been a fiction and more the result of her own guilty conscience. Not her usual modus operandi, but heigh-ho. If she knew anything about the world, nothing stayed the same for long. Like the lay of the land when it came to Lily's affections.

Having Jack at the studio was one thing. Having Jack *and* the prissy clodhopper was entirely different terrain. Picking on Susie wasn't nearly as much fun as picking on Maisie. And even that was beginning to lose its shine.

'Higher,' she demanded as Kiko began to tie off the ropes. 'I said no talking.'

Ruby Rae smiled as the sting of the accompanying slap realigned her focus.

Being here, doing this, reminded her of the essence of dance. Allowing her body to become pure sensation. It was only when she truly submitted to Kiko that she was able to relish the euphoria of the endorphin rush that followed.

Kiko pulled the hoist again. Ruby Rae stemmed her cry, training her focus back to the here and now. She forced herself to savour the unbearable stings of heat singeing her nerve endings as the linen ropes imprinted themselves into her musculature, demanding more of her. The same way she demanded excellence of herself in the studio. Working a sequence over and over, through the blisters, in defiance of the blood, because of the pain. Despite her best efforts, she screamed.

'Breathe,' Kiko instructed. 'Breathe through it, bunny.' She tugged a different pulley and Ruby Rae's legs bent at the knees.

'Aaaaaaaannnghhh!' she cried into Kiko's mouth.

'Do you trust me?'

Ruby Rae was a control freak for nearly every second of every day, but here, with Kiko? 'Always,' she gasped. And it was true.

The pain was so exquisite, so all-consuming, her only choice was to surrender to it.

'Tell me,' Kiko encouraged as she pulled the ropes up ever higher. 'Why does it hurt?'

'I want to win.'

Kiko scoffed. 'So does everyone.'

'I *need* to win.'

'Why?' She pulled again and Ruby Rae's entire bodyweight was now suspended from the reinforced rigging Kiko had designed when she'd moved into the old tobacco warehouse flat. Ruby Rae tipped her head back and looked out through the huge, curtainless windows. If Kiko decided to light so much as a single candle (and she sometimes did), anyone across the river with a good telescope would have quite the show.

'They never should've given me up,' Ruby Rae gasped.

'Who?'

'My mama.' She swallowed against a fresh, deep pulse of pain. 'My papa.'

Kiko looked at her. She never talked about her parents.

'Why?'

'I was worth keeping.'

'Were you?'

'Yes.'

'Who do you want to keep you now?'

Lily.

'You,' she gasped, her nerve endings finally succumbing to the long-awaited waves of endorphins as Kiko's mouth and fingers began to explore her trussed-up body. Before the pain was fully engulfed by pleasure, Ruby Rae allowed herself access to the flares of rage she'd felt when Jack and then Susie had entered her well-ordered life. They were destroying everything. The only person apart from Kiko who had seen through her thick *I don't give a flying fuck* veneer had been Lily. And now, two years into their so-called Five-Year Plan, she feared the guy ropes of Lily's commitment to her were beginning to fray. She'd never wanted to buy this latest doll for her collection, but she'd had to. Terror that Lily was going to kick her out once she moved her own mother, Audrey, in had forced her hand. The slightest thought of it tore her apart in a way she couldn't begin to describe. She'd do anything to stay. Anything at all.

'Tighter,' she pleaded. 'Tighter.'

Chapter Forty-Two

T minus seven days to Susie's exam

'Close your mouth, Susie.'

'Keep smiling, Jack. That's right. Show those lovely teeth of yours.'

He was baring them at Lily, but tempers often flared at this phase in rehearsals. The stress of a poison-wielding murderer in their midst wasn't exactly helping things either.

Which reminded her, 'Susie darling, don't forget we've got to book in a shopping trip and some visits to the beauty salons. Arms! No floppy elbows please.' Lily smiled. She loved it when necessity and sleuthing neatly dovetailed. They did not have time to waste.

'Toe-ball-heel aaaaand . . . *straighten* before you forward walk.'

'Lily, could I just—'

'Not now, Ruby Rae, sorry, darling.'

'Lil, I think we're all right. Suze and I can—'

'Jack. Arms. I'll catch up with you later, Ruby Rae. Jack? Susie. That was rubbish. Opening positions, please.'

Three sets of eyes threw daggers.

Lily beamed her happy face back at all of them. She'd grown a thick skin long before any of them had been born. God bless moisturizer and all her friends.

'En-*gage* those inner thighs. You need to be ab-so-lute-ly *vertical* from your spine through to the top of the head. And stop *grimacing*!'

T minus five days

'Chicken walk, chicken walk, don't chase the music!'

'Chicken, chicken, chicken, cluck, cluck, cluck.'

'Don't *chase*! It doesn't matter which choreography you're using, you've got to stay with the music or you'll look like a little bunny rabbit. I'm late, I'm late . . .'

'Put yourself in the *pocket* of the music! Dum-dee-dum-dee-dum-dee-dummmmm – *there* we are! Beautiful!'

'I hate it.'

'You shouldn't hate anything in your repertoire, darling.'

'It's not the dance. I just hate saying chicken walk.'

'Call it the poultry prance.'

'Can you do that?'

'You can name any step you like, darling, it's your dance. Go and grab a drink of water. Jack? Let me show you this next phrase.'

'One-two – American spin – seven-eight. You see? Bah-dee-bahhh-dee-*bah*-dee-*bah*!'

Jack opened his arms to Susie. 'Right, then. Yahh-kah-yahhh-kah-whoomp-gah-gah!'

'Umm . . . could we just count it out?'

Three days and counting

'Come on, darlings. A waltz isn't a dirge. It was a rather racy dance in its time.' Lily glanced at the clock. 'Give it some zest!'

'If you have somewhere else to be, Lil . . .?' Jack's tone made it clear that he, for one, wouldn't mind a break from her input.

Lily maintained eye contact with him as she pointedly pressed play again.

'You are *framing* Susie, Jack. Not showboating for the judges with a pretty little bauble on the end of your fingertips.

'That's right. Triple step, triiiii-ple step, triple step. No bounce.

'You don't need Jack at all, Susie, if you maintain that strong core.

'Where's that pretty smile of yours, darling? If it isn't pleasure, it's pain, and frankly there's enough of that on offer in this world, isn't there?

'That left leg needs to be strong! Stiff as a board! Like someone's poured Viagra down it.

'Too soon?'

Two days to go

'That's right . . . level, rotate, driiiiive and swing!

'Say helllloooo to the floor, Susie. Don't slap it. Make your foot have a little chat with it. Stroke it. Caress . . . no. Not a thwack. Again.'

'Aren't your other students missing you, Lil?'

'I'm sure they are, but they'll just have to . . . smile, Jack. That's right.

'Legs! Timing! Hips!

'No. Another hour. I want you two to be begging me for mercy. What's that? Sorry, darling, the first-aid kit is just over here.

'And a five, six . . .

'Five . . .

'Perhaps it is time for a cuppa.'

270

One day, two hours and seventeen minutes to go

'The rumba is a vertical expression of a horizontal desire. You two look as if you're about to go to the dentist's!'

'Her exams are *tomorrow*, Lil.'

'*She* is standing right here and has a *name*.'

'Don't worry, Susie darling. You're not invisible. Now, Jack . . .

'Helllooooo! Earth to Lily and Jack!'

'Shush, darling. I'm mid-moment. The entire dance is about Susie. Make sure she knows that! Don't look at the mirror, look at her. Keep looking at . . . right at . . .

'Jack Kelly! What sort of spin release was that? You don't want to send the poor girl flying through the window!'

'For heaven's *sake*, Susie. *Feel* the music. Use the gifts god gave you!'

'Maybe I'm not the same as you. Maybe I don't *have* the gift!'

Lily looked Susie Cooper square in the eye. 'You know as well I do, darling. Dancing isn't a gift. It's graft.'

Susie harrumphed. 'Well, graft doesn't equal sexy.'

'No,' Lily agreed. 'It doesn't.' She looked between the pair of them, facing one another like boxers eyeing up their opponent before a match. 'Don't move.'

She ran to her office and, on her return, changed the music. This particular song had more of a hungry edge to it. A raw longing. In competitions, dancers never knew what music was going to play, only that it would have the necessary timestep.

'Close your eyes,' she instructed. 'Listen to the rhythm. Let it pour into your ears. Feel it surround you like warm sea water. Imagine you're floating in it. That's it. You're floating in the music as it cradles your hips, your arms, your feet, your thighs . . .'

'Hey!'

'Lily!'

'What the—'

'We can't rehearse like this!'

Lily beamed at the pair of them. 'Nonsense, darlings. The rumba's about not being able to keep your hands off each other. Now you have no choice.'

'This isn't fair, Lil,' Jack protested.

'Life isn't fair, Jack. It's time you accepted that and moved on.'

She felt his eyes blazing into her as she turned and headed for the door. Not wanting to end things on an entirely acrimonious note, she stopped, turned, and threw the pair of them a saucy wink.

'Those are some of my favourites. Be sure all the feathers are still on them when I come back.' Despite the storm of protest coming from behind the door as she clicked it shut behind her, something told her that Susie and Jack's rumba was about to become much, much better.

Chapter Forty-Three

'I'm guessing these aren't regulation,' Jack deadpanned, holding their joined wrists aloft.

They both looked at the plum-coloured handcuffs, joined with an arm's length of surprisingly strong metallic gold-link chain.

'Actually,' Susie met his gaze head-on, 'I once brought down a drug lord wanted by Interpol with a pair of these.'

'Seriously? That's . . .' Jack stopped himself then laughed. He jangled the chain that literally bound them then pretended to pull out one of Lily's cherished ostrich feathers. 'I can't even tell you how much this tickles!'

Susie allowed the initial irritation she'd felt when Lily had cuffed them together to take a backseat to watching Jack trying to pull his wrist out of the cuffs.

It wouldn't work. Lily apparently knew her stuff when it came to restraints. Not so tight that either of them would lose circulation, but just snug enough to make squeezing their palms out of them impossible.

How it came to pass that she had a pair of 'perfect for rumba' cuffs to hand was a line of enquiry Susie was probably going to let lie. Some mystery in a friendship was always a good thing.

'If . . . I . . . could . . . just . . .' Jack was folding his thumb this way and that, trying and predictably failing to extract his hand from the cuffs.

'It's not going to work,' Susie said, her patience already wearing thin.

'Not with that kind of attitude,' Jack snapped.

'Ow-uh! Stop yanking it.'

'You're the expert on this stuff. Get us out.'

'I'm a detective not a locksmith.' Susie grabbed the chain and held it tight so that Jack was forced to stop scraping the skin from her wrist. She was having a difficult enough time explaining to her son why he barely saw her these days, let alone why she'd used up their entire supply of plasters. She'd already had to explain away a pair of black eyes. Bleeding wrists weren't really the type of thing she wanted to invent a cover story for. He should never know the risks she was taking now. Not with the murderer. Not with Jack.

She forced herself to take a calming breath. Just a few more days of rehearsal, then the competition and, with any luck, by the time Jack was holding the champion's trophy aloft, she'd be leading someone behind bars for murder.

'Lily took the key,' she reminded him. 'The chain's too strong to break.' She ducked her head so he was forced to look at her. 'And it's not a bad attitude, it's common sense.'

Jack rolled his eyes, tried to walk away and then, when Susie grabbed the chain, was yanked back into that close space Lily was forcing them to occupy. 'Oh, here we go!' Jack cupped his free hand and made the 'out with it' gesture.

'I know you've been dying to give it to me ever since you came to Whitby.'

'What?'

'The lecture.'

'What lecture?'

Jack silent-screamed at the ceiling before pinning his eyes on her. 'The one where you tell me *I'm* a hothead who leaps before he looks and *you're* the sensible one who always knows what's best.'

The comment stung, but only because it had barbs of truth in it. She swallowed down a few accusations of her own and forced herself to ask him, 'Is that what you think of me? That I was basically just a nag?'

Jack was still staring at her, his bright blue eyes boring into hers as if trying to judge whether or not speaking honestly would be a bad decision, considering neither of them could stomp off in a huff. 'No,' he admitted. 'I just . . .' He shoved his hand through his thick waves of straw-coloured hair and sighed. 'You were always the good one. The one everyone went to whenever there was any sort of question about what we were up to. Susie'll know. Susie'll have that covered. Saint Susie would never have let that happen.'

Susie scraped her teeth across her lips. It was true. That *was* how it had been and there had been a part of her that had liked it. But it was also just how her life had worked – how it had to be. After her mum had died, with a father and one much older brother either in the police or training for it, she bore a lot of responsibility at home. Cooking. Cleaning. Shopping. Her family did what they could, but . . .

'You were so *perfect*,' Jack continued. 'And it felt like

everyone wanted to make sure they knew I was so . . . *flawed*. It was frustrating, you know?'

Susie clenched her jaw then, unable to contain herself, let loose. 'You think that was fun for me? I wasn't the one who always dazzled everyone with their panache and flair. Made people laugh with their hilarious banter and jokes.'

'Then why'd you do it? The Miss Goody-Two-Shoes thing. Why, if you didn't like it?'

'It wasn't as if I had a choice, Jack! You never once offered to help. Suze'll do it,' she mimicked. 'Suze is always at the studio first. Susie won't mind making sure my shoes are polished, my costumes ironed, or whatever else it was you were offloading onto me so you had more free time to bewitch your fans.'

'Wow.' The chain jangled between them. 'I can see why you fell in love with me back then. A real prize you won yourself there, Suze.'

The truth flew out of her before she could stem its flow. 'I fell in love with you the minute I laid eyes on you, Jack Kelly. I loved you heart and soul. And I've cursed myself every day since for taking so bloody long to figure out what a mistake that was!'

She hadn't really, but . . . he was so blinking *infuriating*. How could she admit that he was the only one she ever had – and possibly ever would – truly love?

Jack drew in a sharp breath, as if preparing to offload a few more home truths, but then unexpectedly bowed his head and rubbed at the back of his neck with his free hand. When he looked back up she was shocked to see contrition on his face as he admitted, 'I was a bit of an arse back then.'

'What's changed?' she said with a half-hearted laugh.

His posture shifted, as if somehow, incredibly, he had found a way to tap into the younger, more vulnerable version of himself she'd fallen so very much in love with. 'A lot's changed, Suze. You know that. My partner's been killed. Another innocent woman who was meant to dance with me was murdered. And now you and I are targets. And Lily. Marmaduke's gone off his rocker. My studio's a demolition zone. I've not been able to sleep more than an hour at a time for fear of getting you or Lily or anyone else in my orbit killed. And unless we get you up to speed to pass that exam so we can go to Blackpool . . .' He shook his head, unable to put into words what losing this solitary chance to equal Lily's world record would mean. 'So yeah, a lot's changed.' His eyes latched with hers.

Her heart didn't know what to do with itself, so decided to lodge in her throat for safety.

'I wish we'd . . . I wish *I'd* done everything differently back then.'

'Oh . . . Jack.'

'No. Don't, please. It's a long-overdue apology.' He paused as if deciding whether to continue. Then, 'I'm not sure how much you knew about how my life really was back then, but you saved me from the gutters, Suze. Honestly.'

She barked out a laugh. 'I hardly think I did that. Lily maybe—'

'No, Suze.' He cut her off, running the backs of his fingers along her cheek. 'The thing is . . . there were a lot of things I stage-managed so that you only knew half the story.'

Her eyebrows lifted.

'No, not lies – well, not exactly.' His expression wavered and then, as if he'd put one foot off the edge of the cliff, decided he might as well put the other one there, too. 'You know how

I always told you how amazing my family was? Brilliant mum. Epic dad. Brothers and sisters top o' the pops?'

She nodded.

'Well . . . my dad was an alcoholic, Mum liked being anywhere but with us kids. My brother moved to Australia as soon as he was able, and my sister's off somewhere in an ashram in India. No fecking idea where. Might've been eaten by spiders, for all I know. Squished by an elephant. Something awful anyway.'

'No. Jack, I . . . we could find her? Maybe I could see if Madhav—'

He cut her off. 'The point being, Suze . . . my family was shite. It was the one thing I wasn't honest about.'

'But why?'

'I was jealous.'

'What?' She laughed. 'Of *my* family?'

'Ach, c'mon. I know your mammy died, and my heart breaks for you, but you were a unit, you know? An unbreakable unit, and you just took me in as if I were one of your own. Whenever I think of family, I think of you lot.'

Which meant when she'd walked away from him, he'd lost much more than a girlfriend.

'Lily might have taught me discipline, but you showed me how to live.'

'What?'

'You always seemed to know what you wanted, you know? You had a mission. Police academy, dancing, me . . .'

'Jack,' she whispered.

'And I learned from that. I learned from you. If I loved something or someone, I had to stick with it. No compromises. No side tracks. But because I was a dumb idiot, I took everything too far.'

'You didn't,' she said. It wasn't a protest, more . . . an acceptance. He'd wanted one thing, she'd wanted another.

'I did, Suze. Because what I really wanted, more than winning, was you.'

Her eyes shot to his, her cheeks pinking as their gazes held. 'That's not quite how I remember it.'

'And that's why I'm sorry.'

They tipped their foreheads together and shared a few silent breaths as Susie absorbed the new information and he recovered from admitting it.

'Well, then,' she eventually said, 'maybe we should do what Lily suggested.' She pointed at the speaker, still playing sultry rumba music on a loop. 'Shall we give this a go?'

Slowly, because being handcuffed to one another definitely altered their choreography, they began to dance. Awkwardly at first, but more because of the cuffs than anything, and then, eventually, as the shared understanding of what it was they were doing took shape, they reimagined the rumba into something entirely personal.

Jack's hands touched her in a way that felt more intimate than the exact same gesture had an hour ago.

When her leg swept up and round his hip, she didn't tip her torso back with relief, but with an edge of despair, longing for that moment when he'd reach forward and pull her back up into his arms. When she slid down the length of his body, she wasn't travelling from A to B. She was reacquainting herself with a terrain that she hadn't realized she'd missed so very badly.

For the first time since they'd come back into one another's lives, Susie believed Jack was grateful she was the woman he held in his arms. Not Susie the detective. Or Sensible Susie. Or even Susie the nag. He wanted to be with her: Susie Cooper. The girl he'd fallen in love with, despite the fact there'd been a thousand other girls willing to trample her to the ground to replace her. And perhaps something had shifted in her too. A willingness to see the good in him. The best of him. It's what had always frightened her the most, whenever she'd considered opening herself back up to him. Because the very best of Jack Kelly had always held her in thrall.

They danced and danced.

Alemanas. Aidas. Swivels. Spiral turns opening into fan position. Hip twist after hip twist after hip twist.

Susie couldn't get close enough to him, and by the way his hands possessed her body each time he made contact, he wasn't going to give her a chance to find out what it felt like to stand alone. Even if they hadn't been cuffed to one another, they didn't want to. Finally, at last, they'd reconnected with that all-important element of their partnership: trust.

When, after Susie had hooked her leg round Jack's hip one last time, she took advantage of the entire eight-count phrase to make her way back to the floor. Jack shifted his hands from the nape of her neck, to her face, cupping it as if she were the most precious thing in the world.

I'm going to kiss him, she thought. And he's going to kiss me back.

The door slammed open.

'Sorry! Sorry!' Maisie was wincing and already pulling the door closed behind her. 'Sorry, Lily sent me up here before locking up, but I didn't realize . . .' She raced over to them and stuffed a small metal object into Susie's palm. 'Please lock the doors when you go. Sorry, sorry, sorry.'

Susie had to smile as she saw the younger version of herself scurry from the room. She had a soft spot for Maisie and, though she wanted more than anything for Jack to win at Blackpool, she'd love it for Maisie and Darren if they placed well, too.

'What did she give you?' Jack asked.

'Guess,' Susie said without looking.

'Throw it in the corner,' Jack instructed. 'I think I'd like to take one more stab at this.'

Neither of them heard the soft 'ping' as the key hit the wall.

'One more time, Mummy!' Kian pleaded.

Susie glanced at the clock. Chris would be here soon. She looked down at her son's bright blue eyes, sparking with delight, hands held in prayer position.

'Pleeeeeeease?'

She'd managed not to kiss Jack Kelly last night, but resisting a tiny little spin with her son before he headed off to school . . .?

'Okay. Take my hand and spin out to the right.'

Kian was a natural.

'Then a left foot *cucaracha*.'

He dissolved into giggles, which instantly made her laugh, too.

'Someone's in a good mood,' Susie's brother grinned as she twirled Kian round in circles then opened the pair of them up to curtsey and bow to him.

'Aww, Mummyyyy . . . that was fun.'

'Mummy's got to go to work, love.'

'Mummy's enjoying work a lot more these days than she was a few weeks back,' Chris said, tapping the side of his nose as he crossed to the kitchen to pop the kettle on as he always did when he arrived at hers.

'It's hardly a crime,' she said, shrugging on her coat.

'Maybe it should be for repeat offenders,' Chris said. 'Cuppa?'

Susie shook her head, even though her mouth had unexpectedly gone very, very dry.

Chapter Forty-Four

'Mr Fitzgerald, if I've told you once, I've told you a thousand times, there is absolutely no alcohol allowed in the rooms.'

Marmaduke glowered at his latest nemesis. 'Sister, my friend here has brought some Veuve Clicquot. Surely the good stuff doesn't count?'

'It all counts in a hospital,' the nurse replied, removing the bottle from Veronica's hands. 'Especially given the fact that *this*,' she waved the bottle – with no small amount of glee, he felt – in his face, 'contributed to your . . . situation . . . the other day.' She tipped her head towards the part of his anatomy that had failed him in his moment of weakness.

'Whatever happened to patient confidentiality!' Marmaduke bellowed at her retreating figure. It was cursed luck landing in the room served by Nurse Ratched. Once he'd had his heart shocked back into action, he'd specifically asked for a little Swedish number. 'I should've been out of here by now, anyway. Cynthia,' he barked at his wife. 'Go and ask the doctors about discharge again.'

She was toasting Veronica, who'd managed to pour the pair of them some fizz before the nurse had confiscated the rest. 'But I—'

'Go,' he commanded, enjoying watching her scuttle off like the good little minion she was. She'd leave him if she found out how broke they were and, as much as he enjoyed having sex with other women, he liked knowing he had someone permanent on staff. As it were. Which was why Veronica needed to get things rolling.

'How did that shopping trip go?' he asked, trying to pretend he hadn't just spent the last three days attached to heart monitors and being helped to the loo by a man who looked twice his age. 'Maybe you should bring some of the dresses in. Give me a little show. I want to see what my favourite judge will be wearing at Blackpool.'

'Ah.' Veronica's breath caught in her throat. 'Yes, I wanted to speak to you about that.'

'Roni, love.' He pressed his hand to his chest, only managing to get his fingers tangled in some of the wires. She rose and gently began to put everything back in order. He felt a swell of actual feeling for her. 'Did you not go in the end? You could've called me with a video thingie from the changing room.'

Veronica put his hand back on his chest, safely out of the way of the wires, then sat back down in the uncomfortable plastic chair provided for guests. 'No, it wasn't that. I've got a dress.'

Oh. 'What is it then?'

'It's just that . . . well . . .' She took in a quick breath then blurted, 'I'm not going to judge at Blackpool.'

The Duke blinked several times, trying to digest this news. 'Why ever not?'

'It's only . . . well . . .' She looked away, then back at him, 'You see the truth is, Marmaduke . . .'

This got his attention. Roni never called him Marmaduke.

'I'm going to Blackpool with Sam. Sam Pringle.'

'*Scouser* Sam?' Marmaduke was so shocked he let his double chins show. 'What? As a spectator?'

Veronica shook her head, her aqua-blue contacts imploring him to understand. 'As a dancer. We're going pro-am. Sam wants to do it for Topaz.'

Bloody Nora! 'Why?'

'Well, he thought it would be a nice way to commemorate his daughter.'

'No, not the dance for Topaz bit. *Why* are you giving up being a judge to dance with him? If everything goes to plan, we won't need his sponsorship money beyond the next couple of weeks.' He'd probably need it to pay his hospital bill, but that was another story. This wasn't about Scouser Sam, or Roni. This was about him, Marmaduke Fitzgerald, and the legacy he planned on leaving behind. Almost losing his life the other day made putting wheels in motion even more urgent. He looked her in the eye. 'You can't do it, love. I'm sorry. We've got too much on. There are more dancers to recruit. I'm thinking of trying to lure Maisie and what's-his-face away from Lily.'

'Darren,' Veronica supplied patiently as if she were talking to a toddler having a silly tantrum about being out of raspberry jam.

'Yes, him.' He waved impatiently, tangling himself up in his wires again as he tried to tap things off on his fingers. 'We need to find someone for Johanna to sink her claws into. Make training videos for my new dances. And, most importantly, we've got to get that scrutineer on the payroll. I want Lily's judging record falsified so she can be disqualified in front of everyone at Blackpool. So, yes, make sure he keeps the money rolling in. But no, Roni. You cannot dance with him.'

'It's *Veronica*,' she said with a wounded look, and then, with defiance: 'And I'll do what I like. I love him.'

The Duke's heart monitor began bleeping at an accelerated rate. He could feel beads of sweat appearing on his forehead, his skin growing clammy.

'No. You don't. You're just trying to secure the sponsorship money until I kick our little plan into action.'

'No, Marmaduke. I really do love him. I wanted you to be the first to know.'

He was shocked. Genuinely shocked.

His mind reeled as she handed him her plastic cup and he threw back the inch or so of lukewarm fizz.

How could this be happening? Roni had been his ally for years. Decades! His dance partner and confidante all rolled into one. Rage replaced the pain. She'd be nothing without him. He'd been the one to elevate her from an amateur dancer into the professionals. Given her teaching jobs in his studio. Got her a place on the board with the GDC and ensured she had a reputation as a world-class judge. Sure, it was all to benefit him, but she was throwing it all away for a pole monkey?

'He's about so much more than scaffolding,' Veronica said, indicating he might've said that last bit out loud. 'He's really quite interesting, actually.'

'Interesting? What's so fucking interesting about—'

Ah . . . he got it. Sam was rich. Topaz was dead. Veronica was moving in for the kill. And she'd convinced herself she loved him to tease away any guilt she might have for stealing a rich man's lucre.

'Get out,' he growled.

'Marmaduke—'

'Get out!' he shouted, sending his monitor into a string of high-pitched beeps. Nurses swooped in as Veronica turned on her heel and stomped out. 'I'll tell everyone what you've done!' he called after her. 'Every sin you've committed will be broadcast around the world!' And then, as before, darkness.

Chapter Forty-Five

'Straight into the changing room, darling. We don't have time for faffing around.'

Susie didn't budge. 'I think I'm capable of picking out my own dress.'

Not here at Chrisanne Clover's ballroom-gown showroom she wasn't. 'Of course you are, darling. If you were picking up a frock for your holiday,' she said. 'But I'm afraid, Susie my love, you need guidance about what you can pull off on the dance floor. Oh, don't look at me like that. It's not an insult, it's a fact.' Lily flicked her hands in a shoo gesture. 'Go on. I'll start bringing them over.'

Susie knew when resistance was futile. 'Make sure it's in my price range.'

'This is a business expense, darling. Won't you be writing it off?'

She heard a snort of laughter.

'Fine,' Lily said. 'I'll put it on mine, but remember we're also due at the spa, so let's be quick about this.'

'Lily.' Susie stuck her head out of the door. 'You don't have to pay for it, just pick a cheap one.'

'Inexpensive darling. Never cheap. There's a difference.' Lily got to work in what she called 'the business end' of the shop.

The couture section where dresses ran into the thousands and, as such, didn't come with price tags.

Beyond the showroom lay a well-lit, sprawling room filled with every haberdashery item under the sky. At the far end was an inviting array of glue guns, specialized adhesives and threads, if personal embellishment was more your style. Feathers were available in every shade known to mankind. There were pompoms and tassels and enough sequins to bathe in. Reams of lace, Swarovski crystals by the fistful, and even diamonds, depending on the colour of your credit card.

Countless textured and imaginatively coloured fabrics filled yet another enormous hall. Silks, satins, georgette, milk fibre, mesh, chiffon, organza and tulle. Lily allowed herself a brief moment to close her eyes and inhale. It even smelt expensive. There had been more days in her life than there hadn't when she wouldn't have even allowed herself to think of walking in this store, let alone buying one of the couture dresses.

Now, though, she could order a dozen frocks to be brought to the studio. The current state of her finances – above par – was an unexpected phoenix that had risen up and out of the ashes of her longest marriage. Being left on her own in Japan for months on end with nothing to do but teach minted businessmen and women with a penchant for ballroom had its silver linings. The students never thought she had the mental wherewithal to understand their work (or their language) and, as such, were incredibly loose-lipped. Well. Suffice it to say, for ten rather lucrative years, she'd been terrifically well-versed in what to buy and when to sell. If only she'd been as wise with her heart, her life might be on another track now. Poorer. But not quite so lonely.

Onwards.

She began going through the racks, handing frocks to the shop attendant who magically appeared when she saw who it was working her way through the selection of ballgowns. They, in turn, were passed on to Susie.

'What do you think about this one?' Susie asked, presenting her back so that Lily could do up the zip.

'No,' Lily said. 'It's not the one.'

'How do you know? You haven't even done me up.' She looked down at the multicoloured bands of tulle and silk diagonally ruched over the bodice.

'Mermaid cut doesn't suit you. Next!' The shop girl was right there, handing her the next frock.

Half an hour and seven dresses later, Susie wasn't even bothering to disguise how annoyed she was.

'C'mon, darling. It's a marathon not a sprint.' Lily handed her another dress and shut the changing-room door.

'I've had enou . . . ohhh . . . Ooo.'

Lily smiled.

Bingo.

That's what she had been waiting for.

Wordlessly, Susie came out of the dressing room, having already done up the side zip of the pale, spring-green coloured dress. A semi-transparent, pearlescent gold mesh made up the bodice. They weren't obvious hues for her, but they worked, showing off her skin tone and dark hair, as well as adding a romantic pop to her eyes. The dress was exquisite.

'I bet Wonder Woman would wear this if she went to a ball,' Susie said, almost to herself.

She wasn't wrong. It was a powerfully feminine dress. Even without the seamstress's touch, it fitted absolutely beautifully.

More importantly, the dress seemed to give Susie the courage she'd need going into a situation where she would be facing danger head on. Precisely what Lily had been aiming for.

From her shoulders, pale green chiffon 'wings', which Susie could attach to her wrists, fluttered as she twisted and turned, gazing and touching the myriad folds of soft green fabric that made up the skirt. Susie, at last, felt beautiful.

'This is it, darling. This is the dress.'

'I—'

'No time to dither,' Lily tutted. 'Back in the room, off with the dress. We'll get your Latin outfit sorted over at Vesa Design and then we're off to Shaz 'n Baz's for a mani-pedi.'

The Vesa showroom was every bit as divine as Chrisanne Clover's. The women who could afford the very best, as Lily could, were made to feel like brides-to-be. Assistants to help with each fitting. An attendant to hold your hand as you took the one, two, three steps onto the platform in the middle of an arc of mirrors, so you could look at yourself from every angle. It had been pure delight watching Susie give in to the joy of it all. 'It's to die for,' Susie had sighed as she twirled in the performance-ready dress that Lily had picked out for her.

'Worth living for,' Lily had gently corrected as the two of them shared a potent reminder that entering this competition wasn't just for fun and sparkly dresses.

An hour later, Lily gratefully accepted a hi-ball glass filled with cucumber and mint water. She sighed as she dipped her feet into the warm-water pool at the base of her massage chair. 'Ah, now. This is more like it.' She winked at Susie, who was looking the opposite of relaxed as two rather scrummy male manicurists were tutting over her nails.

'I don't want anything pointy. Or too long. Or too—'

Lily intervened, 'Could you please give her a hard gel mani, a hand massage – with the masque – and then a round shape with a simple glitter polish. Something to match this colour.' She dangled swatches of the fabrics from both the ballgown and Latin dresses that Susie would be wearing in just a few days' time in Blackpool.

As tempting as it was to lean back and let the massage chair tease her into a light twenty-minute power nap, Lily knew this was no time to relax. As fortune had it, Baz arrived and began to do half her work for her. He was a portly, smiley-faced, bearded man, sporting a rainbow-coloured yarmulke pinned atop a head of dark curly hair. If ever there was an exemplar for a Jewish hipster, Baz Finkelstein was it.

'Hello, darrrrling,' he cooed as he arrived in a waft of after-shave and product. Married to Shaz straight out of beauty school, this was a man who had tapped into his metrosexuality as if it was pure oxygen. 'I'm not sure if I should tell you this, but . . .'

Lily waited. She knew he would. She didn't come here often, as she tended to meet with her own team of stylists at home or at the studio, but she sent enough business his way to keep him sweet. Some women thought diamonds were a girl's best friend. Lily knew otherwise.

Baz took Lily's hand and started massaging a rose cream into it. 'So. Your "friend" Marmaduke Fitzgerald was sitting in those chairs opposite with VP-W and a little blonde thing the other day. I presume you heard about . . .' He feigned collapsing. 'The epic drama?' Rather than wait for an answer he leant in and whispered, 'We obviously clean between clients but I didn't think you'd want to sit in the same chairs.'

'You think of everything, Baz.' Lily batted her eyelids coquettishly. 'I don't suppose you heard them gossiping about little ol' me?'

'Oh, *sweetie*! There isn't an ounce of old about you!' He turned and glanced at Susie. In a stage-whisper he asked, 'Are we having a consult on this . . . *situation* . . .?'

'Uhhhh . . .' Susie began, clearly affronted at being referred to as a 'situation'.

'Absolutely, darling,' Lily said, throwing a meaningful look in Susie's direction. 'We want to know *all about* the special tweakments on offer.'

'Well!' Baz grabbed a wheelie stool and scooched himself in between the two women. 'Let's see what we've got to work with.' He gave Susie a *you're so cute* smile then brandished a massive magnifying glass. 'I don't think I need to use this to eagle-eye those.' He pointed to the light blue bruises, still staining the pale skin beneath her eyes. 'I've got just the concealer for that.' He leant in and began inspecting her in disturbingly close detail. He shot the odd glance at Lily as he spoke non-stop. 'Anyway, yes. Just thought I should let you know that The Duke was here, downing champers like it was going out of style. He and VP-W – you know that's Veronica, right? Yes. Of course you do. Anyway, they were getting mani/pedi/facial treatments, and being all whispery and conspiratorial, when in flounces this Ice Queen and her diamanté cane.'

Lily threw Susie a quick look. So Johanna had joined them. Interesting.

'She was getting some filler.' Baz pushed his cheeks forward to show where, then he cackled. 'Honestly. For a minute there I thought Veronica was going to do it herself.'

This caught Lily's attention. 'Really?'

Baz fuzzed his lips. 'She offered.'

How horrifying. 'Is she allowed?'

'Oh, yes. She learned how to do fillers and all the extras after the crash back in oh-eight. She's been doing a lot of her own work for a while, but for "legal reasons", we couldn't possibly let her do them here.' He cupped his hand at the side of his mouth. 'I mean, she looks like she's been done by a blind person, am I right?'

They shared a malicious laugh. Lily told herself that breaking her no-gossip rule had been forced on her by the whole 'murderer on the loose' situation but, she had to admit, this was a little slice of *schadenfreude* pie she was happy to eat. And also, very interesting. She hadn't once considered that she was a possible suspect; that it could have been Veronica wielding a syringe. Giving the command? Definitely. But plunging in the needle?

'I think your Ramone is training as well,' Baz said. 'Everyone's getting in on it.'

'Here?' Susie asked.

'No. Not sure where. I saw him post something on one of the cosmetic enhancement forums the other day.'

'Do you know which one?' Lily asked, possibly a bit too casually.

Baz was framing Susie in 'director's hands' now. 'I think it's called Full-Filled in the North. Get it?' He laughed. 'Full-*filled*? Like . . . filler?'

Susie and Lily attempted to laugh along, but Lily knew what Susie was thinking. *Ramone?* He'd been on the periphery of their thoughts, though never a true suspect. But Ramone *had* been the one doing Oxana's make-up the night she'd been killed, and he'd also been at ¡*Oye! Argentina!*

'Speaking of near-death experiences . . .' It was a clumsy segue but it would have to do. 'We were wondering how you were handling the loss of one of your clients. Oxana?' Lily prompted when Baz gave her a blank look.

'Oh, yaaaaas.' He gave a low whistle. 'Gosh, wasn't that just awful?' Baz put down his magnifying glass and turned his full attention on Susie. 'Right, hon, bad news or good news first?'

'Bad?'

Baz grinned at Lily. 'She's a rip-the-plaster-off kind of girl, isn't she?' He gave Susie's knee a pat. 'Chutzpah. I like it. Okay, doll face, here we go.' He rattled off an impressive (or terrifying) ream of treatments that would easily cost several thousand pounds.

Susie glared at Lily.

'What's the good news, darling?' Lily asked, keen to get conversation back to Oxana, the real reason they were going through this entire charade.

'We do each and every one of these treatments here.'

'Amazing. Of course you do. A one-stop shop for beauty.' Lily put her hand on Baz's shoulder. 'Now you come to mention it, we heard Oxana talking about the treatment she got here and how much she liked the beautician. Do you know who that was?'

Baz gave her a weighted look. 'I can't talk about clients, deceased or otherwise, you know that, Lil.'

'Of course, darling. Only, I was thinking of booking my mum and myself in for a whole day of beauty once we're done at Blackpool. The full works . . .' she said in a careless way that suggested if she wasn't given the royal treatment, she might look elsewhere.

'Okay, you win.' Baz reaffixed his yarmulke then grabbed an iPad out of his supplies trolley. He thumbed through his calendar. 'Oh!' he said, frowning. 'She was a no-show.'

'Really?'

Lily's pulse accelerated. She didn't dare look, but she sensed Susie leaning in, too.

'Do you know why?'

Baz flicked through the notes. 'The beautician she'd booked with had called in sick so we got in a last-minute cover . . . doesn't say who . . .' He put the iPad down and shrugged. 'I suppose she didn't want the replacement, but your guess is as good as mine, luvvie.'

'Strange,' Lily said, trying her best to remain calm. 'I would've thought anyone you and Shaz had on your on-call list would be excellent.'

'A hundred per cent,' Baz agreed, belatedly affronted that Oxana would cancel. 'There are so many back-alley faux-toxers these days that the government's had to step in. It's all becoming regulated, but I mean, if you're desperate for a fix? I'm sure there are ways of getting supplies.'

'Does Veronica get her supplies from you?'

'God no!' Baz said. 'I have a reputation to protect, don't I?' And then, a bit more gently, 'I have a few people on speed-dial I help out, but generally? Botulism is a lock-and-key job. It's not the sort of thing you can leave lying around in an open fridge. Who has it, how it's stored and each dose we use is very closely regulated by the suppliers. I can't just order it willy-nilly, nor can anyone else. I mean, people just aren't reliable these days, no matter how close you are.'

Unwillingly, Lily's thoughts turned to Javier and his mentees.

Baz's phone alarm went off. 'Soz, dolls. Gotta dash.' To Susie he said, 'So good to meet you. Just talk to Shaz up at the desk on your way out and we'll get you all young and fresh-looking in no time, yeah?' With a wave and a volley of air-kisses, he swept away.

'Well, that was fun,' Susie grumbled.

'Don't worry, darling. It's how they make their living, isn't it? He can hardly say you're perfect.'

Susie made a face suggesting she wouldn't have minded if he had. Then, more business-like she said, 'We should call my brother and see if Topaz's phone diary indicates if she had any sessions booked here.'

They finished their sessions and called Chris, who was in the middle of booking someone, so she sent him a text asking after the diary entries and a list of her contacts.

A voice message pinged up on her phone from an unknown caller. She shot Lily a look.

'Put it on speaker.'

She did.

The echoey, frightening automated voice boomed from the phone, 'Jack Kelly could eat no fat, Susie could eat no lean . . . and yet with Lily's help, they want to lick the platter clean!'

Lily looked at Susie, only to see that she'd turned as pale as she felt. 'Don't be a greedy guts,' the message continued. 'This is not your banquet.'

'What on earth does that mean?' Lily asked after they'd refused the opportunity to listen to the message again.

'I think it means whoever this is doesn't want Jack and me to compete.' Susie went quiet then said, 'If you don't mind, I think I'd like to get home to Kian.'

'Of course, darling.'

The car ride home was a quiet, reflective one, each of them caught in a silent, intense effort to put the new pieces of the puzzle together.

Was this the type of call Veronica could have made? Johanna? Or maybe even Marmaduke? As much as she'd love to point the finger of blame, she was struggling.

It was so *malicious*! She'd experienced a thousand vile interactions in her day, but never before had she felt as frightened as she did now.

After dropping Susie off with a promise to ring once she, herself, was safely home, Lily was once again on her own.

Normally, she was completely comfortable in her own company. Happy even. But today she was acutely aware of feeling very much alone. So instead of returning home, she asked the driver to take her to the studio. She decided to try on the rehearsal skirt she might have accidentally bought while Susie was in the early phases of I-hate-shopping. It was called the 'Temptress', and for good reason. Jet black, like the rest of her rehearsal clothes, the four-panelled skirt was made of a luxury crepe and featured a thigh-high split on the left. It was perfect for a dramatic dance like the paso doble.

She went into the main rehearsal studio and altered the lights so that they were exactly as they'd been the other night when she'd danced with Javier. Without bothering to turn on any music, she closed her eyes and began to dance. It wasn't difficult to imagine Javier there, across from her. He was the epitome of a proud Latin matador, and she, of course, the wild, uncompromising woman he was trying to captivate with his exacting, staccato moves.

Halfway through her dance she had the sudden, eerie sensation that she wasn't on her own. Goose pimples skittered across her skin. She didn't dare open her eyes.

Was this it? Her moment of reckoning?

Terror swept through her and when, at last, she forced herself to open her eyes to discover who had come to reveal their murderous intentions, she gasped.

Javier Ramirez de Arellano stood no more than a foot away from her, his amber eyes alight not with venom, but with something she couldn't quite put her finger on. He held out his hands, indicating he wanted to take her in his arms, to join her as she finished her half-completed dance.

Had she been a complete fool presuming him an innocent? Perhaps this was a ruse. A way to pull her in close so he could jam a needle into her vein, taking her life just as Oxana and Topaz's lives had been suffocated out of them? Or was he here for the very simple and honest reason that he wanted to be with her?

'No more games,' Javier said.

'I've never played games with you,' she said as her pounding heart shifted gears.

'I've always loved you.'

Her pulse quickened yet again.

'I know.' She loved him, too. But she also knew his love didn't come with the guarantee of a traditional happily-ever-after. That white picket fence and all the trimmings. Would what he had to offer be enough? It wasn't as if she was a spring chicken any more. She was sixty-two. But she still had passion. A sex drive. A heart.

He held out his hands and tried again. 'Dance with me?'

She shook her head. 'No, darling. I've had enough dancing

299

today.' She wanted something else from Javier today because, if anything, she'd just learnt that life was very, very short, and you never knew what lay around the corner.

He took her extended hand and together they left the studio.

Javier's suite was nestled at the back of a boutique hotel in the heart of Liverpool. It was a hymn to masculinity and she the only feminine thing in it. The bed, which dominated the room, featured a vast upholstered cow hide hanging from a wooden beam as a headboard.

'Homesick?' she asked.

He shrugged.

Together they looked back to the imposing bed. Shame she hadn't brought her cuffs.

Candlelight flickered in the next room and, with a tip of her head, she could see a huge claw-footed bath steaming atop a central platform and – yes, there it was – the scent of rose petals. He'd made promises over the years that he'd yet to fulfil. Between the bed, the bath and the fire blazing in a large open hearth, in front of which lay an opulence of cushions and rugs, it looked like he meant to settle his debts tonight.

'You knew I'd come,' she said.

'I'd hoped,' he replied, but his smile told her she was right.

Normally she'd turn on her heel and go. She didn't like anyone thinking she was predictable. It made her feel vulnerable. Tonight, her body pleaded with her to stay.

He gestured at the fully stocked drinks cabinet. 'May I get you anything?'

'Not tonight, darling,' she said. 'I have everything I need.'

She scanned the room again, already picturing where and how they'd make love. He caught her glance with those leonine eyes of his. '*Mi amor.*'

It was time. She stood her ground, wanting him to take the first step.

She knew she was throwing caution to the wind and, for the handful of hours that lay ahead of her, she suddenly didn't care.

She believed Javier was innocent of any crime. She also believed he loved her. In just three days' time, in Blackpool, both of those convictions would be put to the test. Or, perhaps to her detriment, tonight. It wouldn't be a public death, so there was a certain security in that. But if her life were to end here, in Javier's arms, a victim of her own longing, she had faith he would wait until he'd brought her to a climax to kill her. He'd always been generous in that way.

Javier stepped forward and weighted his hands on her hips. His energy surrounded her like a cocoon. He rocked himself forward just enough for her to know how much he wanted her. He shifted his weight back again and she watched his elegant hands at work as he took his time loosening the tie on her wrap-around rehearsal top. Fingertips poised to shift the fabric away, he paused and asked, 'Warm enough?'

She was alight with desire. 'Fine, thanks.'

He smiled and dropped a kiss on her newly bared shoulder. His lips whispered against her skin as he asked, 'Why do you do that, Lily? Downplay how you're really feeling?'

She didn't bother being coy. 'I'm frightened of losing myself to you.'

She felt him acknowledge the confession and, when he rose

to his full height and met her eyes, she saw, for the very first time, that he feared the exact same thing.

He didn't move, but she was so alive with anticipation she could already feel his hands exploring her most intimate curves. His mouth reacquainting itself with her breasts, her belly, her sex. In turn she pictured her nails making their mark on his back. The screams she'd have to stifle in his shoulder. The pulses of sensation she'd feel when she straddled him, rocking her hips back and forth in time with his until she was absolutely certain she had driven him wild.

Words no longer played a role in this discourse. When their lips finally met, she knew she would be perfectly safe tonight.

As he took off her clothes, led her to the bath and helped her submerge herself in the silky water, she knew that before dawn broke, she would walk out of this suite, alive, fulfilled, and completely versed in what it felt like to be adored.

Chapter Forty-Six

'That was . . .' Jack dropped his hands to his knees to regain his breath.

'Intense?' Susie supplied.

'Yeah.' He pressed himself up to standing and was about to sweep his hands through his hair when he thought better of it and grabbed a towel from his gym bag. He knew the samba was supposed to be full-on, but . . . that had been on another level.

In fact, now that he thought about it, everything about today's rehearsal had felt high octane. Maybe Susie had walked away from that handcuff experience the same way he had. Wanting to come back for more.

'Nervous about tomorrow?' He handed her the ceramic water bottle she kept in the fridge.

She gave him that wide, doe-eyed look of hers. The one that reminded him of Bambi's mum when he tried to convince her running into the field during hunting season was safe.

'You'll ace it,' he said. 'You've always had it in you.'

Her gaze sharpened.

He swallowed the slug of water he'd just taken and put his hands up. 'Don't read anything into it, I'm just saying you're an amazing dancer. No matter the whole "dancing isn't a gift, it's graft" thing . . . you've got it, Suze. That intangible something that every dancer wants.'

Her expression softened. 'Sorry. I didn't sleep much last night. A bit tetchy.'

'Is it just the exam you're worried about?'

Something in her expression told him she wasn't worried about the exam in the slightest.

'What?' He crossed to her and dipped down at the knee, waiting until she met his gaze. 'What's happened, Suze?'

She took a drink of water, then made a job of pressing the attached straw back into place. 'We got another call,' she finally admitted. 'Yesterday, when we were at the beautician's.'

'What?' Jack was raging. And freaked. And hurt she hadn't told him earlier. He would've gone to her house. Stayed the night if that had made her feel safer. Anything. She wasn't in this alone. But saying as much – caring as much – scared him. If he held his heart out for her to take a second time, he wasn't sure he'd know what to do with himself if she walked away again. 'What did it say?' he asked. 'Was it that freaky robot voice?'

Susie nodded. 'Yeah. And there was another weird nursery rhyme – Jack Spratt.'

She ran him through it.

'You're not fat,' he protested.

'Thank you, but . . . not exactly the point.'

He shrugged. 'Dancers are weird. They know each other's body fat percentages.'

She nodded as if, yes, it couldn't be entirely discounted. 'I think it was less the content of the rhyme and more *why* they are using rhymes that interested me.'

'How do you mean?'

She shook her head, as if what she was about to tell him was only one in a raft of possibilities she'd been hashing through over the course of the night. 'Maybe the murderer had kids but lost them in a divorce?'

'I don't follow,' Jack admitted.

'Remember Oxana's note? "A clever bunny keeps their appointments." And the second one – "A clever Jack knows how to manage their time."' She paused for effect. 'In the message I received, they talk about missed appointments and being more aware of things. All things you need to do for children, but with cutsie language. And, of course, the threatening nursery rhymes. Maybe they're in the middle of a custody battle.'

'Then why would they kill Topaz and Oxana?'

She gave a 'who knows?' lift of her hands. 'It's just one theory. Whatever it is, the murderer is clearly blaming ballroom dancers for things that have gone wrong in their life. Being loyal is important to them. Keeping appointments. Not being greedy. Maybe they were a competitive dancer whose partnership split up because of some sort of extra-marital affair.'

Jack huffed out a mirthless laugh. 'If those are your parameters, your list is about to get much, much longer.'

She rolled her eyes at him then held up her hands, dropping her fingers with each name. 'Marmaduke doesn't have kids. Or Veronica, as far as I know. Same to Ruby Rae, the Argentines, Kiko and Ramone. Lily's never mentioned Javier having them, but . . . Dunno. That's our whole list.' She shrugged, like it all felt a bit hopeless. 'It's probably an angle that won't pan out, but even though I know life isn't all love hearts and unicorns, I hate thinking that someone with children could also be a murderer.'

Jack gave in to the urge to give her shoulder a soft squeeze and a rub. She glanced up at him and, when the moment shifted into something that felt more intimate, he stuffed his hand through his hair and tried to steer things back to her hypothesis. 'The only people I know who have kids love 'em to bits. If my partner left me and took the little ones, I'd be using my spare time trying to be with them, not turning their nursery rhymes into murder threats.'

When he looked back, Susie's jaw was clenched.

'What?'

'Nothing.'

It *was* something, but he knew Susie well enough to know pressing rarely worked.

He picked up his phone and started thumbing through his playlists.

'Where were we?'

'American smooth.'

'Shall we give it a lash?' Jack bowed.

'With pleasure.' Susie smiled at him and accepted his extended hand.

That was it, he thought as he took her into his arms. She was looking forward to the dances as much as he was.

'This reminds me of us ten years ago,' he said as they swept through the Fred-and-Ginger-style number.

'What? The choreography?'

'No. Well, that, too, but . . .' He led them into a few advanced shadow steps accented with progressive twinkles. 'It's more . . . when we're dancing, the rest of the world fades away, you know?'

She grinned at him, her arms shifting through the air as if her fingertips were trailing fairy dust.

He suddenly felt eighteen again. The age he was when he had

first partnered her and had known in an instant he'd found the person he could dance with for ever. What a fool he'd been ever to let her walk away. 'I'm sorry, Suze.' He stopped mid-chassé. She stumbled and he caught her round the waist, righting her but also, because he'd been longing to do it, pulling her to him.

'For what?'

Not reaching out to her sooner. Not chasing after her when she'd left the café that day. Not being the man she'd deserved to fall in love with. 'For not telling you about granddad. He was such a part of our lives back then, I should've let you know. At least about the memorial. Maybe, if you like, I can take you to his grave. We can lay flowers or something.'

'Thank you,' Susie said, 'I'd like that.' And then, as if she knew he needed to hear it, she said, 'Kian loved you so much.'

He had. Unconditionally. The way he should've loved Susie all these years. His heart hurt. It felt like it was trying to squeeze itself between his ribs to get to her.

'I miss him,' he said instead.

'He was an amazing man,' Susie agreed.

'I wish I'd been a better grandkid to him, you know? It couldn't've been easy, looking after me. Moving over here. Overseeing everything. Rehearsals, costumes, competitions, school, and a thousand other things besides. I should've visited him more once he went into the home, but I didn't. I went to competition after competition after competition. I don't really know who I was trying to prove my worth to. You? Him?' He shook his head, as if trying to physically rid himself of the toxic thoughts. 'Doesn't matter now, I suppose. I lost both of you in the end.'

She cupped his cheeks with her hands. 'You're a good

person, Jack Kelly. Stop beating yourself up for what did or didn't happen in the past. It was seven years ago. We're different now.'

'Not that different.' He took in a shaky breath. He wanted to kiss her. And not in a 'launch his tongue down her throat' kind of way. He wanted to give her one of those proper 'kissing in the rain', movie-moment kisses. The type that would let her know that even though he'd been a selfish, arrogant arse, he'd never stopped loving her and, if there was some way she might consider allowing him to try to win her heart again, he'd do anything for the chance.

The door swung open.

Susie pulled away from him, as if she'd just been caught doing something indecent. He swore under his breath before he turned to see who it was.

There in the doorway was Susie's brother, Chris, if he remembered correctly. He was holding hands with a little boy. Six years old, maybe? Seven?

He had strawberry-blond hair and bright blue eyes. A smattering of freckles leap-frogged over his nose. He had a clean, wholesome aura about him. An innocence. He was wearing a quizzical smile and looking between the pair of them like they were a puzzle he couldn't quite figure out.

'Mummy?' he said.

Jack turned to Susie. All the blood had drained from her face. 'Yes, love.' She held out her arms, panic laced through her voice. 'Kian, I—'

Kian?

'Sorry, Suze,' Chris said through the loud buzz of static that had taken over Jack's brainwaves. 'I got a call. I have to go into the station and Dad's busy. You weren't answering your phone, like. Or Lily. I didn't realize . . .' He tipped his head at Jack.

'No, it's fine.' She knelt down and gave the little boy – her son – a hug, before leaning back on her heels and teasing his thick fringe away from his face.

'I'll leave you to it, then,' Chris said. 'Unless . . .' He shot a glance at Jack then looked back at his sister. 'Do you need me to stay, Suze?'

'No.' Her voice was shaking.

'No,' Jack confirmed, a white-hot rage replacing his confusion. He grabbed his things from a nearby chair. 'We've finished.' And then, without so much as a backward glance, he left the room.

PART FOUR

PART FOUR

Chapter Forty-Seven

'Wait!'

The coach lurched to an ungainly stop. Lily whipped round to see what it was this time. They'd not even made it out of the car park yet, and if there was one thing she couldn't abide, it was being late. Especially for Blackpool.

Ruby Rae was shoving her way down the aisle and out the door of the large, luxury coach filled to the gunnels with costumes, make-up cases, giddy dancers and, as evidenced by Susie's permanently jiggling knee, some very potent nerves.

'You'd better have forgotten a kidney,' Lily called after her.

'Close enough,' Ruby Rae snarled over her shoulder, then ran back into the studio, returning moments later with a large, worn-looking shoe box tucked under her arm.

Lily eyed it the way one might examine a suspicious package left on public transport, until it disappeared with Ruby Rae into the back of the coach. What on earth was she carrying in that ratty old box? Lily hadn't spent much time with her mercurial mentee these past few weeks, and something told her she'd be wise to pay closer attention. She hated to think Ruby Rae might be one of the viable suspects, but if she had to pick one student who might be capable of murder? If she were being completely honest, she knew who she'd pick in a line-up.

'Right then,' Lily held Susie's knee still with her hand and, to the driver, said, 'Let's try that again, shall we? To Blackpool!'

The younger dancers cheered as they finally pulled out of the car park and onto the road, towards the biggest competition many of them would ever compete in: The Blackpool Ballroom Bonanza.

'You all right, darling?' Lily asked once they'd hit the motorway and her students had either plugged themselves into their phones, fallen asleep, or were so engaged in pre-competition gossip they couldn't possibly hear the quiet conversation happening in the front two seats where she and Susie sat.

'Not really, no,' Susie admitted.

'I know it's worrying,' Lily soothed, 'Jack not being on the bus, but the competition isn't until tomorrow morning. There's plenty of time for him to make his way there.'

'He won't come, Lil,' Susie said tightly. 'He didn't call to check if I'd passed the exam. Didn't reply to my text that the competition pack had come through.' Her eyes glassed up. 'He hasn't asked to meet Kian. Nothing. He won't come,' she repeated.

'He will,' Lily said, praying she was right. She, too, had sent Jack messages, telling him about Susie's success at her professional exam, along with reminders that he was more than welcome on the coach, how to find the hotel she'd booked, and just about every other thing she could think of to try to eke a response out of him. This after she'd returned home three days earlier to find his room in her house stripped clean of his belongings, with a hastily scrawled sticky note saying he was off to 'get his head right'. She could hardly begrudge him for wanting to put space between himself and the enormous revelation that he had a six-year-old son. Lily was sure he'd find a way to put things in order by the time the competition started. But he was certainly cutting it fine . . .

'He just needs time,' she said to Susie. 'Men take a while to process things, but Jack's a good man. He'll do what's right in the end.' Susie shot her a look that demanded a change of topic. 'Anyway, we've got plenty to do without worrying about that now. When will Madhav be there?'

Susie's body language regained some confidence as she flicked through a couple of messages on her phone. She flashed it at Lily. 'He and the lads are there now. They wanted to check out the security teams the competition officials have in place. Watch them setting up so they could sort out how they can best cover the areas we can't and, of course, keep an eye out for anyone who arrives before we do.'

'Kiko and Ramone?' Lily asked in a low voice.

'And Veronica,' Susie said. 'And Marmaduke. According to the grapevine, he checked himself out of hospital a couple of days ago and headed straight to Blackpool. There's also Johanna to keep an eye out for. The Argentines.' Susie felt an almost imperceptible stiffening in Lily's spine. 'Lucia and Cristobal,' she quickly clarified, avoiding eye contact as she thumbed through her phone. When she found what she was looking for, she flashed the screen at Lily. 'These are two of Madhav's best security guys.'

'Good,' Lily said.

Susie made a 'not really' noise. 'Depends how you look at it. Bringing them along means he's worried.'

Lily grimaced. The fact someone had a fistful of diet pills and was priming a syringe of poison for one of the three of them – herself, Jack or Susie – *was* worrying. *Terrifying*, if she let herself truly think about it. Especially as she and Susie were no closer to narrowing down the pool of suspects. One solitary person who felt so aggrieved by a perceived lack of loyalty that they had chosen murder as the only means of avenging themselves.

She didn't know whether to feel like an idiot or grateful that the past three nights of lovemaking with Javier had taken the edge off her concerns. But now, with her sometimes lover in his own luxury coach with at least two of their suspects, the nerves were beginning to creep in again. And not just about the murder.

She was worried she had been too free in loosening the ties corseting her heart when it came to Javier. Trying to bundle everything back into submission when he inevitably left would be next to impossible.

She returned to the business at hand. 'Are you still happy to ask around in the dressing rooms to see if any of the stylists we don't usually work with are willing to give you a bit of a freshener before the comp?'

'Absolutely,' Susie said. 'If Ramone can't squeeze me in to do my hair, I'll try to catch him on his own and mention our trip to Shaz 'n Baz's. Tell him about their suggestions for . . .' she mimed getting some filler injected into her forehead 'See if he offers me anything.'

'Good idea. Did you find out anything on the message board?'

Susie shook her head. 'Madhav looked into it, but it was just a general question about income.'

'And . . . the diet pills? You're happy asking about those?'

Susie nodded. 'I'm sure Lucia and Cristobal won't be surprised if I approach them about pills, given that I'm the only pro with more than ten per cent body fat. Especially after they tried to foist them on Maisie.'

They both turned and looked at Maisie. Sweetheart that she was, she was reassuring a nervous pair of amateurs that they would have the time of their lives, especially if they pretended the judges were only wearing underpants.

They turned and smiled at one another, a simple, shared moment of calm before the storm.

Susie broke eye contact first, her smile fading as she pulled her bag up from the floor. 'If it turns out I don't have to dance, because, you know . . . Jack not showing, I'll be able to make sure you are one hundred per cent safe.'

'It won't come to that, darling, I promise.'

'That's not a promise you can make, Lily.' And, without waiting for her to protest, Susie popped in her earbuds, making it clear they were done talking.

Chapter Forty-Eight

Susie looked down at her phone screen for what seemed like the four billionth time and there, beneath her last message to Jack . . .

'Please just tell me you're safe'

. . . nothing.

'Nearly there, darling.' Lily grabbed Susie's free hand and gave it a squeeze. 'I can already smell the sea air.'

Beyond the slated rooftops, Susie caught a glimpse of the Blackpool Tower, already sparkling with lights as night began to fall. The final bundle of nerves she'd been trying to keep at bay with a podcast about serial killers released into her bloodstream.

She pushed herself up from her slouched position and, along with the rest of the coach's inhabitants, glued her eyes to the skyline for another glimpse of the glorious Victorian structure where all their lives would be changed – some for the better, some for the worse – over the next twenty-four hours.

'Who can't wait to go to the top of the Tower!' Maisie called out as she bounced up from the middle of the bus. She and Darren had been holding court with some of the chaperones and the juniors who were performing for the very first time, and had decided to squeeze in a bit of sightseeing as well.

Susie smiled up at her. Maisie was such a good person. Honest as the day was long. A direct contrast to herself. And no, she wasn't being melodramatic. The simple truth was, no matter how perfectly she'd justified her decision to raise Kian on her own, she'd lied to Jack. Robbed him of his son's childhood. If the roles were reversed, she wasn't sure if she'd be able to find a way to forgive him.

She hated to use her next thought as a salve, but she did anyway – at least with Jack not coming, he would be safe from the murderer. It was just her and Lily now. Kian was safe at home with her brother, and with Madhav and his two staffers also going undercover tomorrow, she was hopeful they could pinpoint the killer before any harm was done.

'Honey, we're hooooome,' sing-songed Ruby Rae as the Tower became visible through the huge front window of the coach. The dancers began to shoulder their bags, rising up into the aisles, too excited to sit still any longer. Just one more sleep until they danced upon the world's finest ballroom floor.

Despite a silent promise not to contact Jack again, Susie picked her phone out of her lap as the coach eased up against the kerb of their hotel, directly across from the Winter Gardens where, through the years, the two of them had taken home trophy after trophy.

She typed him a three-word message, then deleted it, pocketing the phone before emotions got the better of her.

You're here for work. Not a long-awaited happily-ever-after.

'Ow!' Susie's hand flew to the back of her head and she whipped round to see what had hit her.

A shoe box held by none other than Ruby Rae Coutts.

Susie looked up at her.

Ruby Rae pulled the box back to her chest. 'Sorry,' she said, mouthing, 'Not sorry' as she turned away.

When everyone had got off the bus and begun claiming their overnight bags from the boot, Susie stood up. 'Right, Lily,' she said, her voice full of bravura she didn't feel. 'Guess we'd best catch ourselves a murderer.'

Chapter Forty-Nine

'It's beautiful in here, isn't it?' Marmaduke sighed.

'Mmmm,' Johanna agreed.

The trophy room at dawn. Not that there was an ounce of natural light in the dark wood-panelled lounge tucked behind the famed ballroom, but . . . by god it was a breath-taking sight. One he made a point of enjoying each year before this, the true pinnacle of Blackpool's ballroom events. One that was mere hours away from being entirely under his control.

'Would you just look at 'em all.' Hundreds of glittering trophies, all waiting to be won.

He spread his arms along the backrest of the ox-blood Chesterfield, glanced at the grandfather clock in the corner and gave it a wink. The number of shags that clock face had seen.

And there would be plenty more to come. Maybe he could even wangle a key to the lift that went up to the top of the Tower. He'd always fancied a bonk up there.

The Bonanza's organizers would be here in just a few hours' time, at which point he'd have to start putting on a show. Scrape and bow to the increasingly aged Cyril de Boeuf. The man's adherence to the rulebook was as tiresome as Lily's. Over the years he'd tried every trick in his arsenal to get Cyril to turn the occasional blind eye, but no dice. He'd considered waiting for him to die naturally, but frankly, life was too short.

Everything would change today.

'Ahh, Johanna,' he sighed. 'I hope you're looking forward to seeing your name on one of these whoppers next year.'

'That'd be nice,' she agreed.

'Better than nice, woman! It'll be glorious! Stupendous! You can't buy that kind of publicity. You have to earn it. Speaking of which . . .' Marmaduke gave her hair a stroke, then gently guided her head back down between his thighs. 'Now where was I? Ah, yes . . . trophies.'

It wasn't just the tables laden with today's awards that tickled his fancy. It was the sagging shelves of cups lining the walls, many of which had his name on them. He never tired of seeing his name nestled amongst other world champions in the same way Caesar and Hadrian and Alexander the Great stood shoulder to shoulder in history books. Men who'd taken charge. Shown the world what a true leader looked like. He wouldn't stop at Constantinople, though. Or the Alps. He'd see his quest through pole to pole.

His gaze snagged on a strip of trophies bearing the one name that never failed to curl his lip.

Lily Richmond.

She was the solitary champion within a forty-year reach who he'd never shagged in here. Or anywhere, for that matter. His hips gave a reflexive jerk. Johanna gagged and he swore under his breath. Even thinking Lily's goddamn name made his cock that little bit harder. He crushed the thought that it was Lily that had that effect on him and focused instead on the series of events he'd be rolling out today.

'Just picture it, Johanna.' He held his hands up above her head, out of her sightline, but this wasn't really for her benefit, so who cared? 'Lily Richmond exposed for favouritism. She'll be struck off judges' panels from here to Timbuktu!'

'Lily's strict,' Johanna said, briefly surfacing. 'No one's going to buy that she plays favourites.'

He wagged his finger at her. 'That's where you're wrong.' He didn't explain. But suffice it to say, whatever money had been left in the GDC accounts was no longer there.

He'd had to double the scrutineer's sweetener – something about orthodontists and twins had made it a trickier negotiation than usual. But he'd got him to agree in the end. Lily's score cards, round after round, would consistently rank her own dancers higher than their rivals. The scrutineer would replace Lily's real cards – which would, as Johanna suggested, be irritatingly fair – with falsified scores, giving Jack and Susie row after row of firsts. Then Ruby Rae and Vlad, and so on. Marmaduke had done the score cards himself, just to be sure. He'd decided not to include Maisie and Darren in the top six after they hadn't answered his calls. That would teach them a thing or two about respect. 'When Cyril approves them, that will make him complicit, too. Ouch. Careful with the teeth.'

'Sorry.' Johanna sat back on her heels and, with a contemplative look, said, 'I've never done it on a crooked one before.'

He chose to ignore that. It wasn't crooked, it was . . . unique. Just like his dances. He gave a pointed look at his neglected member. She gave it a long, luxurious lick.

'I think your plan sounds wonderful,' Johanna said. 'Especially the part when I become a judge.' She took him in and began to bob up and down again.

Ahhh. There they were. Back on track.

He settled back into his daydream. 'Once de Boeuf gives the scores the okay, I'll reveal their duplicity and stage a coup, demanding that the Ballroom Bonanza become a GDC event. And then, of course, when the GDC announces its bankruptcy next week, I'll unveil . . .' He paused for effect: 'Dancing with The Duke.' He clapped his hands in glee. He'd keep Lily around long enough to hear the announcement about Latin dance being erased from the competition. He could already imagine the stricken look on her face. The lifeblood draining from her as the new reality dawned. No more throne for the Queen of Latin.

Always one beat behind, Johanna surfaced and asked, 'Is the GDC bankrupt?'

'Down to its last two cents.' And he'd already worked out a way to blame it on Veronica now that she'd gone rogue on him. 'That's right, love,' he said as Johanna's super-sized pout found its way back to his groin. 'Put your mouth where the money will be. Because once it starts rolling in? There'll be riches galore!'

Chapter Fifty

'Mother-*f*—!'

'Language!' Ramone gestured towards the clutch of giddy children being led from their secure changing room into the hair and make-up area by Brynn and a chaperone, ready to be doused in glitter and hairspray.

'Well, be careful with the tresses then,' Ruby Rae hissed, eyes on the children's costumes, which, true to form, might as well have been nun's habits. *Safeguarding.* God, she'd hated those days. Kneeling down to make sure the hem of your dress touched the floor. No cut-outs in the bodice. No keyhole backs or necklines lower than the top of your armpit. Fishnet tights. *Granny pants.*

'Why did you wash your hair when I told you not to?' Ramone whacked her on the shoulder with his brush. 'It's too slippery now. I'm going to have to put it in a fishtail.'

Ruby Rae slapped the brush away. 'Who peed in your cornflakes this morning?' She might have her kinks, but no one apart from Kiko was allowed to touch her without permission. 'I *want* the snake braid.'

'Who's the expert here?'

He was. *Obviously*. But she wasn't in the mood for his prima donna-ish, 'I'm the best stylist in town and deserve your respect' crapola. He wasn't the only one who could do a snake braid. She'd ask Brynn, if he didn't have his hands full with those awful kids.

She gave her hair a flick. 'Just . . . shut your piehole and get on with it, will you? Time's a tickin'.'

'Morning, everyone!' Lily called cheerily from the dressing-room door, before making a beeline for Ramone's chair. She glanced at Ruby Rae's reflection in the mirror.

'I trust you slept well last night?' she asked, pointedly.

Ruby Rae avoided making eye contact. She'd spent the night with Kiko when she should have followed Lily's 'early night before competition' rule, and she had the dark shadows under her eyes to show for it. Somehow, Lily knew what she'd been up to. She always knew.

'She'd look a lot nicer with a smile on her face,' Ramone snipped.

'Don't we all,' Lily quipped. 'I'm sure our girl will turn it on when it matters. And anyway, there are plenty of ways to freshen up a tired face. Did you see? Even the windows of the Tower were getting a polish this morning. A man was abseiling down from the very top to give them a brush.' Ruby Rae didn't even bother to look interested.

Lily turned away from the mirror, leaning in close to Ramone. In a conspiratorial whisper, she said, 'Speaking of which, I heard a rumour that you have a newly acquired skill?'

Ramone looked briefly shocked, then disguised it with a coy smile. 'How did you know, you little minx? I was trying to keep it quiet until I officially launch.'

'Secret's safe with me, darling.' Lily twisted her fingers in front of her lips and made to leave. 'I won't say a word. But you must tell me where I can see your work. Who've you been practising on?'

Ramone looked furtive. 'Well, I really shouldn't say—'

'No one cares, Ramone,' Ruby Rae interjected, with a couple of finger snaps. 'Less talking, more styling.'

She ignored Lily's frown and Ramone's scowl. She didn't have time to worry about other people's feelings today. She had to keep her eyes on the prize.

'Well then, must dash,' Lily said with a pointed look at Ruby Rae in the mirror. 'This is all looking lovely, darlings.'

Seriously?

'This' so wasn't. Why was Lily lying? Something was definitely off with her. She'd barely seen her in the days leading up to Blackpool. And what was with her sudden interest in injectables? Ruby Rae glanced at the box she was resting her slippered feet on. Was it finally time?

She gave the counter a couple of quick whacks as Lily walked away, bringing Ramone's attention back to where it belonged: on her. 'Chop-chop, baby cakes. You're paid to do what I say. If you won't, I'll find someone else.'

'You booked *me*, sunshine. And you know how I feel about people who break appointments.'

And *he* knew how she felt about looking like shit. 'I don't have to honour anything if I think it's going to compromise my performance. Hey, everyone! Guess what Ramone's been learning to do in his spare time?'

'Fine.' Ramone glowered, grabbing a fistful of her hair and whipping it into three distinct sections. 'One snake braid coming up for Little Miss Viper Tongue. Brynn! Got any dry shampoo I can borrow? Mine's run out.'

In the mirror, Ruby Rae watched Brynn pause his production line of tidy buns. She thought she saw a flicker of annoyance cross his face before he turned, all smiles, and brandished a can in Ramone's direction.

'No problemo, mate. Sharing is caring.'

'*There* you are.' Vlad stomped over. 'I've been all over the place trying to find you.'

Ruby Rae pretended to care. 'Poor Vladdy-pops. Have you been round and round the Winter Gardens like a teddy bear?'

'We need to go over our quickstep. Now.'

She *could* say she'd tried to find him earlier but had seen him disappearing into a dark corner with Felipe, so had run through the steps herself. But, because she needed to keep him on side, she batted her falsies at him and, sweet as a sugar-spun angel said, 'Sorry, honey-pie. I'm afraid I've got to keep my appointment with Ramone.'

Chapter Fifty-One

Jack pulled into a parking spot on the promenade, facing out towards the dark mass of the Irish sea.

He closed his eyes and saw a flash of gold hair and a cheeky grin. *Kian.* The pain was sharp. Like nothing he'd known before. He'd gone to a dark place when he'd discovered that Susie hadn't told him he had a son. Six years lost . . . six years he'd never get back.

He was wounded, angry – at Susie, Lily, everyone. Himself. And so he did the only thing he knew how to do: he retreated. He ignored Susie's calls – there was no way they could go through with the competition now. Their second chance was over before it had even really begun.

But now, somehow, he was here, in Blackpool. He'd just got in the car and drove, without thinking about what he'd do when he got there.

He reached towards the button that turned off the car. His finger hovered over it, just a millimetre away, unable, or perhaps, unwilling to commit.

And that was the crux of the matter, wasn't it?

If he looked in his rear-view mirror, he knew he'd see the

Tower glimmering behind him – a talisman to all who loved ballroom dance. So he didn't look, staring instead at the turbulent waves in front of him. A far more appropriate mirror of his mood.

Susie had kept the fact she was pregnant from him because she hadn't believed he had the ability to commit to her. To commit to a life together that might have curtailed his dreams of becoming the world's foremost ballroom dancer.

Even thinking it tore him up inside. Mostly because he wondered if she'd been right. He'd been so focused on becoming a pro and smashing records that he had sat there in that stupid, Formica-tabled café and watched the love of his life walk away.

He hadn't called after her.

Given chase.

Hadn't waited a week for the two of them to cool down enough to talk things through.

He hadn't even asked Lily, his long-term mentor, for her advice.

He'd just got on with his life, playing by his rules – well, Marmaduke's – and not once bothered to look back.

And what had he done now that life had thrown this extraordinary, life-changing curveball in his path?

The exact same thing. He'd abandoned her, with the added bonus of a homicidal maniac on the loose. Nice one, Jack.

Out of the corner of his eye, he noticed a couple of young dancers taking pictures on the promenade before turning to head towards the famed ballroom, their arms around each other's shoulders. Something about them reminded him of the first time he'd come to Blackpool with Susie; how excited they'd been, how full of big dreams.

At last, he looked up at the Tower – the place where he and Susie could be dancing in a few short hours, if he were to accept the fact that he hadn't been the man he should have been all those years ago.

What's it going to be, Jack? he asked himself as he slipped the car into gear again. *What's it going to be?*

Chapter Fifty-Two

Tick.
Tock.
Tick.
Tock.
Time's running out, my pretties!

Chapter Fifty-Three

Lily quirked her head to the side to catch the emcee's latest update. 'And that's it for the juvenile and junior competitors until the semi-finals at two p.m., ladies and gentlemen. Let's give them a round of applause as they head off for a well-earned rest. Now it's time to turn the floor over to the pro-am competitors in advance of the highly anticipated open elimination round for our professional dancers at high noon.'

Lily scanned the area. She'd tried and failed to find Susie to let her know about her exchange with Ramone. She'd try again after the judge's briefing.

'It's going to be a tough one today,' an unwelcome voice whispered in her ear. 'Are your dancers up for it?'

Lily took an exaggerated step away from Marmaduke, but shot him her brightest smile as she did so. 'I think the real question is, do you have any dancers left to falsify score cards for?'

He narrowed his eyes at her and gave one of those casual, greasy laughs of his. 'You'd better watch your back, Lilian. Your time here among the elite is coming to an end.'

Lily hid her alarm with a smile. Normally his threats were just words. But today, of course, they came laced with the possibility of truth. 'Why, Marmaduke. I thought this was a neutral place where the true spirit of ballroom was allowed to flourish.'

He was just about to reply when Cyril de Boeuf tottered out of the trophy room, decked to the nines in his trademark blue velvet tuxedo. The judges, who had been loitering in a loose cluster, closed in for the traditional pre-competition speech.

'Ladies and gentlemen!' he beamed. '*Mesdames et Messieurs.* Thank you for coming today.' He scanned the esteemed group of well-heeled men and women before him. All champions in their own right. After giving his back a quick crick, Cyril beamed a watery smile at them. 'As you all know, you have been hand-selected to join us here at the Blackpool Tower Ballroom to offer some of the world's finest dancers a *fair and fighting chance* to win the title of world champion.'

Marmaduke gave a derisive snort, as the rest of the judges nodded seriously. They knew what Cyril was really saying. Competitions run by the likes of the GDC could be bought. This one, no matter how hard people tried, had always remained an honourable playing ground.

'Remember,' Cyril added with a flourish of his index finger. 'You must not judge on past results or personal relationships with any of the competitors. The skill the dancers display is all that matters. Each precious moment they have on the floor is all that matters. They must shine in every round.' He scanned each of them, meeting their eyes one by one. 'And more importantly, you must judge them without fear or favour.'

Lily didn't dare meet Marmaduke's eyes this time. She'd always judged by that credo. Today it could be her undoing.

As the scrutineer began to hand out the clipboards charged

with their marking cards, Lily kept her smile in place, but a slight tremor in her hand as she took the board made her suddenly aware of just how frightened she was. The murderer had promised to strike today and she, one of the possible targets, was standing right beside one of their suspects. Had dicing with death sharpened The Duke's will to kill? It certainly hadn't stopped him from trying to pinch Maisie and Darren. Or some of her better amateurs. Though they'd all stayed loyal to Lily, of course.

Lily considered her old rival. She loathed his underhanded tactics, but did she fear him? Could he really be the killer? Or could he be delegating the more gruesome role to his right-hand woman?

Lily sought out Veronica among the judges but, to her surprise, couldn't see her.

'Where's Roni?'

'Dancing,' The Duke gruffed.

Lily stared at him. 'She's what?'

'She's not judging.' He refused to meet her eye. 'She's dancing with Scouser Sam.'

'She's . . . they're . . .' Lily was speechless. 'They're dancing pro-am?' She certainly hadn't seen that coming. The last time she'd seen Sam he'd been consumed by grief, railing against the world of ballroom dance. She glanced at her roster and, after flicking through a couple of sheets, she saw it. Samuel Pringle and Veronica Parke-West – couple number sixty-three in the Over-50s category. How extraordinary.

Why on earth would Veronica be dancing with Sam? Was she innocent, after all? Or had she opted for this tactic so that she'd be free to watch the professionals dance and witness Jack or Susie die in front of the huge crowd assembled here at the Tower?

'And that's about it for now.' Cyril tapped his watch face. 'The first round begins in three minutes. If we aren't on time, we can hardly expect the dancers to keep their appointments.'

Lily turned away from the ballroom, actively wrestling the new snippets of information into place when Susie appeared in the corridor just beyond the Trophy Room.

'Lily!' She hiked up the full skirt of her stunning dress and quickly closed the space between them. With billows of fabric following in her wake, she looked like Cinderella fleeing the ball. Having lost some time to a debrief with Madhav, Lily had done her hair in the end. A simple up-do. Susie's make-up, whilst thick enough to endure the bright lights of the ballroom floor, was subtle enough to make it clear she was a natural beauty.

'Susie, I'm so glad you're here . . . I've just found out—'

'Jack's not here,' Susie cut in, her face creased with panic. She held up his number and four safety pins. 'We've got to go on in less than five minutes!'

What to do? Offer false promises that he would arrive or admit that she simply didn't know?

'Ramone's admitted he knows how to do injections,' she said instead. Time was precious. Once she was out on that floor, she wouldn't be allowed to speak to anyone, let alone a competitor. Without waiting for a response, she continued, 'Marmaduke is on the warpath and Veronica, of all things, is dancing in the pro-ams with Scouser Sam. I'm afraid I don't know what Lucia and Cristobal are up to. Or Javier.'

Susie hard-stared at her for a moment and then, before she could respond, a swarm of dancers began crisscrossing around them, making it clear Lily had to take her place on the ballroom floor.

'He isn't coming, is he?' Susie asked, reaching out to prevent Lily from being dragged away by the tide of competitors. 'He's either decided not to come, or the murderer's . . .' Her breath hitched in her throat. It was then that Lily saw the true panic set in.

'No, darling. Not that.' Lily couldn't allow the possibility that Jack might have become a victim of the killer.

In that moment, Lily felt her will to find the murderer solidify within her. Form into that hard, crystallized focus she'd channelled through the years when she, herself, had been a competitor. As it was then, victory was her only option.

Out of the corner of her eye she saw someone sweep round the corner with a purposeful stride.

Jack Kelly.

'Look, darling.' She turned Susie round.

Jack strode up to the pair of them, make-up done, his jet-black tail suit absolutely immaculate. He looked utterly delectable and completely inscrutable. 'Sorry I'm late.'

'Jack, I—' Susie began, but he held up his hand.

'I'm not going to let you go through this alone.' It wasn't a declaration of love or an actual apology. It was a statement entirely bereft of hidden meaning.

Either one of them could have pressed for more, but they didn't have time, and everything about his body language told Lily not to try. He was here. And that's what counted. She turned him round and instructed Susie to pin one side of his number to his back while she did the other.

From the flex in his shoulder blades, she knew Jack's being

here wasn't only about winning the dance competition. It was about acknowledging that, beneath the layers of hurt, he wanted to keep the woman he loved safe from harm. And that was good enough for her.

'Right, darlings,' Lily said when she'd pressed the final safety pin into place. 'I'm off. You're in the third heat. I'll see you on the dance floor.'

From the moment her leather-soled platform shoes hit the edge of the century-old dance floor, Lily felt a heightened awareness of her surroundings. The movement beneath her as dancers glided onto the thirty-thousand-plus blocks of wood that made up the floor. The balconies heaving with people too far away to identify. Even the shift of silk from her own dress upon her skin caught her attention. There wasn't a detail she could afford to miss if the killer really was going for their moment in the limelight. If they did, no one would miss it. The spotlights were opened to full capacity, so that she and the rest of the judges wouldn't miss a solitary move. Just as well, considering these opening heats were ruthless.

There was silence for a moment and then, on a signal from Cyril, the music began.

At this point in proceedings, early doors eliminations, the music was provided by a DJ. The gilded stage was set, music stands already charged, for the live orchestra, Marvellous Martin and the Swinging Seven, who would take over proceedings from the quarter-finals through to the end.

Time, as it always did when she was judging, lost all meaning.

The lavish decor, cheering crowds and flares of light from the ballroom's many chandeliers blurred into nothing as she took pen in hand and began to mark the dancers. As much as catching a murderer was at the forefront of her mind, her focus was now entirely zeroed in on faulty footwork, poor arm styling and, the biggest of all faults this early in the competition, floor craft. So many collisions in these early rounds. And some of them very nearly with her.

Lily's scoring was efficient, exacting and merciless. She'd been held to the highest of standards as she'd soared to and maintained her status as a world champion, and it was her job to ensure the next generation of champions did the same. Not even Marmaduke's glares from the opposite end of the ballroom could throw her off.

Two heats of professionals later – neither of which contained any of their suspects – Lily's eyes were glued to the main entrance as Vlad led Ruby Rae on to the floor, quickly followed by Darren and Maisie and Cristobal and Lucia. A dozen other couples filed in, until they were only one short of the maximum number of dancers allotted to the floor. And then, as they spread themselves into their opening positions, Jack led Susie to the only remaining spot. Upper right-hand corner, diagonally opposite Lily. If she hadn't seen his emotionally distanced arrival this morning, she would've believed Jack and Susie were nothing less than deeply in love by the way they looked at one another now.

They stood out. Critical at this stage in events where even a national champion could be eliminated if they hadn't brought their A-game. Four hundred couples from around the world would be slashed to two hundred in this round alone. Two hundred to ninety-six in the next. Forty-eight. Twenty-four. Twelve. And then, of course, only the elite dancers would remain. Six couples vying for that solitary, glittering trophy. Two of whom – should Jack and Susie make it through – had targets on their backs.

The music began.

The atmosphere in the ballroom was pure lightning storm. Tensions crackling and sparking as, already, feathers from wrist boas began to fly.

When Lucia and Cristobal waltzed past, they made a point of doing an elongated throwaway oversway so close to her that Lily was almost forced to take a step back to allow room for Lucia's head to tip back into a full extension. Almost.

'*Buenos días, señora*,' Lucia said.

Lily, of course, couldn't speak to her, but she made a point of looking directly into Lucia's eyes, where she saw pure, clinical, cold indifference. The woman didn't care what or who she hurt. The only person she cared about was herself. And Cristobal, while he mattered. But something told her he would only factor in Lucia's grander scheme as long as he was useful. Javier as well, for that matter. After that? *Adiós, muchachos*.

Ruby Rae and Vlad, on the other hand, were hurtling through the one hundred seconds of tango music as if their lives depended upon it. They, too, shone, but not with joy. More, with a sense of determined precision. As a direct contrast, Maisie and Darren were on fine form, the pair of them beaming from ear to ear.

But it was Jack and Susie who took her breath away. They glowed with energy, precision and grace, as if each of the five ballroom dances were to be the very last they'd have together and, as such, they'd decided to actively savour every precious second in one another's arms. Their gazes lingered when Jack sent her into a natural turn, as if neither of them could bear the fraction of a second when they'd be forced to lose eye contact. His hands – when they left her – communicated that they knew they had held a place of privilege and longed to do so again. But it was the connectivity they shared that was most compelling. The way their body language communicated that the pair of them didn't need any of this glitz and glamour, the cheering crowds, or even the music, to compel them into one another's arms. All they needed to survive was each other.

As the dancers spun, fleckerled and chasséd their way through the Viennese waltz, the foxtrot and the quickstep, Lily tried to find a way to put together all the clues they had so far to try to pinpoint the murderer before they had a chance to strike.

They were seeking revenge for being overlooked or ignored in some way. Dismissed. They considered themselves loyal, timely, and careful about earning, not taking what they wanted. They also had access to Argentine diet pills and botulism. And, more importantly, knew how to deliver a lethal dose in such a way as to keep their victim alive long enough for everyone to witness their death.

A boa blinded her for a moment.

As she teased a neon feather out of her mouth, she saw the culprit. Lucia, again. The leggy dancer was shooting the remains of a side-eye to Lily as she curtsied to the judge a few metres down from her, before Cristobal swept her into the opening position for the American smooth.

Then, just as quickly as the round had begun, it finished, and a new wave of dancers glided onto the floor.

Eventually, after two more elimination heats had brought them to the stage where all remaining dancers would advance to the quarter-finals, Lily stepped away from the dance floor and took the opportunity to nip backstage. Though she wouldn't be able to speak to them, she was hoping if Susie and Jack had managed to sleuth out something new, they would be able to indicate as much to her.

The first thing she saw was Susie carefully stepping out of her ballroom gown and into her new Latin dress. Lavished with a glittering diamanté embellishment, the evergreen frock had enough fabric to make Susie feel she wasn't going onto the dance floor naked, but clung close enough to the right curves and featured a high enough split to ensure the judges could see the strong, elegant lines of her legwork, which was so crucial to being marked as one of the top six.

Ruby Rae, on the other hand, might as well have saved herself some money and gone out onto the dance floor wearing a fig leaf and two tassels. Not that Lily blamed her. She had a beautiful body and a passion for Latin that always had the audience roaring for more. Right now she was prancing through to a room marked off limits to the dancers. It was large and had tall windows looking out to the Irish Sea. In amongst the Jurassic mini-golf course that visitors could work their way through en route to the Tower lifts, there were a couple of tables and mirrors set up and signs that read Judges Only.

'Soz, Lil,' Ruby Rae said unapologetically as she parked herself in front of one of the mirrors to check her make-up. 'Light's better in here.'

In silence, Lily stood in front of the mirror next to Ruby Rae, ostensibly to check her own make-up, but really to see if she could get a feel for her fiery mentee's mood. She'd not had much of a chance to talk to her lately, and she'd clearly been out of sorts in the make-up chair this morning.

'Your hair looks nice, Rubes,' Maisie said from the doorway, clearly taking notice of the sign taped to the door.

'Oh, my gawd, Maisie. Have you actually gone blind?' Ruby Rae spoke in a way that made it clear she wanted Lily to take note. 'It's been, like, an actual trauma.' Flicking her hand in the direction of the juniors' dressing room she said, 'I had to get someone else to tweak it because Ramone has been acting funny.'

Lily frowned.

Maisie said something about how everyone was always a bit jumpy at these things and excused herself to go find Darren.

Lily was desperate to ask Ruby Rae to elaborate, but, at just that moment, Ramone staggered through the the doorway towards the pair of them, a brush in one hand and a can of hairspray in the other. His eyes latched on to Ruby Rae. 'You . . . little . . . bitch!'

Lily's blood ran cold as Ruby Rae flounced off in a huff. She'd seen this disjointed, breathless behaviour before. 'Susie!' she called, praying she was still in the next changing room. Surely she was allowed to speak to a dancer if it was a matter of life and death.

Ramone collapsed to the floor, his hands clawing at his throat, as if trying to pull it open and allow the air in. 'Who did this to you, Ramone?' Lily asked, but he said nothing, his eyes glued on the space Ruby Rae had just occupied. 'Susie!'

Susie, her dress covered by a fluffy pink dressing gown, ran into the room, took one look at Ramone, and said to Lily, 'Ring Madhav and the paramedics. I'll be back in five seconds.'

343

Lily dipped into her cleavage and pulled out her phone as Susie disappeared into the dressing room, then came running back with her tote, dropping to her knees beside Ramone. 'Where did they inject you?' she asked him.

He gold-fished at her, his lips already taking on a horrid tinge of blue.

As Lily explained to Madhav what was happening, Susie pulled two syringes from her tote, uncapped the needle of one and held the other between her teeth. She took a small bottle out of a box and carefully slid the needle into the top of it before turning it upside down and charging the syringe.

When she'd emptied the bottle, she handed the syringe to Lily and pulled the waist tie from her dressing gown, cinching it tightly round Ramone's upper arm.

'What are you doing?' Lily asked.

'I need a vein,' she explained as she tapped and pressed on the nook at the inside of Ramone's elbow. 'Syringe, please.' She held out her hand and, after a couple of brisk flicks and a little nudge to the plunger to remove any air bubbles, slipped the needle into his arm.

Jack walked past the doorway then doubled back just as Susie plunged the liquid into his vein. 'What the hell?'

'He's been given botulism,' Susie said, after dropping the spent syringe into her tote and taking the other from her mouth. 'I've got an antivenom.'

'How did you get it?'

'Doesn't matter,' Susie said.

Jack shot her a look. It clearly did.

'Madhav. We got it from his security team last night as part of the "just in case" kit.'

'What's the other one for?' Jack asked.

'Epinephrine,' she said, pressing her fingers to the side of Ramone's throat. 'In case he has an allergic reaction.'

Madhav and one of his security guys arrived, closing the door behind them. 'We've got the situation sorted,' he said.

'What does that mean?' Jack was becoming increasingly irritated.

'It means,' Susie calmly explained, 'that because of the football match up the road and their security needs, we've managed to keep the police out of this.'

'Someone tried to kill Ramone,' Jack protested. 'The murderer's clearly going off-piste. Why would we want to keep the police out of it?'

They all fell silent as two paramedics in private hospital uniforms appeared, deftly loaded Ramone onto a gurney and, with a few whispered instructions from Madhav, disappeared into the large service lift at the far end of the corridor.

'We think the murderer will be scared off if the police arrive,' Susie explained.

'Oh,' Jack mimicked her tone. 'Do "we"?'

Before Susie could launch into him about how his absence over the past three days had made it difficult to pass on all their plans, Lily pressed a hand to each of their forearms. 'Darlings. We've got to stay together on this.'

Susie nodded and turned to Jack. 'If the event is stopped, there's no telling how long this reign of terror will continue.' The defensiveness she had felt dropped away. Jack was scared. They all were. But fear wouldn't help them find the murderer. Believing in one another was their only option. 'If you and I continue in the competition, I'm certain the three of us will be able to figure out who it is and put them behind bars.'

After a quick, terse discussion, they decided they would tell the event coordinators that Ramone had had an allergic reaction to one of the dancer's therapy dogs. The fewer people who knew what had really happened, the better.

Finally able to draw a full breath of her own, Lily went back into the vast sprawl of a dressing room and looked, unsuccessfully, for the one person who would be able to explain what had happened in the lead-up to this dramatic turn of events: Ruby Rae.

Chapter Fifty-Four

Oopsy-daisy.

Mother always said I'd have a problem with my temper. And she should know.

Never mind. Flexibility is the key to success.

One vial left. Two more rounds until the final. And three heads to roll.

What's a murderer to do?

Chapter Fifty-Five

Susie willed the lightness she'd felt in Jack's arms just a few short days ago to return. From their opening kick ball changes, she'd felt fleeting glimpses of it, flutters of connection as he led her through the double time steps. Throwaway fallaways. Curly whips. Stalking walks, sugar pushes and flicks, all culminating in a crisp mooch and spin. Everything looked good. All that was missing was the *feeling* good part. She was pretty sure they'd managed to fake it so far, but they were about to compete in the quarter-finals now. When, and if, they danced the complicated choreography for the fourth time tonight, it would have to be better than perfect. It would have to be sublime. And then a step beyond that for the semis. And a step beyond that for the finals.

Jack cocked his ear at the sound of the emcee on the Tannoy. Five minutes until they were due out on the floor. 'Should we find Lily?' He turned and began walking towards the ballroom without waiting for her response. He had yet to say a single thing about her performance dresses. Or, for that matter, her actual performances, which had seen them through the tricky elimination rounds. Her first victories on the dance floor in years and she was surprised at how much it hurt to have them pass unacknowledged.

It's because you're not really a dancer, she reminded herself. You're an undercover detective trying to find a murderer who has literally just tried to take another life.

'Good idea,' she said to Jack's retreating back. 'I need to give her my phone. Nowhere to tuck it in this dress.' He didn't look back.

She loped a few steps to catch up to him.

She tried to keep her glances at his profile to a minimum, aware that spooking him at this juncture could easily make him change his mind about showing up in the first place. But it was really hard. He was so handsome. So . . . stoic. And this, his Latin outfit, truly showed off what an incredibly sexy body he had. His form-fitting, cuffed-jacket-style shirt with a velveteen collar made Susie's fingers itch to take a peek underneath. But now was not the time to let her thoughts veer off to Sexyville. With the strange dynamic they were sharing – in love on the dance floor, strangers off of it – that sort of intimacy might never come again. Realistically, the best she could hope for was that he would forgive her enough to, perhaps, start a relationship with Kian. They both deserved as much. She saw that now.

She, Jack and Lily converged at the same entrance to the ballroom with only a handful of minutes to spare.

'Lovely work so far, darlings. Keep it up,' Lily said after a quick check to make sure no one was watching them. Susie knew what a risk Lily was taking, talking to them. These types of interactions could easily see her struck off of the judges' roster for life, but seeing as an actual life was on the line, Lily clearly felt it was her duty to exercise a bit of elasticity in terms of observing them. This, after all, wasn't a discussion about putting the pair of them through to the finals.

Lily held out her jewel encrusted clutch. 'Phones?' Just as they were handing them over to Lily, Susie's buzzed. When she realized they'd all received a text, she frowned, instantly thumbing the message open. Lily read hers aloud.

Jack and Susie went up the hill to fetch a pail of water
Who will fall down and break their ballroom crown
Trying to snatch it from the rightful winner?

'That's what mine says,' Susie said.

'And mine.' Jack held up his phone. 'What do you think it means?'

'That the murderer knows their way around a nursery rhyme,' Susie replied. And then, more thoughtfully. 'This is someone whose childhood was not a good one.'

Susie clocked Lily's frown. If she remembered correctly, Ruby Rae had grown up in a series of foster homes. It wasn't a guarantee of an unhappy childhood, but . . .

'It sounds like they're rooting for someone who isn't either of you,' Lily said with a glance towards the ballroom, where her fellow judges were moving into position. 'Whatever it means, I think the killer wants you two to make it through to the finals.'

'They've already struck once today,' Susie said. 'What makes you think they'll wait until—'

'Move it.'

Lucia and Cristobal bashed past Susie without so much as a backward glance.

'Hey!' Jack called after them. 'I think you owe someone an apology.'

Cristobal turned around and made a rude gesture with his fisted hand. '*De acá!*'

'What the hell does that mean?'

'I suspect it means screw you in Argentinian. If not, something close enough.'

Jack made as if to run after Cristobal. Lily stopped him with a hand to his chest but then, at the sound of the emcee welcoming Marvellous Marvin and the Swinging Seven onto the stage, said, 'Sorry, darlings. I've got to get out there. You two should consider getting into position as well.'

'C'mon, Suze.' Jack took her hand. 'We aren't going to be able to figure out what the murderer's plans are now. But if it's those two? I want to knock them out of the competition first.'

Ruby Rae and Vlad shouldered past Susie, knocking her into Jack's chest.

'Watch where you're going, you idiots!' he shouted after them, wrapping a protective arm around Susie. 'This is—'

Susie glanced up at Jack. Had he been about to say 'the mother of my child'? He was looking down at her, his emotions now on full display. He cupped her face in his hands. 'I'm so sorry.'

'No,' she whispered, trying and failing to blink away a blur of emotion. 'I'm the one who should apologize.'

'Look,' he slid his hands down her arms, took both of her hands in his then dropped a kiss onto her forehead, 'we can't get into it now, but I want you to know I wish I'd responded better the other day. I didn't see it coming at all and I was blindsided.'

'Of course. It makes sense that you were angry.'

'I was never angry about Kian. I was angry at myself for not being the man I should have been. It just took me a few days to figure that out.'

'What do you mean?'

'You should have felt safe telling me you were pregnant. I'll always regret that I didn't make it easy for you.' He took a shaky breath, then met her eyes again. 'I loved you so much, Suze. If I'd known, I would've done anything, anything at all that you'd asked.'

Her heart did a pirouette, then stumbled when she realized he'd put his feelings in the past tense. 'Thank you,' she said in the way she might've to a colleague who'd promised to stop stealing her stapler. 'That's kind.'

He frowned, displeased with her response.

Beyond them, in the ballroom, the orchestra began their warm-up.

A few remaining dancers shifted past them. Once they were alone again, with only seconds to spare, he furrowed his brow, as if he was figuring out how best to condense seven years' worth of regrets into one potent apology. 'You're the bravest, most honest, multi-talented woman I know, and I am honoured that you loved me as long as you did.'

She loved him now. *Right* now. More than ever. But she couldn't say as much because he didn't love her in return.

Finally everything was clear to her. The man standing in front of her was the one she'd walked away from. Competition Jack. The one who would stop at nothing to get to the top. The one who'd just described his love for her in the past tense. All of which meant the compliments were nice, but nothing she could take to heart.

Jack's eyes were on the trophies. Hers needed to be on finding the killer.

He crooked his finger under her chin until she met his eyes.

Those bright, beautiful blue eyes. 'But first,' he tipped his head towards the ballroom, 'I think we should go out there and start knocking a few of our suspects out of the competition. Sound good?'

See? It was all about winning. She mustered a smile. 'Sounds perfect.'

Jack's look intensified as he took her hand and tucked it into the crook of his arm, leading them out onto the floor with a camera-ready smile. 'I mean it,' he said, twirling her out to the full length of each of their arms and then, when she'd curled back in close to him, 'What you're doing is selfless. It's not like you actually want to win it.'

She did. More than ever she really, really did. For herself, to prove she could. For Jack, because she loved him. And a little bit for the murderer, because she knew it would grate.

Marvellous Marvin began his intro. And they were off.

Although their talk had been more bittersweet than life-affirming, it had poured countless litres of emotional fuel onto the fires Susie and Jack needed in order to shine the brightest among the remaining contenders. They began with the samba.

As expected, the music was different to their rehearsal song, but the time count and the choreography was the same. Any embellishments they wanted to add to the dance wouldn't be used until the final round. But honestly? Allowing the drum-heavy rhythm into her cell structure was all Susie needed to charge the choreography they had to its highest level. Crisscross voltas. Contra botafogos. And, perhaps, ironically . . . Argentine crosses.

Throughout the round, Lucia and Cristobal made multiple attempts to trip them up, block them when they needed space and, in one critical moment during their jive – literally danced between them so that neither Susie nor Jack had any way to get to the other. But the Argentines' villainy only served to showcase Susie and Jack's skill, as they used the bright and lively music to execute an elaborate push spin around their rivals before reuniting in front of Cyril de Boeuf with a flourish.

When they left the dance floor moments later, still catching their breath, Jack hugged Susie to his side. 'That was amazing, Suze! It felt like the old days. The minute they busted in between us, I didn't even have to look at you to know what you were going to do. It's like we have a psychic connection or something!'

Susie beamed. She'd felt it too. Just as she was about to point out Lucia's thunderous expression as she crossed the backstage area, their number was called to indicate they had made it through to the semi-finals. Jack picked her up and spun her round in a moment of unchecked happiness. It would be so easy to open herself up and tell him how she felt. But she'd endured his rejection once before. She couldn't survive it a second time.

With sheer force of will, she made herself return to detective mode. They were getting closer to the finals now, which meant the killer would be preparing to strike.

As if she'd wished him there herself, Madhav appeared. 'A quick word, Susie Q?'

She gave Jack's hand a squeeze and asked him if he wouldn't mind taking a note of the rest of the semi-finalists while she had a quick chat with Madhav.

Once they found a quiet corner in the dressing room, she asked, 'Anything from Ramone?'

Madhav shook his head. 'The antivenom you gave him saved his life, but he can't recall anything. Only a quick pinching – most likely the injection – at the back of his neck.'

'And he doesn't remember whose hair he was working on?'

'Maisie's,' he said. 'He also mentioned Ruby Rae was there, too. And Kiko.'

Susie tried to connect the dots. Lily had said Ramone had been intent on getting to Ruby Rae before he collapsed. Could she be the culprit? Or the one who'd put someone else up to it?

'Anyway,' Madhav was saying. 'My guys had a quick rummage through his things – his make-up kit and the overnight bag he had in his hotel—'

'His hotel?' Susie quirked an eyebrow. They did many things, but breaking and entering wasn't one of them.

'This is murder, Susie. I was happy to bend the rules to find out if there was a stash of botulism on the loose in Blackpool.'

It was a fair point. 'But you didn't find anything?'

He shook his head. 'Nothing apart from every hair product known to mankind. But no needles. No syringes.'

Susie looked behind her and lowered her voice even further. 'Ruby Rae?'

Again, Madhav shook his head. 'We had a quick look through her bag, but there was nothing. If she's your killer, she's hidden the tools of her trade safely out of sight.'

Susie remembered the old shoe box Ruby Rae had been carrying on the bus. She'd mentioned it to Jack – more because of Ruby Rae using it as a weapon – but he hadn't seen it in the dressing room so couldn't throw any light on the matter.

Could it be there weren't actually any shoes in the box, but rather a stash of pre-charged syringes? She was just about to mention it to Madhav when a stream of Spanish erupted from the far corner.

Susie got an idea. 'Thanks, Madhav,' she said. 'Having you here is a lifesaver.' Hopefully literally. 'We'll catch up after the next round, okay?'

'Right you are,' Madhav said and, before she turned to go reached out and gave her hand a squeeze. 'Susie Q. We're all very proud of you. You are a truly talented dancer.'

She waved the compliment away, but when she turned round to find Jack, she was beaming.

'C'mere,' she said to Jack after he confirmed that Lucia and Cristobal were heading to the semi-finals. 'I want to try something.'

She took his hand and led them over to the corner of the dressing room where the Argentines had set up camp.

Vlad, who had also made it through to the semis with Ruby Rae, was clapping Felipe on the back in congratulations.

'Well done,' Susie said when Lucia finally turned round to face her.

Lucia scowled.

Susie felt Jack's hand tighten on her shoulder.

Cristobal joined them. He was changing out of his white shirt – the shoulder had been streaked with fake tan from an impressive leg extension and spin he and Lucia had executed in their paso doble.

'I thought that move was amazing,' Susie said congenially as if she hadn't been the object of their vitriol these past few weeks. She pointed at Cristobal's shoulder. 'I can't even

356

imagine how much courage it must've taken to do it. What do you call it?'

'Death wish,' Lucia said impassively.

'Oooh,' said Susie, thinking, *gotcha*. She glanced at Jack, who was glaring daggers at Cristobal. She gave his hand a jiggle to break the staring contest but returned her attention to Lucia.

'I'd love to be able to do something like that, but . . .' she leant in and in a sisterly tone said, 'I just can't seem to shake this extra weight. But you!' She stepped back. 'You're gorgeous. So slim and athletic.'

Lucia accepted the compliments the way an empress might endure a bit of kowtowing. A necessity of the job.

'I don't suppose you know anyone who might be able to give me something to . . . you know . . . help with this?' She pointed at her stomach which, whilst fit, was not the concave affair Lucia's was.

'*PU-TA MADRE!*' Lucia exploded. 'My body is my temple! Why on earth would I know something like that?'

'We are pure!' Cristobal declared. 'Vessels made only for dance. Come, Lucia. We will not be stained by this slander.'

The Argentine pair swanned away, their voices rising above them like outraged castanets as they stomped off to put on their ballroom costumes.

'Well, that went well,' Jack said mildly.

Susie smiled up at him. 'We definitely hit a sore spot.'

Felipe approached them. 'Don't pay attention to those two,' he said. 'They're not the paragons of virtue they'd like us to believe. Her father owns a pharmaceutical company. Their luggage rattles with pills and bottles and god knows what else. The two of them have more treatments than the rest of us combined.' He gestured at the dozen or so dancers around them.

Susie gave him a grateful smile. He seemed like a really nice guy. Nice enough, she hoped, that he wouldn't question her curiosity about his compatriots. 'Do you know if they've had any injection-based treatments here, or do they do it themselves?'

'Oh *dios*,' Felipe laughed and clapped his hands together, cackling at the thought. 'Are you kidding me? She's as rich as Croesus. They have staff do everything for them. And it always has to be the best.'

'So . . . no trips to Shaz 'n Baz's Beauty when you were up in Liverpool then?'

'The place Marmaduke recommended?'

Susie nodded.

'No,' he said definitively. 'Not their style. And anyway, someone said they'd brought in a freelancer who was *caca* – you know, shit . . .' They smiled. Yes, they knew *caca*. Felipe's gaze sharpened suddenly. 'Why do you ask?'

'Oh, no reason,' Susie replied, smoothly. 'Just looking for recommendations in case we fancy a freshen up.'

Felipe appeared as if he were about to say something else, but then – distracted –smiled at someone across the room. Susie followed his gaze.

Vlad.

The Lithuanian curtailed a cutie-pie wave when he saw they were looking, and let Kiko continue powdering his face.

Felipe turned back. 'I've got to go find Mirabel. We're due out on the floor soon.'

They thanked him for his insight and then realized that if Felipe was due out on the floor soon, so were they.

'Only one more round to the finals,' Jack said, grabbing her hand as they headed down the corridor to the ballroom. 'You ready?'

She looked down at his fingers weaving between hers. 'As I'll ever be.' And once again the cheering crowd blurred into darkness as the beams of the spotlight fell upon them and the music began.

Chapter Fifty-Six

'Lilian Richmond.'

Alarm bells cut through Lily's intense concentration. She'd just finished marking the pro-am Under-35s, and had sneaked behind a pillar to take her heels off for a moment before the professional semi-final heat began. She didn't need to turn around to know who was behind her.

'How *dare* you.'

Ice poured through her veins. Javier had never once spoken to her with such an accusatory tone. She disguised her dismay with efficiency of movement as she strapped her feet back into her platform shoes, sequinned, to match her pant suit.

'I don't have the slightest idea what you're talking about Javier. Now, if you don't mind—'

'Lilian!' He cuffed her upper arm in his hand. It didn't hurt, but she didn't like the optics. Not. One. Bit. Not to mention the fact that if she was caught talking to him, her career as a judge would be over.

She fixed him with an icy glare.

They were in public. She was working. This could, if she was so inclined, be defined as assault.

He removed his hand.

It looked as if their fleeting romance had reached its customary endgame. Usually there was an excuse. A needy student. A problem with the ranch back home. Something someone else could have easily fixed, used by Javier as a 'get out of a relationship free' card. This time, however, it sounded as though he was genuinely angry.

She opened her compact for a quick glance, trying to keep her voice neutral. 'I can't speak to you right now. You know that.'

'Too bad,' Javier said, clearly not caring.

'Later.'

'Now.'

She snapped the compact shut, glanced over her shoulder to ensure absolutely no one could see her, then met his gaze head on. 'What is it?'

'Your dancers – Susie and Jack.'

Her pulse quickened. 'What of them?'

'They asked *my* dancers how they could get their hands on some diet pills.'

She pursed her lips. No wonder Javier was fuming. This was going to be a tricky one to play. 'Everyone has something here.'

'It's sabotage.'

She barked a laugh. 'And sending Susie flying so that she practically broke her nose wasn't?'

'You know how I feel about pills. I gave Lucia hell the other night. So why press it?'

'Why are you telling me and not them?'

'Your students? Your responsibility,' he ground out.

Oh, ho! So he was choosing that line of attack, was he?

Javier continued, 'My dancers know our bodies are our

purest forms of expression and, as such, should be treated with respect.'

Lily's temper flared. Not because of his ire – pills were triggering for him – but because they'd been here before. He was using this situation to throw a wedge between them so that when he inevitably walked away, she would be left feeling it was she who should shoulder the blame. Well, she was calling bullshit. 'Tell me, Javier, hand over heart, that Lucia's cheekbones are natural.'

It wasn't the point, but she wanted him to separate his anger from what he felt for her.

Silence.

'Or her lips.' Definition of a trout pout if ever there was one.

She didn't bother waiting for yet another silent admission. This entire conversation was ridiculous. Having his morally dubious dancers whining that someone had accused them of something completely feasible should hardly have sent him racing over to accuse her of sabotage.

He wasn't a fool. He *had* to know the dancers he was coaching adhered to a different moral code than his own. Why on earth he'd agreed to bring them over here on this UK tour was beyond her. Unless . . .

No. She couldn't allow the thought that he would compromise his reputation for the sole purpose of seeing her. Unless, of course, he'd truly had no idea about Lucia, the pills, and whatever else it was that had made Susie stir up the hornets' nest.

Her eyes sought his. What was his aim here? To push her away? Or to protect his students? Just as she caught a glimpse of the real Javier, the one she'd fallen for all those many years ago, he said, 'You've just got . . .' He teased a few strands of hair off her cheek and behind her ear. Her skin came alive at his touch. And then, as his fingers left her cheek, she felt a coolness in their absence.

'Thank you,' she said.

'Pleasure.'

She truly wished it was.

There was a moment's silence as the music playing for the final round of amateur dancers switched from the languorous foxtrot into the bright and chirpy quickstep. Oh, to feel that footloose and fancy-free.

'What's this really about, Javier?'

'We never fully trusted one another, Liliana,' he rasped. 'Not with our hearts.'

'How can I trust a man whose forte is blaming other people when he wants an excuse to walk away?' she spat back, turning to glance at the floor where she would be missed if she didn't reappear soon.

She didn't have to turn back to know he wasn't there any more. He may have struck the first blow, but she'd plunged the dagger in and twisted it.

This was their pattern. Seduction. Resistance. Submission. A tempest.

She made her way back onto the ballroom floor, trying and failing to regain her composure.

Johanna, of all people stopped her 'Everything all right, Lily?'

'Sorry, love. You know the rules,' Lily managed, quickening her pace to get to the security of the ballroom floor where she would regain her sense of self. This couldn't break her. She was a stalwart. A survivor. A woman perfectly content to stand alone, and with pride.

She didn't know why she'd thought things would be any different this time. Javier Ramirez de Arellano might believe he loved her, but he had never been willing to prove it. Whatever kept him from choosing her, wholly and without reservation, was buried so deep in his past, the reality was he'd likely never unearth it. Never find resolution. Never experience true, ever-lasting love. She wished she could be sad about it for him, but the truth was, she wasn't quite sure she had it in her.

The music stopped and the amateurs left through the far exits as the senior pro-am competitors floated onto the floor. After the scrutineer handed out the fresh clipboards charged with the names and numbers for this round, Lily was, once more, left with a blank page on which to begin again.

Chapter Fifty-Seven

'We made it to the finals!' Veronica reached out for Sam's hand as the emcee reeled through the ever-decreasing number of pro-am competitors who had made it through to the last and most important heat.

He took it, welled up and curled his other hand into a fist to stem a sob.

'Darling,' she soothed. Then, because she'd grown used to Sam's frequent bouts of tears, always fuelled by the grief that had come in the wake of Topaz's murder, she pulled a tissue out of her décolletage and handed it to him.

Even though the normally deserted bar area had a few punters in it, Veronica led him to a corner for privacy. He was the complete opposite of any man she had ever imagined falling for. He burped for fun, had appalling table manners, and owned far too many matching tracksuits. But he was also an absurdly good novice dancer and, while he insisted they brunched at grungy dockside cafés instead of somewhere Instagrammable, he had more than a touch of the gentleman about him. He always (unless it was bolted to the floor) pulled out her chair.

As much as she wanted to console him, he did have a tendency to crush her much smaller, more fragile hands in his.

'Sam, darling.' She cupped his chin and made him look at her. 'She'd be ever so proud of you.'

'You think?' He squeezed her hand tighter and asked, almost desperately, 'You don't think this is irreverent? Dancing in this competition when my sweet baby girl is . . . is . . .' He couldn't put words to his sorrow.

'No, my love.' For that's who he was to her now. 'No. You are a man of action. And grief is a powerful force. It can consume you if you don't channel it, the way you have, here, tonight. You're representing your daughter. She'd be so proud of you.' Veronica wasn't entirely certain about that last part, but she knew from experience it was best to let the dead lie in peace and, as much as one could, look forward. She too, had loved and lost. Not a child. Nothing so awful as that. But heartbreak, if treated in just the right way, could make you stronger. More resilient. And she was hoping that being here today would put some of her long-held demons to rest.

She gave his cheek a soft kiss, tugged her designer dress back over her hipbones then, after signalling to the barman that she was ready for the small handbag she'd stashed earlier, took a discreet sip from her mini-flask, along with one of her special 'performance pills', disguising the entire act by pulling out her compact and flicking open the clasp with a flourish.

Cripes. Middle age had a lot to answer for. In this world, women weren't allowed to age gracefully and, she had to admit, sometimes the race against time felt cruel. The treatment she'd had at Shaz 'n Baz's hadn't stayed the course at all. Thank goodness she had her own methods of sorting things out.

As she reapplied her lipstick, Veronica saw two competitors enter the bar. She stiffened. Jack Kelly and Susie Cooper. Best nip any unnecessary contretemps in the bud. She needed to be at her best to see this day through to its rightful end.

'Susie!' she cried, in sync with the snap of her compact. 'Jack. *Darlings*. You remember my friend Samuel Pringle, don't you?'

'Of course,' said Jack.

'Mr Pringle,' said Susie.

Sam caught each of their hands in turn and, by the wince on Susie's face, it was apparent he'd not yet mastered a casual handshake.

The two couples stared at one another awkwardly.

Veronica grabbed the bull by the horns. 'So wonderful to see you soaring up the ranks, Jack. As ever.' She nodded at Susie. 'And on such a momentous occasion.'

Jack frowned and then, after a glance at Susie said, 'You mean us dancing together, or trying to match Lily's Ten record?'

'Yes, darling. That's it exactly.'

'Thank you.' He looked bewildered.

She'd not actually meant either of those things, but sure. Whatever he'd just said would do.

'All right there, Roni?' Sam asked, giving her hand a pat.

'Tiptop, darling,' Veronica said with a soft smile. Somehow, the way he said 'Roni' instead of Veronica didn't rankle the way it did when others used the nickname. People like ummm . . .

Her brain was going a bit muddy, to be honest. Between the return to the limelight as a competitor and the bad blood between her and Marmaduke, she was finding the day quite challenging. And still with so much left to do.

Sam landed one of his paws on Jack's shoulder with an almighty thwack. 'I owe you an apology, mate.'

'Really?' Jack exchanged a quick glance with Susie.

'Yes. About all that skip business.'

'You mean, the "skip through the window of my studio" business?'

'Aye. That's the one, lad. Apologies. I—' Sam scrubbed his hand over his buzz cut then pressed both of his hands to his heart. 'I got a little carried away with things when my Topaz came back to me and . . . well . . . now that I've lost her, I see that I probably could have been a little less heavy-handed in trying to give my little girl what she wanted.' His voice wavered as he continued. 'If I hadn't done that, you might've agreed to dance with her and then she wouldn't have. . .' He caught another sob with his fist.

Jack cleared his throat. 'Well. Thank you, Sam,' he said. He gave his jaw a rub then said, 'I feel a bit awkward asking, but you don't happen to know if my laptop was one of the spoils of the incident, do you?'

'Not a clue mate,' Sam replied. 'I wasn't there, was I?'

'I don't know, Sam,' Jack said a bit testily. 'That's why I'm asking.'

Veronica cut in, 'It was probably one of your lackies getting a bit greedy, wasn't it, darling?' To Jack and Susie she said, 'You just can't get the staff these days. No matter how clearly you explain a plan, something always goes tits up. Greedy little bunnies everywhere.'

Before anyone had a chance to pursue that line of enquiry, Veronica pinned her hazy eyes on Susie. 'Lucky business, isn't it? Having Lily as one of the judges.'

'Sorry?' Susie said.

'Oh, you know. With The Duke messing her about the way he does. Trying to keep her off the judging panels. But having her here today must be a bit of a confidence boost for you.'

'Why is The Duke trying to keep Lily off the panels?'

'What?' Veronica asked, pure innocence as she realized she'd quite possibly let the wrong cat out of the bag. 'No, no. That wasn't what I was saying.' Oh, she really was muddling this up. She tried to recover. 'So lovely to see you in the pros, darling.' She grasped for a way out of this mess. 'Isn't it a shame you didn't have time to see to your elevens?' She ran her thumb and forefinger along the taut expanse between her own heavily pencilled eyebrows.

'Yes,' Susie said. 'Isn't it?'

'Who is it that styled you?'

Susie explained that she had 'styled' everything herself, with Lily's help when it came to her hair. The emcee began yet another semi-finals results announcement.

Veronica clasped Susie's forearm in shock. 'You should consider an upgrade, luvvie. No offence to Lily, but some of us,' she wafted a manicured hand along the elaborate twists and curves of her coiffure, 'are better equipped to look after ourselves. I learned from a true master, you see. Oh, I do miss . . .' She shook her head, sadly. 'Divorce can be such a terrible thing, Susie. Although,' she paused to consider, 'the LA lifestyle *does* sound divine.'

'Divorce? Whose divorce—?'

'Suze,' Jack interrupted, 'we've got to do a quick run-through before we go on again.' The emcee was announcing the final pro-am seniors round, after which they'd be back to the professionals for the finals. Susie and Jack's round.

Veronica refocused on Susie, who was resisting Jack's efforts to drag her away. Something about the way Susie looked at her made her feel transparent.

'So you're doing your own work now?' Susie asked. 'Gowns and . . .' she pointed to Veronica's face, 'everything?'

'Yes,' Veronica preened, unable to resist. 'Well, no. I've always been a bit of a slave to the designer dresses. And I don't do my hair, of course, I get someone in.' It was a wig. 'But my make-up kit has a little bag of tricks that can make those pesky lines just disappear.' She winked conspiratorially at Susie. 'A useful skill, wouldn't you say?'

As the emcee's announcements rolled on and Jack succeeded in pulling Susie away so they could run through a few steps, Veronica's thoughts dwelled on her absent stylist. Lily had been the one to recommend her for the job. She was always doing that sort of thing. Seeing an opportunity for someone to take a step up the ladder and being genuinely happy for them when they snapped it up and didn't look back. Veronica had been too dependent on her stylist to suggest anything that might make her leave. Maybe, the thought occurred, she could woo her back. After all, if things with Sam carried on as they were, she'd have more sway in the upper echelons of the GDC.

Yes. Perhaps a trip out to LA was in order. Not now, with all the plans she'd laid in motion, but . . . a short trip for a cut and colour might be fun.

Veronica checked herself. She was getting terribly off track. But before she could regroup and drop a hint to Jack about what she had in store for him later, Sam had wrapped his hand around hers and was leading her off to the ballroom. Her big surprise would have to wait.

Chapter Fifty-Eight

Three blind mice.
Three blind mice.
See how they run.
They all ran after . . . Ha!
Not just yet, my lovelies.
It's really the anticipation of an event, no matter how ordinary,
that turns it into something extraordinary, isn't it? And this
is no ordinary event.
The end, when it comes, will be truly glorious.

Chapter Fifty-Nine

'All right, Suze?'

'Fine.' She shot Jack a quick smile as a cover for her rising panic as she tried to navigate her turbulent emotional landscape, win the competition and find a murderer. 'Good, ta.'

'We were great out there,' Jack flicked his thumb back towards the ballroom where they'd just finished their final Latin round and the scrutineers were busy tallying up their scores. Only one more heat to go . . . International ballroom. And also, the last chance for the murderer to strike if taking one of them down in front of a crowd was the goal.

'*You* were great,' she said. Susie couldn't put her finger on it, but something about her earlier exchange with Veronica had unbalanced her. And Jack had clearly noticed.

'Are you sure you're all right?' he asked.

'Nerves most likely,' she said.

'One more heat and that's it,' he said, almost wistfully. He shook the moment away as they reached their destination. A quiet corner in one of the many back corridors that led from the dressing rooms to the ballroom. Someone had propped open the maintenance door that led to the stairwell that snaked up half of the iron tower soaring above them. The sun had dropped and a thick, misty gloom had consumed the pounding surf beyond them on the miles-long beach.

'Look. The mist is picking up the colours from the Tower lights,' she said, trying and failing to see the beach beyond the promenade. The same way she still couldn't, no matter how she rearranged the chess pieces, pinpoint who had taken Oxana's and then Topaz's life. She had her suspicions, of course. But nothing concrete.

'C'mere, you.' Jack took her hand and began to lead them through one final run-through of the foxtrot. He kept checking in on her, asking if she was okay, if there was anything he could do or get for her. He was being *tender*. And it was killing her. He'd said he admired her for her focus on her work and here she was, failing at the one thing that had set her off on this journey in the first place: finding the murderer.

Jack shifted his hand onto Susie's waist. Choreographed? Yes. Making the butterflies in her tummy take flight? Also yes.

As if each breath they released contained magnetic particles, the air between them vibrated with tension. Longing? Something potent. When Jack slowly brought their final spin to a halt, she looked up to meet his gaze and found herself the recipient of a featherlight kiss.

Susie pulled back, shocked. 'What are you doing?'

'I . . .' Jack also drew back, shoving his hands through his hair. If she was reading him right, the kiss had been pure instinct.

Which made it even more complicated to digest. 'Jack, I thought you didn't want that from me.'

'I don't . . .' he said, then instantly took it back. 'I do, Suze.

I always have, it's just . . . God. When you left it wrecked me. Ruined me for anyone else. I kept myself going by convincing myself I'd been right about competing. About being pro. And since you've come back, everything I'm feeling now is . . . it's like it's in Technicolor, you know? One of those old films where no one's plain old happy or sad. They're exhilarated or devastated. Elated or bereft.'

Susie knew exactly what he meant. Her heart wasn't beating. It was pounding away like a kettledrum. *Boom* boom. *Boom* boom. *Boom* boom. But her brain needed more specifics. 'What are you saying, Jack? Exactly.'

'I'm saying it's complicated.'

She couldn't contest that. 'Yes. It is.'

He tried again, 'I'm saying I want to do right by you, but I don't know what shape or form that takes right now.'

She nodded in response, unable to speak, because if she did she was afraid she'd give voice to the same handful of words that had been running through her head on a loop for the past few days.

I love you, Jack Kelly. And I always have.

Jack ducked his knees so that they were eye to eye. 'I'm saying I want to be in your life again, Suze. And Kian's.'

'I'd like that,' she managed.

Jack's shoulders lifted then dropped, as if releasing a seven-year-old sigh of relief. 'Me, too, Suze. Me too.'

They both gave nervous laughs and then *here we go again* smiles when the emcee called the professionals to the floor for the final round of ballroom dance.

Right. She could do this. *They* could do this. Win this competition and find a murderer.

As they wove their way through the back passage way and then through the main, makeshift dressing room to get to the ballroom, she saw Ruby Rae impatiently tapping her foot as Brynn gave her hair a final shellacking and Kiko swept another layer of rouge onto her cheekbones.

Ruby Rae's eyes met hers. 'Y'all better watch your backs,' she announced to the group, eyes glued on Susie. 'I'm on a mission to destroy!'

And good luck to you, thought Susie. *Because so am I.* When she shifted her gaze away, her eyes met Brynn's.

Oh, crumbs.

Now she remembered why the conversation with Veronica had troubled her. She'd told Brynn he could do her hair, back when they were rehearsing at Lily's, but it had completely slipped her mind and, with Lily's help, she'd done it herself in the end.

She told Jack she'd be with him in a few seconds. 'Brynn,' she said, ignoring the evils Ruby Rae sent her as she swished off to the ballroom with Vlad. 'I owe you an apology. I know I said you could do my hair, but with everything so chaotic—' He cut her off with a quick smile.

'Not to worry, pet.'

'Honestly, I'm so sorry.'

'Nothing to fret about,' Brynn assured her as his attention drifted to her hair. 'Is it all right if I just . . .' He indicated that a couple of hairgrips had come loose in her bun.

'Of course.' How mortifying. Of all the people to have a style failure in front of . . .

As he teased them back in, he smiled at her. 'Don't you worry, love. Everything will come good in the end.'

'Suze!' Jack beckoned for her to join him. 'We've got to go.'

'Off you pop,' Brynn shooed her towards Jack and then turned back to the next dancer in line for a final zhuzhing up.

'All right?' Jack asked.

She smiled up at him. 'Great.' And she meant it. Jack wanted to be in her and Kian's lives. Somehow. Some way. And it turned out that hearing this was all she needed to feel grounded again. Although she knew their dancing had been above par today because of the hard work they'd put in, at last she felt that final click of connection she hoped would propel them to the top of the podium.

Which was just as well because this was the final. The last five dances during which the killer would reveal themselves.

'Scared?' Jack asked.

'Not about us,' she answered truthfully.

His expression shifted, as if suddenly reminded their being here wasn't entirely about the competition.

'I won't let anything happen to you, Suze.'

She smiled up at him. No one could make a promise like that. 'I know,' she said.

He lowered his voice. 'Do you have any ideas who it is?'

She had her suspicions. Especially as she'd semi-deleted a couple of suspects off her list. 'I don't think it's The Duke.'

Jack's eyes widened.

'I know, I know, but . . . I just can't see him . . . you know . . .' She mimed injecting Jack in the neck then looked over her shoulder and made a sign they shouldn't talk about it here, in the crowd.

Jack nodded agreement then bent down and whispered, 'I think you can count Veronica out as well.'

Susie agreed. She'd seemed sort of loopy earlier. If the killer was to strike, they'd need to be on point.

Ahead of them, the final clutch of competitors log-jammed as they waited for the last senior pro-am dance to finish. She could see Ruby Rae and Vlad at the head of the queue. Felipe and his partner, Mirabel, were right behind them. And then a couple she didn't know. Which meant Lucia and Cristobal were behind her and Jack.

A burst of fear skittered down her spine.

The dancers on the floor finished their American smooth. The competitors in front of Susie and Jack began moving in to take their places.

This was it. The moment when, with any luck, she'd beat the odds and take down a serial killer intent on striking again.

The dancer in front of her fiddled with the grips holding her precarious up-do in place. 'It's such a drag Carys moved to LA,' she said to her partner. 'She was, like, one hundred per cent better than Brynn.'

'Two hundred,' agreed her partner, who sported his own rather impressive mane of hair.

'Probably why she left him.'

'I heard their whole business tanked when she went.'

'Sounds about right. He does a mean pony, though.'

'For kindergarteners maybe. I'm using Ramone next time. It's not worth . . .'

The final bit of the dancers' conversation eluded her as they swept off to claim their space on the floor. Jack led her to their starting point, the northeast corner of the ballroom, diagonally opposite Lily's judging post.

Marvellous Marvin tapped his baton against his music stand.

Poor Brynn. She'd had no idea he was divorced. And now he was losing his business? How he stayed so nice was beyond her.

'Ready?' Jack cupped his hand under her shoulder blade.

'As I'll ever be.'

The one-two-three cadence of the final waltz sounded, and off they went. This was the heat when they could embellish their choreography. Add in a weave from the promenade position. Execute double reverse spins and shift into fallaway reverses with a slip pivot. It was fluid and beautiful. The exact same waltz everyone was performing, but with clever little twists that a truly observant judge would appreciate.

As Jack tipped her back into an oversway, Susie caught a movement on the side of the dance floor. Veronica and Sam were slipping into seats in the front row behind Lily.

'Oh, god,' Jack said through his dreamy Prince Charming smile.

Susie followed Jack's gaze and, for just a second, caught a glimpse of Johanna clutching something in her lap.

A shot of adrenaline surged through her. Was this it? The moment they'd been waiting for? A new fear gripped her. What if Johanna came for her with a syringe and hit a vein?

'I don't have the antidote.'

'It won't get that far. I won't let it,' Jack assured her.

Where was Madhav? His support team? Had her goodbye kiss to her son been her last? She looked into Jack's eyes, the exact same colour as their son's, and used them as ballast. A visual aid to overcome her panic. If Johanna launched herself at either of them, Jack was right. Between them, they could subdue her. Unless, of course, it wasn't Johanna at all.

The waltz ended and segued into the tango.

She felt a fractional hint of tension strain Jack's shoulders.

This, of course, was the dance that had seen him lose first Oxana, then Topaz.

Ruby Rae and Vlad approached, performed a series of remarkably sexy 'love to hate you' moves, and then, as Ruby Rae passed, she shot Susie a malicious smile and mouthed, 'Die bitch.'

Susie fought the instinct to stop. To fastidiously reorder all the facts as she knew them. But they were already one hundred and thirty-odd seconds into the heat that could take her and Jack to the top. She couldn't step away from the competition now.

Lucia and Cristobal cannonballed past them as they executed a tango oversway. They altered their steps and somehow, most likely on purpose, managed to get close enough for Lucia's hip to knock Susie's bun free as she tipped back into her full extension.

Hadn't Brynn just . . .

'Suze? You all right?' Jack asked through his smile.

She felt sick. And stupid. All the clues were right there for her to see. 'I know who the murderer is.'

A progressive chassé took them past Maisie and Darren, until their next steps, a back open promenade brought them to Lily's judging station just in time for Susie to realize she'd figured out who it was too late.

Ice poured through her as she saw the glint of the six-inch blade sweep round and catch Lily under the throat. Her face drained of blood as Brynn whispered something to Lily that she couldn't hear.

Then she met Brynn's eyes.

In them she saw a blend of hatred and rage she had never

379

before encountered. Not even in her darkest days in the police force.

A thousand possible responses crashed into Susie's head, but seeing her mentor, her *friend*, caught in the murderer's arms, a knife to her neck, the only thing she was capable of was screaming one, solitary, heart-rending, '*Lily!*'

Chapter Sixty

'Nobody move!' The knife pressed under Lily's chin was almost but not quite biting into the soft skin at the base of her throat.

'Brynn,' Lily managed.

'Keep your distance!' Brynn snapped as Susie took a few careful steps towards them. She froze in place, hands up.

Lily had never truly known complete and total fear before, but at this moment she felt certain this was close.

She forced herself to focus on Susie's steady brown eyes. She needed something to ground her. Something to keep the terror at bay. All else came to her as sensation. The sharp dig of Brynn's knuckle under her chin as he held a terrifyingly sharp blade to her throat. The tang of sweat emanating from him. The cadenced, hot huffs of breath upon her cheek as he dragged her backwards out of the ballroom and towards the lifts. His hands snagging on her sequinned pant suit. She'd never wear it again. Would burn it in a pyre if she survived this.

When she survived this, she told herself. She'd weathered endless turmoil. Overcome so much adversity over the years. Her *mother* was going to be moving in with her in a week's time, for heaven's sake, and if there was one person in this world she refused to let down, it was Audrey. And, of course, the dear girl in front of her. Susie Cooper. Mind almost visibly reeling, trying to figure out how to end this petrifying turn of events.

Surely there was a way out of this. But, try as she might, she couldn't stem the roar of blood in her ears. It seemed an impossible feat to understand how such a gentle and kind man had actually been a devil in their midst.

'Brynn,' Susie spoke slowly, carefully. 'Everyone's watching. You don't want to do this.'

'You have no idea what I want, Susie Cooper,' Brynn sneered. He pressed his sweaty face close to Lily's, stubble abrading her cheek as he spoke. 'Or you, Lily. And now it's time to pay.'

Lily let out a short gasp as the knife bit into her throat, loosening a trickle of blood.

There wasn't much in the way of security at the competition. There'd never really been a need. The odd purse was stolen but nothing like this had ever happened. The Blackpool Tower, of course, had their own staff. Could they rely on them?

'Brynn, please,' Lily said, her voice shaking now. 'Tell me what I've done and I can try and fix it.'

'Oh, come now, Lily. Everyone's got to face the music at some point. And don't anyone here get any big, brave ideas,' Brynn called out in the pin-drop silence of the ballroom. 'You're all going to be evacuated soon. The Tower security staff have just had a call about a "mysterious package" down in the foyer. And as for your three little mice, Susie . . . ha ha!' Brynn's voice turned sarcastic, dripping with unfelt sympathy as he hissed, 'Poor little Susie. Didn't think I knew about your secret team from Dotiwala's Detective Agency, did you? Well, let's put it this way. You can rely on them to show up as much as I was able to rely on you turning up for our hair appointment.'

'Brynn, I—'

'No! No. It's too late for apologies.' He wagged his finger at Susie, the blade of his knife whipping back and forth in front of Lily's face. He sounded as if he was in control, but his actions were making it very clear that the stylist had become completely unhinged. 'You've made your bed, now it's time to lie in it. Ah, ah, ah . . .' He pointed the knife warningly at Jack, who had come up behind Susie. 'Don't even think about trying to be the big hero.' He tightened his grip on Lily's waist and dragged her through the exit, her feet stumbling as she raced to keep up with his long-legged strides.

'Where are you taking me?' Lily asked, astonished that her voice still worked.

'Don't you worry about that, Lily,' Brynn sneered. 'As if you ever worried about me at all.'

She looked up at him and instantly wished she hadn't. His face was full of hate. No matter what she said, he wasn't open to actually hearing her. He dragged her through the empty judges' area, her feet catching on the miniature golf course, tugged her up a couple of steps and then unceremoniously pulled her through a discreet door that led to a gift shop. She desperately scanned the shelves for something, anything she could use as a weapon.

An alarm sounded.

'Ah,' Brynn beamed a twisted, wicked smile at her. 'That would be security figuring out they need to evacuate the building. Isn't it a shame they'll be too busy saving hundreds of lives instead of yours?'

383

Abruptly, he released his grip around her waist and cuffed her at the base of her neck, roughly grabbing her hands and zip-tying them together. The plastic cut into her wrists but she didn't dare complain. Brynn was a madman. One wrong turn of phrase and he could slit her throat.

He dragged her through yet another door reading No Entry: Staff Only. There, Brynn set a brutal pace on a steep metal staircase. Never before had she been more aware of just how reassuring a railing was. She was, after all, doing this in heels. Despite her best efforts, she kept falling behind, tripping and stumbling, only to be caught by the collar of her jacket and hauled up to her feet again.

'Ow!' she cried as she stumbled and came down on the edge of a stair.

'Awww,' Brynn pretended to care then yanked her up again. 'Poor Lily. You'll have one helluva shiner in the morning.' He threw her a wicked wink. 'If you make it until then.'

She was pure adrenaline now.

Uncontained. Frenetic.

Though she was physically fit, her lungs burnt. Her ankles were already wearing raw from the leather bands of shoes designed for standing in, not moving. Every fibre of her body was screaming at her to stop. But stopping wasn't an option.

Finally, Brynn kicked open a door with one booted thrust and there, beyond her, Lily saw a lift entry.

He dropped her a wink. 'Wouldn't be a real trip to the Tower if we didn't head to the top now, would it, Lily?'

He pulled out a key which opened the doors to the lift and before she knew it, they were airborne. It was faster than she remembered. Racing past all five hundred and sixty-three steps the maintenance crews used to affix lights to the exterior of the structure. Where the stairs ended, a seemingly endless row of ladders ascended all the way to the top of the Tower. Before she could catch her breath and acclimate herself, Brynn yanked her out of the glass enclosure and locked it so that the doors stood open.

'Thought someone might nip up and save you?' he asked with a sneer.

'No, Brynn, I—'

'Oh, please, Lily. Let's not, shall we?'

A fierce wind was blowing off the Irish Sea. The Tower lights, usually so cheering, from this angle threw lurid shadows in reds, blues and greens on Brynn's face. He didn't look entirely human any more.

Her heart doubled its pace.

Brynn was a man who not only had murdered poor, innocent women. He had wanted the world to see.

Oh god. She understood now.

'Are you hoping for an audience, Brynn?' Lily bit out.

'We've already got one, love. I told you I had it all planned out.' Brynn swung her so that she all but flew across the viewing platform until her midriff hit the waist-height railing. He laughed when, for one heart-stopping moment, she lurched forwards, thrown off-balance by the move, and saw scores of people, hundreds of metres below her, crossing the road away from the grand complex.

'Been up here before, have you, Lily?'

She nodded, yes.

'Speak up, girl. This isn't a mime show.'

'Once or twice,' she said. In the arms of a lover. And, just a few years back, on her own to look out at the expansive view in the hopes of regrouping after a particularly grim run-in with Marmaduke. On that occasion she had wondered whether all the drama – the living, breathing chaos that made up the world of professional ballroom dancing – was worth it. Then, as now, she knew it was. Every damn second of it.

She summoned all her courage and tried to run past Brynn. He caught her round the waist. She tried to turn her weight leaden, to drop below his grip. Inflamed, he jammed his fist into her hair and dragged her back to her feet. It was a moment when many would have submitted.

But she knew pain. She knew graft. And she knew how to shape them into what she needed to survive.

Brynn was tall. A good foot taller than Lily. And that was with her heels on. She saw now that his outfit, one she'd thought was a sort of trendy combat-trouser-and-desert-boot ensemble, was actually the type of clothing a soldier would wear. 'Brynn?' she asked, desperate to get him talking as negotiators often did in her true crime books. 'Were you ever in the military?'

He barked that icy, pitiless laugh of his.

'Were you?'

'Yes,' he said, not meeting her eye as he dragged her further along the circular viewing platform. 'Army.'

That explained the knife. It was a savage-looking thing. She had no idea if it was military issue, but it was difficult to believe that the government would leave something so lethal-looking in the hands of soldiers who had been discharged. Particularly one who was clearly in need of psychiatric help.

But maybe that hadn't always been the case.

'Brynn,' she tried again. 'What's this about? Really?'

'You'll find out soon enough,' Brynn said, pressing the knife blade back to her throat and a finger to his lips.

Lily felt the sting of tears scrape the back of her throat. For the first time, she realized that she might not make it out of this alive.

She looked down.

A mistake.

Somehow, she hadn't noticed that the floor of the viewing platform was made of glass. As the lights rippled up the Tower, it illuminated just how far they were from the ground. And then, the tiniest flicker of hope: she saw figures making their way up the stairs. Susie and Jack and . . . was that Marmaduke? It was a perilous way to ascend, especially with the wind, but quite possibly her only chance of survival. She gave the area a desperate scan. No doors. How on earth were they meant to get in? She couldn't bear the idea of them putting themselves in such danger only to be stuck beneath that wretched glass floor in time to see her die.

Brynn, oblivious to their approach, tugged another zip-tie out of his pocket and secured her to one of the metal guard rails that curved up from the waist-height railing circling the observation platform. He flashed her a sadistic smile, crossed to an area she hadn't noticed was cordoned off by yellow and black security tape and tore it away.

'Hope you're not afraid of heights.' Brynn contorted his face into a caricature of sadness. 'What's this now? The indomitable Lily Richmond is crying? Well, I never.'

She swore at him, distressingly aware of the unfamiliar tang of hot tears coursing down her cheeks.

'Now, now, Lily. That's not language fit for a lady. But you aren't really as "all that" as you make out, are you?'

'What are you talking about?'

'You and your studio and your fawning students, and everyone at your beck and call.'

Lily bridled. 'What do you mean? I've worked for everything I have and I'm proud of it.'

'No!' Brynn shouted. '*I* worked for everything I had and *you* took it away. So now it's time for a bit of payback.'

Lily's mouth went completely dry. What was he on about? He was a regular hire for her. She used him all the time. She'd even recommended his wife for an amazing job in America that had given their salon an enormous boost. Surely, she'd done far more give than take.

Eyes glued to hers, and in as casual a tone as if he were asking a stranger the time, Brynn asked, 'Do you know how they clean the windows here, Lily?' He didn't wait for her to answer. 'Abseiling!' He unlatched and swung open the section of the secure railing that had been cordoned off. 'Pity they've taken all those harnesses and ropes away.'

Suddenly, they were hit by the bright white glare of a spotlight.

A police helicopter was hovering at a distance, its search beam trained on the viewing platform.

'Help!' she screamed.

'Oh, dear, Lily,' Brynn laughed. 'You think they're going to be able to help you?'

'What do you want from me?' It wasn't a question. It was a desperate plea.

'I want my wife back,' Brynn bellowed in her face.

'I . . . Where is she?'

'She's gone, hasn't she?' Brynn looked at her like she was

an idiot. 'Don't you listen to the rumours, Lil'? She took that fancy job you dangled in front of her. Left me. The business. Our home. Everything. My whole life was like a house of cards. One puff of wind and . . .' He blew a sharp exhalation into Lily's face. 'It all fell down.'

'Get away from her!' Susie blasted through a trap door a couple of metres away from them, not even pausing for breath as she scrambled up the final steps of the ladder and charged at Brynn with everything she had. But he was too fast for her.

With a swift kick he sent Susie crashing to the floor, and then just as quickly caught the newly arrived Jack straight in the chest, knocking him back through the hole onto the ladder. From her angle, Lily couldn't tell if Marmaduke was below him or, more terrifyingly, if, Jack had managed to keep hold of the ladder.

Susie tried to push herself up to standing, but Brynn was on her, twisting her arm behind her back and holding that glinting, vicious knife to her throat. 'Ooh . . .' His voice was pure mania now. 'What shall I do with little Susie?'

'No!' The word felt as if it had been torn from Lily's throat. There was nothing, *nothing* she wouldn't do to save Susie. She twisted and folded her hands in a futile attempt to free them from the zip-ties. 'Take me!'

'That's what I thought.' Brynn heaved a melodramatic smile and pushed Susie away from him. To Lily's surprise, he reached out with his knife and cut the tie holding her to the metal rod. The two women grabbed at each other, pulling close together. And, more importantly, blocking the sight-line to the trap door.

'Awww.' Brynn made boohoo fists beside his eyes. 'Aren't you two sweet?' His expression grew icier still. 'I bet you had beautiful childhoods, the both of you. Loving parents. Siblings who had your back. A cottage garden and Yorkshire puddings every Sunday at lunch.'

'Was that what you wanted?' Susie asked.

Brynn flinched. Whether from the question or the glare of the police spotlight as the helicopter spun round again wasn't clear.

Brynn waved to the enormous crowd below before turning back to his two captives. 'Of course, it's what I wanted! Who doesn't want that? To be loved as a child? Cared for?'

'What was your childhood like?' Lily asked, truly curious despite the terror. Her own childhood had been marked by pain. An absent father and barely enough money to scrape along. She'd endured three very painful divorces. More broken hearts than she cared to tally. Even now, she was on the brink of yet another ending with Javier. And yet she had never been compelled to murder someone. What could have happened to this man to turn him into a killer? Someone who had given years of service to the military, who had had a loving marriage, a successful business. Perhaps, as in her own case, first impressions were ruthlessly deceiving.

'Did you grow up in a children's home, Brynn?' Susie asked.

Brynn mimicked the question in a spiteful tone. 'What do you think, Susie?'

'But you served in the army,' Lily cut in. 'Surely that gave you a sense of pride. A sense of self.'

She held his gaze as Susie gave her hand a squeeze.

'Oh, aye. Killing people who are trying to kill you at the age of eighteen really made my chest swell.'

'A clever jack,' Susie said, almost to herself.

'What's that, Susie?' Brynn shifted the knife to the side of Susie's face. 'Speak up. Don't be shy.'

390

'Clever Jack. You wrote it in one of the notes, but it wasn't about Jack, it's something they say in the army.'

Brynn gave her a hideous smile. 'You want a prize for figuring that one out? A gold star for being so smart?'

Another wave of fear crashed through Lily as Brynn traced the shape of a star along Susie's mesh décolletage, cutting away the diamanté fabric as he did.

'Did you like my messages? I love nursery rhymes. They're all about death, aren't they? Murderous kings and queens. The plague. All sweet and lovely sounding, just like you, Lily.' He drew the knife along her throat. 'Oh, Carys, you're so talented. Oh, Carys, there's a job going in Los Angeles, you'd be just perfect for. Not a thought about me, Lily, was there? No one's ever had a thought for me. Not the teachers when I told them I was being bullied. Not my drill sergeant. Not my fellow soldiers. A brotherhood? Ha! But I finally . . . finally . . . thought I'd got it made when I found my Carys. The most beautiful girl in the world. And she loved me. Loved the man she thought I was.' He grabbed a fistful of Lily's hair again, unable to contain his fury, then spat in her face, 'Right up until you interfered, Lily. I didn't see it at first. The connection. I was so furious with people for cancelling their appointments that I snapped. Oxana. Then that ridiculous girl from America. I thought I'd feel better seeing the last of them. But then I saw you, Lily. Bedecked with jewels. Everyone wanted to dance the tango with you. Real belle of the ball you were that night, weren't you?'

Before Lily had a chance to say a word, to all of their shock, Jack came barrelling through the trap door and, behind him, huffing and puffing, Marmaduke.

But Brynn backed close to the railing, so close that a false move might send him and Lily both through the open gate to their deaths. He screamed at Marmaduke, who was reaching into his pocket: 'Don't even think about it!'

Lily cried out as the knife blade once again threatened to cut through her skin. She could feel the pulse of her jugular against the blade.

'It's a phone,' Marmaduke said, his manner oddly steady. Lily had seen glimpses of this Marmaduke before. Most of the time he was a vile bully. But now, as had happened at other, critical moments in her life, he presented as a trustworthy man with straightforward hopes and dreams. A man who embodied compassion and grace. 'Honestly,' The Duke said, hand slowly easing out of his jacket pocket, 'it's only a phone.' He pinched it between his two fingers and held it out to Brynn. 'They want to talk to you.'

'Who?'

The Duke pointed at the helicopter.

'Oh, well, isn't that nice?' Brynn sneered, using the blade to trace a sadistic journey along the side of Lily's face.

Blood trickled down her throat and into the neckline of her outfit. Susie, normally so calm and controlled, looked absolutely petrified. And that's what scared Lily the most.

'C'mon, lad. Whatever's made you do all this can be sorted.' Marmaduke held the phone out again.

Brynn made a noise indicating he was considering it and then, to everyone's shock, said, 'Nope!' He grabbed Lily by one arm and a leg and swung her as if she were a child playing airplane until, abruptly, he wasn't. Lily felt herself soaring through the open gate into nothingness.

'*LILY!*'

Unbelievably, miraculously, Lily was able to grasp the railing with one hand and then, channelling a sheer will to survive, the other. Her body vibrated with a primitive fear, dangling, as it was, over hundreds of metres of nothing.

The wind had completely died away and she heard the crowd far, far below her cry out.

Susie was weeping now. Her hands grabbed tight to Lily's wrist and Jack took hold of the other, but they all knew the reality. The pair of them had danced seven rounds today. Run up the stairs of the Tower. Then climbed length after length of rickety ladder. What energy they had left was nearly spent.

'Hold on, Lil.' Jack only had her with one hand and, as he tried to realign himself so that he could catch her with the other, Brynn landed a kick in his gut. His grip dropped.

'Don't let go, Lily,' Susie said to her. 'Don't let go. Don't let go. Don't let go.'

Lily felt what little strength she had garnered to get through the ordeal leave her. Deep down, she knew she wasn't responsible for Brynn's pain, but it tormented her that he saw this as the only way out. That he'd let his shattered dreams morph into venom and evil. Taking the lives of first Oxana and then Topaz.

As Jack tried to recover from the blow, Lily was astonished to see Marmaduke grappling on the floor with Brynn. Through the years, she'd taught herself to be cautious with him. Wary. But somehow, incredibly, he had her back now.

'I need you to swing your hand to me,' Jack suggested. 'As if you were going to do a cartwheel across my hips. 'Suze,' Jack instructed. 'Can you try and swing her to the right?'

'No!' Lily protested. Hanging here was awful, but somehow

393

it felt safer than swinging herself about in the hopes she could reach his hand.

'Look.' Jack pointed to a huge girder not too far away. 'I will do everything in my power to catch you, but if that doesn't work—'

'He'll catch you, Lily. On three?' Susie cut in, somehow compelling herself to summon yet more strength, more energy. 'I won't let you go. I will never let you go.'

Beyond them, Lily could see Marmaduke and Brynn wrestling over the knife, edging ever closer to Susie and Jack. 'Don't risk your own life, my darling girl.' Lily wept. She didn't want to die. Far from it. But she couldn't bear to risk Susie's life. 'You have that gorgeous little boy of yours to think of.'

'On three, Lil,' Susie repeated. Their hands were slipping apart. 'One . . .'

Susie's nails dug into Lily's palm and wrist as she did her level best to swing her to the side. A noiseless scream threatened to consume her.

Lily focused on the glass floor beyond her student, no longer able to bear eye contact in case this all went wrong. The knife, stained with her blood, clattered along the floor just a couple of feet away from Susie.

'Two . . .'

Jack grunted as he stretched out his arm as far as he could, legs hooked around one of the wrought-iron bars. Marmaduke and Brynn were each crawling, their expressions grim and fixed, towards the knife.

'Three!'

Lily engaged her core and forced her body to move. It took everything she had but somehow, extraordinarily, she found herself in Jack's outstretched hands. As they pulled her body onto the platform, Marmaduke and Brynn, still entangled, hurtled towards her. It was impossible to tell who had leverage until, with an elephantine bellow, The Duke cried, 'Not on my watch!'

Brynn, caught in the full glare of the helicopter's beam, pressed his eyes shut. The Duke took advantage of his momentary blindness and, with an enormous heave of exertion, pushed against Brynn's chest with such force that Brynn lurched backwards and through the open gate.

There was no time for shock.

Susie and Lily caught Marmaduke just short of falling through himself and, when Brynn's wail of defeat was drowned out by the arrival of armed policemen climbing through the ladder hatch, they all looked at one another in disbelief that they had survived. Each of them was covered in smears of blood and marks that would darken into bruises. Both Lily and Susie's clothing was torn far beyond repair. But as they reached for one another, fell into one another's arms, they slowly, gratefully, began to understand that their ordeal was over.

They had been on the platform for the same length of time it took to twirl and spin through the five ballroom dances that made up the final. But it had felt like hours. Long enough to remember what was truly important in life.

Which was why, when Javier insisted on staying with Lily in the ambulance, and later at the hospital where she was treated for shock and her knife wound, she let him stay.

It was the same reason that compelled Susie and Jack to spend the night together, wrapped in the safety of one another's arms.

It was what ignited Marmaduke to call together all the competitors and their supporters outside the Tower Ballroom. Its shimmering exterior stood proud and true, despite everything.

The building was wrapped in police tape and crawling with forensics teams ensuring the venue was clear of any further dangers.

'But we won't let this make us cower,' Marmaduke proclaimed, orating atop a small stage on the promenade, as if he were Winston Churchill himself. 'We are, above all else, ambassadors for ballroom dance. And we will not let one man's battle with personal demons cloak our lives in fear.'

The competition, he announced, would be brought to its rightful conclusion the next day. A fresh beginning, when the judges and competitors could return to the famed ballroom – without fear or favour – and show the world how truly united they were.

PART FIVE

Chapter Sixty-One

'Brilliant!' Jack hooted and gave an air punch. 'Third place!'

'Amazing,' Susie agreed, clapping loudly as a rosy-cheeked Scouser Sam and a blushing Veronica Parke-West accepted their trophy for the Over-50s pro-am competition to rapturous applause.

Following the chaos of yesterday, the audience numbers had dropped significantly, but those who did attend showed maximum enthusiasm. It had been wonderful to redo the final heat without fear. It hadn't lessened any of the couples' desire to win, but there was, at least for Susie, far more joy in her performance today. Gratitude for Jack, for Lily and, yes, even for Marmaduke who had, against the odds, been the one to end Brynn's reign of terror.

'How do you think we'll place?' Jack asked as the prizes continued to be announced.

Susie laughed. 'There's only one right answer for that, isn't there? But whichever way it goes, Lily warned me to be prepared for a few stilettos in the back. Either stabbing us, or running over us to claim their trophies.'

They both sought out Lily who, unusually, had opted to stand by Marmaduke as the prizes were handed out.

'Oh, Suze!' Jack thumped his forehead. 'I forgot to tell you.'

'What?'

'When I went backstage earlier, I tripped over Ruby Rae's shoe box.' He paused for effect. 'Guess what was in it?'

'I'm presuming it wasn't shoes?'

'Voodoo dolls,' he whispered. 'Or near enough. Barbies and suchlike, made up to look like all of us.'

Susie pulled a face. 'That isn't creepy at all.'

They looked across the ballroom to where Ruby Rae was in a huddle with Johanna and Kiko, and then, a bit further along the red velvet seats to where a cluster of Argentinians, including Lucia and Cristobal, were all toasting Felipe and . . . 'Is that Vlad with them?' Susie asked.

Jack shrugged, the gesture somehow managing to put space between the strange discovery and what was happening between the two of them here and now. 'Dunno. I only have eyes for you.'

Susie's cheeks turned pink. Waking up in his arms this morning had been like coming home. They hadn't done anything, but she'd never felt closer to him than she did right now. 'Do you think we'll make the top three?'

'Top one,' Jack said in mock offence. 'But remember . . . winning isn't everything.'

Susie shot him an amused look. 'I'm sorry. Who's stolen my dance partner and replaced him with you?'

Jack grinned. 'Okay, fine. I'd love to win, but really? When I thought about how close I got to losing you last night?' He pressed her hand to his chest and laid his palms atop hers. 'My heart couldn't beat, Suze. Not the entire time you were up there. And even when I got up there to help, I . . . the only thing I could think was: what can I do to save the mother of my child?'

'I . . .' She didn't know what to say to that. It was factually correct. Who she was. The mother of his child. But she also, deep down, was hoping she was the woman he loved.

'Here we go.' Jack took her hand away from his chest and wove his fingers through hers, his attention glued to the stage as Cyril de Boeuf moved towards the table weighted with the competition's grandest trophies. Those for the Blackpool Ballroom Bonanza Professional Ten-Dancers.

They stood and glanced across at Lily, who crossed her fingers for them both.

Susie closed her eyes and, as Cyril began to announce sixth place, then fifth and then fourth places, none of whom she knew, her pulse fluttered with hope.

Please let us win for Jack. Please, please, please let us win for—

'*Mummy!*'

She opened her eyes and looked up.

'And in third place for the Blackpool Ballroom Bonanza Champion Ten-Dancers we have . . .'

'Kian?' She squinted, scanning the rows of people in the balconies just above her.

'Maisie White and Darren Potter!'

Distractedly she clapped for the dancers as she searched the crowd. The fear and tension she didn't realize she'd still been holding from the night before flooded away, as she saw her son waving at her from the front row of the nearest balcony. Her brother leant over a moment later and gave her a short salute.

'What are you doing here?' she called up to them, not knowing whether to be furious or incredibly grateful to be moments away from being able to hug her little boy.

'Heard there was a bit of a ruckus last night and thought we'd better head down,' Chris said.

'All right, love?' Susie's father leaned over the balcony edge and waved. 'How's our girl doing?' He tipped an imaginary cap brim to Jack.

Jack nodded back then leant in and, in a low voice, asked, 'Do you want to go to them?'

'And in second place for the Blackpool Ballroom Bonanza Champion Ten-Dancers . . .'

She did and she didn't. If they won, she wanted to see Jack's face. If they lost . . .

'Come down!' Susie called to them.

'It's a tie!' Cyril announced. 'This year's second-place position will be jointly awarded to . . .'

Susie held her breath and gave Jack's hand a squeeze. Second place was good. It wasn't first, but . . . it'd be better than nothing.

'Ruby Rae Coutts and Vladimir Zukas . . . along with Lucia and Cristobal Suarez! Which means, the overall winners of this year's Blackpool Ballroom Bonanza are Susie Cooper and Jack Kelly!'

The crowd went wild.

'We did it, Suze!' Jack beamed at her. 'We won!'

Susie was dumbstruck. She knew they'd done well, but . . . Exhilaration replaced stupefaction. 'We *won*!'

Jack picked her up and twirled her round and round. 'C'mon, love. Let's go get that trophy.'

Hand in hand, they made their way up to the podium where, after taking one, two, then three steps up to the top, they were handed an enormous trophy.

'This is for the world of ballroom,' Jack shouted out. 'And for Susie. My partner. I definitely wouldn't be here without her.'

Susie covered her face. She always hated this part.

Jack lowered his voice and said, 'You've always been there for me, Suze. I hope you'll give me the chance to do the same for you.'

Speech defied her, but she didn't have to find just the right thing to say, because Jack took her in his arms and, to the crowd's delight, kissed her as if she were the answer to his truest dream.

'Mummy!'

Kian burst through the crowd and scampered up the podium steps. She pulled him into her arms.

'Hello, love.' She gave his cheek a kiss and breathed in his little-boy scent. Even the idea that she might not have held him in her arms again . . . When he looked at Jack, she said, 'Kian, I'd like you to meet Jack. We're going to be seeing a lot of him from now on.'

Chapter Sixty-Two

Whether a competition had gone well or, like this one, had delivered its share of highs and lows, Lilian always loved this part. When the dance floor was empty, but she could still hear the happy chatter and laughter of the dancers backstage, drawing out the moment when, at last, they would have to leave. She turned, a bit too sharply, to take it all in. She felt her throat to make sure the light dressing she now wore round her neck was still in place.

It was. As was every splendid thing about the ballroom.

Ah, Blackpool.

She felt like she'd grown up here, in this grandiose hall. A home away from home. The things she'd learnt and seen within these gilded walls. Competitions. Proposals. Weddings. Break-ups. And now, the terrifying conclusion to a murder case.

'Lily?'

She looked over and saw Susie at the edge of the dance floor.

'We're going to head off,' she said, flicking her thumb over her shoulder. 'My family and Jack.' She touched her own face to indicate the bruising on Lily's. 'Do you . . . are you all right?'

Lily held out her hands so that Susie would come and join her. 'Of course, darling. I'm fine.'

Susie took Lily's hands without a word, and they looked towards the doorway leading to the Tower. They had both taken risks that could have changed their lives for ever. 'It was quite a competition.'

Lily smiled. That was one way of putting it. 'You always were one for understatement, weren't you, Susie?'

Susie crinkled her nose as confirmation. They stood for a few moments, hand in hand, looking about them and occasionally, almost shyly, at one another.

Lily broke the silence first. 'Thank you, darling.'

'For what?'

'Answering my text all those weeks ago. Believing me.'

'I wish I'd . . .' Susie began and then stopped herself, taking her time to find the right words to express herself.

Sweet little Susie Cooper, thought Lily. *How I've missed you.*

'I think it's me who should be thanking you,' Susie finally said. 'For reaching out. Despite how – you know – how I was after Kian was born. I hope you can forgive me.'

'Hormones, darling,' Lily said, instead of *there's nothing to forgive*. 'They turn a woman into a warrior. And you still are one,' she intoned, before nodding towards the nearest doorway where Jack stood. Kian's arms were wrapped around his neck with his little boy head snuggled into the crook of his father's neck, as if he'd nestled there a thousand times before. Jack beckoned for Susie to join them. 'Not all women are brave enough to take that step.'

Susie's eyes glassed over. 'I'm ready now. Thanks to you. And terrified,' she admitted, laughing as she swiped at her cheeks as a few tears escaped. 'But I'm ready.' She broke eye contact and looked around her, almost surprised to find herself standing here in the middle of the Tower Ballroom. 'I can't believe it's all over,' she said.

'It doesn't have to be,' Lily said. 'After all, now that you're a pro—'

'It's a nice string to have added to my bow,' Susie cut in, a warm smile lighting up her face. 'But I think there would have to be another criminal on the loose to get me back into the fold.'

'Oh, well now,' Lily tapped the side of her nose, 'if that's all you want, darling, I'm sure it'll only be a matter of time before we come up with something.'

'Lily.' Susie shook a warning finger at her, then softened once more. 'Thank you. For everything.' She abruptly pulled Lily into a tight, fierce embrace. Wordlessly, they told one another everything they needed to know. They loved one another. They'd stay in each other's lives. But for now, it was time to go.

'He loves you, darling,' Lily said, holding Susie out at arm's length. 'Whether or not he's found a way to say it yet is another thing, but the fact he's here, holding that gorgeous little boy of yours in his arms . . . that's his way of saying he loves you.'

Susie smiled, leant in, and after checking Lily wasn't saving her make-up for any more photos, gave her a soft kiss on the cheek. 'I'll call you soon, all right?' She winked. 'Who knows? Maybe Kian will want to come to the studio. I know a teacher there I'd happily recommend to him.'

Lily offered a half-wave, too choked up to answer back.

Ruby Rae filled the space Susie had just left and Lily smiled, relieved they could talk at last without a cloud of suspicion hanging over them. 'Congratulations, darling. You should be very proud of second place after all the commotion over these last few weeks.'

Ruby Rae scowled and clutched the shoe box she had tucked

under her arm closer to her. She wasn't the sort to be happy with anything less than first, and Lily respected her for it.

'Are you looking forward to training on Monday?' she asked. 'I think we had a one-to-one scheduled?'

Relief swept away Ruby Rae's irritation. 'Yes, ma'am. I have a new routine I wanted to ask you about.'

'Excellent. And while we're at it, I think we should take another look at that career plan of yours, darling. Perhaps it's time to think about a new partner?'

Ruby Rae pressed her free hand to her chest. 'I'd love that. And I promise, I'll win that first for you one day, Lily. I just know I have it in me.'

'I believe you do. Sometimes it takes a while to know ourselves well enough to know who suits us best.' When Ruby Rae frowned, Lily pointed towards the doorway where Kiko stood, silently waiting for her lover. 'Before you go, darling . . . I was wondering what it was you kept in that old shoe box of yours.' She gave it a tap.

'Ah.' Ruby Rae looked down. 'That.'

Lily tipped her protégée's chin up so that, once again, they were eye to eye.

'They're . . .' She hesitated and then blurted. 'They're voodoo dolls.'

Lily quirked an eyebrow.

'One of my therapists, back when I was in foster care, recommended I learn how to channel my rage and . . . well . . .' Her defensiveness shifted into a sheepish shrug. 'I guess they help me vent without actually hurting anyone.'

'You know, you can always talk to me.'

Ruby Rae's eyes glassed over and, in the blink of an eye, she was her old self again. 'Thanks, Lil, but I'm too much of an alley cat to get all huggy-kissy woo-woo, you know?'

'Whatever works, darling,' Lily said through a laugh and, as Ruby Rae's gaze once again drifted over to Kiko, she added, 'As long as you're happy.'

'Hmm?' And then she was off.

A few minutes later, when the bulk of the dancers had left for their hotels or the pier for a ride on the Ferris wheel, Lily heard her name being called.

Javier.

He walked towards her, pausing for a moment to uncork a bottle of . . . what was that?

Oh, very nice. The price tag for that particular bottle of champagne said it was definitely an apology bottle. Last night they'd barely said a word to one another, let alone mentioned their spat. The fact he'd been there at the hospital, holding her, had been enough.

'Share a glass with me?' he asked. 'It isn't against doctor's orders, is it?'

She shook her head no. He poured. They clinked glasses and drank.

When their eyes met again, she felt a glorious sense of peace come over her.

They wouldn't voice actual apologies to one another. They were past accepting or refusing words as a means of healing wounds. Actions were how they found truth in one another. Or lies.

But something about these past few weeks told Lily not quite as many years would pass between them before they saw one another again.

'Quite a competition,' Javier said, putting out his hand to almost but not quite touch the bruising on her face, the bandages covering the cut on her neck. 'Liliana,' he whispered. '*Mi amor.*'

When the tenderness of the moment had passed, Lily gave a quiet laugh. 'Yes. Someone else just as dear to me said the very same thing not a few minutes ago.'

He quirked his head and smiled at the compliment she'd tucked into her statement.

He took a sip of his drink and then, in a thoughtful tone, said, 'A little birdie told me Marmaduke was going to step down from his role at the Global Dance Council. Said he thought it was time the GDC was led by someone with a fresh outlook.'

'Ha!' Lily would believe that when she saw it. And then realized Javier was serious.

'Oh, not me, darling,' she protested. 'I like my life exactly how it is. Teaching. Coaching. Coming here.'

He nodded, understanding what she was really saying. It's taken a long time to get where I am, and I'm not giving it up for just any old thing.

'Is the stylist who was taken ill yesterday all right?' Javier asked as he recharged their glasses.

'Ramone? Yes.' She gave a nod in the general direction of town. 'He's still in hospital. Will be for a day or so, but it looks like he had a lucky escape.' She touched Javier's forearm with her fingertips and, with a twinkle in her eye, continued: 'His colleague Kiko has renounced the world of dance, though.'

'Oh?'

'Yes. She's decided to return to Japan to pursue a childhood dream of grooming dogs belonging to Tokyo's elite. If I understand correctly, she's going to try to convince Ramone to go with her.'

'There's a big dance scene in Japan,' he said.

The reminder of her years there jarred. She looked Javier directly in the eye to see if he was trying to get a rise out of her. He wasn't. He was just stating a fact. Perhaps she was too hard on the men in her life. Demanding of them in the same way she was demanding of herself. What, she wondered, was she trying to achieve?

Years ago, she'd wanted to be a champion.

She was one now. A legend even, depending on who you asked.

But not so decrepit a legend that she didn't imagine herself deeply, openly, in love one day. She looked at Javier again and raised her glass to him before draining it. Perhaps one day.

'Listen,' Javier said, taking the crystal flute from her hand and setting it on a nearby table.

She cocked her head to the side and heard what he did. Someone had put on a deliciously slow rumba.

Javier dipped his hand into his pocket and said, 'Turn around.'

She half expected him to put another blindfold on her, but instead she felt the cool, weighted presence of a familiar necklace slip over her décolletage.

'Wear this and think of me,' he said.

She turned round and he took her in his arms.

As they began to move across the dance floor, the music flooding her body like a life-force made of moonlight and stardust, Lily knew she was, once again, in her happy place. Whether that was in Javier's arms or on the dance floor remained to be seen. But for the next few minutes, the answer to either question didn't matter, because all she knew, body and soul, was dance.

DANCE DAILY

BREAKING NEWS

As reported by Pippa Chambers

Chaos reigned but the spirit of dance triumphed as serial killer and stylist, Brynn Conway, was brought to justice at this year's better-than-ever Blackpool Ballroom Bonanza.

The dramatic capture was led by dance legend Lily Richmond, after the frenzied stylist held her hostage atop the Blackpool Tower.

Lily's protégés, Susie Cooper and Jack Kelly (champions!), saved her life after Conway hurled her out of the Tower viewing balcony. The pair went on to win the championships, thereby securing Jack Kelly a place in the history books as the only other dancer in the world to match Lily Richmond's Ten for Ten record.

Brynn, who was ultimately overpowered by GDC President Marmaduke Fitzgerald, fell to his death, unfortunately landing on The Duke's cherished Bentley.

Dance Daily reached out to Brynn's ex-wife, Carys Conway, for a comment, but her publicist told us that Carys has closed that chapter in her life and is only looking forward as she #LivesABlessedLife.

When asked about the evening's events, Johanna Gunnarsson of Iceland wept tears of joy as she explained, 'Because of my devastating injury, Jack Kelly was forced to dance with someone else at this year's Ballroom Bonanza.

I could not have been more grateful to Susie for temporarily stepping into the breach. We are the closest of friends and I can never thank her enough for seeing Jack through to his eighth championship as I take on my new role as spokeswoman for the Global Dance Council.'

Jack Kelly and Susie Cooper were enjoying 'some quiet time at home' at the time of publication and were unavailable for comment.

In a statement released by the Global Dance Council's Acting Chairperson, Veronica Parke-West had this to say about the surprise departure of former chairman, Marmaduke Fitzgerald: 'I knew from the moment I began dancing with The Duke that he was a hero. But, even heroes need time away from the spotlight. Along with my soon-to-be-fiancé, Sam Pringle of Scouser Sam's Scaffolding and Skips, I would like to take this chance to announce the opening of the Veronica Parke-West Pro-Am Palace. A dedicated dance school for professionals – like Jack Kelly – to train with amateurs who dream of dancing with the stars.' Ms Parke-West made it clear that Mr Kelly had an open invitation to join her and her ever-growing roster of students.

Get out your calendars and put a gold star on the next big date, the International Ballroom and Latin Extravaganza: Mistletoe and Mirrorballs at London's very own Royal Albert Hall!

Glossary

Professional: A dancer who has passed a series of exams proving a high level of proficiency in Ballroom and Latin dance who also earns their living by dancing or teaching dance.

Pro-Am: A couple who have one partner working as a professional ballroom dancer and another who is still in the amateur class.

Amateur: Amateurs can very often be absolutely stellar dancers, but do not earn their living as a dancer or dance teacher.

Ten-Dancer: Normally when amateurs and professionals achieve a certain level of proficiency, they choose to specialise in either ballroom or Latin. Not the ten dancers. In the professional competitions this book covers, they perform all ten competitive ballroom and Latin dances listed below.

COMPETITIVE BALLROOM DANCES

Waltz: A daring dance in its day, the waltz is a smooth dance performed in ¾ time in which the dancers 'travel' around the ballroom. One-two-three swing!

Tango: This sensual dance is full of passion and requires a couple to gracefully shift from fluid, feline movements to striking, elegant, poses. The oldest competitive ballroom dancer on record passed high level exams just a few months shy of his 101st birthday, proof you are never too old to tango.

Viennese Waltz: Sways, fleckerls, natural and reverse turns 'fly flat' in this swift and breath-taking variation on a waltz.

Foxtrot: Using a combination of slow and quick steps, the showcases smooth fluidity from foot to foot as the dancers travel the floor. A favourite of Fred and Ginger!

Quickstep: Also known as the Quickity Quickstep, this bright, lively dance was born from a combination of dances popular in the Jazz Age including the Charleston and the Foxtrot. It is a highly energetic and characterised by lightning fast hops, skips, jumps and flicks.

COMPETITIVE LATIN DANCES

Samba: A joyful, bright, energetic dance where rhythm, syncopated timing and rolling hips are key. Its Afro-Brazilian roots shine through in its simple forward and backward steps.

Cha-cha-cha: Flirty, energetic and full of fun, the Cha-cha-cha originated in Cuba and is performed to up-beat music. The name of the dance comes from the sounds the dancers' feet make when they perform two consecutive quick steps.

Rumba: With subtle hip movements and exquisite posture, the rumba is a vertical expression of a horizontal desire. It originates from Cuba where, in some regions, the word was a synonym for 'party.'

Paso Doble: This evocative and passionate dance is based on a Spanish bullfight. It is made up of sharp, exacting movements, flamenco footwork and mesmerising body poses. Its name translates as 'double step' and springs from the fast steps of a military march.

Jive: Often performed to swing or rock music, the Jive – or Jitterbug Jive –is an energetic, brightly executed swing dance with lots of kicks and flicks. It was popularised by Cab Calloway, a famous jazz singer.

Acknowledgements

Thank you so much for reading our book! We truly hope you've enjoyed it. Shirley would like, in particular, to send out her heartfelt compassion and support to anyone who has ever experienced bullying amidst the tough knocks of becoming and being a professional ballroom dancer. She knows first-hand how difficult it is and, she has to admit, writing a murder mystery has been great therapy!

And now to the thanks. First and foremost, Shirley and Sheila would love to thank our literary agent, Jo Bell, for introducing us in the hopes we might enjoy working together. She was right. It's been fab-u-lous, so thank you, Jo.

Shirley would love to thank her wonderful manager, Ashley Vallance, for his support and dedication. You are the best in the business, as is the whole InterTalent team! There is no describing the love and gratitude I have for my son, Mark, who, from the moment he was born, lived a life immersed in ballroom and then made it his own. I am so proud of you and incredibly grateful for your insight and guidance in navigating the world of television and social media. Heartfelt thanks, as well, to social media superstar Harry Surplus. Thank you for coming into my life and opening the doors of social media when the entire world was locked down. You are a true Angel of the North.

A huge thank you from us both to our amazing editor Emily Kitchin for championing the project from the get-go. Watching Strictly with you was pure joy. We are so grateful for your editorial guiding light and, when you were bringing new life into the world, for handing the baton to the wonderful Hannah Boursnell and Clare Gordon who shepherded the book through to the printing presses. Thank you to our eagle-eyed copy editor, Penelope Isaac, and proofreader, Linda Joyce. Gratitude to the PR, marketing, design and production teams at HQ for pouring just the right amount of sparkle and style into the book and its launch: Joanna Rose, Dawn Burnett, Georgina Green, Becci Mansell, Angie Dobbs, Halema Begum, Kate Oakley and Emma Rogers. You're all delights as is the wonderful, Lisa Milton who helms HQ with lashings of panache. Thanks as well to the incredible team at Blackpool Tower and the fantastic behind the scenes tour. We have taken a wee bit of artistic license, but the real thing is every bit as inspiring.

Sheila would like to thank Shirley for welcoming her into the extraordinary behind the scenes world of ballroom dancing. It's as glittery and dramatic as she'd hoped. Thanks as well to her friends and family. You're all amazing and you continue to make my heart grow and grow.

Lily Richmond and Susie Cooper return in

DANCE *to the* DEATH

It's Christmastime in London but all is not calm. . .

After solving a series of murders at Blackpool Tower Ballroom, all Lily Richmond and Susie Cooper want is a peaceful Christmas. The last thing they expect is to find a dead body backstage at the Royal Albert Hall. . .

Coming soon

ONE PLACE. MANY STORIES

Bold, innovative and
empowering publishing.

FOLLOW US ON:

@HQStories